FAIRYTALE OF NEW YORK

ZOË FOLBIGG

Boldwood

First published in Great Britain in 2023 by Boldwood Books Ltd.

Copyright © Zoë Folbigg, 2023

Cover Design by Alice Moore Design

Cover Photography: Shutterstock

A CIP catalogue record for this book is available from the British Library.

Paperback ISBN 978-1-80426-942-8

Large Print ISBN 978-1-80426-941-1

Hardback ISBN 978-1-80426-943-5

Ebook ISBN 978-1-80426-939-8

Kindle ISBN 978-1-80426-940-4

Audio CD ISBN 978-1-80426-948-0

MP3 CD ISBN 978-1-80426-944-2

Digital audio download ISBN 978-1-80426-945-9

Boldwood Books Ltd
23 Bowerdean Street
London SW6 3TN
www.boldwoodbooks.com

For my mum, who turned up unexpectedly in New York. At mile 18, cheering my name, just when I most needed her.

PROLOGUE

Charlie curled into a pool of her own blood and inhaled the smell. It seemed a strange, animal-like thing to do when you were dying on the bathroom floor: taking in the scent of your own insides. But as pain seared through Charlie's body, and sadness and betrayal wrenched at her heart, her instinct to survive made her feral.

The cadence of her agonising cries certainly sounded beastly; her blood smelled of rust and warmth.

The smell of death, she imagined.

And as the scent and the pain overwhelmed her, she started to retch too.

I'm dying, Charlie thought as she curled into a clumsy C shape on the tiles. Left alone while suffering the most brutal thing anyone had ever done to her, although she blamed herself.

'Saph!' Charlie howled, as vigorously as she could, but no one was there to hear or help.

As Charlie watched her blood swell around her like a life raft, she remembered the only other time she had seen this much blood. A sticky summer. Legs stretched out in front of her as her eight-year-old self tried to reach the hazy clouds in the sky from her perch on the playpark swing. A slightly older girl with brilliant eyes took the swing next to her and Charlie looked across. Surprised to see someone with dark skin in the park of their very white village, she was envious of the girl's legs because she was reaching her summit much faster than Charlie could reach hers. She was powerful, beautiful, strong. Until suddenly the girl's face contorted and she let out a yelp.

Charlie gasped as the other girl's mouth jarred open, and a torrent of blood poured from her nose onto her lilac sundress.

She let out a pained shout and quickly dragged her flailing legs, scraping her green and white trainers on the ground, to bring her swing to a halt.

'Oh no!' Charlie cried, her innocent face frozen in surprise. Hands gripping the chains of the swing so tight she could smell metal and sweat in the palm of her hands. Paralysed in shock, Charlie let her own swing come to a natural stop while she observed the girl, hands cupped and blood streaming into them. 'Oh dear!' said Charlie's sweet voice. 'Are you... are you all right?'

'No,' the girl said calmly. 'I get nosebleeds.'

'Where's your mummy?' Charlie asked, looking around, but the playpark was empty.

Five minutes later they were in the kitchen of the Brown family's stone cottage, a trail of bloody dots and splatters leading back down the front garden footpath, to the playpark and the tarmac under the swing. Charlie's dad, Ray, was helping the girl, who leaned over the sink, blood still pouring, mixing in with the stream of cold running water from the tap, where thin pink, red and brown ribbons diluted and swirled, disappearing down the plughole. Charlie watched, alarmed, wondering if the girl's brain was going to land in the sink with a thump.

Charlie's mum, Ruth, ran in clutching old towels, saying something about The New Family, and how she would go and find the mother. Charlie watched her dad help the girl, surprised by how proud she felt seeing Raymond Brown being so tender towards another child.

My dad looks like a superhero.

Now, as she lay on her bathroom floor, her dad was all she wanted.

'Dad!' she called, even though she knew he was over two hundred miles away, probably washing up at that same kitchen sink. 'Saph?'

Charlie lay, overcome with an irrational fear that the blood on the floor might seep back into her, through her eyeballs, nostrils and mouth, as if her own blood were poison. She edged her head back a centimetre or two, away from the expanding pool in front of her, taking comfort from the fact she knew this was irrational; she knew she was still conscious.

She touched her eyebrow with a shaky hand. At floor level she could see the white grout of the hexagonal grey tiles gradually turn oxblood as the grooves filled up.

The pain ripped through Charlie and she cried again as she moved her hand from her forehead to her core. She tried to comfort herself, but her hand was too shaky, she felt too dizzy.

Charlie's kitten, Mabel, a silvery grey ball of fluff who had only come to live with Charlie a fortnight ago, sprang into the bathroom as if this were a game. Mabel froze, blue eyes wide and alert. Her ears twitched and her tiny black nose wrinkled as she sniffed the blood and turned her head in vigilance, like a nurse deciding what to do. She encircled Charlie, gently butting the back of her, while making sure she didn't get blood on her paws.

'Saph!' Charlie cried weakly. But Saphie wasn't there. Mabel couldn't get help. So as the waves of pain and righteous rage washed over her, Charlie knew she would just have to bleed to death. All over her nice new bathroom tiles.

How could he leave me like this?

PART I

1

FOUR DAYS BEFORE CHRISTMAS

'And the winner... of... series sixteen... of... *Look Who's Dancing!*... is...'

The studio darkened and atmospheric music pulsed while hundreds of hearts pumped in anticipation as the audience, contestants and crew held their collective breath for the result.

All except Charlie Brown, who was already dreamily weaving through the corridor-like edges of the TV studio, amid a labyrinth of black curtains and jigsaw flooring, using the sensation of the balls of her feet through her black DMs to negotiate the familiar terrain of cable under tape beneath her. Charlie snaked quietly, respectfully absent-minded, as she scrolled her phone for the weather forecast in New York.

Seven degrees and sunny. Lows of minus two.

Charlie didn't mind *who* the winner of *Look Who's Dancing!* was. She had become a fan of all three finalists: the cricketer who had done a balletic showdance; the newsreader whose Argentine tango was talked about at Prime Minister's Questions; the soap star whose samba would go down in *Look Who's Dancing!* history (although he had danced at stage school, but that titbit hadn't been leaked). All three finalists were genial and polite to Charlie and her team, despite the pressure cooker they had been living in for the past four months.

As long as the terribly rude sitcom star hadn't won, but she'd gone out early, so Charlie really didn't mind now. And her mind was elsewhere.

She rubbed her eyes as she meandered, looking at her phone, dressed head to toe in black. Charlie only ever wore black on studio days, or to the occasional funeral. Every other day, Charlie was a colour-clashing, blocking and popping make-up artist whose bright wardrobe offset her own blank canvas perfectly: clear peachy skin and khaki-green eyes sitting wide and lovely under thick brows on a heart-shaped face. If you were to ask people what colour Charlie's hair was, some would say blonde, some would say brown. In truth it was both, as ombre and shimmering as her eyes and her mood, which was mostly upbeat but right now she was so tired she felt like a zombie.

As director of make-up to a team of ten, Charlie had curated and executed the looks for cute quicksteps and quirky charlestons; she had gone above and beyond for Halloween specials and Hollywood week, and tonight she had led her team in powdering the A-list faces for the last show of the season, the finale of *Look Who's Dancing!* – note the exclamation, *Look Who's Dancing!* always had an exclamation, even when it was abbreviated to '*LWD!*' on a call sheet. It was that fun to work on. And it was the most popular show on British TV.

Most of the hair and make-up team went home as the show was going live on a Saturday night, rather than stay until midnight and crawl into cars, but Charlie and her senior assistants, Eva and Phoebe, were always waiting in the wings for touch-ups and powdering; the quick changes for professionals to do a pro dance and then get back into their show outfits for the results. Now

Charlie had to get off, but she knew Eva and Phoebe would take care of the sweaty foreheads and retouch the lip gloss for the post-show interviews. Charlie had a flight to catch.

She scrolled to the weather for the week ahead.

Christmas Day, a chance of snow!

Charlie stopped at a small makeshift desk against a breeze-block wall that had been painted black. On top of the desk was a bank of switches and knobs with lights glimmering green, blue and red. Underneath the desk was a tatty-looking fridge to keep the studio drinks cold. This was the workspace of sound engineers Bill and Simon, who stood in the shadows whispering all night with boxes and cables and sound packs that did things Charlie had no clue about. She tucked her phone into the pocket of her black denim skirt and raised her arms, as if she were going through airport security.

A white Christmas! How romantic.

Bill and Simon, also dressed for the studio, head-to-toe in black, took their cue to start silently unwiring cables, lifting packs and removing Charlie's headset and earpiece.

'I've got fifty quid on Lana...' Bill whispered.

Ashlee, the female host, repeated her line for maximum tension.

'The winner of *Look Who's Dancing!* is...'

'Come on...' Bill whispered under his breath.

'Hrithik!'

The studio audience, dancers and crew all stood up in a collective roar. He was a popular choice.

'Fuck!' Bill sighed quietly.

'Bad luck,' Charlie conceded.

'Always bet on the cricketer,' said Simon, who was younger and more mathematically minded than his boss.

Bill rolled his eyes and pulled the cable from Charlie's neck and down her spine through her black jumper, entangling it on the belt of brushes that sat around her waist as he weaved it free.

'Oops, sorry.'

Charlie shook her head as if to say *no problem*. Occupational hazard.

Bill handed the pack and headset to Simon and nodded to Charlie she was good to go.

'See you at the party?' Simon asked hopefully as glitter cannons burst above the studio floor, creating a gold rain that Alina, the runner, was already waiting for, poised on a large broom handle, to sweep up for Health and Safety.

'No, mate, I've got my flight to catch.' Charlie pushed a wavy strand of hair off her face and tucked it behind her ear.

'Shit, tonight?'

'Well, no, tomorrow morning, but I've not even packed, I'm so behind!' Charlie gave a smile that was a mixture of excitement, fatigue and mania as she pictured the pile of clothes, teabags, magazines and Fortnum & Mason treats that littered her flat as she had left for the studio this morning.

Simon looked a little lost, and Charlie surprised him with a hug. 'Catch up when I'm back though, eh...?' she said, releasing him. 'In March.'

'Sure thing.' Simon forced a smile as Charlie gently punched Bill on the arm and carried on weaving towards the make-up rooms to pack up; via the green room to say goodbye to the contestants, their families and the guests, although most were still on the studio floor, gossiping and being interviewed by the Behind the Scenes team, contents of the glitter cannon in their hair.

Charlie popped her head into Wardrobe on her way around.

'Annnnd, that's a wrap!' she joked blearily, huge eyes dulled by exhaustion as she walked in and plonked herself on a stool.

'Ufff!' Leyla puffed as she whisked hangers along a clothes rail at lightning speed. The sound of metal scraping on metal always made Charlie wince. More so when she was tired.

'Happy for Hot Hrithik though, eh?' Charlie smiled. She and Leyla both had a bit of a crush on Hrithik. His bright eyes jumped out against his dark skin and he was the nicest contestant they had ever had on the show. Which made him even sexier. Although Charlie and Leyla were both happily loved up with their respective partners of course. And so was Hrithik. Married to a Bollywood megastar who had given Charlie plenty of brilliant make-up tips of her own while she watched her husband getting ready to go on air.

'You all set?'

* * *

Leyla was the head of Costume – the person Charlie worked closest with beyond her own hair and make-up team – and a long-time industry friend. Leyla and Charlie had met in the theatre, when Charlie had recently graduated from art college and was working on musicals. Both Charlie and Leyla moved into TV around the same time; crossing paths on game shows, comedies and dramas; but they became close friends six years ago when Leyla brought Charlie to '*LWD*' as *they* called it, without the exclamation mark, as Leyla had already done two seasons and the show needed a new senior make-up artist. Since then, their annual cycle of work and friendship had strengthened with each season.

The rhythm of *LWD* was usually the same: in late spring, once the talent booker had secured the celebrity contestants, and the commissioner, exec and dance-team producer had worked out who might go with who, Charlie and Leyla would sign their NDAs and be told who the fourteen celebrities were – usually followed by gossipy WhatsApps about their reputations, their lovers, and their fashion and beauty styles. These would graduate to evenings over wine at Leyla's house in Crouch End or at Charlie and Harry's flat in Finchley, eating crisps and olives and discussing all the fun they could have with each celebrity contestant and their look.

By summer, in the early production days, Charlie and Leyla would meet more formally at Broadcasting House or the studios in north London to run through song ideas with the choreography and music teams, and there the ideas would fly, before the production line would hit turbo in August, with Leyla's sewing crew getting into full swing and Charlie briefing her team with sketches and mood boards about the looks they would be creating hair and make-up for.

The *LWD* half of the year from July to December was usually Charlie's happiest. It was more fulfilling than the stop-start work of smaller TV shows, adverts, video shoots and make-up artist gigs in partnership with beauty brands. With *LWD* a bonded team would reconvene, pretty much like getting the band back together, and have a rip-roaring, fun and exhausting ride ahead.

In preparation, Charlie and Harry would take an early summer holiday – Montenegro, Ibiza or Sardinia – also handy because their holiday destination of choice was never swamped with kids in June. Then Charlie would return, tanned and happy and ready to throw on a bright autumnal beret – and herself into another exciting season of *Look Who's Dancing!*.

Only this summer, Charlie had felt flatter than usual, some of her sparkle had gone. Her eyes hadn't shimmered so brightly. Harry had just left London to start a two-year sabbatical in New York; Charlie's best friend from art school, Saphie, had moved in while she was on a break from her boyfriend, Prash, and suddenly Charlie had felt as if she'd gone backwards more than ten years: the pair of them eating Häagen-Dazs on the sofa while they watched *Gossip Girl*. Only now they had Charlie's cat, Mabel, for company, and Saphie preferred Booja-Booja vegan ice cream because Prash had enlightened her to the evils of dairy.

This season, Leyla hadn't been able to help but notice the absence of Charlie's usual robust and resilient sense of humour on set. She'd been intolerant of diva demands. She'd got more tetchy with the more unreasonable celebrity requests. She'd even snapped at the sitcom actor, and Charlie was not a snapper.

'I'm thirty-two and back living like a student...' Charlie had confided to Leyla one night in Finchley, eyes welling up after her third rhubarb gin.

'I doubt you and Saph drank gin from gold-brushed Oliver Bonas glasses at Bournemouth?' Leyla had said with a raised eyebrow.

* * *

Now another series of *Look Who's Dancing!* had come and gone, and Charlie was about to be reunited with Harry, in an amazing city she might also call her home. It would make the stress and longing of the past six months all worth it.

Leyla kept whizzing sparkly outfits along metal rails. She was clearly immune to the screech after all her years in Costume.

'Nope.' Charlie winced. 'I've got ten hours to hone my capsule winter wardrobe. Not even hone it. I've got ten hours to pack, and then hone it.' She said it with near despair.

'Shit,' said Leyla, her face sweet under a soft brown bob.

'I'm so excited, but I've been so bloody busy, I just haven't had a chance.'

Leyla gave Charlie a knowing look. She had barely seen her nine-year-old twins since they went back to school in September. For Leyla, the end of another series meant collapsing at Christmas and not getting out of her PJs for the best part of a week.

'What do you reckon? New York for ninety days. What would Leyla wear?'

'Why ninety exactly?'

'Well, ninety days max, it's all my visa will allow. I might come home earlier, well, hopefully not.'

'OK, so that's December to March; winter into spring. It's cold there, way colder than here, so you need knits. Lots of them. Layer and layer. New York isn't showy – you've been, right?'

Charlie shook her head.

'You've never been? Oh, goodness, Charlie, how did I not know that?'

'Probably for the same reason you haven't spoken to Jeff and the kids and I haven't had a proper conversation with Harry or anyone in months.'

'You're going to love it.'

Leyla was ten years older than Charlie and very good at hiding her frazzled interior under her calm and capable exterior: the thought of an escape to New York filled her with memories and yearnings she'd forgotten in the melee of Lycra, sequins, packed lunches and Lego. It was where she and her husband Jeff had honeymooned twelve years ago.

'Can you just pack me?' she pleaded softly.

'Sorry,' Charlie apologised.

'OK, well, New York is very understated, you won't need much. Neutrals, cashmere, merino. Less is actually more there, and if you need anything, just buy it.'

Leyla realised as she finished talking that what she was saying was ridiculous to a woman like Charlie. 'Oh, hang on a minute...'

Despite the all-black studio staples, Charlie was never a less-is-more sort of woman. She liked to clash apple-green dresses with royal-blue DMs; hot-pink cigarette pants with a red sweatshirt. Topped off with a yellow bomber jacket or a lilac wool coat. And too many accessories. Always too many accessories. New York neutrals were never going to be Charlie's thing.

They laughed.

'Maybe just close your eyes and do a lucky dip?' Leyla suggested.

'It's all I have time for.'

That was more Charlie's style anyway. Winging it.

The dressing-room door burst open and Blake, the male presenter with perfectly quaffed hair and a very taut face, blustered in.

'Leyla, darling! Get me out of these pants. They are so tight I think I've scent-marked them.'

'What?' Leyla said, with a small curl of her nose.

'OK, skid marks. I'm commando. Were they gifted or loaned?'

Leyla winced as she cautiously looked in the waistband of Blake's trousers and made sure she didn't inhale.

'No, you're all good,' she said, calmly. He still smelled of citrus and sandalwood. So much of it, Charlie thought as she watched the spectacle, Blake must bathe in Tom Ford.

'I have been sweating my arse off in them.'

Leyla dared to peer closer.

'Drat, they're borrowed. Maison Margiela.'

'Well, you can't send them back now.' Blake winced as he clenched his buttocks and rose on his toes briefly. 'Tell them I loved them so much I couldn't part with them. I'll do an Insta post or something, darling, don't worry.'

Charlie and Leyla exchanged a look over the clothes rail. 'But I do need something for the after-party. Something looser...'

Lee, the senior producer, peered around the door before coming in.

'Ahh, you're here!' Lee was clutching Blake's emergency cue-cards.

'Great show, Blake, I think that went really well. You smashed it.'

'You think?' he asked. 'That last gag before the results, about the wigs, do you think I'll be cancelled...?'

Lee was used to reassuring Blake after every link – and at the end of every show he always needed a debrief before he could truly unwind and party.

'Brilliant. You delivered it brilliantly, mate. I reckon that was your best final yet.' Blake looked so pleased with the affirmation that Charlie felt a little bit sorry for him. His neediness made her feel sad. Leyla held up some clothing options to Blake's waist and they all looked at his very handsome reflection.

'I'm going to get off...' Charlie said as she smiled at Leyla, Lee and Blake in the mirror. Blake turned around sharply.

'What about the after-party, darling?'

'I'm going to New York in the morning, aren't I?'

'Of course! But, God, who am I going to duet to Gloria Estefan with?'

Blake looked around the room at no one in particular for comedy effect.

It was their party piece of end-of-seasons past. Blake Perry, the highest-paid TV presenter in Britain, dancing on a table with Charlie Brown, unassuming Lancashire lass, to 'Rhythm Is Gonna Get You' or Erasure's 'Respect'.

Leyla and Lee gave polite *not me* shrugs.

'You'll be fine, I'm sure!'

Blake looked sceptical. He'd had a soft spot for Charlie since she joined *LWD*, always requesting that she do his face.

Charlie sang Erasure into the hairbrush as she whipped out of her belt, pointing at Blake and giving an eighties wiggle. He was assuaged by her reassurance, and decided he would, in fact, let her go home and pack for her big trip.

'Hug?' Charlie suggested as she moved along the line of three in height order, shortest to tallest (Leyla, Lee, Blake), and slipped out to get her kit from Hair and Make-up, where Eva and Phoebe were already packing away their tools, as well as Charlie's for her.

'Girls, you're my heroes. Thank you,' Charlie said as she put a palm to her heart. 'For everything.'

'CBDT!' Phoebe cooed.

'CBDT!' Eva and Charlie replied as they huddled for a hug.

Charlie Brown's Dream Team had assembled for the past six series, the past three with Charlie as Director of Make-up, and Eva and Phoebe knew Charlie would be back in contact for the next series in the autumn. As long as she didn't stay in New York.

'You're coming back, then?' Eva asked longingly as she pulled away.

'Of course! Wouldn't miss this world... for the world!'

Charlie did have an internal thrill from the unknown though. Might she stay out in New York? Might Harry suggest something crazy and wonderful? Might she be working for NBC out of the Rockefeller Center this time next year?

She would definitely miss this, the most prestigious gig in the UK TV industry. She'd worked hard for it. But it wasn't as if there wasn't film and TV in America.

Charlie picked up wraps of brushes and see-through bags of pots and paint, liners, eyelash glue and gloss the girls had tidied for her, and packed them expeditiously into her silver make-up case on wheels, rubbed her eyes and said, 'Happy Christmas, eh?' almost maternally as she pulled each of them in again. Charlie was the queen of good, heartfelt hugs. The love-heart contours of her face seemed to become more pronounced as she closed her eyes and smiled when her arms were wrapped around someone else.

The door burst open and the huddle broke.

'You *have* to take this hairpiece out!' Ashlee demanded. 'Give me something more free.' She looked at Charlie. 'I want to do "Proud Mary" at the after-party and this makes me nervous.' She tugged at the long blonde ponytail attachment, circa Madonna 1990. Ashlee looked like a Barbie doll, tall, blonde and sculpted, but she was surprisingly no-frills and fun off-duty, and even confessed to sleeping in her studio make-up on a Saturday night to try to eke it out at family lunches on Sunday.

'I'll do it,' Phoebe said. 'You go.'

* * *

Charlie walked out of the studio for the final time that season, looked at the lights on the Christmas tree of the hotel opposite, and inhaled the dampness of the December night air.

'Evening, Barry,' she said as she slumped into the car, silver case packed with primers and pigment safely stowed for her three-month freelance hiatus, and headed back to her flat in Finchley, her friend Saphie and her cat, Mabel. Her and *Harry's* cat, Mabel. They had bought Mabel together, even if she had always felt like Charlie's. Giddy at the prospect of seeing him tomorrow, for the first time in months.

2

THREE DAYS BEFORE CHRISTMAS

'I bought pastries!' Saphie smiled as she poked her head around Charlie's bedroom door and looked at the hot mess of clothes and panic in the light, bright room. Charlie's bedroom was a corner room on the third floor of a once-grand art deco mansion block off the Finchley Road, with high ceilings and a small balcony terrace that overlooked a leafy side street away from the London chaos.

Charlie was sitting, her thighs straddling her suitcase, hands wrapped around her waist like a stubborn toddler mid tantrum.

When Harry moved out in June to start his two-year secondment in New York, Saphie moved in. Her boyfriend, Prash, had proposed to her by surprise while they were on holiday at Iguazu Falls last May, and Saphie's reluctance to say yes had put an awkward tinge on the holiday to say the least. So when they got back to London, Saphie decided to move out of their flat in Kentish Town, to have a breather and take some time to think if she wanted the marriage and kids that Prash so desperately desired. She moved into the spare room – her old room, in fact – starting a Sunday morning brunch tradition. It was their biggest indulgence of the week and so different from how their art-school breakfasts were in Bournemouth: Basics Rice Pops served with milk on the turn.

Sundays were Charlie's only days off when *LWD* was live, so she spent them leisurely. She and Saphie would go to Hampstead Village, Primrose Hill or Belsize Park for poached eggs on toast (or mushrooms on toast for Saphie), and perhaps walk the canals, parks or heath as they made their way back with the papers. Sometimes they would meet their friends, Phil and Aidan, in The Queens or the Duke of Hamilton, but that usually ended in hangover and regret the next morning.

Charlie bought her flat when she was on a break from Harry in her mid-twenties, and then-single Saphie moved in to help pay the mortgage when she got an art-teacher job at a school in Camden. And even though Saphie had moved out, and Harry had finally moved in, the flat had never felt more of a sanctuary than when she, Saphie and Mabel were flatmates. At first in the early days when Mabel was a kitten; and now she was older and Saphie was an established artist.

The friends met when Charlie was studying Media Make-up for Performance and Saphie was doing Fine Art, and, despite breadline years of creating and composing, Saphie had started earning a reliable income, first as an art teacher, and increasingly receiving commissions for paintings and neon artworks with every exhibition she was invited to be part of. Saphie had just been offered her first solo exhibition, opening in the market of Covent Garden in March. So while Charlie was in New York, Saphie would have the flat to herself to work on her exhibition, consider her future with Prash and look after Mabel, who at nine was a feline grand dame.

But there was no time for brunch this morning. There hadn't been enough time all December, as Charlie was so wrecked on her day off, she tended to sleep in. She felt a pang of guilt as she looked up gratefully from her case.

'Thank you. I love you.'

'Almond croissant, vegan cinnamon bun, or both?'

'I'll go almond, thanks.'

She took the pastry but didn't budge from the case she was trying to close. 'Perhaps this'll seal the deal,' Charlie joked hopefully, taking a hearty bite as she edged down and put further pressure on the case with her bottom.

'Selflessness amid a packing panic. I like it,' Saphie said coolly as she leaned her willowy frame on the bedroom doorway. She was long and languid in stature with blonde straight hair and a gentle, celestial face like it should be on the moon.

'I can't believe I'm still not packed!'

'It's a big deal. You want to get it right.'

Saphie took a bite from her cinnamon bun as she observed.

'Leyla's "New York minimal" is *not* going well.' Charlie winced.

'Charlie Brown maximal is a thing, I'm sure,' reassured Saphie, who wore the same chambray shirts and slouchy trouser style, dressed with thin gold necklaces and beaten-up espadrilles, that she had been rocking since they met.

'I might need to rethink...' Charlie admitted, bouncing up and down on the case and pulling the zip.

'You cannot go to New York without your standard too-many accessories, missy,' Saphie ordered.

It was true, the case was probably half full with berets, snoods and scarves, all of which took up too much space alongside the Liberty ties Harry had put in a request for, three boxes of Fortnum & Mason Rose & Violet Creams (for a guy who mostly weighed out his food, Harry's sweet tooth was always satiated by a small 10 g confection) and the bundles of magazines he had put an order in for on Tuesday: *GQ*,

Men's Health and *Esquire*, along with teabags and Marmite. No wonder Charlie barely had space for her colourful staple separates, and the one party outfit and heels she packed in case she didn't have anything in time for New Year's Eve. And make-up. Charlie always packed too much make-up, of course, even though she wore little herself.

The zip groaned, Charlie swallowed the last bite of her croissant, and – bingo – she closed the suitcase.

'Uff!' she exclaimed, standing up exhausted and fanning her face.

'What time's the car coming?'

'Forty-five minutes. Shit, shit, shit.'

'You'll be fine! As long as you've got your passport. Harry will have anything else you need.'

Charlie walked into the airy living room with the little deco balcony going off it, to retrieve her pint of water. She sighed. She would miss Mabel, Saphie and the flat. She would miss the brightness that Saphie had brought to it in the past few months. The neon macaws on the wall above the television. But not enough to quell her excitement.

Saphie's neon art creations that now peppered the flat added a vibrancy that had been absent when Harry lived there. He liked minimalism and muted tones. Everything he owned was digital to avoid clutter: his music, his photos, his everything. His life was on his laptop and not the walls of his home, and when he did live there, you would have only known from the clothes hanging neatly in the wardrobe, the protein powder in the cupboard and the macro boxes in the fridge if he was going through a 'shred'. Friends joked about how Harry's minimalism and Charlie's colourful chaos were the perfect complement for each other. Saphie's flatmate style was something in between and easier to live with.

'Are you going to be OK?' Charlie asked. She'd been so

obsessed with work and New York, she hadn't checked in on Saphie for a while, and she felt terrible.

'Of course! We'll be OK, won't we, Mabes?'

Charlie's velvety grey cat tiptoed across the living room with confident, sassy paws, jumped up onto her favourite spot on the lid of Charlie's record player, and closed her eyes.

'Rude,' Saphie joked. Then she looked at Charlie's expectant face, still waiting for her real answer. 'No, really, we'll be fine. This gives me three more months to leap or leave.'

'You seem to be getting on better?'

Prash's visits to the flat had begun again, like in the early days after Charlie and Saphie had met him at a yoga retreat and he and Saphie had fallen head over heels – or heels over head in the case of their exquisite plough poses – when they were in the tentative days of dating. Lately, Saphie was starting to spend the odd night back in Kentish Town at the flat they had bought together.

'We'll see,' Saphie said cryptically. 'But don't worry about anything here, we'll be fine.'

Charlie's eyes welled up.

'I know.'

* * *

When the message came in to say the Uber driver was outside, Charlie went over to the record player. She gave Mabel a gentle kiss between her ears and carefully lifted up the turntable lid, Mabel still on it, and placed it on the sofa so she could put Saphie's Christmas present on the turntable. Her beloved record player; her beloved cat, and a small gift-wrapped box with gold hoops from Les Néréides for her beloved friend. She replaced the lid.

'Shhh, don't tell her until Christmas Day...' Charlie whispered, but Mabel didn't flinch. Saphie came in from the little balcony where she'd been having a cigarette. She hadn't smoked for a decade before taking it up again after Prash proposed, and she did all the rituals for Charlie as she would if she were a teenage girl, hiding it from her parents. She only smoked on the balcony; she always wrapped her cigarette ends in an old tissue, which she would deposit in a street bin; she always used breath freshener afterwards.

'I think your car's here,' she said, shutting the balcony doors on the arctic blast whipping their leafy corner of NW3.

'It is.'

'Here, let me help you with the case. That is definitely over twenty-three kilos.'

Together they hauled Charlie's cumbersome orange suitcase down three flights of stairs and to the communal door that, irritatingly, had been left open by another tenant, as was often the case.

'For fuck's sake,' Charlie muttered, but her excitement overwhelmed her annoyance and she wheeled her case to the car on the pavement outside.

'You are going to have the *best* time!' Saphie said, opening her arms out. She smelled of cypress, oakmoss and cigarette. A combination that worked on only Saphie.

'I know!' Charlie squeaked.

'New York has it all. The lights and the smells and the galleries and the attitude. And Christmas!' Saphie marvelled. For someone who loved neon lights so much, New York plus Christmas was her happy place. Unlike Charlie, Saphie was a seasoned visitor.

'And Harry,' Charlie added, with a slight frown.

'Oh, yeah, and Harry!' Saphie laughed at her own oversight. 'Have the best time, yeah? Let us know when you land.'

'Will do, love you.'

* * *

In the Uber Charlie took a deep breath, sent Harry a text to say she was on her way, texted her parents to say the same, and then hovered her thumb over the circle with Jasmine's face in it. She thought about sending a text, but left it. Her friend Jasmine was too young and too carefree to care for the mechanics of getting somewhere. She would be more impressed with a selfie in front of Radio City Music Hall, the Empire State Building or the Lincoln Center, so Charlie threw her phone in her bag and checked, for one last time, that she had her passport.

3

Seven blissful hours in the sky without Wi-Fi or texts from Eva, Phoebe, Lee, or Charlie's parents checking she was OK was liberating after the chaos of the past few months.

On the plane Charlie curled into the window and drifted off, in and out of sleep, which scuppered her in-flight entertainment plans to watch *Pitch Perfect*, the new *Star Wars* and all of *I May Destroy You*. She didn't even make it beyond north Scotland before first passing out. Being off-grid and in the air meant she didn't have to worry about work or what she was going to pack. It was done now.

Charlie had felt a pang of guilt about missing Christmas with her mum and dad. As an only child, she bore the responsibility for them all on her own, but they assured her they would be OK. Charlie, Ray and Ruth had celebrated Christmas early in late November when Charlie had whizzed up to Lancashire and back for NovembMas, Brown style.

Ordinarily Charlie and Harry would have driven up the Sunday after the *Look Who's Dancing!* finale. They would have spent Christmas Eve in their favourite pub halfway between the

Brown family cottage in the Ribble Valley and Hawksworth Hall where Harry lived. Sometimes old schoolfriends would join them, but increasingly those friends were having babies and staying home. After too much mulled cider and a Slade singsong, Harry would get in a taxi to his parents' pile and Charlie would go back to Ray and Ruth Brown and her old bedroom. Christmas Day would be an endless, happy feast of Scrabble, eggnog and the *Corrie* Christmas special, and she and Harry would reconvene on the twenty-sixth at Hawksworth Hall for the infamous Taylor Boxing Day bonanza, which was more of an uptight cheese and wine party than a familiar jamboree.

With Christmas being brought forward to November due to New York, and Charlie having to work, she wasn't even able to get sozzled. She had borrowed Saphie's Fiat Uno and driven up on the Sunday morning, enjoyed her mum's full Christmas dinner with all the trimmings at lunchtime, exchanged presents (a Tatty Devine EU passport brooch for her staunchly Remain mum and gaiters for her dad) and played Trivial Pursuit (Charlie won, but her parents were always terrible). She had set off from Lancashire at 5.30 a.m. on Monday in time for the production meeting at eleven. It had been jazz week on *Look Who's Dancing!* – so she'd had to be there or she'd have been on the back foot for the show. Still, it had been lovely. Her mum and dad had bought her a nice new orange Samsonite suitcase for her big trip.

As Charlie weaved through sleep and time zones, she dreamed about painting oranges with her dad and her mother's marzipan-infused stollen. She could smell the spices hanging in muslin bags over the fireplace in the cosy millstone cottage and she could feel the warmth of her family home. Guilt fizzled away like the contrails from the jet engines behind her as she dreamed of her parents, knowing that they were thrilled for Charlie's New York Christmas. And with that knowledge she didn't wake up again until Greenland, when the smells of the dinner service – or was it lunch? – wafted through the cabin.

* * *

Charlie rubbed her eyes and looked out of the window. The seat between her and the man in the suit along the row had been empty, so she hadn't had to worry too much about dribbling and personal space, her bag making a convenient barrier on the seat between them. All she could see was sea. The Atlantic, she assumed. Excitement fizzed in her stomach when she realised she might even be in Harry's time zone.

She had missed him so much. Reliably charming. Boyishly handsome. His fair sticky-up hair and muscular shoulders. His blue eyes that sparkled mischievously when he said something controversial. They had got together at school: Harry, the youngest of four, had joined Charlie's local comprehensive when he was kicked out of boarding school for dealing weed to the vicar's son.

Of all people to be a secret stoner, let alone deal weed. Harry was now obsessed with macros (meticulous about his balance of proteins, carbs and fats); micros (vitamin supplements) and meal timings (hours fasted versus hours fed), who only poisoned his body with whey protein or Rose & Violet Creams. And the vicar's son! The vicar had been surprisingly unforgiving about the incident and pressed the governors to expel Harry. Despite Henry and Clarissa Taylor's pleas to the headmaster, and the reminders just how much money they had furnished the school with in fees over the years for four children, he had been expelled, and Harry Taylor had had to slum it at the nearest comp. 'To teach you a lesson!' his father Henry had roared.

Slumming it had brought Harry to Charlie, when they'd locked eyes across a Bunsen burner in double science.

Charlie couldn't remember what colour her hair was the week Harry joined the school: black; red; plum; fuchsia; blue-tipped. All she remembered was that it was Chemistry. Now, as she fluffed the flat side of her hair that was neither brown nor blonde despite it being a thousand shades of in-between, she felt burning excitement as the plane sounds started to alter, and she knew they were about to descend.

Harry.

He was her right arm. A focused, hard-working and disciplined one. 'He'll go far, that one,' Ray proudly said of his daughter's boyfriend, putting his expulsion from boarding school down to financial ambition. Until he went too far, and Ray couldn't bring himself to look Harry squarely in the eye again.

Charlie and Harry were together when they took their GCSEs and A levels. They stayed together despite going to colleges at opposite ends of the country: Charlie to Bournemouth, Harry to study economics in Durham. Although they weren't always together, and Harry wasn't always there for Charlie: when he was taking his economics exams or trying to get into LSE, or when they were taking a break.

Charlie didn't care what Saph said or what her parents said when she was in her darkest hour. They had come round. Because Harry was her reliable city boy who knew how to keep a tidy flat, which pension plan was best for her as a freelancer, and how to invest his bonus so they could go to Australia one day. And he was about to support Charlie while she lounged around the very cool, very minimalist Chelsea apartment in New York for three months, while she thought about whether she might relocate there too.

* * *

As the cabin crew took their seats, Charlie looked out at the finger of Manhattan Island, jutting out of a continent beneath her, and saw buildings start to come into focus. Some skyscrapers shimmered as the pink sunset lit the sky and looked as though it might just reach all the way over to the West Coast.

Wow.

Charlie wondered which building Harry worked in out of all of those in the Financial District, although he wouldn't have been at work today. How would he have spent his Sunday? She imagined him cleaning an already pristine flat and going to the Farmers Market on Union Square; or to Whole Foods to stock up on shopping that came out of brown paper bags. The flight was due to land at 5.50 p.m. and it was only 5.20 p.m. They were going to be early.

As Charlie scrutinised the view, she could see landmarks start to come into focus: the Empire State Building, One World Trade Center, the Chrysler Building. Was that... was that a tiny Statue of Liberty over her left shoulder?

'Can't be,' she whispered.

It was.

'Oh, wow!' she said to the businessman two seats away, stopping short of hitting him on the arm. 'Statue of Liberty! Looks really small!' she marvelled.

The man looked nonplussed.

Miserable fucker.

She remembered the landing card she hadn't yet filled out and grabbed a pen from her bag on the seat between them, feeling a slight panic.

Name: Brown. Charlotte Florence.

Date of Birth:

Month first!

She was careful to write 02/11 instead of 11 February.

Number of family members traveling with you: NONE.

US Street Address:

Fuck.

Charlie looked through her phone notes, her message history, her WhatsApp search and any downloaded emails to try to remember the address of the apartment in Chelsea.

Shit, what was it?

Now Charlie thought about it, she wasn't sure if she ever *had* known Harry's address in any more detail than 'Chelsea'. She hadn't ever had to fill forms in with it; she hadn't felt the need to send Harry post in the digital era.

What if they don't let me in?

A panic crept up Charlie's neck as the landing gear was lowered under the fuselage. She looked briefly at the man in the suit, considering asking him his address so she could put that, but she suspected it wouldn't go down well.

Blake!

Charlie remembered the card of the upscale/downscale B & B Blake Perry had slipped her earlier in the series, which she had duly put in her bag thinking she wouldn't need it. His 'go-to bolt-hole in the Village', he called it. Charlie hadn't really known what upscale/downscale meant when he had said it conspiratorially, as if Charlie were privileged enough to know the secret to the universe, but it must be nice if Blake stayed there.

'There's no front desk and it feels like you live there. Like *Friends*, but chic, darling...'

Charlie scrambled more frantically now, among her Ishiguro and her iPhone, her Rescue Remedy and her boiled sweets, and was relieved to find the card tucked in an outer pocket of her leather bag. Blake hadn't really listened when Charlie had said she was reuniting with her boyfriend who *lived in New York*. But Blake was famous, and most famous people liked to talk at you and not really listen. Charlie was now grateful she had humoured Blake and taken the card anyway.

Thank fuck.

She wrote Jane Street Guest House, Jane Street, Greenwich Village, 10014, New York, New York on her landing card, before putting on a slick of Nars under her tired eyes and some peachy Bobbi Brown balm on her lips. She would thank Blake later.

* * *

Landed!

Charlie messaged Harry as soon as she switched off airplane mode and got her thumbs-up text to roam. Harry hadn't replied but he wasn't much of a texter and she knew it would be more special to just see him on the other side. So she sent her parents a message to tell them she had slept most of the way and had landed safely, then slipped her phone in her culottes pocket and regretted not wearing something warmer when she saw the New Yorkers on the plane unpack bobble hats and scarves.

* * *

As Charlie weaved through the Arrivals labyrinth of JFK airport she was struck by how tatty it looked. Not like the polished new terminal she'd flown from at Heathrow.

She clutched her passport and looked down at her colourful Frida Kahlo socks atop her bronze brogues as she walked through to Immigration with a spring in her step. Sunday evening in New York. Cold, starry, romantic.

A stern border patrol officer beckoned Charlie forward and she suddenly felt as if she had done something wrong. People always thought Charlie was younger than she was – so she teetered into teen mode and got defensive, even though technically she had done something wrong by lying on her landing card.

Greenwich Village was meant to be near Chelsea, she reasoned.

'Why are you visiting the United States, ma'am?' asked the glum and broad-set official.

'For a holiday. Er, vacation. To see my boyfriend,' Charlie replied proudly.

The man's face showed no emotion.

'Where will you be staying?'

Charlie's cheeks flushed pink.

'Here...' She pointed. Terrified. Showing the man the guest-house card she clutched in her hand, as if that made it official.

'How long will you be staying, ma'am?'

'A couple of months...' This was the part she was most nervous about. More than the address lie. 'I won't be working—'

'No, you won't, ma'am.'

'It's just a reunion. I haven't seen my boyfriend for six months!'

A tiny flicker of irritation curled on the corner of the border patrol officer's mouth as he whipped through the pages of Charlie's passport. She silently cursed herself for always saying too much. It was clear the official didn't care for bleeding-heart stories.

He gave a forceful stamp of an antiquated mechanical machine, handed Charlie's passport back to her and looked at her with a grave expression.

'Benjamin Steakhouse,' he said as he extended his arm to let her pass.

Charlie wondered if that was the man's name.

'Pardon me?'

'Benjamin Steakhouse.'

Cute.

'East 41st Street, between Park and Madison...'

His accent was so thick, and Charlie was so caught off guard, she still looked flummoxed. 'Best flank in the city and most romantic restaurant in the world. My wife loves it.'

'Oh. Thank you. Noted!' Charlie said, pointing an index finger to her temple and giving a huge smile.

'Welcome to America, ma'am.' The officer nodded, and a relieved Charlie whizzed through to Baggage Reclaim and the Arrivals hall, full of butterflies for the relief and the reunion.

4

Charlie had hoped the doors to the Arrivals hall would be sweeping and slick, to make her big entrance to the Big Apple even more magical. But they were nondescript and office-like, propped open by two black plastic door stoppers.

She didn't care. She was about to see Harry. The airport didn't matter, only the reunion, she thought as she came through, heavy orange case on its wheels by her side as she scanned the faces looking back at her eagerly. The drivers, the delegates, the lone lovers, the entire families. Airport reunions were so romantic, even though she'd never had one of her own. But she'd seen *Love Actually* when she was sixteen, and then every Christmas thereafter, and she knew that if she was ever going to have a heart-swelling airport reunion of her own, this was going to be it.

Where is he?

She laughed to herself, imagining a taxi crisis making a flustered Harry about to enter stage left, golden hair flopping as he pushed it back upwards. Disciplined gym-toned arms bursting out of his Sunday shirt. But he didn't. Charlie laughed again, except this time it was tinged with slight exasperation.

This is something I would do!

Her bemused smile dropped as her eyes darted left and right, scanning the scene, but she *still* couldn't see Harry's face in the crowd. After a few minutes of looking and lingering, she knew she had to shuffle out of the way, along with The People Who Had No One, so as not to cause a bottleneck.

This was not how it happened to Hugh Grant and Martine McCutcheon.

* * *

Charlie snaked through with her case. Flicking over the blissful faces of people already reunited: the lovers in their embrace, the drivers leading clients out to cars. Scanning the hot faces of people rushing to Arrivals. Hoping Harry would emerge from the throng of people arriving by taxi, metro and car at JFK. But however much she scrutinised the barrier, at the Travelex currency booth, the coffee shop or the Dunkin' Donuts, Harry was nowhere.

What the fuck?

She found a seat on a bank of chairs outside a paper shop called Metro News, parked her case and slumped down, getting her phone out of her pocket. She looked at her message to Harry. Two grey ticks. Delivered but not read. Perhaps there was a network issue with her new provider. She called his phone. A singular dial tone she had become familiar with over the past six months rang, but it rang through. Usually if he was in a meeting or Charlie had messed up the time difference, it would ring about ten times before going through to voicemail, but this time it didn't. It rang and rang.

No answer. She pictured his phone on the floor of a yellow cab, or in the pocket of his coat.

We'll laugh about this later, she thought, until she pictured his phone mangled, smashed, screen broken after Harry had been hit by said New York taxi and gone flying twenty metres into the air.

Shit.

She looked around the terminal again and then back to her phone, not knowing what to do, then looked around and saw a cashpoint.

Money! I'll get money. I need it anyway.

That would kill a few minutes while she waited. First she fired off another text before standing up and walking in a small circle as she stared at her phone.

I'm here! In the Arrivals hall. ICYMI.

She sent another.

Landed half an hour ahead of time but I'll sit and wait.

And another.

I've been here an hour now.

Where the hell are you?

As she sent that she felt a punch of panicked guilt in case the Flat Harry scenario was the correct one.

Hope you're OK, love you x

* * *

Two hours later, Charlie had got cash, been to the loo, cried, touched up her make-up and cried again.

Three hours I've been in America! Three fucking hours! WHERE ARE YOU?! Pick up!

She was furious with Harry now. But also worried. Was he OK? Was he dead? She thought about their last actual exchange and looked at her phone to remind herself of it. That she had communicated the correct day to him (she had) and flight number (yes, V137 from LHR). Their exchanges had mostly been to do with the stuff he wanted Charlie to bring out. He had texted on Tuesday with a shopping list: Marmite. Tea. Liberty ties. Rose & Violet Creams. Magazines.

See you Sunday babycakes.

He *knew* it was Sunday she was landing. She did have a missed call from him on Saturday evening – lunchtime in New York – when Charlie had been in the throes of doing Ashlee Niedermeyer's make-up. It wasn't the sort of face you could stop to take a call during. So she'd ignored it, finished Ashlee's finale face (she went smoky eye *and* red lip), and fired off a message to Harry.

Going live, call you after the show.

She hadn't called him. Now she thought about it, they hadn't spoken all week. She'd been so busy, so elated about going to New York, scrabbling around Soho and Sainsbury's to get ties and Marmite, she hadn't had the chance to align the time zones and chat. Perhaps she had subconsciously not called because she wanted to save all their gossip for the blissful New York marathon of sex and conversation she had so been looking forward to. She'd just been so fucking busy.

Maybe something happened, she worried. *Maybe he was calling to say he couldn't collect me. Maybe something came up.*

Charlie pouted. Surely nothing could be more important than this.

But then he would have sent her a message.

Fuck!

Charlie felt such despair, she stared at her phone and wondered what to do. Charlie was not a stare-at-your-phone-and-wait sort of person. She had looked through the slew of pictures that had come in from the *LWD* after-party and all the messages that had wished her 'Safe flight!' 'Happy travels!' and 'Have a wonderful time in New York!' She'd never felt so lost and impotent. Charlie had never suffered FOMO, she was active, not passive, and if plans didn't include her she tended to find something better to do with her time anyway. She had never felt like such a passive, powerless bystander as she did now.

What do I do?

She thought about Jasmine. What would Jasmine do? But was too embarrassed to text her. She'd exchanged a couple of excited texts to her parents to let them know she had got through safe and well; then she'd lied and said it was great to be reunited with Harry – she didn't want to worry them – but she considered calling Saphie. Except it was now 9 p.m. in New York, and would be two in the morning back home. Plus she knew how Saphie would react.

* * *

By 11.30 p.m. Charlie felt too unsafe to leave the sanctuary of the airport alone, so she decided to stay there the night, and moved around. From bench to bench. Arrivals. Departures. Pretending she was early for an imaginary flight or waiting for a scatty sister. Nursing hot chocolates. Sleeping fretfully where she could, wrapped in her oversized lilac coat and huge yellow scarf, suitcase strap clipped to her wrist. At 3 a.m. she called all the hospitals she could find on her phone in Manhattan, and asked if there was a Harry Taylor in the emergency room. Most had been helpful, the Eye, Ear & Throat Center aside. No Harry Taylors in any of the hospitals or psychiatric centres listed for Manhattan. As her anger rose, she called Harry for what felt like the 104th time. No answer. Not funny any more. I feel like Tom Hanks.

Where are you?

'What do I do?' Charlie said out loud in a quiet, exasperated voice. She had seen so many people come and go she was worried Security would notice her and ask her to move along. But no one had. It was almost as if she were invisible.

Did I fucking die in a plane crash and not realise it?

At 4.30 a.m. Charlie heard a small cry coming from somewhere around a corner, under a flight of stairs and an escalator that led to the departures hall upstairs. Charlie looked around to see if anyone else had noticed the cry, or if there was a responsible adult around as the cry sounded as if it might be coming from a child. A cleaner pushed a cart and changed the liner of an airport bin. A young Asian couple walked past oblivious. Charlie tentatively stood up and unhooked herself from her case.

She peered around the corner towards the underside of the stairs.

'Are you OK?' she called softly, one hand still on her suitcase, one toe pointing towards the direction the noise was coming from. 'Everything all right?'

Sniffs and whimpers started to get clearer; Charlie heard a panicked little cry, so she stepped away from her bag, suitcase and coat on the bench to investigate further.

Under the stairs was a small child, of about seven or eight, huddled in a ball, sobbing softly. She wore red dungarees over a pink roll-neck and had buttery brown hair, but her face was tucked into her knees.

'Oh dear!' Charlie said in her lightest, gentlest voice. The one she usually used for Mabel. 'Are you OK? Are you lost?'

She peered closer.

'I can find your grown-up for you if you let me know who you are travelling with...?'

The girl didn't lift her head but quietly whimpered into her knees.

'Hang on, let me just get my stuff, and then I can help you. We can go find your family.'

Charlie went back to the bench where she had spread herself out and hurriedly stuffed her scarf, book and ear buds into her green leather bag, along with her phone and its waning battery, slung it on top of the suitcase and labouredly heaved it around in the direction of the stairs. 'Just coming!' she called to the girl as she rounded the corner, but she stopped abruptly when she saw the girl had gone.

'Hey!' Charlie said to the empty stairwell.

She looked up and down the hall, a couple of times in each direction. The cleaner was sweeping litter into a tall dustpan. A jaded-looking cafe worker carried a stack of paper cups. Two cabin crew strode through efficiently, lamenting their schedules and rotas as they passed.

'Did you see a little girl just now?' Charlie asked the cleaner,

who had earphones in. The cleaner looked up at Charlie with a
quizzical face. She obligingly took her earphones out.

'A little girl here – she was crying under the stairs. Lost
maybe...'

'*No sé lo que...*' the cleaner replied in Spanish and shrugged.

Charlie looked up and down again. There was no sign of a girl
in red dungarees.

5

TWO DAYS BEFORE CHRISTMAS

At 6 a.m. Charlie called Saphie, from her new perch outside another Dunkin' Donuts franchise that smelled of sugar and deep fat fryers in need of a change of oil. It was a smell she didn't like at any time of day, let alone sunrise after a fretful and sleepless night.

Saphie answered and even before she could speak, Charlie burst into tears.

'What's the matter? Are you OK?' Saphie stopped the screeching sound of pulling brown parcel tape from its roll – she had been wrapping a neon clock she had been commissioned to create for a store on Brick Lane – and muted *Sky News* on the TV.

Charlie managed to speak just about clearly enough to tell Saphie that Harry hadn't turned up.

'What the fuck?' Saphie gasped. 'Where are you?'

'In the airport.'

'Still? What time is it?'

'I spent all night here, waiting for him.'

There was silence on the other end.

'Saph?'

'Sorry, Charlie, I'm fuming.'

'I am too, but I'm also worried. What if something's happened to him?'

She could hear Saphie let out a sigh and pictured her rubbing her forehead with her palm.

'Are you OK?' Saphie asked, after catching her breath and making a mental note not to berate Harry too much. That wouldn't help now.

'Yeah, I'm safe. I found a nice bench.'

Charlie looked around, surprised at the small relief a new day brought her: staff opening up their airport shops, baggage-handling agents walking through with lanyards flapping, cabin crew weaving to meet their flight team for the day. The footfall of eager passengers gradually, positively, trickling into the airport, making the place seem a little less terrifying and lonely than it had in the middle of the night.

'You've spent the night on a bench in JFK?'

Charlie didn't bother saying she'd spent the night on several benches and seats in JFK.

'You poor thing. Can you not just go to the apartment?'

'I didn't want to in the middle of the night.'

'Get a cab, sweetie, he must be there. Maybe he got the day wrong. I missed my flight from KL to Bali, remember? Because I turned up a day late...'

'Slight problem, Saph.'

'What?'

'I don't have his address.'

'You don't have Harry's address?'

'Work helped him secure the apartment; the documents were all electronic. I've looked through all our emails about the move but I don't think I *ever* had his actual address.'

'You've not ever sent him anything?'

'We send each other messages every day,' Charlie said defensively, before softening. 'Until recently. Work—'

'But can you remember, have you ever sent him something physical to the apartment? Maybe there's an address or postcode on one of those Post Office receipts on the fridge.

'No,' Charlie said, almost with shame. Prash and Saph were corresponders. Postcards. Love notes. Aerogrammes. Thoughts, feelings and mementoes jotted down and sent with a stamp. Prash treasured his archive.

'Have you called his office?'

'It was Sunday night, but I will soon.'

'What can I do?' Saphie asked despairingly. Charlie was sure she heard her mumble 'motherfucker' under her breath.

'Maybe there is some paperwork somewhere. In the flat...' Charlie said, clutching at straws, wondering how to find out Harry's address without the shame and embarrassment of calling his parents. They never were terribly supportive of Charlie over the years. And even as the words came out, she realised it was futile – why would there be paperwork pertaining to the move lying around? Everything about Harry's move to New York, visits to the American embassy aside, was sorted through email, through Goldcrest, through his relocation app. When Harry was choosing an apartment from an online edit he was sent by the relocation manager and Charlie had excitedly looked over his shoulder, they never specified anything more than the district. Tribeca. Grammercy. Greenpoint. Chelsea.

Charlie scratched her temple. She could tell Saphie that the apartment they chose – the apartment *Harry* chose – had exposed brickwork, and one of those chutes that went from the sink to the garbage disposal. She knew it looked quite industrial and minimalist and Harry would have kept it as tidy as it looked in the virtual online tour. She knew that, like her flat in Finchley, the only sign of him living there would be his neatly hung clothes and a cupboard with protein shakes in it. But she couldn't tell anyone the address, other than that it was in Chelsea.

'Where will I find it?' Saphie asked, scrabbling at the remaining photos and pieces of paper attached to the fridge. 'Is there visa stuff? Did he leave any paperwork here? Or a forwarding address, for fuck's sake?'

'I... I just don't know...'

Saphie was trying to be helpful. She felt desperate for Charlie and could hear the fear in her voice. It was rare to hear hopelessness in her bold friend. Unsettling even, because it reminded Saphie of *Then*. Saphie looked at the fridge door with its many notes, photos and papers, as if she were an FBI agent with a case to crack. As she studied it looking for clues, clutching the phone to her ear, Saphie remembered putting her arms around Charlie in their university kitchen, pulling her in, and telling her he wasn't worth it. She remembered looking at flats with her and telling her that she could totally do it on her own. She remembered scooping Charlie up off the bathroom floor, bent double and bloody, and telling Charlie that her dad was on his way.

Motherfucker.

'Actually, you know what,' Charlie decided. Now she thought about it, she really had never known Harry's New York address. She felt guilty that she didn't ever stop to ask, or send Harry an actual tangible housewarming card to greet him on his arrival, or a love note. Saphie would have sent Prash a love note, even if they were apart. 'I don't think I've ever written it down. God, I'm a shit girlfriend.'

'You are *not* a shit girlfriend,' Saphie countered, anger bubbling in her throat.

Charlie sighed as she pulled the card of the guest house Blake Perry had given her out of her pocket.

This is karma, she thought, shaking her head, *for lying*. She rubbed her thumb over the embossed text.

Jane Street Guest House, Jane Street, Greenwich Village, 10014 New York, New York. She needed a shower and a base. And when Harry was back at work later that morning, this whole confusion would be cleared up. If his phone had died; if he'd lost her number; if he had totally got the wrong day/week, she would be able to get hold of him at the office and relocate to his apartment after work.

'It's OK, Saph. I have a plan.'

'You do?'

'I'm going to check into somewhere for today, sort my shit out, get Harry to pay for it and go BALLISTIC when I see him. Unless he's died.'

Saphie let out an acerbic laugh. She hated the thought of Charlie, alone in a hotel in New York, and thought there must be another way.

'Can you call Lord and Lady Taylor?' she said with disdain. 'Oh, or what about Xander?'

Charlie had come close, in the darkest corners of the night.

'Nope. I'm going to sort it. Don't worry. Blake Perry gave me the name of his "upscale/downscale go-to bolthole" in New York, whatever the fuck that is, but I do remember he said it's near Chelsea because he loves that part of New York best. I've got the card here.'

'Well, let me know when you're safe and showered. You must be going crazy!'

'Will do. Thanks, Saph.'

'Love you.'

'Love you.'

'Oh, and Mabel sends a miaow. She's clawing at my bubble wrap right now, the little tinker.'

Charlie's heart flooded as she pictured Mabel, her face oval and flat, almost like a teddy bear, pouncing on bubbles. How her eyes lit up looking at Saphie's neon artworks. Fluoro pinks and yellows reflected in her now-orange eyes that were once baby blue, and suddenly she felt a warmth she hadn't in hours.

'Oh, I love you, Mabel,' Charlie cooed, wishing she were cheek to furry cheek with her right now.

'Yeah, she's being a terror. Get off!'

Charlie laughed.

'Right, better call this guest house and hope they have a room.'

'Let me know how you get on, OK?'

'Will do, bye.'

Charlie hung up to a 20 per cent low battery notification, swore again, and dialled the number on the bottom of Blake's crisp card.

6

Charlie's disappointingly-not-yellow taxi peeled away from the noise and traffic of a blustery Manhattan Monday morning and stopped on a quieter, cobbled street. The street was lined with trees shielding redbrick houses with tall stoops and wrought-iron lattice railings.

'Wow!' Charlie exclaimed as she rubbed her eyes. Some of the buildings were two storeys and elegant, some were five storeys high with fire-escape ladders that just looked so New York.

The branches of the trees that punctuated each pavement were bare and black, leading out like a Broadway chorus line all the way to the Hudson River at the end. Charlie got out of the taxi and looked down the road, glimpsing a slice of water at the far end, bobbling under a cold blue sky. The invigorating wind was certainly enough to wake Charlie's tired senses. It was 9.38 a.m. and she had barely slept all night.

'Sixty dollars, please,' said a man in an accent that sounded more Russian than New York.

Oh.

She rubbed her eyes. Charlie had done all-nighters before: with Saphie at Glastonbury when they had danced until dawn under the headphones and the canvas of the silent disco (Harry hadn't gone, the only festival he would deign to go to was with VIP tickets to the V Festival in Chelmsford because they had Portaloos with mock wooden toilet seats). She'd done all-nighters with Phil and Aidan on the beaches in Haad Rin, Thailand, dancing under the light of the full moon (Harry hadn't gone there either – they had been on a break). And she had done all-nighters in Brixton, tumbling out of the Academy and dancing with Saphie and her friends under their neon artworks in basement flats (which Harry also eschewed as he didn't like Saphie's arty friends). But this was a first. Up all night in New York: what she'd thought was going to be sexy and rampant and eye-opening and fun. A heady reunion in Chelsea followed by dancing with Harry's *new* New York mates. It had been one of the most traumatic nights of her life.

Grow up, Charlie chastised herself as she carefully counted out notes of money that all looked the same.

'There you go, mate,' she said, her joviality belying her broken-ness as she stood by the boot of the battered car.

The man lifted Charlie's heavy case out and gave her a sympathetic nod. As if he were in on the joke. Charlie smiled. So far New Yorkers had been kind to her. It was the Brit in the city who hadn't. Yet still, Charlie couldn't shake the guilt and worry that Harry might *not* be OK.

She looked up at the beautiful town-house-turned-guest-house and vowed that once she'd checked in, had a shower and charged her phone, she would call Harry's best friend, Xander, back in London, to see if he knew what the hell had happened.

* * *

The Jane Street Guest House had a small and nondescript oval plaque next to the front door that made it look nothing like a hotel. In fact, the whole street seemed residential, except for a cafe, bagel shop and convenience store at the end that crossed with the bigger, lateral avenues. There was a shoe shop in the building next door, a rare white façade among the mid-nineteenth-century red brick, but it looked so subtle and elegant, equally it could have been an art gallery or someone's home.

Charlie knocked on the door, wondering if it really was a hotel or one of Blake's special places, and a young man with short hair and sparkling blue eyes opened it, giving an actor's smile.

'Charlie?' he said warmly.

Was he in on the joke too?

'That's me,' she said, raising a hand.

'Come on in.'

'I wasn't sure if you would be expecting me. I only booked online a couple of hours ago.'

'You got lucky. The gentlewoman staying here left yesterday, after a month-long stint. Gone back West for the holidays. It's our last room.'

'Thank goodness.'

'I'm also Charlie,' the man said, extending a hand. 'Black though, not Brown.'

'No way!' Charlie laughed.

'Can I help you with that case?'

Gosh, people in New York were surprisingly friendly, thought Charlie as she shook his hand, said she'd be fine with the case, and lumbered it up the small stoop, into a little lobby that wasn't really a lobby but just a coffee table with a couple of chairs.

'I'm Charles though,' he admitted, with some regret, it seemed.

'Charlotte.'

'Welcome to New York, Charlotte. If I can just get your passport, please?' he asked, sitting primly at the laptop on the coffee table.

Charlie Black took Charlie Brown's details, handed her an old-fashioned set of keys, and wheeled her case to the grille door of the old-fashioned elevator and pressed a button.

'You take the elevator, third floor, I'll run up and see you there,' he said, closing the golden grille on her with a smile.

Charlie wasn't sure if the elevator would take the weight of her plus her orange case, the cage felt so rickety, but that, too, was kind to her, and when she squeezed out at the top and walked down the short corridor to the room where Charlie Black was standing in the open door, she wanted to cry with relief.

'It's lovely,' she said, looking around. The room's opulent touches were all artfully downplayed: the crimson walls looked in need of a refresh; the four-poster had no canopy or curtains; the gilded picture frames housed kitsch artworks that looked as if they might have come from a thrift store. It was luxe-looking but downbeat; opulent yet slightly battered.

Upscale/downscale.

It felt confusingly like home.

Charlie Black showed her how to work the TV, the heating, and said that there were blankets in the long thin wardrobe behind the small velour sofa.

'So you only booked for one night, was that right? Because if you do want to stay – for Christmas especially – it might be gone.'

Charlie stopped, bewildered, and looked at his face. It was so handsome, his quiff so neat, he looked as if he might be in a toothpaste commercial in the fifties. 'No pressure,' he said, holding up his hands. As if he might know that Charlie was really a donkey on the edge. 'But just so you know.'

Charlie ruffled her flattened hair and tried to look composed.

'Oh. I'm sort of up in the air. Need to work out what I'm doing.'

And work out the maths. She couldn't exactly afford to live here for a month, let alone three. Where the fuck was Harry? Where was Chelsea, come to think of it?

As the taxi had weaved its way from JFK on to Manhattan, Charlie had looked at the island and wondered where Harry was on it. What his coordinates were. Which downtown skyscraper was his office. Where had he been sleeping. If he was still even alive.

She just wanted to get showered and make some phone calls. Charlie Black got the message.

'No pressure. I tell you what, if I get a call for availability, I'll check in with you first. I've got your cell.'

'That'd be great, thanks.' Charlie smiled gratefully as the other Charlie carefully closed the tall door behind him.

Charlie wheeled her case next to the bed and went to the bathroom, which was exactly how she had imagined a New York bathroom to be. Not the sleek modern one from the photos of Harry's apartment: all floating loo and shiny teal units. This had white tiles, black fixtures, a very old toilet with a high cistern and long chain and a tiny window, which opened out onto the back brick walls of the buildings on the parallel street.

She pulled down her culottes, sat on the loo and looked at her phone while she peed.

'Where the fuck are you?' she asked it pleadingly as the battery went flat and the screen went black.

* * *

After Charlie showered she stopped to consider the room. If she weren't loath to unpack – hoping desperately she wouldn't be here longer than one night – it did perhaps look like somewhere she might want to stay. When she stopped to appreciate the colours – the plum cushions against the turquoise velour of the sofa, the crimson walls – it was her style, which felt that perhaps the universe had conspired for her to spend the night here. Just the one though. Maybe it was one big joke.

She regretfully rummaged in her case for her hairdryer, careful not to concede to unpacking while needing to look her best. If she was going out looking for Harry, she couldn't do it with wet or straggly hair. But she couldn't wait any longer to call Xander. It would be mid-afternoon in Westminster, where he was a policy advisor to a Tory cabinet minister.

The way her day was going she half expected him not to answer.

'Chazbaps!' Xander shouted as he, in fact, did. 'How's the New World?'

'Erm, great?' Charlie said unconvincingly.

'Hang on a minute, Harry doesn't call me for weeks and you're there ten minutes and you call to brag. Put him on, the weasel!'

Charlie laughed, utterly confused and totally lost for words. Xander clearly knew nothing about this in joke, or what had happened to Harry, and expected Charlie and Harry to be reunited too. She was so discombobulated she thought about hanging up, but she had to know anything Xander might, even if it was limited.

'Erm, have you spoken to Harry lately?'

'Not since he was in London.'

'Oh. That was ages ago,' Charlie said, but he hadn't seemed to hear.

'Put him on!'

'I can't, he's...' Charlie looked at the open door of the bathroom, wondering whether to lie. She had already lied in text to her parents. She was so terribly embarrassed – or she would be if there wasn't anything wrong with Harry and he was alive and well and had just not turned up. But this was too important. She had to be truthful. Xander wasn't her most favourite person in the world, he was lazy and entitled and his table manners were grim, but his charm was that he didn't realise how funny he was. And he was Harry's best friend. 'It's just that...'

It was hard to it say out loud to anyone other than Saphie. She was dreading the moment she might have to tell her parents. 'It's just that... Harry's not turned up. To meet me. At the airport.'

'What? What's happened? He's not still chained to his desk, is he?'

'I arrived on a Sunday. He shouldn't have been.'

'And he's still not with you? Fu-u-u-uck.'

'Well, quite. But I'm in a hotel. Safe and well, *thanks for asking*, but I have no clue what to do. When did you last hear from him?'

'Like I said, not since he was in London.'

'Since June?'

'And then I was pretty miffed with him, I have to say.' Xander sounded as if he was munching on an apple and spitting it everywhere, as was his toothy and messy way of eating. 'Hang on, June? No, when he was last here. Didn't call me, the weasel. I only found out he was here because Hugo bumped into him on the Fulham Road.'

'Wait, what?' Charlie stopped rubbing her hair and dropped the towel. 'What are you talking about?'

'When he was here a few weeks ago.'

'Harry was in London a few weeks ago?'

'Must have been late November because we joked that he was spending his first American Thanksgiving back here, but he said it was just a flying visit.'

'Xander, what are you talking about?'

Xander went quiet and Charlie could hear him scratching his mop of black curls.

'Harry was in London? Are you sure?'

'Well...' He started to bumble and shuffle like a Tory at a press conference. 'I-I-I-I... I didn't see him, Hugo did by chance and I was pretty miffed he hadn't told me he was in town, but he said it wasn't worth telling anyone about, the visit was so flying.'

'Well, clearly it wasn't worth telling me.'

'*You* didn't know?'

They stood in silence for a few seconds, both frozen with embarrassment and duplicity, on opposite ends of a line and an ocean. Perhaps Harry was still in London.

'Did he mention me coming to New York? *You* knew I was going! He knew! He was messaging me with requests for *fucking magazines*...'

'Yes, I knew you were going after the finale. Great show, by the way. Katie was plumping for Hrithik, bloody good-looking bugger. Shit, I hope Taylor's OK.'

'Well, that's what I'm worried about.'

'Have you called him?'

'Of course I've called him!' *You prick*, she thought. And then felt bad. 'He's not answering.'

'Have you checked hospitals and suchlike.'

Only Xander used words like *suchlike*.

'Yes, and no luck. Well, great luck in that he's not in any of them.'

'But he's not answering his mobile?'

'No. I wonder if it's been stolen, but I did wait and wait at the airport. I was there all night.'

'Oh, you poor thing.'

'I've had to check into a $280-a-night guest house. I can't live here for three months.'

'OK, don't worry, let me think.'

Charlie could hear the tapping of a pen on wood and remembered how useless Xander actually was.

'Look, don't worry, just try to remember what your last texts were like, just in case he was having some sort of breakdown we didn't notice or something, yes? I mean... London? Are you sure?'

'He did text me when he was back in New York, I think feeling bad we hadn't been for a beer, asking me to put a word in with the chancellor about something. I told him for the four hundredth time I'm DCMS.'

Charlie didn't know what DCMS was and right now didn't care. She just wished Xander hadn't confused her even more.

'But I'll have a look at my correspondences.'

Correspondences. Only Xander would call texts correspondences.

'OK, thanks,' Charlie said.

'Shall I call Mater and Pater?' he offered hopefully.

Not yet. She couldn't stand the thought of them knowing; she pictured the vicious giggles she had been privy to in the past when the Taylors closed rank. What if *they* knew about his UK visit when Charlie hadn't? That would be even worse. But Xander must have got that wrong. He was pretty hopeless.

'No, don't worry, I'll call them,' Charlie lied.

'OK, let me know how you're getting on, yah?'

'Xand...?' Charlie asked nervously. 'I don't suppose you have Harry's New York address, do you?'

Xander spluttered.

'Do you not?'

'No.'

'Erm, well, I don't either, sorry. No one does snail mail any more.' Xander's chortle annoyed Charlie. This wasn't funny.

'Have you tried work?'

'That's my next step. He'll be back at work, all going well. I'll head there soon.'

'OK, good luck, Chazbaps.' Xander was the only person who called Charlie Chazbaps, and it sounded so preposterous coming from his mouth that it usually made her laugh. It didn't now. 'Keep us posted, yah? And punch him in the nuts for me when you do get hold of him for keeping you waiting all this time, eh?'

When Charlie woke three hours later, her hair was dry, her phone fully charged and Jake Tapper was presenting news on CNN. She had got off the phone to Xander, cried, and felt such fatigue that she had fallen asleep, hair damp and tousled, half in heartache and half in body shock, onto the plump bed beneath her and caught up on some of the sleep she had missed overnight on the airport benches.

This isn't me, she thought as she tugged at her face in the bath- room cabinet mirror, smoothed a gentle sheen of strobe cream over her peachy skin, roughed her thick eyebrows with a brush and rubbed balm into her lashes and on her lips.

I'm in New York, for fuck's sake.

Charlie was not going to be defeated. She grabbed her red beret, lilac coat and bag with all the things she might need for the next few hours, and decided to walk the fifty-one minutes it said to get from Greenwich Village, through Soho, Tribeca and Lower Manhattan to the Financial District. She wasn't the gym bunny Harry was – she had never had a gym membership, despite Harry's efforts to sign her up – but she could walk an hour on the flat, she reckoned.

As Charlie turned right out of the Jane Street Guest House onto Jane Street she looked at the blue dot on the map on her phone. It pained her to walk away from Chelsea, which was just to the north according to the map, edging away from wherever Harry's apartment was. But she knew she had a better chance of finding him at the offices of Goldcrest, the Anglo-American bank Harry worked for, which she had an actual address for, than walking aimlessly around Chelsea while Harry was at work.

Something about the Empire State Building, anchoring Charlie to where she *shouldn't* be going, elegantly signposting her to where she should, gave her a reassurance as she walked, wrapped in her layers, through crisp air and neighbourhoods she recognised, even though she'd never been before. Past flower sellers and bakeries; coffee shops and little playparks; past hip pop-ups and grimy-looking stalls selling fakes, until the buildings started to crowd the sky and she lost sight of the Empire State Building.

You OK bud?

Saphie texted.
Charlie took a selfie outside Wall Street station and joked:

Sod Harry, I'm looking for Leo instead!

Just to reassure her that she still had her wits and her sense of humour about her. Then she took a photo of the rainbow bagel she had bought en route, and was the size of her head, in front of her face so she looked like a swirl of cream cheese and colour.

Go girl!

Saphie replied with the rainbow emoji.

Just before 4 p.m. Charlie arrived at the American HQ of Gold-crest, a bird etched onto a gold plaque over the revolving doorway, and looked up. A long way up. She had phoned the switchboard and asked to speak to Harry Taylor on her walk there, but the operator said he was unavailable right now. When Charlie tried her luck and asked for Harry Taylor's home address, she got the answer she expected.

'Sorry, ma'am, we don't give out personal information. Can I leave a message?'

Charlie had left enough of those. She knew turning up was her only option.

* * *

In the vast marble lobby Charlie was surprised to see there were about four hundred different offices within the Goldcrest skyscraper, all departments she didn't even understand the names of.

'Hello, hi...' she said, with affectation, trying to downplay her Lancashire accent. The one she had kept but Harry had lost quickly, somewhere between going to Durham to study economics, doing his masters at LSE, getting his internship at Deutsche Bank and landing his first job with Goldcrest, although Charlie wondered if Harry had ever sounded as if he was from the Ribble Valley. She couldn't remember an accent at school. 'I'm wondering which floor Harry Taylor works on, and whether I can speak to him, please?'

The man with the headset started typing slowly with two fingers.

'Which department, ma'am?'

Fuck.

Charlie tried to remember what it was Harry actually did.

'Umm... currency hedging perhaps?' she said hopefully, as if she were answering the million-dollar question in a quiz. Why did it feel as if she were breaking into a fortress when she was just trying to catch up with her boyfriend of sixteen years? She looked around for him. At the stairs, the lifts, the building he came to and from every day, and hoped this was all a total misunderstanding.

'Thirty-third floor, ma'am. Sign in here, please. Do you have ID?'

Charlie handed the receptionist her passport – he took it, typed in her name with two fat forefingers, and printed out a docket and put it in a lanyard for her.

It was the same deal at the thirty-third-floor reception area. Although Charlie felt a pang of optimism and nervousness at being closer.

'Harry Taylor, he works on this floor...'

The receptionist with flame-red hair called Harry's line, but there was no answer.

'Oh, there's a note here,' she said, pressing her finger at her screen and hanging up. 'He's on annual leave. For Christmas.'

Charlie's shoulders slumped. Could he really be in London? Surely Xander was talking nonsense as ever. Harry would have told her if he were in London.

'Wait, what?'

She looked at the clock on the TV behind the woman. It was 4.11 p.m. on Monday 23 December.

'He's gone *for Christmas*?'

'Back January.'

'January?'

Charlie felt sick; the receptionist shrugged.

'But Harry Taylor is my—'

'Oh, you sound just like him!' interjected a woman with a black shiny bob as she waited for the lift. 'You must be his sister! Oh, your accents are adorable.'

'Back 3 January, that's what the note says,' the red-haired receptionist repeated. 'Most workers take the whole holidays off. Two weeks if they're traders... to spot for irregularities,' she said helpfully.

'Oh, he's gone to Isabelle's, upstate,' the woman said as she repeatedly jabbed the lift button. She stopped in her tracks and pivoted, a delicious smile softening her sharp features. 'Are you here to *surprise* him?'

The woman with the shiny black hair had a high short fringe, a killer suit and scrutinising eyes as she looked Charlie up and down. She already knew her colourful clothes didn't fit in around the Financial District.

'Isabelle's, you say?' Charlie asked, as neutrally as she could.

'Yah, for the holidays. You have his cell, right?'

'Yes, but I did rather want to surprise him...' she said, affectation sounding more Harry Lancashire than Charlie Lancashire. 'Where does Isabelle live?'

The lift doors opened and the woman slunk in.

'Oh, you can't miss the Irving house!'

The woman said it with a smile as the lift doors slid shut and Charlie wondered why the woman hadn't thought to hold the lift for her – she was clearly on her way out too.

'Happy holidays!' the woman called before she disappeared,

although Charlie wasn't sure if she was saying it to the receptionist, to her, or to neither of them.

* * *

Charlie slumped into the first Starbucks she saw on the block, comforted by the fact it smelled just the same as any of the Starbucks branches in London, Lancashire or anywhere else in the world, and ordered a hot chocolate. As the darkness settled in the slice of sky between the buildings, Charlie accepted that she would be spending another night alone.

'Fuck,' she mumbled into her canned cream, which tasted like the stuff her dad had wrecked her with during a game of Pie Face last Christmas. She so wanted to see Ray and Ruth right now. At least she had a warm safe bed for the night.

But Harry wasn't dead. He was on holiday. *Upstate.*

Unless there was another Harry Taylor at Goldcrest. Who happened to be English too. Neither name was unusual. As Charlie stirred aerated cream into hot milk and watched it evaporate, she remembered Leyla telling her about a girl in her twins' class. First name Penelope. Last name Keith. They had speculated about poor Penelope Keith and whether her parents had chosen the name ironically, or whether they just hadn't put two and two together. Perhaps they didn't grow up in eighties Britain and had no clue. Harry Taylor was a more common name than Penelope Keith surely?

But how could he have forgotten Charlie was coming for Christmas? Unless he thought she was coming for New Year. But he *knew.* The emails, messages and phone calls had always referred to Sunday. They had joked about having pastrami bagels for Christmas dinner; she had said she'd leave New Year's Eve plans in Harry's hands, while secretly hoping they involved a proposal or some kind of gesture of commitment. They'd had a conversation about the relief of not trudging between Charlie's family cottage and Hawksworth Hall two villages away. Of doing Christmas *their* way. Even if they did eat pastrami bagels, although Harry wasn't big on bagels. A bagel was his whole day's carb allowance if he was doing keto or on a shred.

What did he want to say on Saturday night?

Charlie sipped her hot chocolate that wasn't hot enough to comfort her and watched the city workers pack up for the holidays. Tomorrow would be Christmas Eve.

What do I do?

She wondered who to call.

Do I just go home?

She still hadn't even told her parents that Harry hadn't turned up. She didn't dare tell Jasmine, who had told her before, with the confidence of her youth, that she thought Harry was an 'utter prick' and Charlie should use New York as a chance to cut him loose.

Maybe I just get the next flight home, rock up on the doorstep and surprise Mum and Dad.

But here she was. New York. She couldn't come all this way without seeing it. And she couldn't go home without seeing Harry.

Charlie awoke her phone, opened Google and searched up Isabelle Irving and Goldcrest. A blonde all-American girl with blue eyes and bright teeth popped up, along with news stories and images of her walking out of restaurants, at fundraisers, or completing charity pursuits. There were photos of her with women who had to be her sisters, they all looked as if they were cut from the same cloth. Charlie zoomed in on one photo of three blonde young women sitting lovingly and obediently around their parents, Seymour and Cathy. A quick Wikipedia link led Charlie to Seymour J. Irving Jr, a businessman who had founded Irving Inc., a company that did something in refining and pipelines and words Charlie glossed over. But she did see that Seymour J. Irving Jr lived in a sprawling mansion in Bedford Hills, Westchester, New York. A quick search of 'Irving house Bedford Hills' revealed the Irving mansion had been the backdrop of photo shoots with *Forbes*, *Elle Decor* and *Town & Country*. Most of them with Isabelle and her very blonde sisters shining like jewels at their parents' feet.

What a load of bloody bollocks.

Yet the word *upstate* had got caught in Charlie's ear and left a tiny tingling pain.

That couldn't be where Harry was.

The Irving house.

It was clearly one of the grandest homes in the state, if not the country, and another search said the train to Bedford Hills took one hour twenty-one minutes from Grand Central Terminal.

Maybe I just rock up on their *doorstep.*

Charlie sipped the dregs of her hot chocolate and told herself not to be ridiculous. This must be the biggest practical joke Harry had ever played – Harry did like a practical joke. He was known for them at school and even now among his friends. His favourite was sticking a picture of Nicolas Cage to the underside of the toilet lid to scare visitors when they went to pee. Charlie didn't find Harry's practical jokes all that funny, especially not when she went to the loo in the night. Maybe this was just an elaborate, more grown-up practical joke. Like an escape room. Harry had done an escape room for his thirtieth birthday and loved it, so perhaps this was one huge city-sized escape room that would result in a beautiful proposal. Charlie shook her head.

Isabelle Irving, please fuck off.

She decided to head back to Greenwich Village via the subway before it got too dark and scary for her to really start panicking.

8

_____

CHRISTMAS EVE

Charlie woke on Christmas Eve bathed in sweat and steeped in determination. Her clammy skin was the result of a nightmare, the first she'd had in months, and was so terrifying, she pulled the vest of her pyjama top up from her waist to her collarbone to mop her clavicles dry. In the dream she was back in the airport, on one of the many godforsaken benches where she had spent Sunday night. Uncomfortable and cold and lonely and scared. The girl under the stairs was curled into a ball again. Little cries and whimpers coming from an echo between her knees. Charlie was paying more attention this time. Desperate to be helpful. She looked closer at the girl; swore she wouldn't lose sight of her. Her attention and focus were so heightened, she could see a small ball of fluff attached to one ankle of the girl's red corduroy dungaree legs, which she must have picked up in her dusty corner.

'Oh dear...' Charlie had said gently. 'Are you OK?'

In her dream she could see her own hand reaching out in front of her, yellow under the airport strip light that was flickering slightly.

Her hand, which she was observing as if her dream had been

filmed with a shaky point-of-view camera, reached out, edging nearer to the girl. Charlie couldn't work out if it was predatory or soothing, but she only wanted to help. She reached out to the girl, getting nearer. Charlie was going to touch her on the shoulder. Feel the softness of her straight hair.

'Are you los—?'

Before Charlie had even got the word out the girl looked up and roared. A distended mouth like a cage of fangs jumped out at her and what smelled like bile and death blew towards Charlie in a shrieking gust of air. The girl's eyes, which she'd imagined to be sweet and sad, were angry and chilling, piercing and sharp despite their milky veneer.

'No!' Charlie shouted as she jolted awake, boiling hot in a bed with too much bedding. She looked at her phone and it was 6.30 a.m. Not too early to get up, especially when she had A Plan.

She fired off a text to her parents, telling them that she and Harry were having such a brilliant time she hadn't taken many photos yet but would today, and one to Saphie to tell her not to worry, she was fine and going to do some sightseeing.

But did you catch him at the office?

Saphie had asked again. Charlie hadn't replied to her three texts last night. Typing it out would only confirm Saphie's already questionable opinion of Harry, and she just couldn't face disappointing or worrying her. Or the crushing reality that was looming ever closer. She was too shattered.

As Charlie showered in the small white and black bathroom, hard beams of water pummelled her beaten skin. A text came in from Xander to the phone on the bed, which she leaped for as soon as she got out of the shower.

Sure you've caught up with him by now but in case you haven't – this is all I have!

Wrapped in a towel, Charlie examined the screenshots. Harry, a martini glass raised to his lips, looking at the camera smugly and a message below saying:

Happy birthday from the Big Apple

Xander's reply had been:

Fuck off lucky bastard.

It must have been early October, Xander's birthday. Charlie studied the picture closely. A rooftop bar. Relaxed looking in a pale shirt, open at the neck, rolled-up sleeve showing his muscular fore-arm. A sparkle in his eye. Charlie tried to guess who had taken the photo to elicit such a sparkle. Isabelle? How tall was she? They were both sitting down. He didn't look as if he was missing Charlie much.

Charlie decided not to answer. She had nothing to say. A photo from over two months ago was so lame and added neither insight nor hope. This predated the exchange about Harry being spotted on the Fulham Road in November.

As Charlie got dressed and dried her hair in the mirror above the tiny white sink, the TV kept her company. Jake Tapper chatting with a jovial meteorologist in a Santa hat, who said a deluge was coming to the Midwest.

Charlie grabbed the remains of the giant rainbow bagel in its paper bag, plus a muffin she'd bought yesterday at Magnolia Bakery, and put them in her bag with her wallet, passport, phone and assortment of woollen accessories (red beret, yellow scarf, cream cable-knit mittens) and left her room, wishing she could be as excited about Christmas as the glamorous meteorologist, but she had never felt so utterly let down and miserable in her life.

As Charlie trod the streets of Greenwich, she called the most recently dialled number in her phone again. Harry Taylor. That solitary, hollow dial tone. Again, it rang through. This obviously wasn't Harry's phone number any more. Whether his phone had been stolen, squashed, or tucked away in a drawer.

At the corner of Jane Street and 8th Avenue, Charlie stopped outside a closed tavern with a green awning and looked on her phone for directions to Grand Central. An Uber looked as if it was what most locals did, so she tapped open the app and called one under the UberPool option she hadn't used in London before.

Two minutes. Licence plate ending 4528.

I love New York! Charlie thought, except there was something of a barrier stopping her from really loving it, and she felt a kick of resentment to Harry for that. Two and a half minutes later a weatherworn grey Honda Accord pulled up with the corresponding number plate and Charlie gave the top of the Empire State Building's elegant art deco tiers a nod before opening the back door.

As she was about to slide in, she saw a signpost on the pavement opposite, showing a walking sign to Chelsea Market behind her.

Chelsea!

Charlie hadn't realised quite how close she was to Harry's district. As she wavered with the car door half open, she wondered if she should just walk and walk around Chelsea. See if she might recognise Harry's building from the virtual tour they had been given last summer. See if she could spot where Harry lived from deep memory or instinct. What use was it if he wasn't even there?

She teetered on a mental tightrope: get in and go to Grand

Central, or pace the streets of Chelsea. It must have been another
Harry Taylor who had gone upstate to the Irving house.

'You gettin' in or what, miss?' gruffed the driver.

And there it was. Charlie finally had her first experience of an
abrupt and grumpy New Yorker, straight out of *Copland*, *The
Sopranos* and *Trading Places*. All the films and TV shows she had
watched with Ray and Ruth that had made this place seem so
familiar. Everyone had been so unexpectedly nice so far. She
almost wanted to thank the driver for not throwing her another
curveball, but instead she did what all good British tourists did,
and she apologised.

'Sorry,' Charlie said, still flummoxed. She leaned her head
down and saw the expectant face of the fellow carpool passenger,
waiting to see if she was getting in; whether they would be splitting
the fare today or not.

'Erm, yeah, Grand Central?'

'Come on already!' the driver huffed. 'We're on green!'

Charlie jumped in, closed the door and apologised to the
waiting passenger, a man with dark brown hair, olive skin, a
burgundy tweed blazer and a deep grey scarf. His liquid brown
eyes were enormous, but patient.

'I'm so sorry,' Charlie apologised again. 'I just wasn't sure...'

The light changed red just as the Uber driver pulled away from
the kerb and he cursed under his breath.

'No problem!' The man alongside her shrugged casually, trying
to offset the driver's negative energy. He felt bad for the indecisive
woman with the English accent. It was only him she was inconve-
niencing, and he didn't mind. But he did feel responsible for the
driver being an asshole.

'Where are you going to?' the man asked.

Charlie looked at him across the back seat. His jacket looked
something between an heirloom and an afterthought and she

couldn't work out which. It wasn't like the tweed jacket Harry's dad wore when he was shooting – it looked frayed around the edges, as if it might have patches on the elbows and was loved.

'Grand Central station.' Charlie smiled, laying a copy of *People* magazine she had picked up at the grocery store across her lap. Harry and Meghan on the cover, looking up at her.

'No, but where to from there?'

'Oh! Sorry. Bedford Hills. Somewhere in Westchester.' She avoided saying upstate. She hated the woman who had said *upstate*. 'Do you know it?'

The man looked impressed, as if it was the sort of place he would like to go to but hadn't.

'Nice. For Christmas?'

'No. Yes! Oh, I'm not sure.'

'Not sure? Wow. It's Christmas Eve. You're a fly-by-the-seat-of-your-pants kinda woman, huh?'

Charlie frowned at him for mentioning her pants, before she remembered he didn't mean *those* kind of pants. This was America.

'Oh, I'm just looking for someone.'

'Someone in particular?'

'You ask a lot of questions.'

'It's what I do,' the man said.

'Are you a journalist?'

He frowned in mock horror.

'Hell no! I'll leave that to those guys...' He nodded to the magazine. 'I'm a geologist.'

It was Charlie's turn to give a caricature of an impressed face, raising her eyebrows and turning her mouth downwards so her little V-shaped chin crinkled.

'At Columbia.' He pointed ahead out of the taxi window as if it were nearby, but in truth Charlie didn't know where it was. Perhaps he even meant South America. 'We're curious types,' he said as if he were apologising. 'I ask a lot of questions in my research and I ask a lot of questions of my students. Sorry, I didn't mean to intrude.'

Charlie widened her eyes, lined with a smudge of golden green today. She always did feel a bit more kickass with a blaze of smoky liner or a Dior feline flick along her long lids. Today she wanted to feel more kickass.

'But you just asked me a question so we might be even.'

This guy had a flirty sparkle Charlie tried not to like, except it was nothing but warm and she felt safe in the car with him. It was the longest conversation she'd had with anyone since she had left London.

'We're definitely not even,' she batted back. 'You're about four–one up. Not that I'm counting.'

'Not that you're counting.'

They paused and both smiled to themselves as they looked out of their respective windows and the traffic lights turned green again.

'So are you British?'

'Five–one. Yes.' Charlie smiled with some self-satisfaction and the man laughed. 'You're American? Five–two, catching up.'

They both laughed.

'Well, you could have passed that off as more of a statement than a question, but yes, I'm American,' the man said, rolling his eyes almost by way of an apology. Charlie had become accustomed to doing that when she was abroad, although she hadn't yet in New York. People had seemed enchanted whenever they heard her speak.

'You going to Grand Central too? Five–three.'

'No, the library just up the road.'

'Let's stop counting.'

'*I* already had!' The man put his hands up in submission and gave a smile that lit his warm features, and Charlie felt as if she could tell him a little bit more.

'I'm here to find my... erm. A friend. Up in Bedford Hills.'

'And hope they take you in for Christmas?'

'That's a question too far.'

'Sorry, it's just you're travelling light.'

'No, just to... to catch up. See how they are. Someone who's sort of missing.'

She looked out of the window and her eyes filled up a little, reminding her of her reality. This was all so crazy.

The man saw the sadness flicker over her face in profile and was relieved to point out the Flatiron Building propping up a junction, in the road and their conversation.

'You been in New York long?'

'No, just a day. Two,' she said with some irony that was lost on her fellow passenger. 'It's my first time here, so keep the landmarks coming...' She had a humour about her the man hadn't come across before.

He laughed. They were about to pass the Empire State and the Chrysler Buildings, but the British woman wouldn't see them from inside the car, with the density of the streets' crowded skylines.

'Well, if you are in a fix tomorrow, I'm having Friendmas in the Village. I'm not good at missing persons but I make a mean *melomakarona*.'

Charlie smiled. Even though she didn't know what *melomakarona* was, and it sounded like a wonderful geometric scientific decoration *thing*, she would rather spend Christmas on her own than with strangers.

'Thank you.' She nodded.

He opened his jacket and took out a Sharpie from the inside pocket.

'May I?' He gestured to the magazine.

'Sure.'

The man wrote the name 'Pete' across Prince Harry's forehead and underneath it a stream of digits. Underneath those he drew a Hitler moustache on Harry's upper lip, and a more flamboyant, curly one on Meghan. It seemed a bit of a left-field thing for a stranger to do to her crisp new magazine she had just paid five dollars for, but it made Charlie chuckle anyway. She covered her mouth and realised she hadn't laughed in days.

'Pete,' she said, regaining herself.

'Pete,' he confirmed. 'If you get in a fix over Christmas... my friends are real friendly.'

'Well, thank you, Pete, I'm Charlie.'

'Charlie,' he repeated slowly with a nod.

'And I appreciate your generous offer,' she said, knowing that they would never see each other again.

'Grand Central!' announced the driver, accent a bit less thick now he didn't seem so angry.

'I'll get out here too,' Pete told him.

'Oh, are you sure?' Charlie asked, worried that she had inconvenienced him.

'Yeah, it's just two blocks up there...'

Pete gathered his small backpack, got out of the car and stood on the pavement. He was tall with chocolate-brown hair pushed up above his large forehead, and a slow, sweet diction.

Charlie walked around to join him, dropping a mitten in the gutter as she stepped on the pavement. Pete picked it up and handed it to her.

'Thanks,' she said.

'No problem,' he replied as he straightened his jacket over his shirt and jeans. He looked underdressed compared to the bustle of people walking in all directions around them, wrapped in duvet coats and parkas; twirled in hats, scarves and mittens. Almost as if

Pete must travel with his own personal beam of sunshine above his head. In truth he had cursed himself when he'd left his apartment and realised how cold it was, but he was so keen to get to the New York Public Library that he couldn't be bothered to turn around and walk back up the stoop.

Charlie straightened her beret and wound her scarf up around her neck.

'Well, thanks for making my first UberPool an OK experience and not being a serial killer.'

'How do you know I'm not?'

'Good point. I don't think serial killers ask that many polite questions. Or wear jackets like yours,' she said, hitting him with her rolled-up magazine.

Pete wasn't sure if that was a compliment or gentle mockery.

'I must try harder to be weird,' he acknowledged as he slipped his backpack up and over his shoulders.

'You didn't ask me if the lambs are still crying...'

'My boiler suit is in the wash.'

Charlie smiled, tucked her magazine in her bag and put on her mittens, before looking all around her.

'That way!' Pete said, pointing to the terminal.

'Thank you!' Charlie hollered as she walked off, feeling hope for the first time in days.

9

Charlie slumped into the large blue train seat and opened *People* magazine on the table in front of her. She couldn't focus on it. She couldn't focus on anything as the train emerged from the arterial tunnels of the impressive Grand Central Terminal. She felt sick with nerves. Like the first time she met her first group of cancer patients and had to stand up in front of them. Sick. Nervous. Inadequate. The light hit her face and she adjusted her eyes as she soaked up the views outside the window. As Harlem turned into the Bronx, and the city's boroughs gave way to outskirts followed by leafy expanses, she congratulated herself on sitting on the left-hand side as the train hugged the Hudson and its choppy contours showed glimmers of blue amid the brown.

Charlie ignored her magazine and looked at her phone instead. An article and interview with Seymour J. Irving Jr from *Architectural Digest* in 2003, with a photo of him, his wife Cathy and their three very prim, teenage daughters in navy-blue separates and pearls, leaning against a vintage car on a circular driveway with a fountain in the middle of it. Behind them a stone manor house, large yet discreet behind triangular, topiary-trimmed trees and creeping ivy.

No, this cannot be where my Harry is, Charlie thought as she swiped through the photos of the grand interior. A dark mahogany wood study with leather-bound tomes and gold curtains. A white marble bathroom with an opulent rectangular bath raised in its centre. A sitting room adorned with Louis XV zebra-wing chairs, an eighteenth-century tapestry and a chandelier.

The article focused on the house and how impressive it was, but Charlie didn't give two hoots for stuffy interiors. She just wanted to know where Harry was, so she searched again for Isabelle Irving and scrolled through pictures of her on Google Images. At society events in New York. Representing Goldcrest in a boating competition on Long Island. Walking the red carpet at the Tribeca Film Festival alongside her Argentinian polo-player boyfriend. She clicked on the Getty Images link and saw that was last June.

No, Isabelle Irving definitely wasn't who *her* Harry Taylor was spending Christmas with.

So where is he, then?

She was on the train now. She might as well hunt around the millionaires' haven of Bedford Hills. Call Saphie while she was there and let her know she was OK.

Charlie thought about Saphie and Prash. Prash would never do anything unreliable, or play a practical joke. Prash was a carpenter and his word was as solid as oak. As solid as the wood he carved and caressed and fashioned into beautiful things: wardrobes, tables, fruit bowls. Charlie hoped Saphie and he could find a way forward. Prash would have met her at the airport. Prash wouldn't have left her in a pool of her own blood on the bathroom floor.

The train was half empty and the rhythmic hum of the wheels on the line and the cables anchoring them overhead pulled

Charlie into a delicious yawn. After another frantic night and that awful nightmare, she had to be careful not to fall asleep and miss her stop. Bedford Hills was not the last stop on the line and she didn't want to end up in Canada on Christmas Eve.

Charlie still hadn't got to the Harry and Meghan gossip in *People* magazine by the time the train pulled into the sleepy station of Bedford Hills, but picking it up and looking at their moustaches did remind her of Pete from the Uber and how sometimes people were sent to us for even just a sliver in time, to point the way. The girl in the airport was a sign to get the hell out of there – the version of her in Charlie's dream was anyway – and Pete the geologist had ensured Charlie went the right way and got to Grand Central. She'd needed a nudge to come to Bedford Hills today, even if it was pointless.

As Charlie walked up the stairs and out of the quiet two-track station that was so different from the terminal at which she had embarked, she almost expected to see a horse and cart waiting in the taxi line. It was lunchtime on Christmas Eve, she figured: everyone would be inside with family. Or perhaps it was always this quiet, which was why those who couldn't handle city life lived here. But the station approach had a blandness about it that made Charlie feel uneasy. It was neither sprawling countryside nor teeming metropolis; in Lancashire and London she loved both. She hugged her coat around her and approached the lone taxi with its light on top and asked the driver if he knew the Irving house.

'Who doesn't?' he replied with a smile. 'You wanna go there?' he said with slight derision. Perhaps the commuter-belt cabbies were as grumpy as the city one she had met this morning.

'Yes, please,' Charlie replied primly, before the driver switched on his meter and she got in.

As they drove past white clapboard houses and vast boxed hedges, Charlie realised just why the man in the UberPool – why Pete – had raised an impressed eyebrow. Once she was out of the station approach, Bedford Hills was pretty. And fancy. All the houses looked grand. Most of them were tucked behind double gates, and when the driver pulled up outside billionaire petrochemical magnate Seymour J. Irving Jr's house and said with a smile, 'Here you go!' Charlie realised she was being ridiculous. What was she expecting would happen? Would the family say they didn't know *her* Harry Taylor, but invite her to join them for a long lunch, stay the night in the pool house, and celebrate Christmas with them? Would they pity the mix-up and just take in a stranger – even a charming Englishwoman in colour-popping brights, with wide friendly eyes and a smile that lifted her entire face? She pictured the happy scene of her spending Christmas with another family, all wearing novelty jumpers. She could offer to update the slightly passé hair and make-up of the Irving women, which aged them each by twenty years – although Charlie would put it more politely than that.

More likely, they would just not open the door.

This is crazy.

She looked at the grand closed gates through the windscreen; the security intercom to the left of them.

'You know what... is there, like, a town centre around here? Somewhere I can get a cuppa?'

'A whatta?'

'A drink. A coffee.'

'You're not a long-lost cousin of the Irvings, then, because, you sorta sound like a princess.'

Charlie laughed.

'No, I am not.'

'Don't worry, honey, we all wish we were. I'll drop you in the centre. There's a bakery. Or Richard Gere's place is up the road if you wanna fancypants drink?'

That sounded funny. Charlie's mum loved Richard Gere. Ruth, Charlie and Saph had all watched *An Officer and a Gentleman* when Ruth was down last summer, and even Charlie and Saphie fancied him in that. Perhaps lunch there would be fun before getting a train back to the city. She could take some photos and make it look as if she were there with Harry. Or maybe just call her parents and come clean.

'Perfect!' Charlie smiled.

Except nothing felt perfect about being in this outpost, on her own, on Christmas Eve, with only her phone for company. Perhaps she would call Saph. It would be early evening in London.

Five minutes further down the wintry lane, the car swung into a quiet gravel driveway.

'Here you go. Give Dickie my best!'

The taxi driver was all chummy now.

'I will!'

Charlie paid, got out, looked at the Ferraris and Range Rovers in the car park with a sigh, and headed to the elegant and low colonial country building built of stone and grey clapboard. Fairy lights strung across the property's frontage warmed the starkness of its winter wood backdrop.

'Can I help you, ma'am?' said a young woman with pink cheeks at the reception desk.

'Yes, I'd just like a drink and some lunch, please.'

'Would that be in the main restaurant, or the barn?' she asked, looking Charlie, dishevelled and colourful in a heap of wool, up and down. Ironically it felt like Charlie's own *Pretty Woman* moment. Was she being judged for not looking the part?

Don't be ridiculous, Charlie told herself. She had always been proud of her ability to walk into any room with self-reliance, and make a friend.

She peered at her two options. A pewter-and-platinum-looking restaurant with fancy candelabras to her right, or a rustic refurbished barn across a small courtyard with decorative horse saddles and large leather chairs.

'I'll go there.' She nodded towards the barn. It looked more cuppa than coupé glass, but only just.

'Very good.'

As Charlie slumped into her chair and ordered the chicken club sandwich and a New England IPA, she unravelled all her layers, grateful for the open window bringing in crisp cold air. The hot taxi and toasty rustic inn were making Charlie's skin turn pink. Her phone pinged. It was her mum.

Everything OK love ?

Shit.

She so wanted to talk to her mum, who was funny, often without knowing it. To hear Ray's calm and concise wisdom. He was a man of few words but those he did say were warm and profound and he always had *time* for people. He was patient and forgiving. So although she knew she could tell them, they would be so utterly heartbroken she was on her own on Christmas Eve, she couldn't bring herself to do so, and therefore ruin theirs. By avoiding them she could blame her silence on sightseeing but a longing pulled at her core, to be playing whist around the table at home. To say to Ruth, 'He didn't fucking show up, Mum, and I've been a wreck.' To cry into her dad's arms as she had when he scooped her up. She was desperate to speak to them but didn't know how to. She couldn't call when Harry wasn't around or they would ask why. And there was no way of calling them when Harry *was* around. Besides, she wouldn't be at this sort of a restaurant on Christmas Eve without him. She *really* wanted to tell her mum she was at Richard Gere's restaurant, even though she hadn't known it existed twenty minutes ago.

She was halfway through firing off a vague reply about what a fun time she was having with Harry – too fun to talk right now – when she thought she heard a familiar laugh.

What?

Her ears sharpened, she flicked her head, straining to hear a familiar sound in an unfamiliar place among the low tinkle of Nat King Cole.

It couldn't be.

Charlie stood up and left her chair, strewn with her layers, to go back to the busier-sounding restaurant on the other side of the courtyard when a waiter in a white shirt tucked into black jeans brought the most mouth-watering-looking chicken club sandwich through the doors. Charlie froze. There it was again! An English exclamation. Plummy tones. A laugh that always ended in a sigh. *Harry's* laugh.

The waiter stopped and looked confused, as if he had got the wrong order for the wrong table.

'Oh, over there, thank you.' Charlie gestured to her seat. 'I'm just going to the bathroom...'

'Very well,' the man said in a French accent and nodded sweetly as he delivered Charlie's lunch and she lingered at the entrance to the restaurant, where she had come in from the car park. Poised, frozen. Like Mabel listening for a pigeon on the balcony. She heard the laugh again, more distant now, so she went another way, back through the patio doors to the courtyard and the back end of the restaurant, where Harry's undeniable chortle was filling a room of chinked glasses, Christmas songs and chefs shouting orders.

Charlie walked past the back of a kitchen as flames roared, to the outside of the restaurant, past a row of rectangular, colonial-style windows, each decorated with a bountiful wreath with a bow at the top. She heard it again. Harry's unquestionable laugh. And then she saw him.

10

Harry was sitting at a large round table in the far corner of the restaurant, facing the window she was looking through. Charlie slumped to her haunches and waddled, as low as she could, to the corner, so she could peer up and in, but not in his direct eyeline.

What the fuck?

She rose slowly. There he was. *Her* Harry Taylor. Holding court at a table with those three blonde sisters, now all adult yet still dressed in a similar style as they had in their teens; now more confident in their skin; their hair blonder; their brows filled out. Next to each blonde sat a man with a thick head, an oxford shirt and a blazer. Charlie recognised Harry's blazer. She had been bored in TM Lewin when he bought it. Around the curve of the table was an older woman – Cathy – with Martha Stewart pearls and a sharp silver bob. And next to her, Seymour J. Irving Jr, who looked more like Blake Carrington than he did in his *Architectural Digest* interview.

Harry was laughing, telling an anecdote Charlie couldn't hear, but also couldn't understand how it might not have involved her. Of course it didn't involve her, this was a different life now. Her thighs burned as she squatted under the corner window and rose a little higher to see Isabelle Irving stroke Harry's temple while he clutched her hand in his and kissed it with adoration.

'Mother. Fucker,' Charlie whispered.

'Are you OK, ma'am?' asked the sweet French waiter with a tray full of glasses and plates.

Charlie wasn't even embarrassed by how strange she must have looked. Spying on Bedford Hills' first family.

'Not really,' she said, still squatting, pink cheeks now ashen.

The handsome waiter had a look of concern.

'Can I help you up?'

Charlie shook her head apologetically.

'Is there something I can get you, ma'am? Perhaps your club sandwich, it's at your table.' The man gave her an encouraging smile.

Charlie stood slowly, gripping onto the external wall to support her. The waiter went to put the tray down on the floor so he could help.

'I'm OK...' she said, ushering him away as she put her hand over her mouth to suppress the vomit she felt rising up her oesophagus. 'I have to go! Sorry!' she half wailed as she strode, as fast as the soles of her brogues would take her, back along the row of wreaths shielding her face from view; back past the kitchen to the courtyard and the barn restaurant, where she grabbed her coat, scarf, beret and mittens from the cosy chair with the club sandwich in front of it and ran. Out of the sedate property, across the gravel drive and onto the tree-arched road, towards the centre, towards Bedford Hills station. Heart wringing and tears streaming.

* * *

As Charlie lay on her back, in the shape of a star, on her bed at the Jane Street Guest House, she looked up at the ceiling and her eyes burned.

How the fuck did I get here?

She could barely remember the woman with the grey plaits who picked her up in her truck, crying so hard she could barely speak on the sparse highway – the woman's sage, lined face smiling serenely as she dropped Charlie at Bedford Hills railroad station and told her to look after herself. She couldn't remember how long she waited for her Metro-North train to Grand Central. And she couldn't remember walking the forty-five minutes down East 42nd Street and 5th Avenue, past Bryant Park, the Empire State Building, the Flatiron and the sign pointing towards Chelsea Market, which she mumbled 'Fuck you,' at before collapsing into her room just as the sun was setting.

She only half remembered the phone call with Saphie as she walked. She remembered Saphie saying, 'Fucking cunt, I knew it!' and then something about how if Charlie could get a night flight home, she would be there to pick her up at Heathrow on Christmas morning. Charlie couldn't even remember what she'd said in response. Only that she didn't have that kind of energy.

All she knew as she stared up, eyes raw with anger and betrayal, was that the ceiling felt infinitely lower than it looked, as if it were falling in on her and her shattered future. She replayed the jolly family scene over and over in her head. Harry's guffaws and Nat King Cole. She saw her future, her babies, her life, crumble away and dissolve in front of her without so much as an explanation. An apology. A message to say he couldn't meet her.

Now it was quiet but for the sounds of the traffic, helicopters over the Hudson, the rush for people to get to loved ones for Christmas, and Charlie closed her eyes, defeated.

PART II

11

THREE DAYS AFTER CHRISTMAS

Charlie reckoned she must have checked out all the coffee shops in Greenwich Village by now as she stood in a bright, light cafe with exposed brickwork painted white, waiting in line for a no-nonsense Americano to wake her up. In the past few days she'd sampled no-frills cortados at the old-school Italian cafe with the green bubble-shaped awning that had been open since the twenties; she'd had an oat-milk latte with an Instagrammable piece of strawberry shortcake on the side at the vegan cafe by Washington Square; she'd drunk coffee made by baristas who took the process so seriously, colleagues weren't allowed to talk to each other while they were creating their artisan brews, and she'd sampled peanut-butter-flavoured macchiatos in a coffee shop where there were board games galore. She nearly asked an old man drinking alone if he wanted to play Connect 4 with her.

Christmas Day had been a low. The cafes were shut and Charlie's tear ducts were open, so she stayed in all morning and watched TV, before hitting her lowest ebb by lying to her parents on FaceTime.

'Happy Christmas, Mum!' she cheered into the phone – a reindeer filter conveniently masking the swollen red rings around her eyes.

'Give us a tour, then, love,' Ruth had demanded as Ray came running into the picture to join them.

'Happy Christmas, my pudding!' he chortled, paper hat askew, his cheeks ruddy.

'Well, this is the bedroom...' She gave a super-quick spin. 'And there's the en suite... but there are fireworks going off out of the balcony so I can't show you the living room at the moment, I won't be able to hear you!'

Her dad peered into the camera.

'Isn't it daytime there?' he said, squeezing his misty eyes.

'Oh yes, they're mad for them here! Been going off non-stop since midnight!'

Ray looked doubtful, but took his daughter's word for everything.

'Where's Harry? Put him on!' demanded Ruth.

'He's popped to the liquor store...'

'On Christmas Day?' asked Ray again.

'This is New York, Dad! The city that never sleeps.' Ironically it felt pretty sleepy as Charlie glanced out of the window onto Jane Street. It was the quietest she had known it all week. 'He's gone to get champers.'

'Oh, are you celebrating something, darling?' Ruth gave a hopeful look.

'No, Mum,' Charlie replied, trying to sound as if it didn't cut her. 'He's bought me... he's bought me a... a helicopter ride, out to Liberty Island.'

Charlie was a quick thinker. She needed to come up with a gift she couldn't show. She felt wretched lying to her lovely parents. They were usually so honest with each other. About periods; about clothes that didn't suit them; about the time she had tried Marlboro Lights at a party; about life, London and jobs. About the moment that broke all their hearts. And now she was lying. She felt dreadful.

'Oh, wow, a helicopter! Be careful, love!' Ruth said nervously as her smile dropped.

That afternoon, as Charlie walked through a quiet Union Square, she cropped the photo of Harry drinking the cocktail, the one he'd sent to Xander, so you couldn't see that it was taken on a balmy outdoors roof terrace, and sent it to her parents with a terrible pang of guilt.

Not quite as good as your eggnog, Dad, but good enough for me!
Happy Christmas from Harry too!

The cafes were closed on Christmas Day, but Charlie walked more than she'd ever walked that afternoon and evening: thirty-two thousand steps according to her Fitbit, through every nook and cranny of Greenwich Village, across Manhattan to the Brooklyn Bridge – where she scrutinised every man she passed to see if they were Harry. And just for a second she considered jumping off it so she wouldn't have to tell everyone excited for her back home what had happened. So she didn't have to let them down.

But she knew that was ridiculous. She didn't jump and she didn't celebrate Christmas. Instead she walked and walked, alone with her own thoughts. Imagining Harry's happy new life without her. Thinking about her parents. Wondering what the man from the Uber's Friendmas might be like. Until she was so tired she collapsed on her bed, watched *Home Alone* and cried herself to sleep.

* * *

Three days after Christmas and Charlie was feeling stronger – or perhaps that was the aromas of java and cinnamon making her rise on the balls of her feet in the queue. She had returned to her favourite coffee shop, a Pinterest-perfect one that sold colourful zingy smoothies and breakfast jars of granola, yogurt and compote that were almost too pretty to eat. Which was another fly in the ointment. Here she was in New York, the most photogenic city in the world, on an enforced social media blackout so people didn't realise she had been dumped. For now she was mentally putting it down to living her best life and not curating it, but she knew her friends back in London and her family in Lancashire would start to wonder where the New York scapes and loved-up photos of the happily reunited couple were. She knew Jazz would be onto her soon.

'You found Manhattan's best breakfast, then?' said a warm slow voice over Charlie's shoulder. She turned around and almost gasped in confusion when she saw Pete from the UberPool standing in line behind her. She had never been happier to have a stranger speak in her ear, and her response was a little zealous.

'Pete!' she said, as if he *were* in fact an old friend. She checked herself and pulled back a little. 'Oh, hi,' she said more formally.

Pete smiled.

'What are the chances, huh?' he said, rubbing his jaw.

'In this metropolis of a gazillion people!'

'Well, technically we did both get in a car around about the same place, so I guess that cuts the odds down,' Pete figured. 'And there's a reason this place is called The Village...' Pete seemed to be a man of reason.

A nineties supermodel walked in with her teenage son and Charlie remembered she had seen her twice already this week: once picking up dog poo on the tiny green of Abingdon Square, and the second time outside a thrift shop on Bleecker Street. Maybe it was a small world.

'True,' she said, trying not to look at the supermodel again.

'How was your Christmas? Did you find your missing person?'

Charlie shook her head and tried not to cry. Pete's wide brown eyes flashed with commiseration. 'Well, did you have a good Christmas?' he asked hopefully.

Again, Charlie shook her head, not saying a word, her eyes getting glossier. She thought about lying but it was much harder to fib without a reindeer filter on her face and Pete had the sort of quiet, intelligent face you couldn't lie to. He could see she was upset and changed the subject to spare her feeling as if she had to tell him anything.

'Wanna get this coffee and take a walk? I'm just meeting my friends and their daughter – my goddaughter – in the playpark...' Pete nodded out of the huge window to 8th Avenue.

Charlie remembered it was Saturday, during Twixmas, so normal people weren't at work. People like Pete: clever, solvent New Yorkers – people with friends. On a Saturday they would be grabbing coffee and going for walks with theirs, as she would in London. He was the only friend she had in New York, and it seemed like a better prospect than spending another hour on her own, looking at her step count.

On Boxing Day she had headed north to Times Square and the Rockefeller Center, cursing Chelsea as she'd walked through it, and taking photos she hadn't dared to send anyone or post. And yesterday she had taken a subway to Columbus Circle and got lost in Central Park among the runners, rollerbladers and tourists all wrapped up as they had meandered through the paths dotted with trees and rocks. As Charlie had watched couples and families skating on the ice rink, the loneliness had set in like rot.

'That would be wonderful,' she replied, realising how British she sounded saying it.

She paid for her coffee and breakfast pot lined with blueberries, yogurt, mango compote and granola, stripes of lilac, cream and yellow bleeding into each other, and Pete ordered three coffees and a banana smoothie that somehow turned out to be green at the till next to her, and she waited for him by the door, trying not to look at the supermodel again.

'This way,' he said, propping the door open for her with his foot and pointing to the right. As Charlie went through, Pete saw her face up close and the sadness in her eyes and made a note not to ask her too many questions. *Keep it light.* As they walked side by side through the sunny chill, 8th Avenue turned into Hudson and everyone around them looked as if they had a purpose Charlie lacked.

'I'm glad you got the memo about how New Yorkers match their food to their clothing...'

Pete gave her a nod of approval as he warmed his hands on the hot coffees in his tray. Charlie was wrapped in a lilac wool coat with her oversized yellow scarf coiled around her neck loosely, and her cream cable-knit mittens, layered in a similar way to her blueberry and mango granola pot. She held her breakfast up to her lapel proudly.

'Always,' she said with a smile. Another Instagram moment she might have photographed but wouldn't. 'But speak for yourself, Mr Mocha...'

She studied Pete's sepia-coloured cords, mahogany jumper and brown and black down North Face coat and concluded he did perhaps look like a cup of coffee, and they both laughed.

'I know, I know!' Pete conceded. 'I am so unstylish. Who dresses like *coffee*?'

'I think you're onto something...' Charlie said, appraising the pair of them.

As they walked to the Bleecker playground they considered which American celebrities would carry what foodstuffs in their hands: Beyoncé would accessorise with a delectable cream horn with sparkly cinnamon sugar sprinkles on top, of course. Gaga would be carrying uncooked steak; Donald Trump would be a three-day-old tuna melt; and Andy Warhol would be brandishing a Mister Whippy – although Charlie had to explain that a Mister Whippy was an ice cream as she giggled at the surprise turn the conversation had taken, with the nerdy Columbia academic comparing famous people to food.

'Ah! They're here.'

Pete carefully propped his card tray of drinks on one hand so he could open the gate to the playpark with the other. 'After you...' he said as Charlie nervously entered.

Is this weird?

It was certainly nice to see *life* as a New Yorker saw life on a Saturday morning.

'Mike, Erin, this is my friend Charlie...'

Friend? That felt nice.

A tall, well-built man and a petite woman smiled and waved a casual *hi*. 'Charlie's over here for... well, how long are you here for?' Pete asked, turning to her.

'Who knows?' she said, her jovial smile belying her heartache.

'She's British!' Pete said, as if Charlie were a treasure he had discovered in quartz. 'First time in New York.'

'Wow,' the couple said in unison, his voice deep and soft; hers high and shrill, as if they couldn't believe there were people on the planet who hadn't been to New York before.

'Charlie, this is Erin, that's Mike...' he said as he hugged them himself.

Both Mike and Erin shook her hand and said hi, which felt weirdly formal given they were being friendly. 'And *where*...' Pete said, as he looked around, '*where* is that monster...?'

A little girl with big hair came running at Pete's legs with glee. 'There she is!' Pete braced himself for impact as she slammed into his body.

'Whoa!' Charlie seamlessly took the tray with the steaming cups and smoothie out of Pete's hands so the hot coffees wouldn't spill everywhere as Pete lifted the girl by her armpits, rolled her up his long body and perched her on his right shoulder so she looked like the parrot to his explorer.

'This mucky monster is Téa!' he said, beaming up at her. Charlie expected Téa to squawk, but the little girl folded her arms and checked Charlie out from her vantage point, eyeing her with suspicion.

'Are you Pete's new girlfriend?' the girl asked, before losing her stern façade and bursting into a giggle.

'God, no!' Charlie nearly choked on her Americano. 'I mean, no offence, but I've only just met him!'

'Cheeky little sparrow!' Pete said as he pulled Téa off his shoulder, cradled her in his arms and tickled her tummy as she kicked her legs gleefully in the air.

Erin pretended to scold Téa while Mike smiled. Charlie observed their family unit. Mike was a beautiful man with a black beard and thick rectangular glasses framed by a baseball cap; Erin had birdlike features and a tired face.

Charlie, Mike and Erin exchanged pleasantries by the swings and they asked where in Britain she was from ('Lancashire – you won't have heard of it – via London') and where she was staying ('A cute little guest house on Jane...') which weirdly they hadn't heard of either, given they lived in the Village, but they knew Jane Street well. Their smiles were warm and real and Charlie felt at ease with them both. Erin always had one eye on Téa so she was a little harder to talk to, but Charlie soon discovered Mike fused his two biggest passions, hip hop and science, to go around schools engaging kids with science through pop culture. Erin was a teacher who fell in love with Mike the day he visited her class ('His passion was so *hot!*') although she didn't love her job as much as Mike loved his because she was very much looking forward to her impending maternity leave. Charlie couldn't tell Erin was pregnant under her long down coat but said, 'Oh, congratulations.'

Erin was friendly but had a blunt demeanour Charlie quite liked. She always admired straight-up people. People who were honest and wore their heart on their sleeve were much more Charlie's kind of people than liars who would say anything rather than disappoint. Which made her feel even more hoodwinked by Harry. Erin asked the questions Pete had been cautious about asking, and that was OK.

'So are you in New York on your own?'

'I wasn't meant to be...'

She told them about how she had flown out almost a week ago, expecting her boyfriend of sixteen years to meet her at JFK, but he hadn't shown up. Pete's face dropped.

'Is that who you were looking for, in Bedford?'

Charlie nodded.

'Yup,' she confessed, slightly guilty that she had lied in the coffee shop. That wasn't very straight-up. 'I found him all right!' Charlie was trying to put a brave face on it, but Pete, Mike and Erin could all see her mouth tremble a little in the corners as she spoke. 'And his new girlfriend.'

'The ratbag!' Pete rebuked.

'And the girlfriend's entire family.'

'No!' gasped Erin.

'And he looked pretty comfortable with them too. Quite the

Christmas scene it was!' Charlie's soft cheeks flushed dappled shades of rejection and shame.

Pete gave a pained sigh and shook his head.

'I'm so – so – sorry,' he said, rotating his coffee cup in his hand to find the last of the warm bits, but it had all gone cold in the chill. He turned to Mike and Erin. 'We met on Christmas Eve morning in a cab – I feel dreadful.'

'Oh, it's fine!' Charlie batted, although clearly it wasn't.

'You could have come to us for Christmas!' Erin bemoaned, hitting Pete on the chest. 'Mary and Elle have been to London!'

As if ensuring that Charlie would have got along with Mary and Elle on Christmas Day, whoever Mary and Elle were.

'I did invite her...' Pete said to Erin in his defence.

'Was it that obvious I was about to be totally humiliated?' Again, Charlie's jokey manner belied her distress.

'No, I just—'

Erin frowned at Pete for not trying harder.

'You should have come!'

Mike stole a concerned glance at Pete.

'It's OK!' Charlie felt bad about them feeling bad for her. 'It's all a learning curve, isn't it? I have seen more of New York and got more steps than I ever would have in a week holed up in the apartment with Harry, I'm sure.'

Pete continued to shake his head gently.

'How long did you say you're here for?' Erin's small face knitted under her concerned brow.

'That's a good question, I didn't.' Again Charlie said it as if she were doing stand-up. Making light to make everything nice. She really didn't want these kind New Yorkers to fall out over her or feel sorry for her. Dammit, they were even nicer than the people back home in Lancashire. 'The guy at my guest house is keeping my room open for me – giving me first refusal if he gets a booking enquiry – so I'm not going to be turfed out on my arse or homeless any time yet.'

Charlie didn't want to say that she couldn't afford to eat *all* of her three meals a day out for three months, living in a hotel room without a kitchen. Nor could she face the shame of going back to London, alone, after just one week.

'Well, at least keep in touch with us,' Erin said, looking warmer and more sisterly than her face first allowed.

Charlie looked at Pete. His doleful eyes seemed to express all the pain she was trying to gloss over as he stared into space. He felt crestfallen that the woman in the Uber had been about to go off and have such a humiliating experience he hadn't been able to prevent. It cut Pete more than Charlie could know.

* * *

'What are you up to today, buddy?' Mike asked, changing the subject, encouraging Pete to invite Charlie along to whatever it was he would no doubt already have planned. But mentally, he already had.

On Saturday mornings, Pete would always bring the drinks to meet Mike, Erin and Téa in the playground before Téa's piano lesson with Mrs Pyne on Perry Street. Before Pete would go off and do whatever activity he had in store. Sometimes Mike, Erin and Téa would join him at The Whitney, Chelsea Market or Union Square. Although today they wouldn't because they'd hung out all Christmas and Boxing Day and they wanted some family time, even though Pete was pretty much family.

'Well, it was a toss-up between Basquiat at the Guggenheim or Nature's Fury at the Natural History.'

Erin rolled her eyes as if to punctuate the conversation with a silent *again*.

Pete turned cautiously to Charlie.

'Would you like to come to either of those? If you're at a loose end.'

Charlie looked hesitant.

'Or I can take you somewhere touristy if you like?'

'Oh, I don't want to be any bother!' Charlie said, waving her hand. She really didn't want to be a pain. She had become accustomed to walking around New York on her own before collapsing on her bed with Wolf Blitzer (on CNN; not her duvet). 'Really, I'm fine. I saw the Basquiat at the Barbican in London though – it was amazing.'

'You mean you *don't* want to hear about the science of natural disasters? How earthquakes and volcanoes could destroy us at any minute?' Pete said it in a slow, self-deprecating tone.

'Natural disasters in Manhattan?' Charlie asked with a raised eyebrow.

'There was a tornado here in 2012!' Pete said, almost with pride.

Charlie looked surprised.

'But don't worry, you are safe from impending doom.'

Téa sipped her smoothie between whizzes on the slide with a look of total joy on her face and Charlie wished she were a child who was never at a loose end, she looked so full of energy and zing.

'In which case, I'm in!' Charlie decided. 'Natural disasters sound... fun!'

'Great!' Pete said, putting the coffee empties back in the card for the recycling.

'But really, only if you didn't mind me tagging along, I am OK on my own.'

'I tell you what, I'm going to London to deliver a paper in March. You show me around London on my day off, I'll show you New York today. Deal?'

Charlie didn't really have to think. She had no other plans.

'Deal.'

'Great!' Erin said sharply. 'You kids have fun. We have to get Téa to Mrs Pyne... Last one, honey!' she called out to her daughter back at the top of the slide.

Erin had said it a bit too quickly for Charlie's liking. If they were matchmaking, they were barking up the wrong tree.

12

At the 14th Street subway station Charlie proudly showed Pete that she already knew how to negotiate the underground system as she casually wafted her MetroCard at the barrier. They strode down the grey wide stairs to the platform, boarded the train, and she told him what she had seen in the five days since they had met – which was most of Manhattan, except for the John Lennon monument in Central Park, which she wanted to take a selfie next to for her dad.

'You covered a lot.' Pete sighed, impressed. 'More than most New Yorkers in a year.'

'I didn't have much choice.'

'A weaker person would have turned around and got on the first flight back to London.'

Charlie didn't feel terribly strong. She'd been moping around New York and lying to her parents, but Pete's words gave her a boost. Despite her heartache, a tiny fragment of her fibre enjoyed remembering she was self-reliant. She was so hung up on her reunion with Harry, she had forgotten that, actually, she had been OK on her own for the past six months.

'I didn't feel very strong. I haven't even had the balls to tell my parents,' Charlie confessed.

'They don't know?' Pete put his hand over his mouth. 'Are you not close?'

'We are close – that's why I feel so terrible for lying to them. They'll be heartbroken.'

'Have you told *anyone*?'

'My best mate, Saphie. She's housesitting my flat in London. Looking after my cat, Mabel.'

'Cute name.'

'Saphie or Mabel?'

'I meant Mabel, but Saphie is cool, I'm sure.'

Charlie nodded knowingly. The train pulled into 34th Street and Pete and Charlie looked at the people getting on and off before resuming their conversation.

'What did she say?'

'Mabel? She can't talk, she's a cat.'

'Very funny. What did Saphie say?'

'Words I cannot repeat. And that she's going to break his balls.'

'Well, I don't know the guy, but I'd like to break his balls.'

As they sat side-by-side they both laughed and jabbed their arms into each other at the same time.

'So have you heard from this chump?'

'Harry.'

'Harry.' The way Pete repeated his name came with a side order of scorn.

'I sent him a text on Christmas Day.'

'What did it say?'

'Happy Christmas you motherfucker.'

'I like it. To the point. Punchy.'

Charlie gave a smile.

'I don't know if he got it, I didn't hear back. He might not have got any of my messages. He might have buried his phone in a drawer, I have no idea. One minute he was texting me lists of stuff to bring him; the next I get here and he ghosts me.'

'Shit, man, I'm so sorry.'

Pete didn't want to dwell on Harry. Charlie was clearly better off without him.

'So what do you do back in the UK?'

Charlie looked up and saw a small poster for *Wicked* on Broadway on the strip of adverts above the opposite passengers. A witch with a green face and red lips. A white witch whispering into her ear. She nodded at it.

'That.'

'You're an evil witch?'

'No!'

'The good witch, then? Suits your complexion better...'

'I'm a make-up artist. I used to work on *Wicked* in London. But I do mostly TV and film now. The odd workshop. Occasional celebrity wedding.'

'Sounds fun.'

Charlie thought about the last few stressful months on *Look Who's Dancing!*. Working her socks off. Pining for Harry. It had sort of lost the fun lately. She reflected for a second on what she used to find fun about it. The things that motivated her and gave her buoyancy in her stride. Charlie wasn't ready to tell Pete the real reason for getting into make-up, but she didn't want him to think she was shallow.

'I do charity workshops too.'

Oh, God, now I sound like I'm virtue signalling.

'What kind?' Pete asked, shifting his body round to Charlie.

'I work for a couple of charities. One that helps women – and men – after cancer treatment. If they've lost their hair, eyebrows and lashes... a lot of people are knocked for six after chemo and need advice on how to navigate those tricky months. I do wig workshops too, as I use a lot in my day job.'

'That's amazing. You volunteer?'

'Yes, for teens too. Usually through another charity, for people with visible differences, who are self-conscious, and scared to go out.'

Pete pondered this.

'Like what sort of differences?'

'Scars from self-harming, or rosacea or vitiligo – skin conditions that aren't just fleeting...' She paused and thought about how lucky she was. 'Permanent visible differences that can have a huge impact on someone's emotional well-being. Some people – like my older cancer survivors – they can be more comfortable in their own skin. Some younger people are crippled by how they look. Although some wear their differences with pride.'

Charlie was never drafted in to help the people who were comfortable in their skin, but she thought about Jazz Jenkins. Jasmine as she first knew her. A snippy and sassy teen whose mother had contacted Charlie when she was fourteen and her life was falling apart. How proudly she wore her differences eight years later.

Pete studied Charlie's face and liked that she looked comfortable in hers. He had no clue there had been a time she wasn't.

'I like turning people into different versions of themselves, unleashing a side of their personality they never knew existed.'

'Sounds really cool. All the different things you get to work on.'

Charlie nodded.

'It is.'

'What's your favourite kinda work?'

'Stage make-up and prosthetics are great. I do like a big transformation. But actors revel in becoming someone else. I like it best when I work on real people. Like the teens who try skin camouflage for the first time and feel able to go out. Or giving people a totally different look for work or helping them leap out of their comfort zone to feel a different power.'

'I'm sure they do,' Pete said, sold, looking at her in mellow awe.

Charlie straightened her back and dropped her shoulders. She looked at her distorted reflection in the window opposite and thought about her teenage self as they comfortably rode together, chatting all the way to 81st Street.

13

It might ordinarily have felt strange to Charlie, to be standing in a darkened hall in a corner of a grand museum space in New York with a man she didn't know, but today it didn't. The wonder of the real-time earthquake monitor on a huge screen in front of her and Pete, lighting up their eyes, was a fascinating distraction.

'That's one to watch,' Pete said confidently, pointing to somewhere off the west coast of Africa. 'Cumbre Vieja. It's a geological cooking pot.'

'Really, how?'

Charlie stood on her tiptoes and considered the Canary Islands, remembering a big holiday with Harry and all their friends to Tenerife, the summer they finished their A levels. Before life got hard. For the first time.

'There's a volcano there, on a fault line that's at risk of landslide. If it erupts, or if there's an earthquake big enough, it could break off and cause a mega-tsunami. It could reach the Eastern Seaboard and decimate this little island.'

Pete seemed very relaxed about impending catastrophe. In fact he didn't look as if much rattled him.

'That sounds horrific.'

'It's amazing!' he said, his deep eyes widening. 'And horrific.' Charlie could see more of Pete since he'd unwrapped his scarf and thick puffa jacket and they'd put their coats in lockers. As she appraised his enthusiasm she realised he looked less chunky without a thick coat or a tatty tweed jacket on. Dare Charlie think it – buff, in just his jumper pushed up at the sleeves and cords.

Pete had got a first proper look at Charlie too, without a red beret, yellow scarf and lilac coat. She looked unlike anyone he'd ever met before in her polka-dot dress, tights and brogues, as they weaved through exhibits, information boards and interactive displays about earthquakes, volcanoes, tornadoes and hurricanes.

'The destructive power reminds us how small and vulnerable we are.'

Charlie had certainly felt that this past week, but she didn't relish it the way Pete seemed to. 'How dynamic the planet is,' he continued. He looked across and saw a slight panic in Charlie's eyes. 'Oh, don't worry, this only happens every hundred thousand years.'

Charlie was suitably reassured.

'Is that your field, then? Earthquakes?'

'Physical geology is a huge field: rocks, minerals, tectonics... a lot of my colleagues specialise in the chronology of it: mapping out our geological past. And a lot of my friends work in environmental sciences – finding new green-tech resources for the future. Looking at the interactions between humans and the geological environment to solve problems like resources and climate change.'

'That sounds cool. So what's your specialism?'

'The here and now.'

'The imminent doom.' Charlie laughed as she looked back at the earthquake board, red lights flashing under an island in

Indonesia. 'Well, I'm just an earth sciences teacher. Jack of all trades, master of none.' He said it so casually, so happily.

'I don't believe that,' Charlie said, leaning her arm into his again.

'It's true. I'm too excited by all this. The shape of our planet right now and how much of it is mighty and out of our control. The beauty of it! And getting that across to the young people who are going to study it so *they* can come up with the answers. Look at this!' he said, diverted, as he led them to a set of double doors that looked as if they might lead to a cinema. A steward was ushering people in for the last spaces before the doors closed.

Pete hurried, stopping short of pulling Charlie by the hand; Charlie wanted to tug on the sleeve of his jumper so she could keep up.

'What is this?' she asked as she followed him in. The room was dark and circular, with curved bars for the museum-goers to lean against, leaving the centre open and lit with a dim blue light.

'Ever been in a hurricane?' Pete asked excitedly. 'Or seen a tornado?'

Charlie shook her head and smiled.

A group of children streamed in behind them as the doors closed, an adult admonishing them for being noisy, as they filed around to the opposite side of the room. Young boys were bundling into their friends; girls were swinging on the curved railing. Charlie thought they looked like a school group but figured perhaps they might be a church or community group on a Saturday between Christmas and New Year. There were about twenty kids of about eight or nine years old. Their excitement and anticipation almost as palpable as Pete's.

A siren went off and ambient lights flashed blue. A theatrical voice came over the speaker.

'Ladies and gentlemen, boys and girls, the doors are now

locked. You are about to experience high winds and devastating gusts. Hold onto your hats... and watch out for the flying cow!'

Giggles tinkled through the room as a wind machine whipped up and the circular screens that wrapped the room started to show darkening skies and light debris, building up along with the rising 'Ooohs' and 'Ahhs' from the museum-goers. Families, couples and kids all beginning to feel the force of nature as the wind machines started blowing hair and rippling cheeks. Charlie and Pete looked at each other in anticipation as Charlie went to clutch her beret before it blew off, forgetting that it was in their locker until she pressed her hand to her hair and laughed.

The noise was roaring and furious, the odd scream coming from a little mouth.

'There's the cow!' one woman shouted as a brown and cream Hereford hurled around the screen and off into the distance. People were screaming and laughing against the wind and the security of staged force.

And then Charlie saw her, the girl from the airport among the group of children. The girl in the red dungarees and the pink polo neck, who was crying under the stairs. Amid the chaos and furore of her cohort she was still, looking in Charlie's direction, almost in a trance. Charlie could see the girl's face now. It wasn't evil and jagged as it was in her dream. It was soft and sweet and she had pale eyes under her bobbed hair, which didn't move ferociously in the machine-induced wind as everyone else's did. It framed her gentle features as she looked through the tornado in the middle of the room and in Charlie's direction. Charlie pointed her finger to her own chest as if to ask 'Me?' before turning around to see if there was someone behind her, but the wind was whipping her hair and making her eyes stream to the point she could barely see. She narrowed her eyes enough to see the girl was still looking at her.

'HELP ME,' she slowly mouthed at Charlie, who grabbed Pete's arm.

'You OK?' he asked, his laugh stopping in concern, his thick dark hair pushed backwards by the force. Charlie nodded as best she could and held onto Pete as if she might blow over. 'It's OK, I got ya,' he said.

The wind started to slow down and Charlie looked back to the children opposite. The girl had moved. There was a space where she had been. Her cohort all started to shape-shift as the adults shepherding them told them to behave themselves and get ready to file out.

Small world, Charlie thought, as the end siren sounded and she flattened her hair and dried her eyes on the sleeves of her polka-dot dress and followed Pete to the exit.

* * *

In the volcano room Pete helped a boy press a button to generate a virtual volcano and the whole room, lit in reds and oranges, started to heat up as the temperature hiked. A man who sounded like James Earl Jones started narrating – perhaps it was James Earl Jones – and Charlie remembered the last time she and Harry had spent an entire weekend watching all the *Star Wars* films in chronological order.

She wondered if Harry ever thought about her, whether little things like a voice or a song could trigger memories that Isabelle Irving couldn't take away. Was he wondering if she was still in New York, whether she had hung around like a bad smell? Would he be looking over his shoulder? Or had he never looked back? He was obviously so good at compartmentalising – like his little macro dinners in their tubs – perhaps he hadn't thought about Charlie at all. What would he make of her being in the American Museum of

Natural History? In a hot, rumbling room, living the dynamics of the planet with a handsome native? He probably wouldn't care.

A sudden simulated eruption brought the room to a standstill.

'Wow!' Charlie said, her face flushing.

'Cool, huh?' Pete said, encircling the outer edge with his hands in his pockets. 'You ever been to a volcano?'

'Harry and I went to Iceland for a minibreak once, we bathed in the sulphur pools.'

'Eyjafjallajökull?'

'Bless you,' Charlie joked, as if Pete had just sneezed.

'There you go!' Pete said proudly, as they were both taken by surprise by the fact she could make such a joke.

'I thought it was called a number or something.'

'E15?'

'That's it!'

'Yeah, same volcano. Eyjafjallajökull, E15,' Pete said casually. 'Caused the ash cloud,' he said with wide eyes. 'Took down European aviation for the first time since World War II.'

'Well, we went to a nice spa there.'

'You know there are almost fifty active volcanoes in Europe?'

Charlie's eyes narrowed.

'Define active...'

'They've erupted in the last ten thousand years. But some erupt daily. There's this one I really want to go to, in the Aeolian Islands.'

Charlie was ashamed to have never heard of the Aeolian Islands. They sounded Greek.

'Off Sicily,' Pete said, perhaps reading her mind. 'Every night the volcano erupts, like the most phenomenal firework display you could ever see.'

'Can you go near enough to see it?'

'You can climb it, while it's erupting.'

'Shut up!' Charlie said hitting him.

'No, for real. Only because it's a certain type of volcano that falls back in on itself, so it's safe-ish.' He gave a wry smile. 'You hike up there mid-afternoon, it takes a few hours...'

Charlie didn't want to say she wasn't really the hiking type, although she had walked more in the past week in New York than she had in the whole year they were coming to the end of.

'By the time you get up to the summit and the sun sets, you see this most amazing thing.' He cupped his hand, put his fingers together and opened them out like a peony going from bud to bloom in a second. 'Strombolian activity it's called, after the volcano. Stromboli.'

'Stromboli,' Charlie repeated, liking the way the word sounded; marvelling that she had never heard of it. An active volcano. Fifty active volcanoes, on her doorstep.

'I'm hoping to tag it onto my trip, after London.'

'Sounds amazing.'

The volcano simulation rumbled again and the sequence restarted, signalling it was time to move on.

'Euw, who farted?' said one of the little boys from the tornado simulation room, after the volcano let out a low, deep rumble. His comrades laughed.

'This is why you teach university students, right?' Charlie said, rolling her eyes.

'Totally.'

In the fourth-floor cafe Charlie bagged a table under a mural of a triceratops while Pete got two paninis stuffed with mozzarella and basil and weaved through to join her with a tray.

'Oooh, thanks. I'm starving!' she said, helping move the plates and the Cokes onto the table. Pete said, 'No problem,' in a way she was becoming accustomed to, and sat down.

Charlie took a bite, put it down, then tried to sort her unkempt hair with her fingers as she pondered disaster. Pete's mellow manner really did jar with the hypotheses he had put to her earlier.

'So if it's out of our control...' Charlie lingered. 'The mega-tsunamis and tectonic plates – how can the students *you* teach come up with the answers to stopping said disaster you seem so excited about?'

Pete put his sandwich down and pushed the sleeves back up on his soft brown jumper. These were obviously questions he relished.

'It's not about stopping them, it's all about the response. You can't do anything to stop an earthquake or a collapse or an eruption – a lot of stuff is out of our hands.'

Charlie suddenly felt very powerless in the shit situation Harry had put her in, and a rage and heartache ripped through the tectonics that anchored the soles of her brogues to the floor of the bustling cafe.

'When Cumbre Vieja goes – if there's a landslide and a megatsunami – it'll go. That part is out of our hands. But it's the earth scientists' job to work out what can be done to prevent catastrophe – loss of life and habitat. It'll be *how* we react to it that's the difference between whether we sink or swim. Our response to what happens to us is more important than that which we cannot control.'

The spark in Charlie's eyes extinguished as she looked at Pete, defeated. As uplifting as his enthusiasm was, she just couldn't push Harry's betrayal out of her mind.

'Are you OK?'

She nodded, assuring him with a weak smile while they both returned to their lunch. Pete put his panini down again.

'I'm sorry, have I upset you?' He spoke like one of those candid New Yorkers Charlie had heard about, like she thought Erin might be, yet Pete's voice was gentle, his manner lackadaisical. The two didn't marry up. But it gave Charlie permission to be honest too. She took a swig from her can of Coke then tugged at the ruched cuffs of her dress.

'It's the lack of control, I guess...' she said ruefully. 'Everything that happened this week, it's all been taken out of my hands.'

'It's shit,' Pete said with compassion.

'I'm not accustomed to my life being so out of my hands.'

Pete nodded.

'I guess my job is to make things nice. Make people feel great or powerful, like they can accomplish anything. I give them control and I love being in control of that myself.'

'Like a puppet master yielding a make-up brush.'

'Exactly!'

'Only nicer,' Pete added. 'I don't wanna make you sound like a despot.'

'Thanks.' She paused. 'Physically, it's what I do. It's my superpower.'

'It's a cool superpower,' Pete concurred.

'But Harry took everything away from me, and gave me no choice in the matter, or a chance to talk about it. I've become totally powerless.' She looked around, in despair, then realised she was perhaps oversharing. She had only told Pete about being stood up this morning.

But Pete seemed to listen with his eyes, such was the calm intensity of his gaze, which gave her the confidence to continue.

'I don't mean Christmas or three months in New York. He's taken my whole future away. Marriage and kids.' She swallowed hard and felt a sickness she couldn't convey. 'It was all stolen from me. By the guy who was supposed to be my best friend.' She shook her head. 'It's fucked up.'

'It is fucked up. People can be assholes.'

Charlie looked at Pete and paused.

'I'm sorry. Debbie Downer here! You just wanted to go to a museum on a Saturday and you got me.'

'Hey, don't mind me. And don't be hard on yourself.'

But Charlie was bored of talking about it, of thinking about it, of dreaming about it. Of it consuming her. She had to come up with a plan.

'Well...' she pondered as she looked at Pete twiddling his ring pull sadly. 'I need to toughen up. React better, as you say.'

She sat up in her chair and straightened the cuffs she'd been tugging at. 'I'm being a self-indulgent twat. The earth doesn't stop turning, you know that.'

Pete smiled.

'You're being hard on yourself. Human emotion is part of any planning strategy. Seismologists and volcanologists can plot earthquakes or predict eruptions: science enables us to assess whether these events are likely or not. *You* and only you can act based on what you know *and* how you feel. But you were blindsided. You didn't know any of this was coming.'

'Denied of the facts. The motherfucker.'

She tried to laugh.

'But look at your response!'

Charlie met Pete's eye as if to ask *what of it?*

'It looks pretty fuckin stoic and powerful to me.'

Charlie swallowed. That was the kindest thing anyone had said to her in a long time and her eyes sparkled under the saltwater of her tears.

'Hey, wanna see something beautiful? My favourite room in this entire place...'

* * *

They finished their lunch and meandered past a blue whale, a woolly mammoth and the trunk of a one-thousand-four-hundred-year-old sequoia tree to reach the darkened hall of gems and minerals that seemed to have its own gravitational pull.

'Whoa,' Charlie said as she was drawn in by a towering amethyst quartz geode that looked as if a thousand tiny planets glittered within its purple galaxies.

'Geology rocks,' Pete said quietly as he marvelled at Charlie's face marvelling at the geode.

She turned to him and raised an eyebrow.

'Really?'

'It's the bumper sticker of my people.'

'Your people...' Charlie tried to mock, but this was the coolest thing she had seen in ages. She leaned over and examined the shimmering minerals.

'I wish I could capture this colour and put it in a palette. It's like nothing I've ever seen.'

Pete stood with his hands in his pockets, his shoulders rounded and a quiet, satisfied smile.

* * *

As they meandered through the darkened gem hall Pete pointed out his personal highlights.

'Star of India. Biggest sapphire in the world,' he said as Charlie studied the milky blue hue and lightning-bolt markings of the golf-ball-sized gem. 'Stolen from this very place in 1964 by some chancers from Miami Beach, they took a haul worth the equivalent of three million dollars, while the director of the museum was having a tooth pulled out.'

'Wow, that's quite some extraction.'

'Took a load of gems, with the DeLong Star Ruby and the Midnight Star Sapphire...' Pete looked around to find them. 'Over there!'

'How did they get them back?'

Pete gave a look of mock modesty and rubbed his fingertips against his chest.

'Well, I don't want to take the credit but...'

'What?'

'Just kidding. They were rescued from a Miami bus station and back on display and the thieves in Ryker's Island by 1965. Even I wasn't born then.'

Charlie looked at Pete in the low light and narrowed her eyes as she wondered how old he was. Definitely older than her. He had a wisdom in his warm, mournful eyes; a couple of grey strands sparkled at his darkest of brown temples.

'How old *are* you?' she asked. 'Not quite as old as the dinosaurs, surely?'

'Thirty-six.'

'Wow, thirty-six. That's, like, really old.'

'Ha ha,' he said sarcastically. 'Those there...' He pointed to a rock of greeny-brown tourmaline crystals that, as Pete had suspected back in the cafe, were the same unusual colour as Charlie's eyes, although he didn't say it. 'They're 1.8 *billion* years old.'

Charlie couldn't quite get her head around it as they ambled among emeralds, organdies and a metre-tall fuchsia-pink elbaite tourmaline that shone as if it must have come from another planet.

'Stunning, stunning, stunning!'

'Put your ear to this one...'

Charlie stopped at the huge block of vibrant blue azurite and green malachite and leaned over the barrier as close as she could. Pete held her upper arm so she could lean over.

'It's the Singing Stone, from Arizona.'

'What does it sing?'

She leaned further into the green and blue, Pete anchoring her.

They stayed silent, staring at each other as they listened, eyes wide in concentration.

'Your Song' echoed in her mind, but she shrugged.

'Well, I've never heard it, but apparently it lets out a high-pitched squeak when it's humid.'

'Why?'

'Its minerals have water molecules that come and go, and can make the structure change its shape, depending on the temperature. But it's kept so constant in here...' Pete looked around the low-lit hall, almost disappointed.

'No, I can hear it!' joked Charlie. 'I think it's calling you.'

She emitted a small squeak of 'Pete!' through her almost-closed lips.

'Get outta here!'

* * *

It was already dark when Pete and Charlie came out of the museum and onto Central Park West. Headlights were glimmering as cars flew north, a busy avenue dividing luxurious apartment buildings on one side with the stark black trees of the woods in winter on the other, laced with a white dusting of snow that couldn't quite reach the park's perimeters.

'Oh, wow!' Charlie said as she faced the park and soaked in the sight. It looked creepily magical, like a Tim Burton movie brought to life in front of them.

'In the spring all this is a bounty of green,' Pete said, sweeping his arm out in front of them. 'In fall it's golden.'

'I imagine it's beautiful at every time of year...' Charlie said, entranced.

'Wait!' Pete put an arm barrier across Charlie to stop her walking out into the road, the lure of the park tempting her to leap five lanes of flying cars. They stopped and waited for a clear enough run.

'Go!' he said, wrapping his hand around the upper arm of her coat as they ran.

Charlie let out a reckless laugh as they darted and dodged and made it to the other side, their hearts racing.

'Whoa!' she said, looking back to the grand porticos to the east entrance of the museum, which took up whole blocks of Central Park West.

'Actually this sidewalk is best. For the architecture and the park,' Pete said, as if colluding with Charlie's recklessness.

A man selling pretzels from his stall on the pavement was shutting up for the night and noticed Pete trying to catch his eye.

'You gotta have a Big Apple pretzel if you haven't—'

'I haven't!'

'I'm just closing, I'm just closing!' the vendor protested.

'Well, have you got any left, buddy?' Pete asked politely.

'A couple...' said the man as he shut the metal awning onto his hut.

'That's all we need...' Pete said calmly as he dug in his pocket and handed over a five-dollar note. 'Keep the change,' he said, killing the man with kindness, who conceded with a smile. 'Have a great night.'

'You too, man...' said the man as he clicked the padlock on his hut.

Pete handed Charlie her pretzel wrapped in parchment and they walked the park side of Central Park West, Charlie taking a bite with gusto.

'It's a bit on the... stale side... end of the day...' Pete said apologetically, giving in after a couple of bites.

'It's not just me, then?' Charlie said with a mouth full. Before managing to say, 'Chewy!' between chews. As they binned their stale pretzels and sank into their scarves, Pete pointed out the landmarks: the Beaux-Arts twin towers of the San Remo on Central Park West; the white ornate lace of the wrought-iron Ladies Pavilion nestled among the stark trees of the park. The lake behind it, glimmering under moonlight and frost.

'Didn't Carrie and Big live in one of those apartments?' Charlie said, pointing back to the built-up side of the road, to a redbrick building with classical inspired gargoyles, stone draping and a very polished-looking entrance canopy.

'No, but Michael Douglas and Catherine Zeta-Ya-Know do.'

'Cool.'

'Carrie and Big were the other side of Central Park. Opposite the Met.'

Charlie looked at Pete in awe.

'Not that I ever watched it...' he said with mirth in the corners of his mouth. 'Oh, that's the Dakota! You know, where John Lennon lived?'

'Oh, are we near Strawberry Fields?' Charlie asked. 'I couldn't find it the other day. I was walking around in circles and my phone died.'

'Right in there.' Pete nodded as he put his hands in his pockets. 'Shall we?'

As they weaved into the park Charlie told Pete her dad was a huge Beatles fan and had told her she must make a pilgrimage to Strawberry Fields.

'Who isn't?' Pete replied.

'Oh, but my dad's from Liverpool. Wavertree. John and George came from Wavertree.'

Charlie said it as if that meant her dad would always win Beatles Top Trumps were there a game, and she laughed at how ridiculous she knew she must sound. The smile soon snuffed away in another pang of guilt. Her poor parents.

Charlie took a deep breath and looked at the curve of the path leading into the wood. It had a gothic beauty, the way the frost kissed the trees and rocks in front of them.

They stopped at a black and white mosaic starburst on the floor, with the word 'Imagine' written in black lettering over a white circle.

'Oh,' Charlie said, abruptly, seemingly underwhelmed. 'No wonder I couldn't find it! I probably walked right over it!'

Pete laughed. At Charlie's face and her honesty, his hands still in his pockets.

'You wouldn't have walked over it.'

A few well-trodden carnations skitted across the circle in the rising wind and Charlie put her mittens on and hugged her body.

'I just expected...' She looked around, at a few wrought-iron benches.

'Strawberries? And fields!' They both said it at the same time, deadpan, and laughed.

'Well, my dad will think it's pretty cool anyway. It *is* cool.'

Pete hugged himself in his thick puffa coat.

'Here, will you take a picture?' Charlie asked.

'Sure.'

Charlie handed Pete her phone and instructed him to swipe the screen to go to camera, as if he were such a dinosaur he wouldn't know how.

'Sure, I got it...' he said as he walked around to get the best angle and Charlie straightened her beret and smoothed those bits of hair poking out from underneath it. 'I gotta get the word in!' he said, crouching and angling, before realising he had a better bet standing on tiptoes.

Charlie smiled and Pete stopped for a second, taking in her smile, the apples of her cheeks.

Imagine.

She put one hand on her hip and held her other hand up in a salute.

'You can't see I'm making a peace sign in my mittens, can you?' She laughed. 'Do I look weird?'

'You look amazing, I'm sure your dad will love it. Say "strawberries"!'

'Strawberries!'

Pete took a burst of photos.

'Actually...' Charlie said gingerly, 'if you squat a little – make yourself shorter – it might look like Harry took it.'

Charlie felt shame creep up her neck even as the words came tumbling out. She wasn't proud of herself as she watched the smile fizzle away from Pete's face as the icy wind whipped up. The change in his features disconcerted Charlie. He had looked so warm. So friendly.

Pete obligingly bent his knees a little to make himself shorter, and tried to see Charlie through Harry's eyes. It made him feel pretty horrible.

'OK, then, smile,' he said wearily. 'Cheese!'

'I am the walrus!' Charlie said, still holding her peace sign.

Pete took a few photos, stood back up, scrolled through them and spoke gently but sincerely.

'You know you don't have to pretend.'

Charlie looked crestfallen as she walked towards Pete to reclaim her phone.

'You have nothing to be ashamed of.'

Pete handed the phone back with a shrug and took his woolly hat out of his coat pocket and rolled it onto his bouncy hair.

'I know.' Charlie flushed red as she spoke. 'I just... I just can't tell them. Not yet.'

'Hey, I'm not being judgy, it's not my place...' Pete held up his hands.

'They'll be so disappointed, so sad for me.' Her eyes welled up. 'So fucking angry! They'll be so angry.'

Pete nodded, calm eyes soothing her wrath.

'I can't put that on them, not when I'm so far away. Not when I'd be ruining their Christmas holidays and New Year too.'

'I know.' Pete gave a sad smile. 'But you didn't do anything wrong. And I'm sure if they're as lovely and supportive as I imagine...'

Charlie wondered how Pete knew her parents were lovely and supportive, but let him continue. He was so bloody nice. 'They will be understanding and will only want to help you in whatever you decide to do.'

They locked eyes as Charlie blinked out a tear, surprised it didn't freeze midway down her cheek it suddenly felt so cold. She thanked Pete with a nod that sent the tear to the monochrome mosaic floor. A Japanese couple dressed to the nines in Chanel cooed to come around the corner and find the living memorial, smiling at Pete and Charlie as they passed.

* * *

'So what do you want to do?' Pete asked purposefully, putting his gloves on now. The cold felt especially biting away from the buildings and he clearly didn't want to hang around. 'I can drop you back in the Village. Or I'm going to see my friend DJ on the Lower East Side if you fancy that? Get a bite to eat and a drink.'

Charlie looked surprised. Pete didn't seem like the sort of geologist academic who had DJ friends, although Mike did say he was a hip-hop science communicator and looked pretty cool under all his winter clothing.

'Mike?'

'No, it's my friend Mary. Mike's more hip hop. Mary is classic soul and blues. More my bag.'

'Oh, really?' Charlie raised an intrigued eyebrow. She was immediately intimidated by how cool Mary sounded, and felt a weird pang of *something* to imagine a faceless woman entwined with a guy she had only just met.

'Little Richard, Jackie Wilson, Etta James. That kind of thing.

She plays the last Saturday of the month at a sort of bakery-turned-record-store, down near Alphabet.'

Charlie was so shattered from a day of heartache and sight-seeing that she wanted to go back to the Jane Street Guest House, put on the TV, collapse, think of Harry and cry herself to sleep. But something made her check herself.

'You know what,' she said, getting a second wind, 'that sentence sounds so bloody New York, how can I say no?'

'Excellent.' Pete smiled as he put a thumb up. Charlie responded with a woolly one of her own, and they put their hands back in their coat pockets as Pete led them to the subway.

15

'So let me get this right, you've never been to New York and Pete took you to see a bunch of rocks and the twister exhibit at the AMNH?' A long languid woman called Elle with razor-cut cheekbones and a pretty scowl passed her smoke on to Charlie, who duly took it. 'Jesus!' Elle complained as she hit Pete on the chest, sitting on the sofa next to her.

It was 1 a.m. and they were back in Pete's apartment in the West Village listening to 'In My Tenement' by Jackie Shane. The night at the cake-shop-turned-basement-club had been wonderful. Mary, a tiny woman with a blonde pixie crop and headphones that covered a large percentage of her head, had been a powerhouse on the decks. Pete explained that he and Mary had met on the old-school soul and blues music scene ten years ago and Charlie couldn't help but notice Mary had one protective – or was it possessive – eye on Pete while she was tending to her vinyl.

Mary had total control of the club, where the atmosphere was so optimistic it permeated Charlie's bones and lifted her soul; she also had the command of her rapt friends, who were happy to be ending the year of monthly soul nights worshipping at Mary's turntable temple. Pete's friends were as convivial as, but cooler than, Charlie expected. Mike was there too. Along with a dishevelled guy called Isaac, who had a mass of curly brown hair and said the three had met at Syracuse university 'way back when'. Elle was a jewellery designer and the most beautiful woman Charlie had ever seen without make-up, and other friends had come and gone but all been warm and sincere.

Pete had unravelled his layers, even the jumper, and looked steamy and swarthy in a white V-neck tee as he and Elle beckoned Charlie to get off her little pouffe and dance as if they had known her for years. When Elle went to the decks to give Mary a drink and plant a kiss on her lips, Charlie felt weirdly relieved to realise Mary wasn't Pete's girlfriend, and that Elle was hers.

The club was packed with the spirit of soul and the unexpected brilliance that only an unplanned night of dancing with new friends could have. As Charlie danced in her polka-dot dress she realised she felt free and happy for the first time in six days – six months, if she thought about it. Self-reliant and strong, dancing to '(Your Love Keeps Lifting Me) Higher and Higher' by Jackie Wilson.

Now they were back in Pete's apartment, which was small and cosy, with hanging plants tumbling like stalactites from the ceiling; records stacked like stalagmites from the floor, and an olive-green bookshelf lining an entire wall. Most of the books looked as though they were about earth sciences and geological wonders, but among them Charlie spied political biographies and Borges.

'Oh, no! I had a great time!' Charlie said, in Pete's defence. As she said it she realised it had been one of the most exhilarating days of her life. 'I mean, the Singing Stone!' she said, eyes sparkling in the sweet spot of intoxication and animation, messy bob looking blonder next to the floor lamp.

The ring in her ear from Mary's fervent tunes reminded her of the echoes in the gem hall as she studied Pete, getting up to get another round of Brooklyn Lagers out of the fridge in the open kitchen and walking back slowly in his threadbare tee. Elle put her hand on Charlie's knee. Her fingers were decorated with delicate gold bands and semi-precious stones.

'Seriously, you need to do something touristy. Not like one of Pete's field trips.' Elle turned and shot Pete a flirty look as he handed the beers out and slumped back down on the sofa next to her. Elle seemed to flirt with anyone whose gaze she held. Mike was rolling the next joint beyond Pete, and Mary was sitting cross-legged on the floor rifling through Pete's new second-hand vinyl purchases.

'Oh, I've done loads of touristy things,' Charlie assured Elle. 'I've been to One World Trade Center, and I went to the Empire State Building and the Chrysler. And I've been to Central Park.'

Elle nodded her approval.

'I failed to find Strawberry Fields until Pete showed me today.' She looked at Pete and wrinkled her nose as she smiled. 'Oh, and Grand Central station.' Charlie's smile dropped when she remembered Harry's proprietary arm slung around Isabelle Irving's twin-set-clad shoulders.

Not now.

Charlie felt as if all the joy had suddenly been punched out of her stomach and she wondered if perhaps it was time to go back to the guest house.

'How long are you here for?' Elle asked, brown eyes penetrating her while Mary talked to Mike about the records in Pete's collection.

Pete was listening in, wanting to help Charlie dodge a question he knew she probably didn't want to answer.

'And, er, you walked the Brooklyn Bridge, didn't you?' Pete's stoned voice sounded even more relaxed than usual.

Charlie was grateful for the pivot.

'It was so cool.'

She didn't say that a tiny fibre of her wondered whether everything might be easier if she jumped off the bridge.

'She needs to do a proper tourist day, Pete, before she goes home.' Elle was almost whining. She hadn't realised that Charlie hadn't answered her question, she didn't know when she was going home. Elle was good at asking questions but not noticing if the answers never came.

'I'm going to my parents' for New Year's,' Pete said, putting his palms up as if he were off the hook. Charlie looked at Pete looking at Elle and felt a sense of panic. Was she being a total drain? Had she outstayed her welcome? 'Then I'm back at Columbia on the second.'

Charlie shuffled on the sofa.

Time to go.

It had only been one actual day but Pete was her only friend in New York, and the thought of not seeing him again sent a displeasing feeling shimmying down her spine. Charlie already pictured these friends as *her* friends and felt a crushing disappointment when she remembered how fleeting this all was. The misery of her reality.

Pete stood up, hitched up his cords that had started sagging, and turned the record over to the B side. A rasping song called 'Comin' Down'. As he put the needle down he tried to concentrate.

'Tomorrow is all I have, I guess...'

'I could do tomorrow,' Charlie said keenly.

'Take her to Statue of Liberty,' Mary ordered. 'You been to Liberty?' she asked through heavy lids. Charlie shook her head.

Elle took over again. 'You know *I've* never been to Liberty Island!' she gushed, as if it were a sacrilege, or a badge of honour, that a girl from Austin who had lived and worked in New York for fifteen years had never bothered. 'I've been up The Monument in London but never the Statue of Liberty.'

'Oh, how disappointing Monument must be!' Charlie said apologetically, remembering it mainly for the studio she sometimes shot in on the corner of Eastcheap and Pudding Lane and the nearby sandwich shops. How dull it must be compared to the Statue of Liberty.

'Oh no, I love all that shit!' batted Elle. Mary nodded to say *that much is true.* 'I'm a real Anglophobe.'

'Phile!' Pete shouted as he got a pint glass of water from the kitchen, and another for Charlie. 'Anglo*phile!*'

Elle laughed.

'Oh, yeah. I love it. Henry VIII, Great Fire of London, yadda yadda...'

Mary leaned in conspiratorially as she relieved Charlie of the smoke.

'Elle's Halloween costume of choice is "bubonic plague victim".'

Charlie's mouth hung open in awe as she imagined Elle would make sixteenth-century death look chic.

With the words bubonic and plague, Mike remembered he would be in serious trouble with Erin if he didn't get home sharp. Erin had texted him to say Téa was running a slight fever before bed and could he check on her before sleeping on the sofa.

'Shit, I gotta go!' He sprang up, eyes bloodshot.

Charlie thought she better had too, in case she had outstayed her welcome and Pete was just being polite about taking her sightseeing.

'Yes, me too, I'd better get back.'

'I can walk you,' Pete and Mike both said in unison.

'Yah, I'm not going anywhere,' Elle declared. 'I'm having your bed, Pete…' Mary overruled her and said they'd tidy up and get a cab back to their Washington Heights apartment.

'You'll be thankful in the morning,' Mary told her as she tucked a strand of hair behind Elle's bejewelled ear. Elle pouted.

'Really, I can walk you…' Mike offered.

'You're going the other way,' Pete protested, hair dishevelled and stumbling a little as he put his jumper back on. 'It's OK, I'll grab my coat…'

* * *

On the brownstone stoop of the Jane Street Guest House, Pete stood with his hands in his pockets and looked up at Charlie. Both of their eyes were bloodshot and bleary after a day that started in a coffee queue and felt like a decade ago.

Pete rubbed the back of his head and spoke nonchalantly.

'We really don't have to do a tourist day tomorrow if you need the break. You must be all New Yorked out.'

'My feet do ache…' Charlie observed, wiggling her toes to check in with herself and only realising then that the balls of her feet were sore from all the walking and dancing.

Pete nodded acceptingly.

'And I don't want to be a pain…' she added, not wanting to impose on Pete's entire weekend. It was the last weekend of the year and he surely had better things to do.

'You're not a pain at all. Don't worry about that.' He gave a slight nod, and Charlie wasn't sure if that meant he was free or he wasn't. Whether he wanted to take her sightseeing or not. For a teacher he was a rather relaxed communicator, although perhaps it was different when he was talking about rocks. His face had lit up and his pace quickened earlier in the museum; his words had been crystal clear. They looked at each other through dreamy stoned eyes and held the other's gaze for just a second too long. A man on the other side of the cobbled street, wrapped up and carrying flowers, broke their impasse, and Charlie craned her neck to look at him.

When Charlie had checked into the Jane Street Guest House she had texted Harry to tell him where she was staying, just in case. And even though she had since messaged him to say 'Happy Christmas you motherfucker', she still had 1 per cent hope that he might have realised his huge mistake in cheating, ghosting and dumping Charlie for a billionaire's daughter, and raced back to Manhattan to make things right.

The faceless hooded man on the other side of the street clutching flowers walked on, and Charlie looked crestfallen.

'Really,' Pete said, 'it's cool, I should probably—'

'I'd love to,' Charlie blurted. Thinking of Jazz suddenly, and how proud she might be of Charlie for doing something so kickass. She was still too embarrassed to tell Jazz.

Pete nodded at his feet, smiled, and looked back up.

'Cool. I'll come by... ten-thirty?'

'Uff!' Charlie said, looking at her Fitbit. 'Better get my beauty sleep.'

'Nah, you're good.'

'Great, see you then.'

Pete didn't actually say goodbye as he turned to walk back up Jane Street towards the junction, and Charlie tried not to take it personally. This was something she had observed since she got to New York. People ended phone calls abruptly – not quite hanging up in a huff, just without saying goodbye to confirm that it was time to hang up. People walked off when an exchange had met its natural end, in a grocery store or Uber. Charlie tried to remember if people said goodbye or goodnight in London. Perhaps it was a Lancashire thing. But it felt as if something wasn't quite right with how the brilliant night had ended. Then it hit her, the drunken urge to ask a question that had been niggling her all night.

'Pete!' Charlie called in a stage whisper down the dark street.

He'd only got a few metres away before he stopped and turned around.

He looked at her expectantly.

'How did you know my parents are lovely?'

He looked confused, drunk and stoned all in one serene expression as he stopped to ponder his assumption.

'It's written all over your lovely face,' he said as he raised a hand, turned around, and walked on.

Charlie smiled, key in hand. She didn't say goodbye either.

16

FOUR DAYS AFTER CHRISTMAS

Pete was sitting sideways on the stoop, legs stretched out across the step, black and brown puffa matching the coffee in each hand, as Charlie sprung out of the guest-house door at 10.40 a.m.

'Sorry!' she said, looking back as she closed it, wondering where the other Charlie lived. She hadn't seen him for at least two days and he had such a beautiful face, one she would love to get her hands on and paint.

'No problem, coffee might be a bit cold though – I shoulda got lids but... you know... plastic.'

'Oh, thank you!' Charlie said, gratefully taking the corrugated card cup as Pete stood. 'Couldn't open my eyes this morning...'

'You too?' Pete lamented. Although Charlie had an energy in her she hadn't had for ages. She could sense it too, despite her fatigue, bubbling loose and free like a balloon inside her when she remembered how far she had come in just one week. Last Sunday morning she was rushing to the airport, about to get on a plane to face the most humiliating and traumatic night of her life.

Second most humiliating and traumatic night of my life.

She had come far.

Yet the push and pull of achievement and self-reliance over heartache and dejection came with a fragility and a constant sense of impending doom. Perhaps she should slow down on the coffee, she thought as she gratefully took a sip.

'So where are we going?' Charlie asked, coffee in one hand, huge caramel-coloured scarf in the other, which she artfully coiled around the collar of her lilac oversized coat. Pete marvelled at her skill, and how she didn't even look hungover, but then that was her job.

'The Battery.'

'The what?'

'We're getting a ferry.'

* * *

'This is us!' Pete said as the boat pulled up to the jetty of a small island that was dominated by a grand redbrick building with four towers capped with copper cupolas. Charlie had been surprised when Pete said they *weren't* getting off at the first stop, Statue of Liberty, with most of the other tourists, but Pete assured her the view of Lady Liberty was best seen from the harbour itself, and a glimpse of her dignified beauty from the water was more pertinent to something better that was to come.

'What is this place?' Charlie asked, really hoping it wasn't another of Seymour J. Irving Jr's houses, internally cursing herself for thinking about Harry *again*.

'Ellis Island,' Pete said, extending his arm to lead her out. 'Museum of Immigration. You will learn more about this country from this building than by climbing into the crown of that one...' he said as they carefully stepped off the boat and onto the jetty. 'Not that you can climb her any more...' He shrugged.

Charlie wanted to link arms with Pete to steady her recovering sea legs but she stopped herself.

'Wow!' she said, looking at the majestic French-Renaissance-style building, shielding her eyes from the sun.

'You say "wow" a lot.'

'New York is a very wow place, Pete. Not just the bits I'd heard of.'

They walked up to the stately museum entrance alongside the other passengers from the boat, mostly tourists from all corners of the world.

'Well, this is a big deal. Over *a hundred million* Americans are descendants of immigrants who walked through this building.' As Pete said it, he sounded as if he couldn't believe it, even though he was one of them. 'That's, like, a third of the country,' he enthused. 'Not just immigrants to New York.'

'So was it, like, a prison?' Charlie thought about her own country and its response to immigration: barriers, detention, suspicion, expulsion. The building had an imposing and faded HMP grandeur about it.

'Quite the opposite, the way I see it. It was a gateway to freedom. People in search of the American dream.'

'The American dream...' Charlie repeated, thoughtfully.

'Yeah, it was a processing centre. They passed through here, had health checks, and went on to start new lives.'

Pete looked poignant as he said it, looking up at the redbrick and limestone palace in front of them, jutting out against a bright blue wintry sky. The clouds that had generated last night's dusting had completely disappeared and sun beamed down on the cold harbour as they walked through a set of glass doors, into a huge open entrance that reminded Charlie of the railway station in Mumbai, when she and Saphie had travelled through it. It had felt as if there were a hundred million people walking through that station just on the day she and Saphie had.

The signage on the ceiling made it feel like a railway station too, arrows leading to journeys: The Peopling of America; The Registry Room; A New Era of Immigration. A display of antiquated suitcases piled on top of each other. Above it, huge black and white and sepia photos of that baggage at the feet of immigrants, standing in lines wearing hats and expressions of hope. Waiting to be processed.

'Wow!' Charlie exclaimed. Again. As Pete showed a museum official tickets on his phone and they meandered through the baggage hall to learn about why people left their homeland: the promise of land and opportunity. How they journeyed to North America. The routes they took from Europe, West Africa, China and the Far East. The routes they travelled up through the Americas.

'"All journeys begin by leaving one place to venture to another,"' Pete read out, and looked at Charlie. She thought about her big leap a week ago, and the many more she had made since. But seeing these exhibits and photographs, the testimonials, put her journey into perspective. They made her feel small and grateful.

Pete and Charlie lingered at the back of a group where a tour guide in a beige hat and tight bottle-green shirt with a name badge that said 'Dorothy' was telling the group about the six-second medical check, and that medics marked chalk letters on the shoulders of those who were suspected of having an illness. A letter C for conjunctivitis, a G for goitre, H for heart problems. An X denoted suspected mental illness.

'That's a bit of a strong assumption to make in six seconds,' Charlie whispered.

'Only took me six seconds to realise you were nuts,' Pete joked with a slow raised eyebrow. She hit him on the arm, then it hit her.

She had done tours like this of Auschwitz in Poland and S:21 in Phnom Penh – processing and chalk marks had usually led to something far more sinister. This was a completely different gateway, one full of hope. Dorothy had the sparkle and pride in her eyes of a woman who loved her job. Pete and Charlie smiled and naturally peeled away to look around together, at their own pace. They worked well as a pair.

As they walked through rooms themed on all elements of journeying – from leaving and making the trip to arrival, struggle and survival – Pete and Charlie soaked up every artefact, sign, and photo. One, blown up on the wall, of a large group of olive-skinned people, was carefully scrutinised by Pete.

'My great-grandparents came through here,' he said, narrowing his eyes as he looked at the faces.

'No way!' Charlie held his arm as she said it, before putting her palm on it to apologise. 'You didn't say! Where from?'

Pete had swarthy, olive skin but New York had the beauty of making the physical characteristics of someone seem inconsequential. Charlie hadn't wondered why Pete looked dark or where his ancestors had come from. He had just been the friendly guy in the Uber who invited her to join him for Friendmas. Now she thought about it, he could be Latin American, or southern European. Mike was black and looked as if his family might come from West Africa. Mary was pale and could have been Irish or Icelandic, or from some other planet, her features were so small and ethereal. Elle had cheekbones that made her look Slavic. New York seemed to be a place where you only thought about where people came from later. All that mattered was right here, right now.

'Southern Greece,' Pete said proudly. 'They were farmers, escaping between the wars; impending civil war in Greece, a declining agricultural economy, their shitty lot.'

'And they actually came through here?'

'Yeah, they did. My great-grandpa was only sixteen. Luckily *he* didn't have an X chalked on his sleeve.'

'What were their names?'

'Makris. It's my name. It was one of the few Greek names that weren't anglicised or shortened in the arrivals lists. My *proyaya* was called Panayiotopoulou. Eliza Panayiotopoulou, although she changed her name to Makris, they met here. They're both on the database,' he said, nodding back to a room of computers they had already passed. Pete sighed as he gazed up at the large pixelated photograph. 'But try as I do to find him in a photo here, he's not. Of all those handsome men. But he was here, in this building.'

'That's amazing.'

Pete nodded.

In the vast Registry Room, where the sun beamed through large semicircular windows onto the red-tiled floor, Pete and Charlie sat on a bench and Pete opened his backpack.

'Want a sandwich?'

'You brought lunch?'

'Just a couple of bagels I grabbed with the coffees this morning. I didn't remember if you were veggie or not so I got one cream cheese and one pastrami...'

'Thank you,' Charlie said, unpeeling her scarf and coat, suddenly realising she was famished. She hadn't eaten properly since the plate of bao buns they'd demolished at Mary's DJ night, and that probably didn't qualify as a meal.

'God, I am starving, I'll take whichever you don't want, thanks.'

He held up two brown paper bags and offered her the pick of lucky dip. She took one, opened the bag and her eyes lit up. Now this was a New York bagel, even better than the rainbow one.

'So do your family still work in agriculture?'

'Well, my great-grandpa didn't come to Manhattan to be a farmer, so they went upstate, and opened vineyards, actually.'

'Oooh, do you have a family wine? Makris Merlot perhaps?'

Pete laughed and shook his head.

'It didn't lead to much. The winters are not so forgiving. Eliza was from a family of academics, so academia soon trumped agriculture. My parents and grandparents, they're all teachers and scholars. Some of my siblings too.'

'How many siblings do you have?' Charlie gave an exaggerated expression, as if he were about to say twenty.

'Three. Two sisters and a brother.'

'No way! Harry has two sisters and a brother.'

Pete didn't look as if he cared much for Harry's family, so Charlie got back onto the subject of his.

'Where do you fit in it all?'

'I'm the oldest. Boy, girl, girl, boy.' Charlie didn't say that Harry's family was also boy, girl, girl, boy, but that Harry was the baby. 'But my sister Irenie is an academic too – has a master's in linguistics, she's now a freelance translator since she became a mom.'

'You're an uncle!' Charlie stated.

'Yeah.' Pete looked proud.

'So what do your parents do? Or what did they do...?' Charlie's own parents had recently taken early retirement.

'My dad is a psychologist, Mom a nutritionist. An epic feeder. They met at Syracuse.'

That sounded somewhere Mediterranean but Charlie remembered Mike telling her last night that it was a university in upstate New York where he, Pete and their friend Isaac had met. 'Oh, cute.'

'What about you? Any siblings? What's your heritage?' Pete studied Charlie's muddy green eyes, her irises spreading colour across her gaze in the sunlight under thick dark brows and her brown-blonde hair. He couldn't work her out.

'Oh, I'm so boring!' Charlie waved. 'Such a disappointment. I'm an only child. And as Anglo-Saxon, white and northern as you get.'

'But you're all descended from Vikings, right? So that's interesting…'

'My dad *is* very good at making and carving things out of wood – maybe that's why!'

Pete smiled.

'Is he a carpenter?'

'No, he's a model maker. He made props and models for theme parks and attractions across the UK. If I ever needed a prop for school, or a creepy wooden hand for Halloween trick or treating, he was my man.'

'How about your mom?'

'Americans are so obsessed with *where* people come from and *what* they do, aren't they? Heritage plus profession, it's so intrinsic in who you are… I think that's why I usually get on well with Americans – I ask a lot of questions too.'

'Ain't that the truth!'

Pete went quiet as he pondered it as he hadn't before. He thought about all his siblings, his friends, and realised Charlie had a point. He did define them by where they came from and what they did.

'Are people not usually like that in the UK?'

'I don't think as much. But maybe this is why.'

Charlie gestured to the big hall around them.

'All the people registered through here. Their heritage and what they could do were so important to whether they were let in, and where they went on to in the next part of their journey. The American dream!' She rested her bagel on her lap and waved her palms as she said the word 'dream'.

Pete chewed thoughtfully.

'Anyway, Mum works in a farm shop, local to us, just to keep her brain ticking over. They retired, but she used to be a dental nurse in Lancaster.'

'Hence why you have good teeth...' Pete said.

'Another thing Americans are obsessed with! But yes. She was militant about fluoride and flossing, and for that I am very grateful!'

'So you get your artistic talent from your dad?'

'I suppose...' Charlie thought. Remembering that it was her crippling anxiety that had made her want to become a make-up artist, as much as she loved watching her dad in his workshop.

On the boat back to Castle Clinton at the foot of Manhattan, Charlie watched Ellis Island and the Statue of Liberty shrink away beyond the choppy waves of the boat. She thought about the White Star Line room at Ellis Island, all the dreams that had been put into motion on this body of water. The fresh starts. How what looked like a prison to the ignorant eye was actually a door to opportunity and hope for those who had the courage to knock. Hope that Charlie herself had had stolen from her this past week. She turned to look ahead, at the skyscrapers glimmering in the last of the cold day's sun. The year coming to an end. She knew that, however sad she felt about her journey, she was going to have to find a way to push on through it. To deftly adapt, as Pete's ancestors had.

As a tourist helicopter whizzed overhead, Charlie wondered whether Harry was back on Manhattan. What he might be doing to see in the new year. Then she internally cursed herself.

Dammit, Charlie thought. She wanted to cry again, but instead she took her phone out of her pocket, to capture the sight before the sun set beyond the city and into the heartland. The sparkle against the skyscrapers could disappear any second.

* * *

Charlie turned to Pete, his elbows propped over the side of the boat, eyes taking in the city from a vantage he knew he didn't appreciate enough. He looked thoughtful and lovely, and she wanted to capture it.

'May I?' she asked cautiously, wondering if it would be weird to take a photo of him. Pete was such a big part of her short New York story, even though she didn't really know him.

'Sure!' he said, looking over his shoulder at her, before attempting to flatten his hair as it bounced in the wind.

An elderly woman in a silk headscarf also struggling with the wind smiled from her seat on the deck as she watched Charlie taking a photo of Pete's bashful smile.

'Want me to take a picture of the both of you?' she offered help-fully, in a southern American accent. She was obviously unaware or too old to understand the concept of the selfie, and Charlie smiled politely.

'Yes, please!' she said, handing the woman her phone. She took it in her shaky hands as Pete turned around to reposition himself, back against the side of the boat with the city's skyscrapers behind him. He put a friendly arm around Charlie's shoulder.

'Say... "New York field trip!"' he joked at his own expense. They both laughed while the woman squinted and pressed the screen with a fragile index finger. She kept taking photos – or perhaps she was only taking one – or perhaps she had the camera the wrong way round and she was in fact taking a selfie, Charlie thought as she and Pete held their pose.

'What a darling couple!' the woman gushed as Charlie and Pete's smiles became more forced and less certain.

'Want me to do a boomerang?' the woman said, taking them by surprise.

Charlie and Pete laughed again.

'We're good, thanks!' Charlie said, pressing her palms together in gratitude.

'Just give her back the phone!' said a curmudgeonly man with a walking stick, seemingly embarrassed by his wife's mere existence. Charlie felt sorry for her.

'Thank you so much,' Charlie said, accepting her phone back.

'You two are adorable. I love the British accent,' she said, clasping an arm of them each with her hands.

'Thank you very kindly,' Pete said, in the most terrible British accent Charlie had heard since she watched Don Cheadle in *Ocean's Eleven*.

The woman smiled and turned back to her grumpy husband as Charlie gently hit Pete's stomach with her phone.

'Terrible!' she admonished.

* * *

Warm and toasty in a Mexican restaurant back in the Village, Mike and Pete were discussing the Green New Deal for public housing while Charlie did Téa's make-up using a set of face paints Erin had grabbed from Téa's dress-up box. Téa's fever had amounted to nothing and she had asked Charlie if she would transform her into a favourite character. As Charlie held the girl's tiny chin in her hand and got to work, Erin took the opportunity to eat her dinner before it went cold, wolfing down tacos while her daughter was quiet; before her baby gave her heartburn.

'What are you guys doing for New Year's?' She spoke quickly, with a mouth full of pumpkin, corn and salsa verde.

It was a clumsy question really, given she knew Charlie's predicament, but Erin had a teacher's way about her, as if she fired off questions in her sleep.

Charlie didn't take her eyes off Téa's face.

'Nothing, really. I'm so tired I'd happily sleep through it,' she replied. 'Hold still...' she reminded the little girl. 'Probably best I say goodbye to this shitty—'

Téa gasped, although her mouth and eyes were already wide open as Charlie applied whiskers to her face.

'Oops, sorry.' Charlie gave Erin a furtive glance before continuing. 'Best I say goodbye to this – difficult – year.'

Pete had stopped listening to Mike's musings and had one ear on Charlie.

'I'll wake up on Wednesday and start afresh.'

'Oh, I am with you!' Erin said, in her matter-of-fact way. 'Except I guess my fatigue is born from this and not...' Erin hadn't meant to sound insensitive as she pointed to her bump, she was trying to show compassion, but she realised halfway through her sentence that perhaps she ought to back up a few paces. 'And not... you know... so I'm not complaining.'

Charlie felt the punch again. The reminder. Even though she knew Erin hadn't meant to deliver such a blow. She took a deep breath and focused on Téa's pretty face, full of optimism and energy. Pete interjected, picking up a flauta as if it were a cigar.

'You know, you're welcome to come up to the Hudson Valley. My folks always have a New Year's party...'

Erin was glad of the change of tack.

'Oh, they do! You should go. His folks are adorable.'

Mike gently nodded as he grabbed a quesadilla.

Pete leaned in and Charlie looked at him quizzically, a pause button pressed on painting Téa's face, Téa's lips still pursed for her transformation.

'They got married on New Year's Eve, so that's always when my family convene over the holidays. To celebrate. New Year is like our Christmas.'

'For real,' Mike concurred. 'Hey, buddy, isn't it a big one?'

'Forty,' Pete said proudly.

'Wow, it's your parents' fortieth wedding anniversary on Tuesday?' Charlie asked.

'Ummm... excuse me?' Téa protested.

'Sorry, sweetie,' Charlie said, and resumed artfully shading white and black face crayons onto her soft brown skin.

'They always have this mega Makris dinner on New Year's Eve – the best food in the world – and then a party with friends New Year's Day. Soulla's food is *insane!*' Erin said, shovelling in a tortilla fully loaded with guac.

'Ahhh, that's so sweet,' Charlie said, adding the finishing touches of fur effect to Téa's forehead. 'But I don't want to take the piss. Oops—' She put her hand over her mouth and winced. Charlie wasn't accustomed to dining with five-year-olds; she made a note to herself to monitor her language.

Erin hadn't seemed to register.

'Take the piss?' Pete asked with a raised eyebrow. He knew about being pissed *off* but not taking it.

'You know,' explained Charlie. 'To be cheeky, ask too much. To mock someone. You know... "take the piss" out of them?'

Mike nodded as if to say he knew that – he had been backpacking with a British friend around South America – and Pete looked suitably impressed.

'What I mean is, I wouldn't want to crash such a special celebration, you've been kind enough to me already.'

Everyone looked a little disappointed, except for Téa, whose expression was still obligingly frozen. 'I'll be fine here, I promise!'

'Well, it's not a problem.' Pete shrugged and Charlie wondered if anything ever was a problem for Pete. If Charlie had invited a house guest to a huge family party at short notice – not that the Browns ever threw huge family parties – Ruth would have had kittens.

'You gotta see the Hudson Valley, Charlie, it's beautiful,' Erin said with authority.

'There you go!' Charlie declared, happy to shift the focus. 'Grizabella!'

Téa precociously belted out a line of 'Memory', not minding that the entire restaurant could hear, and Charlie was enthralled. Something about Téa reminded her of Jasmine. Both were born performers.

'It's brilliant!' Erin gushed, looking adoringly as she took photos of Téa's face on her phone.

'Baby, you look amazing!' Mike said in awe.

Pete stole a sidelong look at Charlie, as Charlie watched Téa make faces at herself in Charlie's hand mirror, proud as punch: growls, frowns, cute kitten faces. It reminded Charlie why she loved what she did.

'So what are you cool cats doing for New Year's Eve?' Charlie asked Mike and Erin.

'Us?' Erin squeaked. 'Times Square on TV. I'm seven months pregnant, I am not going anywhere.'

17

NEW YEAR'S EVE

Shortly before 1 p.m. on New Year's Eve, Pete pulled up outside the Jane Street Guest House in a battered brown Saab and honked the horn twice.

'Coming!' a flustered Charlie called out, even though Pete clearly wouldn't hear her from inside his car, all the way up to her room.

She hadn't known what to pack for a homely sounding family's homely fortieth anniversary celebration dinner in a homely house upstate. Then a bigger party with aunts, uncles, cousins and friends on New Year's Day. And she had more items to choose from after spending Monday on her own, traipsing the Midtown beauty halls and drugstores for trends. Any make-up artist worth their salt scrub knew that a holiday could equate to a research trip: a Balinese supermarket lip balm or a Greek foot oil might be the next big hero product; no trip to France was ever complete without stopping to look at skincare in their treasure-trove pharmacies. Now the bed was covered in the contents of her washbag, a few new beauty treats to try out, and all the clothes she'd brought to America. At the last minute she grabbed the black jumpsuit and heeled boots from her capsule wardrobe, and, with Leyla's voice in her head, she grabbed a long gunmetal cardi too.

Layer, Charlie, layer.

The long-sleeved tiered dress she was wearing in a pixelated print of brown, pink and white dots worked well over black tights and brogues and would look smart enough to carry her through to the family dinner she pictured tonight; the jumpsuit would do for the bigger party tomorrow – she could dress it down if it were too much. The only other things she needed were washbag, make-up, jewellery and phone. And maybe her passport. She was only going for one night, why was she panicking so much?

It's a big night.

She had to think to remember what she did last New Year's Eve. Dinner at Xander and Katie's, which, now she thought about it, was probably one of the dullest she'd ever spent. Jasmine had invited her to a party with some of her drama school grads at a warehouse near Old Street, but Harry had said they were far too old to hang out with drama students quoting Coward, Kane and Butterworth. Harry hated the theatre. Charlie loved Jazz's drama school friends, they were so bright and bolshy.

She put her on her lilac coat and camel scarf then hauled her slouchy overnight bag over her shoulder, gave one hurried look around the room, then cursed herself as she almost forgot the gifts lying on the bed. Harry's demands that would now double up as presents for Pete's family.

Fuck you, Charlie whispered to herself as she threw them into the bag too.

On the stairs she saw Charlie Black mopping.

'Hey!' he said, eyes lighting up.

'Hiya! Oh, I just wanted to let you know – I won't be in tonight, New Year plans!' Charlie said, as if she was surprised too. 'But obviously I'd still like to keep the room. Definitely not sorted my shit out...'

Charlie Black leaned on his mop and Charlie Brown expected him to break into song.

'No problem. Do you want to leave the key with me or take it with you?' He almost sang. 'No problem either way.'

Charlie paused.

'You know what, the way my trip has gone so far, I'd better keep it on me, so at least I can access a bed tonight if I need to.'

Charlie wanted to ask loads of questions. He often applied back stories to guests, some of which were boring, some were intriguing. The British woman had an interesting back story given she turned up out of the blue and didn't know how long she was staying. He wanted to go for a coffee with her and ask what the hell happened, but he was polite and professional and held back.

'Where are you off to?'

'Oh, I don't know. Somewhere in the Hudson Valley.' Charlie laughed when she realised how reckless it sounded out loud. Then frowned when she realised that she hadn't once considered her personal safety. Another honk came from Pete's car outside as an alarm went off in her head. She didn't know any of these people she was spending the night with. But she'd thought she'd known Harry. And even though Pete didn't seem like a serial killer, she made a mental note to send her Live Location to Saphie on WhatsApp from the car.

'Cool!' Charlie Black said. 'It's a pretty part of the world.'

Charlie Brown pictured lush mountains and peaceful valleys, with her limbs strewn all over them.

Not such a pretty part of the world.

'How about you? What are you doing tonight? I hope you're nearly done mopping.'

'Yes! Going to a friend's in Williamsburg. Low-key. I'm not one for New Year's.' Charlie imagined Charlie didn't drink much with that fresh face of his and wished him well.

'Have a good one!' she said.

'You too.'

* * *

'Sorry!' Charlie said getting in.

'No problem, I'm always disappointingly on time. It pisses most my friends off. Sometimes, I'm even a little early,' Pete said in mock confession.

Charlie looked at Pete with mock suspicion as she slung her bag on the back seat.

'How dare you be punctual?' she joked, assessing the battered dashboard of the car that was going to take her *upstate*. 'It sort of jars with your cool and casual... you know... I would think you tardy.'

'Oh, really?'

'But then you are a scientist... I suppose you're more reliable than me.'

'Yeah, don't be fooled by that, some scientists give or take sixty-five million years when they're due to be someplace. I just like to be where I say I'll be.'

Pete's voice had a little bite, as if he didn't like people who weren't, although Charlie didn't feel it was directed at her.

'Well, sorry, I am always five minutes late, which I blame on being an artist of sorts.'

'Better late than never,' Pete said cheerily, 'and you really weren't that late at all. Good to go?'

'Good to go.'

* * *

As Pete drove up through Manhattan past Chelsea Piers, the George Washington Bridge and onto the Joe DiMaggio highway, Charlie wriggled out of her coat and scarf and took charge of Spotify, looking through Pete's recently played tracks and playlists on a phone tethered to a threadbare cable plugged into a USB.

By the time they got to Yonkers, which made Charlie chuckle, she asked Pete for the lowdown on his family as if she were cramming for a test.

'So my dad is called Dimitri and my mom is Soulla.'

'The psychologist and the nutritionist.'

'Correct.'

'Wow, you must be very balanced of mind and body.'

'The irony!' he said drily. 'They're semi-retired though now. Dad spends much of his time in the garden.'

'Agriculture runs through his veins, of course...'

'Mom is the best cook. Although she does tend to go on about the benefits of magnesium in cashews and selenium in Brazil nuts when she's making her baklava...'

'Yum.' Charlie licked her lips then reapplied her tinted balm. 'And they're celebrating forty years of marriage... shit, today?'

'Correct.'

'What gift did you get them?'

'My siblings and I booked them a trip to Hawaii, to go stargazing, then stop over and see Alex and Conor in LA. They've always wanted to go to Hawaii.'

'Who are Alex and Conor?'

'Alex is my brother.'

'The baby of the family, right?'

'Yes. I'm the oldest.'

'Oh yeah, the ancient thirty-six-year-old.'

Pete gave a downbeat roll of the eyes under another large green road sign overhead on the highway hugging the curves of the Hudson.

'Next is my sister Irenie – she's the linguist, married to Jack, with two boys, Theo and Elias. They live in Chicago. My nephews are crazy, adorable, exhausting...' Pete said proudly. Charlie nodded and soaked it in.

'Theo and Elias. How old?'

'God, I don't know. Like seven and five. Maybe eight and six. I never forget their birthday but often forget how old they are.'

'That'll be your age again.'

'Funny. Then there's my younger sister, Agata, and her husband, Ollie – they live in the city too. Brooklyn though. Agata is a nurse. She's pregnant with their first, due this spring.'

'Oh wow. Everyone's at it! OK, Agata, check.'

'And my baby brother, Alexander. He lives on the West Coast. He's a lawyer in Pasadena. Has a ridiculously handsome husband from Ireland, Conor, who's a teacher.'

'All married? Even your baby brother?'

'Yeah, he got married this summer in Big Sur, he's twenty-nine.' Pete drummed his fingers on the dashboard to The War On Drugs. 'All married, except me. Great tune, by the way.'

Charlie sat a little higher in her passenger seat.

'I'm a big disappointment to my parents.'

'Oh no! How can you be?'

'No, not at all...' He paused while he considered how fortunate he was. 'They're wonderful, supportive. We have no cross to bear.'

Charlie thought about her parents and how lucky she was too. They had never been anything but supportive of all her life choices. Even the dodgy haircuts and colours. She was hit by another slap of guilt, which gradually dissipated as they chatted through The War On Drugs, Interpol, and an artist called Jeanette 'Baby' Washington, who Charlie had never heard of but she had topped Pete's Spotify Wrapped artist of the year, so she must be worth a listen.

As a song called 'That's How Heartaches Are Made' came through the car's speakers, the light was starting to fade.

'Fuck!' Charlie cursed, looking at the familiar terrain. Metropolitan Manhattan had led the way to rocky and bendy highways whose stark trees arched over wintry roads as if pointing the way. 'I know this place!'

She looked through the rear window, just to be sure.

'What?' Pete asked, shuffling in his seat, looking in the rear-view mirror as if they were being followed.

A chill ran down Charlie's spine as she recognised little signs. The bakery closing up. The Western Union. The drugstore. Richard Gere's place couldn't be far away. Charlie felt nauseous and upended. She opened the window and sucked in the cold air.

'You OK?'

She took a few seconds to answer.

'This is where I came. Where Harry was.'

'Oh, yeah, right. Bedford Hills.'

She shook her head and stuck it a little further out of the window.

'Oh, man...' Pete lamented as he took his eyes off the road and glanced uneasily at Charlie, who was gripping the handle on the inside of the door and taking deep breaths, like a child trying to outwit car sickness. 'I shoulda gone another way, I'm sorry.'

Charlie shook her head as if to say don't be silly and inhaled big gulps of frosty air.

'Are you OK? Want me to stop?'

'I absolutely do *not* want you to stop.'

Pete went quiet and let it pass, let her breathe.

'Take your time...' he eventually said, quietly.

'Shit,' she half whispered, the optimism of their road trip now crushed under the wheel along with the squirrels, opossums and racoons that punctuated the road. 'It's OK, sorry,' she apologised.

'Did you go to her house? Is that where you caught him?' Pete didn't say what they were both thinking.

Nice houses.

'Sort of. It was hard to miss.'

Charlie didn't want to sound like a stalker. 'But actually I chanced upon them in a restaurant. Harry and his girlfriend.'

'She's not a friend of the Irvings, is she?' Pete joked. 'I imagine everyone up here claims to be.'

Charlie wound the window down a little further. An icy blast helped combat the nausea.

'She is an Irving.'

'Fuck!' Pete slapped the top of the dashboard with his palm.

They drove in silence for a few miles.

'Which one?'

'Isabelle.'

'Your boyfriend cheated on you with Isabelle Irving?' Pete rubbed his eyes and refocused on the road.

'You know her, then...'

'I pick up *The New Yorker* and *Page Six* in the waiting room at the dentist.'

'And he didn't even have the decency to tell me.'

'What an asshole.'

As they drove past a sign to say they were leaving Bedford Hills, Pete wound down his window and the cold dusk wind whipped through the car.

'Fuck you, Bedford Hills!' he bellowed out of the window, to no one in particular. The ridiculousness of it took Charlie by surprise and made her laugh out loud, wind her window all the way down and lift herself out of her seat to fully lean out.

'Yeah, fuck you, Bedford Hills!' she shouted, towards cornfields and quiet, and they both laughed, her laugh coming through tears, as a song called 'Leave Me Alone' by Baby Washington came on and Charlie turned it up.

* * *

After a quiet period where Pete watched the road and Charlie watched the spartan trees turn to white, where snowfall left its dainty layer over gnarly branches, Charlie came to a conclusion.

'I think I need to call my parents.'

She had been picturing them, sitting in the living room, drinking Bailey's and watching Jools Holland, thinking about her, and realised she couldn't sustain the lie any more.

'I didn't want to pry,' Pete said calmly, 'but I think that sounds like a great idea.'

He looked over at Charlie, who was still looking out of the window at the evolving landscape.

'They'll be devastated.'

'I'm sure they will, but they will want to know you're OK. The important thing is, you *are* OK. Look at you. Pretty fucking damn OK.'

Charlie laughed as she tidied up the mascara under her eyes in the flip-down mirror.

'I just always want to protect them. It's just me, so I'm sort of responsible. For them and for their happiness.' Charlie said it as if she were a massive let-down.

'Well, firstly, you're not responsible for anyone else's happiness. Not until we're parents anyway. As humans, I mean.'

Charlie looked at him.

'And you need support too. Want me to pull in?' he said, gesturing to a gas-station sign. 'I gotta fill up anyway...'

* * *

At the small roadside service station Charlie wrapped up again, found a loo and paced in circles as she spoke to Ray and Ruth, who were indeed watching Jools Holland, an hour off midnight in the UK.

'Oh, darling!' Ruth cried. 'Why didn't you tell us?'

'Don't ask questions, Ruthie! Let her speak!' Ray said, although it sounded as if he was choking up too.

Charlie explained what had happened – how Saphie knew and was keeping her spirits up, and that actually she had made a couple of friends and would be safe and well this New Year's Eve.

'I'm celebrating with a friend in the Hudson Valley,' she said reassuringly.

'A friend! Who?'

'Pete.'

'So when are you coming home, love?' Ruth asked.

'Let her work it out!' Ray snapped.

Charlie sighed as she looked around the forecourt. Pete was putting air in the tyres so as not to make her feel rushed, unhurried and casual as ever.

'I just don't know what to do. I'd like to catch up with Harry. I need answers before I just get on a plane home. Or I'm sort of accepting it. Allowing it.'

'I think you probably do need to accept it, love...' Ray said.

'Oh, I do, Dad. But he can't just dump me without bothering to tell me. There's so much I deserve to know.'

'That bastard...' Ray rued, before stopping himself.

'Are you sure it's not a mix-up, darling?' her mum asked again, completely baffled.

'No, Mum. Absolutely not a mix-up.'

* * *

Pete was chatting to an old man by the air pump when Charlie returned to the car. The man was patting his motorbike, explaining how rarely he rode in winter yet always took a drive on New Year's Eve to see his son in Albany, snow permitting.

'You and your wife have a happy new year!' the man said as he clipped his helmet and got back on his touring bike that looked more like an armchair than a motorcycle.

Charlie nodded and smiled.

'You too, man.' Pete waved as the man's motorbike engine chugged like the snore of a sleeping bear.

Charlie walked around to the wrong side, then the right side of the car, a combination of relief and sadness sweeping her face as she did her awkward little dance.

'You OK?' Pete twisted the valve cap back on the last tyre, wiped his hands on a cloth, and got in.

'Not really. But thanks.'

He nodded, and readjusted his rear-view mirror, as if someone else had been driving.

'They weren't upset about me lying.'

'I told you, huh?'

'Just upset for me.'

'Of course.'

Pete had a calm about him that Charlie appreciated. Despite first impressions in the back of the UberPool, he didn't ask too many questions and when he did they were thoughtfully and respectfully put. Even the more controversial ones, which he asked when they were a few miles down the road and Charlie had put on a Motown mix.

'Have you heard anything from the douchebag yet?'

'After my "Happy Christmas you motherfucker" text on Christmas Day? Funnily enough, no.'

'Oh, man...'

Pete seemed to say, 'Oh man' as much as Charlie said, 'Oh wow'. Charlie wasn't saying wow now, she was letting a sigh out of the side of her mouth.

'It just feels like... I've been totally robbed. Like I haven't had the right of reply.'

'I hear ya.'

Charlie became more animated.

'I want answers I can't get. I want to see him. Square up to him. Look him in the eye and say, "What the fuck?" I'm so angry!'

'Damn, you need to put on some angrier music. You need rage anthems not Motown! Put on a rage anthems playlist!'

'Yeah right.' Charlie sighed as she looked out of the window. She wasn't ready for Taylor, Kelly or Eminem.

'Or you could have a candy. I got some while I was paying, in the glove compartment...'

'Oh, brilliant...'

Charlie opened the glove compartment and a large bag of Reese's Peanut Butter Cups tumbled out.

'Are these good?'

'You've never had a Peanut Butter Cup? You don't have them in the UK?' Pete exaggerated his astonishment.

'I might have seen them but I've never tried them.'

'The food equivalent of rage anthems...' Pete said knowingly. 'Taste good too.'

Charlie was dubious – she'd had a Hershey's bar in desperation from the grocery store on the corner of Jane Street and 8th Avenue before she'd remembered she could tuck into Harry's chocolate. Before she forgot to again. But these were good.

'Want one?' she asked Pete.

He held out his flat palm and as he unwrapped a Peanut Butter Cup and popped it in his mouth, he thought some more about Charlie's situation.

'You know... maybe it's better if you never see him again.' There was a sad tinge in Pete's voice. 'Looking him in the eye. It could be so hurtful. So raw.'

She looked over at him, one hand on the wheel, the other squishing a foil wrapper into a tiny ball.

'And I can't imagine any explanation would suffice.'

Half an hour later – four hours after they had left Manhattan – Pete turned off the A road into a curved one lined with bony sugar maples, red oaks and hickory, all of which had shed their red and russet leaves for winter. The trees were peppered with the evergreen hues of cedars and pines, tall and proud, pointing the way to a Georgian house tucked behind a neat hornbeam hedge.

'This is where your parents live?'

'Yeah. It's where I grew up.'

'Oh, wow!'

The house was spacious-looking and symmetrical with eight windows framed by sage-green shutters, divided into two sets of four. The windows, two up and two down on each side, were separated by a large white front door topped with a Palladian arched window. The house was capped beautifully by a roof with grey slate slopes and two chimneys at each end.

It looked like a family home from a Steve Martin film, not the ramshackle cottage with grapevines, cypresses and terracotta pots surrounding it that Charlie had imagined.

The couple who came out onto the white porch were not the old, shrunken, Greek parents Charlie expected either. Dimitri was a tall and strapping man who wore cords, a dark blue shirt and a blazer. Soulla was slim and elegant with short silver hair, glasses framing a pretty face and she wore a housecoat over slender trousers.

Still, she clutched her heart then opened her arms out when she saw her son, as only a Greek mother could.

Pete parked the car to the side of the house where other cars were gathered in front of a double garage and a side door, which was framed with another neat white porch. This one had a narrow set of steps leading to a boot room. Pete opened Charlie's door then walked round to greet his parents at the front.

Charlie got out and put her hand to her brow. She was grateful to have just caught the house in the last of the light. It was beautiful.

'My darling!' Soulla said, pulling her strapping son in and kissing him robustly on the cheek.

'Happy anniversary, Mom.' Pete hugged her, then his dad, as they clung to each other, gripping each other's backs.

'Thank you, darling,' his mum said as she watched her men in an embrace. 'What a gift. And you must be Charlie!'

Soulla's accent was 100 per cent American and not European, and Charlie felt ridiculous for her assumptions of a hunched old woman in a headscarf, painstakingly working at a rustic kitchen table.

'You knew I was coming, then?' Charlie let out a big mock *phew* while Soulla appraised her. Charlie could already tell she liked the British accent too. 'Thank you for having me,' she said, hamming it up a little. 'Happy anniversary.'

They gave each other a kiss on the cheek.

'Not at all, any friend of Petros...'

Charlie shot Pete a look and was heartened to see his brown cheeks turn slightly pink. She raised one comedic eyebrow at him.

'Do come in,' Dimitri said, shaking Charlie's hand then

ushering her up the steps. 'I've just this minute finished setting up the fireworks.'

'What a beautiful home you have!'

* * *

In the capacious kitchen Soulla made everyone a fresh peppermint tea and placed a tray of cups on the large island with dark granite worktop in the middle of it. Irenie came in from the garden in a quilted coat and wellies, black and shiny, took them off and put them next to the large stone hearth.

'Hey!' she said, grabbing her brother gratefully, hugging him, then releasing him. She put a palm on each cheek and asked him if he was OK. It was tenderness and protectiveness Charlie had never seen between Harry and his sisters.

He nodded to reassure her, as if they were speaking without talking.

'Where are the boys?'

'Jack took them to see the tractors in the Dessner field. Elias has gotten heavily into tractors.'

'You don't see many of those in Chicago,' said Pete.

'You get everything up here!' Dimitri said, proud of his enclave, as if he were selling it to Charlie. 'Lettuce! Apples! Beets! Wine! Plus antiquities and the arts in Hudson.'

'We have tractors in Illinois, for God's sake, Dad!' Irenie said coolly.

Charlie thought it a bit odd that Irenie hadn't said hello yet, but perhaps she was shy, and Pete sought to correct it.

'Hey, Reen, this is Charlie, all the way from London.' He had clearly primed all his family that he was bringing a friend.

'Hi.' Charlie waved, big scarf, big gloves, big smile, all of which she started removing as Dimitri held out his hands like a butler and took her coat and scarf off to a closet. She just about held onto the smile. It was such an amazing house it could easily have its own cloakroom and butler.

Irenie smiled and waved a polite 'Hi,' which wasn't as effusive as her mother's.

'My cousin lives in London,' Soulla confided as she pushed her glasses up her nose and kept a deft eye on pots on the hob and trays in the oven. Dimitri declared it was far too early to be drinking peppermint tea and opened a bottle of red.

'Do you know an Eleni?' she asked, stirring something on the wide range hob. 'From a funny part of London, what's it called, honey?'

'Cockfosters,' Dimitri said as he uncorked the wine.

'That's it, Cockfosters.'

Pete and Charlie exchanged a bemused, knowing look.

'I don't know an Eleni. But I do have something from London for you...' Charlie smiled as she flung her bag onto a stool next to the island and rummaged for the Liberty and Fortnum & Mason treats inside.

'Obviously I didn't know I was coming until yesterday – thank you so much for having me, by the way.'

'Not at all!' Soulla waved.

'But I never travel without these,' she lied as she presented Soulla with an artisan-looking packet of Chorley cakes that cost ten times the price of a packet twice the size in the village shop. She also gave her a pretty cylindrical tin of loose-leaf English Breakfast tea with a merry-go-round horse on the outside. Harry's favourite.

'What is this, "Chorley cake"?' Soulla pushed her glasses up her nose again and examined the packet. 'It looks like a British mince pie!' she said with curiosity. 'We had those once, didn't we, darling?' she said to Irenie, who nodded and smiled. 'Only these look like flat mince pies.'

'Shh, don't say that in Lancashire!' Charlie whispered theatrically, while Dimitri elaborately poured the wine and he and Irenie pondered what an odd thing a mince pie was, the time they went to London one December.

'Your sister liked them more,' Dimitri said to Irenie.

'Where is Aggie?' Pete asked.

'She and Ollie went into Hudson to pick up some apricots I needed. Silly me,' Soulla said. 'They'll be back soon.'

Soulla opened the large oven and her glasses steamed up as she removed an enormous tray of what looked like one giant filo pie, but it was about to be cut into an artful jigsaw of squares, rectangles and triangles.

'Oh, my goodness!' Charlie said, a little embarrassed by her well-travelled Chorley cakes. The syrupy, bejewelled confection sent scents of pistachio, citrus and spice rolling through the kitchen, and Charlie felt even more grateful to Pete that his family had welcomed her into their home.

* * *

After a quick tour of the house and its rambling garden, where they met two excited, pink-cheeked boys returning from a walk with their dad Jack, uncle Alexander and his husband Conor, Pete led Charlie to the large creaky staircase and showed her to her room at the top and on the left of a spacious wooden landing.

'This OK for you?' he asked.

'Is it OK? It's gorgeous!'

Standing side by side with Pete in the doorway, Charlie was almost too nervous to go in. It looked like something from *Anne of Green*

Gables, with floral wallpaper and sage-green skirting the same colour as the shutters on the outside of the sash windows. The wooden floor looked older and less polished than the darker floorboards of the landing and stairs, but it had a chintzy cotton rug in stripes of faded pastels. Under the window was a white wrought-iron bed with a pretty quilt over it that had apparently been made by Soulla's mother, and next to a standing mirror and dresser was an en suite bathroom that Anne of Green Gables definitely wouldn't have had, but Charlie had seen *Selling Sunset*: modern Americans were crazy about bathrooms. Pete walked in, drew the curtain and turned on the lamp on the bedside table, as if the room didn't look warm and hospitable enough.

'It's a bit twee,' Pete apologised. 'I don't think it's been decorated in decades.'

'It's wonderful, I love it.' Charlie pressed her palms together as she soaked up the room. It looked like going back in time. To a simpler time. 'Thank you.'

'Hey, no problem.'

'Where are you?' she asked.

'Down the hall, other end. Just holler if you need anything, huh?'

'Sure thing.'

Pete smiled and walked past Charlie as she dared to step into the room and put her bag onto the patchwork quilt.

'Oh, Pete!' she called to him, already working his way across the landing towards a commotion of boys being shepherded to the bathroom.

'Yeah?' he said.

'Will this frock do?' she said, holding her arms out at her sides.

'Frock?' He gave a quizzical laugh.

'Yeah, frock. My dress.'

'Oh, right.'

'How smart do you go for dinner? I don't want to get it wrong, but I've barely brought anything.' She laughed more lamely than she should. Charlie was not the sort of woman to worry about how to dress for people, but the delicate balance of wanting to make an effort and being out of her comfort zone tripped her up a little. Plus she hadn't realised Pete's family were so fancy.

Pete rubbed his temple.

'You look great! It's relaxed anyways. I'm just going to change my shirt, but that's mainly because of the car journey and I probably smell.'

Charlie only just registered how Pete did smell. Of cedar and sandalwood. She wondered if that was why she felt so comfortable with him in the car; he smelled of pencil shavings and nostalgia.

'You don't smell,' she assured him.

He smiled. His smile reminded Charlie of simpler times too.

'It's more of a relaxed thing tonight. The cocktail party tomorrow is a bit fancier, but I'm sure Agata has something in her old room if you need anything?' Pete tried not to look at Charlie's body as he mentally noted they were about the same size, before Agata was pregnant, anyway.

'Great, thanks. I'll just freshen up my face, then.'

Pete nodded an OK as Charlie closed the door, pressed her hand against it, closed her eyes and inhaled.

18

Dinner was a robust and lively affair; Charlie's gifts had been a great icebreaker. Dimitri and Alexander loved their Liberty ties, and when Charlie had apologised for not having anything for Conor, Jack and Ollie, Conor had said not to worry, he would share Alex's. Soulla, Irenie and Agata loved their pretty boxes of Rose & Violet Creams and when Theo and Elias had asked where their gifts were, Charlie had deftly turned them into Spiderman and Hulk thanks to the colourful Urban Decay palette she had happened to grab on her way out of the guest house. Irenie had been impressed, until they got a little too into character and spent much of the evening defeating imaginary foes (and knocking over a heavy candelabra).

'Anyone want to pretend 10 p.m. is midnight?' Irenie whispered to Charlie, who smiled. Irenie had definitely warmed up as the meal had gone on. But the wine was flowing and Charlie could feel herself getting giddier with each course that seemed to extend into the next one until the abundant table was packed with meze, tomato and orzo soup, lamb stew in wine, roast pork loin, stuffed cabbage, vine leaves and dips galore. All lovingly made by a family team effort (under Soulla's instruction and tutelage). And olives. An abundance of olives, because, Dimitri explained, olive trees grew for at least one hundred years, so they symbolised longevity and fertility at the family table.

Dimitri was full of stories. The genial host, revering his wife, adoring his children and grandchildren – while still managing to remonstrate about poor table manners if Spiderman and Hulk got out of line. Always ensuring that glasses were topped up and plates were furnished with the feast.

When he, Soulla and Pete brought desserts through from the kitchen, Pete and Dimitri tried to explain each confection to Charlie, with interjections and corrections from Soulla if Pete wasn't selling them quite as well as he should: the platter of doughnuts drizzled in orange syrup were called *loukomadies* and it was against the law to only have one; the custard tarts on filo were Pete's personal favourites; the chocolate and orange blossom baklava was the most popular, so dig in quick, and the honey biscuits drizzled in sweet sticky syrup were called *melomakarona*, which reminded Charlie of the beautiful way he'd said it in the Uber to Grand Central.

Soulla lovingly placed the centrepiece on the table, a beautiful bread-like orange cake called *vasilopita*, made in honour of St Basil. In Greek homes it was St Basil who brought the gifts, not St Nick, and the cake had a coin placed inside it before baking, said to bring the finder of it luck all year.

'We tend to eat that a bit later,' Pete whispered. Charlie gave a nod to say *got it*.

When all the desserts were laid out in front of them, despite everyone already being fit to bursting – especially Agata under her beautiful baby bump – Dimitri looked at Soulla and proposed a toast.

'To my wonderful wife. To forty years of friendship and family

– old and new,' he added, turning his glass to Agata, who rubbed her stomach protectively, and then to Charlie opposite him, meeting her eye. She raised her glass back. 'I must be the luckiest man in the world...' Charlie looked around the table and saw a sadness sweep over the faces of the Makris children, followed by flashes of gratitude, all told in the different ways their features wore them.

Alexander, at the end of the table opposite his mother, had a handsome confidence that told Charlie that whatever had passed had passed. Agata's sadness contained a blend of excitement and fear, for all the wonderful and harrowing things she knew were coming for her. Irenie's sadness had a maternal look, as she caught Pete's eye across the table; and although Pete was sitting next to Charlie, and she couldn't see sadness in his liquid brown gaze, she guessed the family had been through the mill, despite Pete's relaxed arm slung along the back of her chair. She remembered the grip with which Pete and his dad had clung onto each other. She wondered if he might open up to her on the drive back tomorrow.

'*Ya mas!*' he said decisively.

'*Ya mas!*' everyone around the table chimed back, and Charlie too, as they chinked dainty cut wine glasses and smaller ones swilling with ouzo. Charlie would have felt as if she were imposing if the Makris family weren't so warm and welcoming.

It was so different from the tense family dinners at Hawksworth Hall where the biggest noise was the chinking of cutlery on china, the conversation was so sparse. Harry's parents, Clarissa and Henry, barely acknowledging each other's existence in the long wood-panelled dining room. His uptight older brother, Lawrence, with carrot-coloured hair, who Charlie always thought walked about as if he had a carrot up his arse, although she rarely said because Harry thought Lawrence was the bee's knees. Harry's middle sisters, Lucinda and Felicity, one mousey, one strawberry blonde, both with the same gummy smiles and horsey mouths, were hideous to each other and talked to Charlie as if they were craning away from her, as if something about her wasn't to their liking. And charming Harry, the youngest, doted on but at a cold arm's length by everyone for being handsome; for knowing all about finance and macros. Desperate to impress his parents and do well after being kicked out of the boarding school his older siblings had all drifted through and underachieved at. Who would have thought it? Harry would come good at state school – thank *Christ* – because he had got a job in banking and had made it in New York.

This same boy-girl-girl-boy Makris family couldn't have been more different from the Taylors. They couldn't have been more animated and warm. And they were getting warmer with each glass of ouzo. Ollie kept topping up the shot glasses for everyone except for Agata, but made sure she always had a full glass of whichever artisan tonic it was he'd picked up in Hudson with the apricots.

Soulla's angular cheeks were getting rosier. She looked more like a powerhouse politician than a Greek mama who had spent all day in the kitchen. When she spoke about the nutritional benefits of each dish, she said it with gravitas, not fuss.

'So good to have all my children and their partners here!' she said, resting her chin on her curled fists propped on her elbows at the head of the table. She hadn't meant to make an assumption about Pete and Charlie, her eldest did say he had only just met the girl, so Soulla corrected herself straight away, reaching her hand out to cup Charlie's. 'So good to meet *any* friend of Petros.' She looked emotional now.

'Oh, Mom—'

'Petros!' Charlie smiled. There it was again, Pete blushing.

'My given name is Petros. Peter.'

Alexander, his Liberty tie loose and proud, draped around his neck, paused his wine glass at his lips.

'Our parents' gift, Charlie – other than giving us the gift of life, of course – is that the names they gave us have become what we went on to do as a career.'

'Really?' Charlie was enchanted.

'Petros here,' Alexander said, leaning over Irenie's husband, Jack, and the space where the boys had been sitting to squeeze his brother's forearm, 'means rock or stone. And he is an eminent geologist, his papers devoured the world over.'

Charlie looked impressed. She knew he must be good at his job to be so impassioned and to be delivering a paper in London, but she hadn't realised he was quite so respected.

'Solid as a rock too,' Soulla said as if she were selling him. Pete blushed and Charlie looked between him and his mother.

'Irenie – means peace,' Alexander continued. 'She used to work at the United Nations in New York before Jack stole her to Chicago.'

'Alex, I was a translator! That doesn't work.'

'Yes, it does. You're always a peacemaker between those two monkeys.' He nodded towards Theo and Elias, curled up on the sofa in the room on the other side of the hallway watching an *Avengers* movie. Jack half guffawed, as if Irenie only added fuel to the boys' fires. She raised her chin and narrowed her eyes at her husband.

'It's true,' Dimitri concurred, solid and authoritative and, dare Charlie say it, quite hot for a man in his early sixties – but perhaps that was the ouzo too – as Dimitri adjusted the centrepiece candles and relit tea lights that had gone out. 'Irenie *is* a peacemaker. She always got you and Agata in check when you were fighting,' Dimitri said.

'I rest my case,' Alexander said, looking guiltily towards Agata about the fights they used to have, before blowing her a brief kiss.

'Agata... Agata means good-hearted – she's a nurse and she always looks after everyone...'

'But mostly her papa...' Dimitri said gratefully. He looked at his youngest daughter sitting next to him, while her husband, Ollie, stroked her shoulder proudly.

'And Alexander!' Dimitri took over from the talker – for he and Soulla were the ones to have bestowed these names. 'Alexander is the defender of man.'

'Lawyer,' Alexander said apologetically as he put his hands up. 'In the entertainment industry, so I defend the *real* criminals.'

Conor laughed and looked at Charlie as if to say *It's true*. Conor and Charlie had talked while she was doing the boys' superhero make-up, and bonded on account of both being from the British Isles. As lovely as the Makris family were, they all seemed sickeningly accomplished. If Charlie hadn't been as comfortable in her own skin she would have felt intimidated; still Conor's quiet chat gave her a comforting feeling of the familiar in an unfamiliar place.

'Wow, what a gift! I will think long and hard before naming any of my children, if I am ever fortunate enough to have them,' Charlie said.

'What does Charlie mean?' Soulla asked as she tucked her short hair behind her ear so she could really listen.

'Well, my full name is Charlotte. It means free woman,' she replied as she raised herself a little in her seat and Pete softly stroked the thumb from his hand resting on the back of her chair to a disc near the top of her spine.

Charlie felt it.

* * *

After dessert, the assorted Makrises, Mullen, Wilsons, Brooksbanks and Brown played cards – a New Year's Eve family tradition for good luck – a game called 31, where Charlie kept catching Pete's eye to make sure she was doing the right thing, and he duly nodded, to encourage her to kick his siblings' arses.

As midnight neared they cut the *vasilopita* (Charlie found the coin in her slice, to great cheer), and Irenie realised she was too late to pretend to the boys that midnight was any earlier.

'Time to go outside,' she prompted, so everyone got up, put on their coats, and walked through to a study with French doors that led to the back garden for the fireworks display Ollie had helped his father-in-law set up earlier in the day. Everyone except Agata, Theo and Elias were tipsy to various degrees.

'Boys! Turn off all the lights!' Soulla commanded as she sent Theo and Elias back into the house. They charged back in over the stone step of the laundry room that led to the flagstone-floored kitchen and a thundering roar came through the house of boys in wellies charging to be the first to turn out each light.

'Is that just to tire them out?' Charlie asked.

'They're tired enough,' their father, Jack, said with a look of peril.

'The lights have to be out for the best view,' Soulla said.

As the adults gathered on the patio slabs facing a rambling orchard, Pete quietly explained the next Makris tradition.

'After the fireworks, we all follow one person into the house, in the dark, making sure our right foot is the first foot to hit the step.'

'Like a slow conga?' Charlie said, looking as though she was feeling giddy enough to dance.

Pete laughed.

'More measured than that.'

'Why the right foot? What if I'm left-handed? I might accidentally go on my left foot as it's stronger.'

'Are you left-handed?'

'No.'

'Well, I don't know why it's the right foot, but it's good luck, for the year ahead.'

'Who do you follow in... your mum?'

'It changes every year. Last year it was Theo.'

'Oh, cute.'

'Who's doing it this year?'

'Well, a family email went around early December and we all put in suggestions. Agata and her baby are going through first.'

'That's lovely.' Charlie smiled as the bonfire Ollie and Conor were tending to in a firepit started to gain momentum. It lit Charlie's happy cheeks.

'What time have we got?' asked Conor.

'Ten minutes,' said Agata.

'Where are the boys?' asked Irenie, craning her neck.

'Here, sparklers!' Soulla handed them out, urging everyone to take one.

'Look at the stars!' said Alexander, marvelling at the most speckled and crisp sky Charlie had ever seen, midnight blue with glittering dots and milky wisps. The night sky in upstate New York looked different from the night sky over NW3.

Conor prodded the firepit before returning to Alexander, who handed him his wine glass and slid an arm around his waist.

The boys came tumbling out of the study French doors again, as if it were an unspoken rule that you exited the house one way, and entered another, to cries of 'Careful!' and 'Calm down!' and 'Mind your step!' from their parents and *Yia-yia*.

Dimitri emerged from the orchard, a tall shadow, patriarch of a family who felt more grateful for him this anniversary than ever, and calmly said, 'Ready.'

Charlie felt Pete's hand guide her back, even though he wasn't touching her, and she put the giddy feeling in her stomach down to the stars – she could clearly see Perseus, Cassiopeia and Orion – and the ouzo. Everyone shuffled forward a few paces while Dimitri ran back into the orchard.

'Careful, Dad!' Agata called.

'Can *we* light some?' Elias looked up to his mother, whose stern shake of the head was enough to quash that idea.

At five to midnight, the first rocket shimmered into the sky and burst into a sparkly umbrella far larger than the Bonfire Night fireworks Charlie last saw in her parents' garden.

'Oooh!' everyone gasped.

This is America, she thought.

'Aaah!' they chorused.

'They're a bit wonky, Dad!' Alexander shouted.

'That's old age for you!' came a muffled chuckle from the orchard.

'Go help him,' Irenie urged Jack, who obliged. 'But be careful,' she told him.

On the terrace, Charlie and Pete stood next to the firepit, the warmth of his left side drawing the fatigue in her right side into him until she became aware of them touching, through the wool of her tights and the tiers of her dress. Until their hips were touching and the sides of their arms too. They were both surprised but neither protested. It felt like a safe, comforting, and rather nice way to see out this roller-coaster year for both of them.

Ollie stood behind Agata and stretched his large hands around her bump, as if he were using it as a life raft. Irenie kept a boy attached to each leg with a palm pressed to each of their chests. Soulla stood on the other side of Alexander to Conor and linked arms with her son. He kissed her cheek and said, 'Happy anniversary, Mom.' She appraised his face with a smile that reeked of pride and contentment. Charlie had never yearned for a big family before – Harry's dysfunctional and cold clan had made her grateful to be a treasured only child. But for the first time, she thought it would be a nice prospect. That she might have liked what Pete had. That children of her own might have been nice.

Boom.

She felt a pounding to her stomach, as if her insides were being ripped out. A pain so searing she remembered what it was like to want to crawl under a rock and die.

Bang.

She was relieved that her gasp was drowned out by the firework.

'It's OK, it's OK. I'm taking you home.'

A voice in her head made her feel both shame and comfort.

It's OK, it's OK, I'm here and not there, thought Charlie as she focused on the sky's bright lights and her eyes became veiled in glittery tears.

She pressed further into Pete for safety and with each boom and bang, their thighs seemed to become more stuck.

'Almost midnight!' Ollie declared.

'Make it a good one, Dad!' called Alexander.

'Ten, nine, eight... Wooooo!'

Dimitri had saved the crescendo for midnight and an umbrella of blooms in purples, reds and pinks, like allium and dahlia, were thrust towards them, a gift from the night sky.

'Six, five, four...'

Charlie swayed into Pete. A grateful thank-you nudge for rescuing her New Year. They looked at each other and smiled in the light of the fireworks and Pete curled his arm around Charlie's shoulder, half embrace and half shield.

'Three, two, one...'

Charlie rested her head on Pete's shoulder for a second before the collective cheer of 'Happy New Year!' startled them apart.

The Makris family and their spouses all turned to each other, Dimitri coming out of the orchard again to hug his wife and children. Elias had started crying at the last bangs while everyone went around in circles hugging everyone else, trying to comfort the small boy as they passed him. Charlie hugged Pete first, slipping her hands under his arms and up his back inside his coat. It might have been the ouzo but she swore she felt his heart beat against hers.

'Happy New Year,' he said warmly, falling into her embrace, which was broken by Conor wrapping his arms around both of them for a group hug.

The family swirling the dark and smoky garden looked like an ill-choreographed Viennese waltz. Charlie's hug with Irenie was short and sweet. Agata's belly had pressed into her so wholly that it frightened Charlie somewhat. Ollie and Jack were functional and polite, Jack even going to offer a handshake before Irenie hit him and snapped, 'She's not the Queen, Jack!' Dimitri was warm and effervescent, Soulla was seemingly grateful to Charlie, even though Charlie must have been more grateful to her. Alexander gave Charlie a hug so hearty he almost picked her up. He was definitely the drunkest.

'*Kalo podariko!*' declared Dimitri, indicating it was time for the *good footing*, to return to the house, Agata and her unborn baby leading the way.

Agata was followed by Theo, who nudged Elias out of the way in a fight ahead of Uncle Ollie to be the first of them in.

'Boys!' Irenie hissed, from further back in the line.

Ollie ushered his mother-in-law, Soulla, to make her *kalo podariko* ahead of him, and Dimitri followed her, his hands on his wife's shoulders.

Ollie slotted in ahead of Jack and Irenie, closely followed by

Alexander and Conor holding hands, stopping to give each other a little kiss on the threshold.

'Happy New Year, *husband*,' Charlie heard Conor say quietly through their kiss, their first as a married couple.

Pete was last, looking back into the orchard to check for embers.

'What do I do again?' asked Charlie from in front of him, a little light-headed as she stopped just short of the stone step to the laundry room.

'Go in with your right foot first, have a little pause, and wish for whatever you want for the year ahead, if you can.'

Charlie carefully pressed her right shoe onto the flagstone step and turned back to Pete, to check he was still there. He almost walked into her, their noses bumping, as she froze on the step and saw the moonlight catch his face.

She didn't say anything as they paused, and then kissed. Gently and thoughtfully at first, gradually becoming more fervent as they took in the taste of aniseed on each other's tongue, protected in the dark by the lights going on in the kitchen. As the commotion ensued of tables being cleared and kids being sent to wipe smeared make-up off their faces and brush their teeth, Charlie and Pete kissed feverishly under the light of the smoky star-filled sky.

19

NEW YEAR'S DAY

Charlie awoke to a new year with a furry tongue, a fuzzy head and a sense of utter embarrassment. She looked across the expanse of her Anne of Green Gables bed: the crumpled sheets and the empty space. The pretty quilt Soulla proudly said her mother had stitched was half fallen into ruffles on the wooden floor, flowers on the quilt merging into the pastel shades of the rug. Anne of Green Gables wouldn't have felt so slovenly.

The coldness Charlie felt on her shoulders and the thump in her head were eased a little by a glimmer of sunshine slicing through the thin curtains; a crack in the sash window let in determined birdsong and the distant sound of trickling water. She rubbed her eyes and felt a desperate pull to be outside, feeling that cold, invigorating sun on her closed eyelids; seeing it thaw the frost that enveloped the trees, fields and woods to the back of the Makris house.

She could hear young voices sounding smaller as they headed away as if they were bubbling on the brook. The boys, she assumed, off on a ramble with the most willing or the most subservient adult. Her money was on Jack.

Charlie looked at her phone. She'd had a message exchange with Saphie before she had fallen asleep: Saphie had sent a photo of her wearing the Les Néréides gold hoops Charlie had left her on the turntable; Charlie had sent drunken declarations of love to Saphie, Mabel and Prash, and Saphie told Charlie that she and Prash had decided to make a go of it.

I'm so happy for you <3

Charlie had texted.

Although can you hold fire until I get back? Prash can eat my cocoa nips if he likes, I won't even mind.

Charlie had to think about that for a second, to put herself into her drunken mind as she remembered that Saphie and Prash were officially back together, which was wonderful news, and that he could eat Charlie's *cacao nibs* if he wanted, damn autocorrect. She had bought them on a health kick last summer, fourteen pounds for a small tub from Holland & Barrett, then complained about the cost of them so much she forgot to eat them. Prash would appreciate them more.

Prash was the rare man who could spend all day building a complicated understairs cupboard system or a beautiful wardrobe, and put his feet up with a mug of oat-milk hot chocolate in the evening. He made the best wardrobes and he made the best hot chocolate. He was nurturing and patient and he had patiently waited for Saphie without any pressure or duress. For that, Charlie thought he was even more wonderful. Her health kick had only been for Harry's benefit, which she also felt wretched self-loathing about. For thinking she didn't feel good enough for a man who wasn't good enough for her.

She rubbed her eyes again and looked at a message from her parents, the ping that had woken her. It was a selfie sent from her mum's phone, of their windswept faces, Ruth's cheeks pink under her silver bob; Ray's moustache looking as if it might spin away in the wind. It reminded her of the tornado machine at the museum and gave her a lump in her throat.

New Year's Day stroll along the Ribble !! Hope you had a good rest of the night love . Here's to a bright new year . Love you c

The message had her mum's customary spaces before full stops and an accidental c instead of an x, which made her mother both infuriating and endearing.

PS X

PPS Dad's gaiters are 'very nice' he says ! Working well . mum c

I mean x

There was nothing from Harry, of course. He hadn't had a New Year epiphany. He was as much of an arsehole in this year as he was in the last. Charlie threw her phone on the bed, blinked hard and caught her reflection in the freestanding mirror by the bathroom door. She gasped when she saw her shoulders were bare, until she remembered she had forgotten to pack her PJs and they were still under the pillow of her bed at the Jane Street Guest House. She swiped the dark circles under her eyes and cursed herself for breaking the make-up artist's number-one rule: melt all of your eye make-up off with a vigorous yet soothing tonic before bed. She really did know better.

The tiny voices outside had disappeared into the woods and there didn't seem to be any other apparent noise in the house. Perhaps the Makris clan were late sleepers. Perhaps they had all already got up and gone out on a family hike. Charlie couldn't work out which it was, so she got out of bed, quickly showered, put on some strobe cream, culottes and a leopard-print sweater and headed downstairs.

The kitchen was empty but scattered with the detritus from the night before, which added to the late-sleeper evidence and which she decided to attack. As she washed plates, dried glasses and wiped the big table in the dining room, she processed what a mistake she had made.

She was glad no one had interrupted her cleaning or told her not to. She had wanted to pay her way somehow. When she was done, she contemplated the kitchen with a feeling of satisfaction and a sense of urgency. The slow moves on creaky floorboards upstairs made Charlie hurry to get out, so she wrapped herself up and headed out for a walk in the woods, so she could process her shame before facing it.

Charlie meandered along a light frost-strewn path on the edge of a brook; she passed fields fallow and fertile, reminding her of all the signs she had seen on the roads leading to the Makris house.

'Juicy apples here!'

'Best corn in Columbia county!'

'Welcome to Waddledown watermelon patch!'

The fecund fields were abundant with lettuce, squash, corn and snap peas. She'd seen signs for arugula and tart cherries, whatever they were, but didn't know if they were visible on her walk. She figured the watermelon farm must reap its yield in another season.

Charlie could hear a tractor – Elias' tractor perhaps – in a nearby field, the farmer not even taking New Year's Day off. But the hum of the engine in the distance, the sound of lark, American robin and chickadee, the trickle of the water, thickening into a fuller body that she might follow to a lake if she was lucky, were all steady distractions as she replayed a memorable New Year's Eve in her mind; as she thought about the dinner she needed to walk off. The secrets a family had let her into, and those she suspected they hadn't.

She thought about the fireworks, the tender kiss on the stone step, and how she and Pete couldn't stop entangling their hands secretively behind their backs once they were back inside, through 'Goodnight!' and 'Happy New Year!' wishes to the family, as they clicked closed the doors of their rooms. How Charlie and Pete paused at the top of the stairs, about to go their separate ways, when she pulled him into her room and pushed him against the door to close it behind him.

* * *

Their second kiss was more frenzied, even though they had more time. As Charlie pushed Pete up against the door and pressed her body into his, she could feel his bewilderment entangled with his longing.

'Charlie...' he murmured between kisses. Not quite a protest, not quite reverence. His lips were full and strong, his chest dark and soft as she unbuttoned his shirt and pushed it back off his shoulders so it almost clung to the door inside out.

'You're so lovely you're so lovely!' she repeated drunkenly as she smattered Pete with kisses, bit his lip, and removed her dress, stepping clumsily out of it until she could re-glue herself to his body, like Velcro, in her bra and wool tights.

Pete kissed Charlie's neck as he lifted her by the bottom and up around his waist, where she wrapped her legs around him in a lock. He swung her around, walking backwards to the bed where he sat and she straddled him, still in her tights, and he unfastened her bra as she pressed against him.

She caught a glimpse of them, spinning in the mirror, her breasts in his face.

'Uhh!' she gasped and froze, her lips stopping, her head pulling back. She jumped off Pete, off the bed; as if he had just given her a sharp electric shock.

'What?' Pete asked, alarmed.

'I–I—'

'Are you OK?' His eyes were wide and glassy.

Charlie put her hand to her mouth, as if she had just seen a hideous truth in the mirror.

'No!' she said.

Pete recoiled and looked for his shirt, still hugging the door from the hook it landed on.

'I'm sorry, I thought—'

'No, no, no, no, no!'

'What?'

'What am I doing? This is so wrong!' Charlie was wincing, her nose curled up as she started to cry, standing in just her knickers and tights. Feeling stupid as she saw herself in the mirror. She pulled her forearms against her chest to cover the nipples Pete had just been kissing as she clasped her hands to her ashen face. Gold eyeshadow moved around her lids like molten metal.

'Hey, I'm sorry.' Pete clasped his hands together in a prayer.

He really hadn't meant to make her cry.

Charlie looked as if she was going to be sick. Pete slowly stood and collected his shirt.

'I can't, I can't...'

Charlie started hyperventilating as she shook her head and slumped into the spot where Pete had been sitting on the bed, her arms still covering her chest.

'Hey, it's OK...' Pete wanted to comfort Charlie but didn't want to touch her body any more.

'I can't...'

'Hey, it's cool, don't!' He looked at her. 'Get some sleep, huh?'

Charlie shook her head ferociously.

Pete had never felt quite so repellent.

'It's really not anything you did...'

'Hey, it's OK, it's OK.' Pete was standing at the door putting his shirt back on, wanting to go to her but not daring to take a step closer.

Charlie cried as inky tears rolled down her face.

'I was meant to be with Harry and I feel sick and my heart hurts and—'

'I know.'

Pete picked up Granny Ekkeshis' quilt from the floor and gently placed it over Charlie's shoulders.

She kept her forearms pressed to her boobs and her fingertips pressed under her eyes.

Pete sat back next to her on the bed, all his warmth from the garden disappeared with the smoke from the fireworks, but he didn't want to leave the room with either of them feeling so grotesque.

She shook her head, aware that she had snapped at him as if he were the predator he certainly wasn't.

'I'm so sorry, it's not—'

'"It's not you it's me"?' Pete gently offered with a friendly nudge of his arm against the quilt.

'It's most definitely me.'

'I think we both know that it's entirely because it's me, and I'm *not* Harry...' Pete said as they both looked at the rug on the floor under their feet.

'I'm so, so sorry,' Charlie whispered.

'Hey...' Pete said, before coiling the copious quilt around Charlie until she looked like a caterpillar in a chrysalis. 'Don't worry about it. You get some sleep, huh?' He gave her two friendly and perfunctory taps on the shoulder before standing and fastening the remaining buttons on his shirt wonkily.

He opened the door and paused. She looked at him and shook her head.

'Happy New Year's,' Pete said with doleful eyes.

* * *

As Charlie inhaled the scents of pine trees and fields of collard greens she felt mortified that she had ruined what had been a brilliant evening and what was becoming a friendship she felt enormous gratitude for; embarrassed that Pete might tell his sisters, brother or friends. Worried about how she was going to get through the fancy cocktail party and the evening road trip back to Greenwich Village. As she got further from the house, the invigorating air lifted her – she could almost smell the clarity of the river water, trickling its soundtrack to her steps.

After a few kilometres Charlie saw a wooden lodge up in a clearing, like it ought to be decorated with sweets. As she approached she saw that the structure wasn't a creepy cottage but a modern escape, someone's bolthole. The wall between the lodge and the river was glass-panelled and she peered in to see a piano and a sofa covered in cowskin hide. An empty kitchen at one end was small and clean. Above a small dining table hung a light fitting made of wine glasses, which turned Charlie's stomach when she remembered how much she had drunk. The property looked compact, plush and deserted. And like it was none of her business, as she made a frame around her eyes and peered in.

She remembered how badly spying upstate had gone before and thought perhaps she ought to turn around before, perhaps, Harry and Isabelle Irving returned from a New Year's yomp.

'Morning, Charlie!' came a voice out of nowhere.

She turned around, startled. Conor was standing with his hands in his pockets and the sun in his eyes.

'God, you terrified me!'

'I'm sorry.' He gave a sheepish smile and pushed his jaw-length hair back under his hat. 'You're up with the larks too?'

'Needed to clear my head.'

Conor grinned.

'Yeah, it's a Makris hazard that. The ouzo-woozos I call it. Next-day shakes. It's why I stick to wine,' he said in a soft Galway lilt.

Charlie smiled. There was something of a tonic in Conor's handsome features that took the edge off her self-loathing.

'What are you doing up here?' she asked.

'Oh, I took a walk with Jack and the boys. He took them fishing over by Credence Creek, but I wanted to check out this place. It's for sale.'

Conor peered through the glass as Charlie had, but more confidently, as if he knew no one was home.

'It looks beautiful,' she said.

'Doesn't it?'

Charlie looked again and they stood like two children, pressing their noses against the window of a sweet shop. At second glance it looked even more idyllic.

'Who owns it?'

'I don't know – someone musical, it looks like. Beautiful, eh?

Right by the water.'

'It's an amazing spot. So peaceful. Near the in-laws...'

'We'd like a place near them out East. We thought about Hudson City for the vibe – it's a nice town, gay-friendly, like a mini Brooklyn upstate – but I like the remoteness here.'

Charlie looked at Conor's eyes in profile. Bright and sharp as he drank in the property.

'It's stunning,' Charlie said.

'It's small,' Conor lamented. 'I don't think we'd fit everyone round that table.'

'Well, there is that.'

'Alex doesn't see the point anyway. Says it's too close to his parents and we may as well stay there. But it would be nice to have our own place out here. It can get a bit chaotic when everyone is around. With all the entertaining.'

'Do they entertain a lot?'

'You thought the Irish like a party. These guys are next-level sociable.'

They laughed.

'Every weekend there's an eminent scientist friend visiting from Columbia, Syracuse or Massachusetts, or a cousin from Chicago, Australia or Greece. And there will be more and more grandkids coming, hopefully. I'm sure we'll need our own space.'

As Charlie pressed her hand to the glass, closed her eyes and listened to the sound of tufted titmouse and American tree sparrows against the trickle of water, she thought what a world away from Finchley this was, remote and peaceful. She imagined summer nights and fireflies, and wished this were a place she could escape to. That she might be welcome back.

'How does it work over here? Buying a house...'

'Oh, it's less complicated than the UK. But the complicated thing is getting Alex on board. He struggles to leave California.

The Greek sun-god in him is strong. Anyways...' Conor looked at his watch. 'Speaking of parties...' He nodded back towards the path. 'Wanna walk back with me or are you heading upstream?'

Charlie couldn't think of anyone better to talk to right now than Conor. She almost forgot how awfully the night had ended.

* * *

As they wound back through frozen fields, stopping to take in a flash of red from a northern cardinal, Conor told Charlie about his move to California. How he had done American Studies at Galway and taught at camps in the US every summer he could, before becoming a teacher at a fancy school in LA.

'My accent opened lots of doors here,' he said. 'I imagine yours has too.'

Charlie explained she wasn't supposed to be in America for long – she didn't even have a work visa; she was meant to be on an extended holiday visiting her boyfriend and what a disappointment that had turned out to be. Charlie was delighted to hear Conor use the word *eejit*, as if she didn't believe Irish people actually said it, and he said she was clearly better off without him. She told Conor about how Pete had been a bit of a hero, offering her Christmas and New Year plans when she was in turmoil.

'Not that you need rescuing, I'm sure,' Conor said. 'I've been on a night out in Blackpool and I know for a fact that you Lancashire lasses are the hardiest.'

They laughed.

'But Pete is a solid guy for sure. One of the best.'

'Oh, it's nothing like that...' Charlie dismissed, recoiling at last night. *Did Conor know?*

* * *

As they walked back Conor told Charlie all about life in Pasadena and LA. How wonderful their wedding was in Big Sur last summer. How it was nice to have something so positive after such turmoil in the family with Dimitri's illness. How they hadn't wanted anything too OTT as they didn't want to be insensitive.

'Insensitive?' Charlie asked, before stopping to get a stone out of her shoe.

'Here,' Conor said as he offered her an arm for balance. She grabbed onto it as the tiny stone flew out of her brogue.

'What happened to Dimitri?'

'Did Pete not say?'

It occurred to Charlie how, in the little time she had known Pete, and although they had talked a lot, she didn't know any of the important stuff about him. She knew what he did for a living and what music he loved, but she didn't really *know*. Had he been married? Might he even have kids? Had he almost lost his dad?

'He's come through treatment for bowel cancer...'

'Oh my God, poor guy.'

Conor wasn't sure if Charlie meant Dimitri or Pete.

'And he looks like such a strapping picture of health!'

'He's hot, isn't he?' Conor said behind his hand.

'Well, I didn't want to say...'

They sniggered like schoolgirls until Conor's face dropped.

'But it was touch and go at one point. Really hard times. Alex was terrified. Soulla was totally lost. We all were. And then, just when he was coming through it and it looked like he might make a recovery, the shit hit the fan with Pete.'

'What shit?'

'Uncle Conor! I caught a fish, I caught a fish!' Theo shouted as they rounded back onto the path that led to the side of the house, running in wellies that looked as though they were going to fall off him.

'Well done, buddy!' Conor fizzed. 'How big was it?'

Theo looked up at Conor and chuckled while he internally worked out how far he could push it.

'*This* big!' he said, making himself as wide as he could, before jumping up into Conor's arms as he swung him around and onto his back for the last stretch. Theo proceeded to talk Conor and Charlie through every moment in the river and how bad the maggots smelled.

By the time they got back to the house, cars and catering vans had already pulled up onto the driveway, and ornaments, food and flowers were being unloaded from the back of them by suppliers and staff. Apparently Soulla loved to cook the New Year's Eve dinner, but they always got caterers in for the New Year's Day party. She was directing people where to go while Dimitri took custody of crates of hired glassware.

'Oh, there you are!' Soulla said as she saw Conor, Theo and Charlie approach.

'Theo, your mother wants you in the bath, go back inside and get that river smell off you. Darling, Alexander was looking for you, something about who's wearing the Liberty tie in lieu of a bow... you see, Charlie, they're already fighting over who's going to wear it!'

Charlie looked at the comings and goings over Soulla's narrow shoulders, but Pete wasn't there. 'I'm not sure where Alexander went, but can you help me with the flower arch?'

'Sure,' Conor said obligingly.

'Anything I can help with?' Charlie asked, desperate to be useful; desperate to see Pete, even though her stomach was in knots.

'Actually, Charlie,' Soulla said, turning to her and looking at her over her glasses, 'there is.'

20

As Charlie followed Soulla up the stairs to the master bedroom, they walked across the Persian rug on the floor of the landing – a gift from an old colleague from Beirut – past Irenie and Jack's room, where a bath was running. Irenie was visible through the open door, deep in conversation with someone inside the room, maybe two people, but their conversation halted as soon as Irenie saw Charlie.

'Who is it?' she heard Agata whisper.

'Guys...' Pete said to his sisters in a beleaguered voice. Soulla seemed oblivious to it all and continued along the hallway, talking about something Charlie wasn't focusing on.

'Morning!' Charlie smiled cheerily at Irenie.

Irenie gave Charlie a mechanical smile as Charlie followed Soulla to her room, hearing Irenie and Jack's door gently click shut in her trail.

They all know.

'Ah, here we are!' Soulla said, walking into the large bedroom with thick carpet and windows to three sides of the house.

They must think I'm awful.

Soulla and Dimitri's room was grand but not showy. She imagined Pete as a little boy, standing at his mother's bedside, eyes wide and hair bouncy as if he'd had a nightmare but didn't want to disturb his parents, and her heart melted.

'I'm sorry I'm asking you to work on New Year's Day, but given we have you here...'

'Oh, it's not a problem at all!' Charlie said, looking around. 'In fact, it would be an honour. I'm just sorry I don't have that much kit. And I used up my reds and greens on Spiderman and Hulk!'

Soulla sat on the stool at her vanity table, the light of the back garden beaming in.

'Well, why would you, darling? You're on vacation. I have plenty of make-up anyway. All this stuff I barely use...' She opened a drawer of Clinique, Bobbi Brown and Laura Mercier. 'The girls always buy me palettes and pretty-looking things, or give me the freebies in sets they don't want. I don't often get round to using it!' Soulla said it as if she were too busy to try, although she clearly used the same well-worn favourites. 'I stick with the same look...' she confessed.

'We all do that,' Charlie confided as she rummaged at the packs and packaging, all of it familiar. 'That's great,' she said. 'Plenty to work with. And I wouldn't want to use anything you're not comfortable with anyway.' Soulla looked up at her and smiled.

'Thank you, darling.'

'Is that your outfit?'

Charlie nodded to a navy trouser suit that was hanging on the wardrobe door over a cream silk shirt.

'Yes.'

'Well, I know just what to do.'

* * *

As Charlie quietly did Soulla's make-up, Soulla reflected on forty years of marriage to Dimitri, and confided that it wasn't always a bed of roses. That you had to work at marriage and not run away. Especially when there were four children involved.

That was another thing Charlie loved about being a make-up artist. Not just the power to boost someone's confidence or reclaim it, but the confidences clients entrusted her with.

'But "In sickness and in health," they say...' she added, with a wry smile. Charlie nodded. She didn't want to ask about Dimitri's illness unless Soulla volunteered it, so she asked about what the wedding was like.

'Oh, it was wonderfully eighties!' Soulla said. 'At St Sophia's in Syracuse. We met in college there. We were juggling our PhDs with wedding planning, it was all very exciting. People came from all over the world. It was very special.'

Charlie's eyes lit up as she imagined, not just a wonderful Greek wedding, but an eighties one too.

'Obviously Princess Diana was my inspiration – everyone wanted a dress like Diana's at the time – but I'm not really the Diana type, am I?' She laughed, looking small and learned. 'Such a shame, what happened to Princess Diana...' Soulla added dreamily as she looked out of the window as Charlie blended her eyeshadow.

There was a gentle double knock on the open door, and Soulla beamed when she saw her son standing in the frame.

'Petros, darling, I hope you don't mind me borrowing Charlie?' she said mischievously. Charlie carefully leaned the heel of her palm on Soulla's cheek as she blended a midnight eyeliner across her upper lashline, and looked up so briefly she barely registered Pete's face. Concentrating on her craft could be convenient some-times. It was a tactic she usually employed when there was a diva celebrity or a stroppy stylist in the make-up room.

Always focus on the face in front of you.

'Hey,' Charlie said, still looking at his mother.

Pete gave an awkward smile that was so brief Charlie wouldn't have seen it even if she had been looking over.

I hate this.

'Hey...' he said quickly. 'Dad can't find the skeleton key to the bureau with the fancy bottle opener in it. Do you know where it is? The caterers only have one between them...'

Soulla tried to sit still. She didn't look accustomed to sitting still.

'Keep your lids closed, please,' Charlie said softly, wanting to look over at Pete and mouth 'What the fuck did we do?', except she didn't avert her gaze. Soulla spoke through closed eyes. She knew her way around her house with her eyes closed.

'It's in the cutlery drawer, next to the tray with the cocktail stirrers.'

'Great, thanks...' Pete said, before heading downstairs to retrieve it without another word.

Charlie kept blending Soulla's eyeliner and focused on the laughter lines around her eyes, and tried not to cry.

* * *

'Mom looks incredible,' Agata said as Charlie came down the stairs. She had deliberately taken her time to change and do her own make-up so she wasn't in the way or making Pete feel any more uncomfortable than he already had. The annual New Year's Day anniversary party was in full swing; this year made extra special with a floral arch over the doorway with a number forty at the top.

Charlie looked understatedly incredible. She wore a black jumpsuit with spaghetti straps under a gunmetal cardigan, black

heels, delicate layers of gold jewellery and dark grey eyes. It was
almost like being in the *Look Who's Dancing!* studio again, trying to
blend into the background in black, although she had wanted to
make the effort to look suitably celebratory.

'She looks so glamorous, thank you.'

'My total pleasure!' Charlie said as she squeezed Agata on the
arm. 'Navy eyes would look pretty on you too.'

Agata had warm brown eyes and what Charlie assumed was
dyed blonde hair, long, lustrous and reeking of pregnancy.

'Can we keep you?' Agata joked. 'Sort my tired new-mommy
look, God willing.'

'I charge too much,' Charlie joked, relieved that not everyone
had frozen her out.

A waiter walked past with a tray of drinks and Charlie took one
quickly, cursing herself that she'd taken champagne and not elder-
flower. Hair of the dog didn't seem like a good idea when she
hadn't even spoken to Pete yet.

'Want this?' She proffered it to Agata.

'Are you kidding me? So badly!'

She hadn't realised Charlie was joking anyway. Charlie decided
to take a few sips before accidentally on purpose losing it.

'Aggie!' an older woman with a stiff cloud of hair cooed as she
stepped into the house. 'Look at you!' she gushed as she kissed
Agata and placed her hands on her bump. Charlie felt a lurch in
her stomach and stepped back. 'How are you feeling? You look
spectacular!'

Charlie nodded to the older woman who had no interest in
anything other than Agata's bump and whispered, 'I'll leave you to
it,' as she slipped off to look for Pete. She walked through the
kitchen that didn't look like the family hearth it was yesterday –
more like a hotel kitchen – as staff milled around replenishing
trays with drinks and canapés. She saw a flash of a small boy dart

past on his way in from the garden. Elias in a little shirt and bow tie that already had leaves on it.

Dimitri rushed through, looking for a wine aerator a psychologist friend had given him as he wanted to give the impression he and Soulla used it often.

'Are you OK there, Charlie?' Dimitri asked. 'Do you have a drink?' Charlie raised her glass to reassure him.

'Yes, thanks.'

'Attagirl,' he said as he scratched his head, opened the drawer and said, 'Here it is!'

There must have been eighty or a hundred people milling around the Makris residence, but there was just one person Charlie wanted to find, so she weaved her way through the living room, past academics, relatives and the Hudson Valley illuminati, into the dining room where they'd had dinner last night and a woman was gushing to Alexander about how wonderful his wedding was. Alexander had looked up and seen Charlie, but hadn't made an effort to ingratiate her into the conversation, so she thought she'd try the garden, despite the chill.

She opened the door to the study, remembering the French doors they had exited last night, and was startled see Pete step backwards, flustered, as if he'd seen a ghost. He was pulling himself away from a small woman in a skintight white dress, her shoulders bare, and a curtain of shiny black hair swishing to her waist.

'Charlie!' he said, with forced happiness.

'There you are!' Charlie replied, her face trying to hold a smile. Pete was wearing a black tux, white shirt and a thick black bow tie, his shoulders broad yet slumped, his eyes sad and defeated. He looked more handsome than Charlie had realised. 'Are you OK?'

'Yeah, erm, this is Martha,' Pete said. The word *Martha* hung thick in the study air as if it had a million connotations, of which

Charlie knew none. Charlie looked blankly back at Pete, who rubbed the back of his head with a flat palm.

Unlike Pete, Martha didn't look flustered as she turned to Charlie with only a slight sliver of inconvenience in her smile.

'Martha, this is my friend Charlie.'

Martha pivoted slightly on an elegant ankle and Charlie could see the love-heart neckline of her white dress, barely containing her Betty Boop chest. Charlie wanted to congratulate Martha on her magnificent breasts, but it wasn't the sort of thing you could say to a stranger. Martha smiled fleetingly but didn't speak, and Charlie suddenly felt as if she should explain herself.

'I was just checking to see if you were in the garden, couldn't find you, that's all!'

As Charlie spoke she could feel Martha's eyes burn into her; her full and glossy lips parted into a curious smile as she slowly took in Charlie from the shoes up.

'Yeah, I was just—'

'And where did you come from?' Martha asked haughtily, one thick eyebrow raised, as if Charlie were a woodlouse who had just crawled out from under a stone.

'Martha!' Pete admonished.

'Well!' She tried to laugh off the caustic bite behind her white teeth. 'I know everyone here! I've not seen her before, that's all.'

Pete cleared his throat.

'Charlie's from London...'

Charlie didn't think that was what Martha meant, but she played along.

'Well, Lancashire, via London, but what's the difference?' Charlie joked. Her joke fell flat while Pete and Martha exchanged looks.

'Sweet,' Martha said, a disdainful smile making her pretty face seem not all that sweet.

Pete looked at Charlie apologetically and folded his arms as he perched back on his parents' desk. He felt the bumbling and uncomfortable need to fill the air, when Charlie just wanted to walk back out, or, better still, go through the French doors and into the garden for some air. Both options seemed a little dramatic.

'Martha is a...'

'Family friend,' they both said, sternly, at the same time.

Fucking hell! Charlie wanted to laugh at the awkwardness, but something in Pete's face, the coldness, pissed her off.

'Nice to meet you, Martha.' Charlie smiled.

'Yes,' Martha agreed, as if the pleasure really were all Charlie's. Her shoulders were feeling the chill, goosebumps forming on her arms.

'I'm just going to... go,' Charlie said as she backed out of the room. Pete looked as if he wanted to stop her, but equally as if he could not wait for her to go. 'Catch up later,' she said, and Pete looked lost for words.

Martha said nothing but smiled, giving Charlie's shoes one last cursory glance.

Charlie left hastily and circled around the party, trying to look both part of it and inconspicuous. She met a behavioural economist from Baltimore, a child psychologist from Ottawa and a psychiatrist from Stanford, although she wasn't sure where that was exactly but figured that, between them, the Makris family would have a solution to every disorder and disfunction within these walls. She met Dimitri's ninety-year-old mother, and Soulla insisted Charlie tell her about Chorley cakes, much to Charlie's embarrassment because the ancient woman couldn't understand her accent; and she crouched in a corner with Elias singing 'A sailor went to sea, sea, sea...' while teaching him how to clap their palms together to the rhythm. That killed a good ten minutes, until

Irenie came over with a look of adoration that dropped when her eyes met Charlie's.

Jeez, what is with everybody?

Charlie had a sudden and compelling urge to be on her own, on her bed in the Jane Street Guest House, even if she were crying. She looked at her watch, wondering what time exactly Pete planned to leave. She knew he had to be back in the city tonight to teach tomorrow.

'Again!' cheered Elias, who was just getting the hang of it.

'OK...' Charlie said, pressing her palms together, trying to remember if Elias was six, seven or eight, and what it meant if he was.

'A... sailor went to sea, sea, sea...'

Pete sidled up to watch the spectacular, which got faster and more out of control with every clap until Elias lost his rhythm in a tangle of hands and giggles.

'Ahhh, you got good!' Charlie said.

'Whoa, buddy!' Pete said proudly.

Charlie, self-conscious and sad, got up from her haunches and stood straight.

'Again!' Elias demanded. 'With Mummy this time!'

'Oh, I don't know...' Irenie said, unsure of herself, but Charlie reminded Elias of the rhythm, showed Irenie, and let them get on while they slowly gained pace.

'That's it!' Charlie said.

'You OK?' Pete asked quietly, almost guiltily, in Charlie's ear. 'Been a bit crazy today...' They both kept their gaze on Elias and Irenie before Charlie turned to Pete. She thought he looked beautiful in a tuxedo. He was stunned to see her looking so grown-up and glamorous. Both were a little lost for words.

'Yeah, yeah I'm great,' she answered hurriedly, feeling terribly in the way. 'Great party!'

'Yeah...' Pete said, looking around the room and beyond it, and Charlie saw an unease in his features she hadn't noticed before. He was awkward and shifty and suddenly Charlie thought Pete might not be the safest person in the room faced with natural disaster, and that unsettled her.

She wanted to ask him if he was OK, but in truth she had felt a little abandoned by him after what happened last night. She thought Pete of all people would have handled it better than her. Been more of a grown-up about it.

'What time did you want to—?' she was asking when Alexander chinked a glass with a fork and asked all the guests to congregate in the large entrance hall at the bottom of the stairs.

'Oh, this is us, siblings assemble. Hang on.'

Ollie paused the Chopin coming from the speakers in the dining room and Jack told his kids to quieten down as the golden winter sun beamed through the arched window above the front door, lighting the happy couple. Soulla and Dimitri dutifully stood a few stairs up, as instructed by Agata and Alexander, Soulla one step higher than her husband so they could link arms more comfortably.

Alexander gave a beautiful speech on behalf of his siblings, who were dotted around among the guests, to thank their parents for their love and for being such wonderful role models; to congratulate them on forty years of marriage they could only aspire to achieve – which led to a few uneasy looks between aunties and elders – and to tell them about their special gift from him, Agata, Irenie and Pete: a stargazing trip to Hawaii.

'A place of great seismic activity,' Pete whispered to Charlie, forgetting himself, reminding her of how much easier things had been at the museum. Everyone cheered and raised their glasses to forty years of love and marriage.

* * *

At 6 p.m., Dimitri and Soulla stood at the boot of Pete's car while he loaded his overnight bag into it and Soulla pressed her hand to her heart.

'Can't you stay the night?' Dimitri playfully pleaded, a palm on his son's shoulder, a proud glint in his eye.

'Don't be ludicrous, Dimitri,' scolded Soulla. 'He has classes!'

Pete nodded.

'Sorry, Papa,' he said, giving his dad a huge bear hug. Dimitri looked so adoringly at Pete that Charlie wanted to melt as she shuffled behind him, still in her black one-piece, which felt a bit flimsy in the freezing cold now, brightened by her big lilac coat.

Soulla told Charlie it was always fortuitous when New Year's Day fell on a Saturday. Better still, a Friday, because they had the entire weekend together after, but she would take any time with Pete over nothing. Charlie looked at him and could see why. Which only made her feel worse about how last night had ended.

'Thank you so much for your generous hospitality,' Charlie said, taking Soulla's outstretched hands. 'You have a home with warmth like no other.' Soulla squeezed Charlie's hands vigorously in each of hers.

'You're welcome!' she said, looking almost teary.

'Any friend of Pete's is a friend of ours,' said Dimitri with a wink, and Charlie tried not to blush.

'Next time we're in London we'll look you up,' Soulla said matter-of-factly now, pulling herself away from her emotions. 'Get together with Eleni. Go out for tea and Chorley cakes.'

Charlie laughed internally at the way Soulla said Chorley in an American accent.

'That would be wonderful,' Charlie said, knowing it would never happen.

Pete threw his tux jacket over the back seat and opened the passenger door for Charlie.

'Good to go?' he asked.

'Yes,' she said.

They got in and Pete lowered the windows and ordered his parents to return to the party while he demisted the windscreen of his battered Saab. As Pete wiped the windows with a hangdog-looking cloth, Charlie watched his parents walk back into the house, his dad waving an arm behind his back as he hurried to get back to their guests.

'Right, let's get you back to Jane Street,' Pete said as he looked at the sky and noticed snow starting to fall. From the way the jagged flakes fell on the bonnet it looked as if it might settle on the road. Pete stopped wiping, cranked up the heaters and looked at his phone, tilting the screen away from Charlie. 'Traffic looks OK, so unless the snow gets worse, I should be able to drop you in... two and a half, three hours?'

Pete sounded as if he couldn't wait to get rid of her.

'Great, thanks.'

He slipped his phone into the pocket of the driver's door.

'You want to use your Spotify?' Pete suggested, inviting Charlie to plug her phone into his threadbare cable. Did he not entrust her with his any more? There was definitely a more busi-nesslike tone in his voice and she could imagine Pete the lecturer, impassioned about magma hotspots and fault lines, telling a coasting student that they should have done better in a test.

'OK,' Charlie said quietly as she kicked off her heels, put her stockinged feet against the heaters, plugged in her phone and tried to pick something suitable. She thought of the most Pete-like album in her recently played list – one she loved to put on back in the flat in Finchley for comfort. She stopped at *Pearl*, by Janis

Joplin. And Pete gave a nod of approval as 'Move Over' kicked off the album.

They sat in silence for a few minutes as Charlie looked out of the window into the blackness of the passing trees, turning white liked shocked ghosts. She couldn't see the jolly signs regaling the road with their crop yields. The Hudson Valley suddenly seemed barren.

Janis' raw confidence gave Charlie the nudge to address the elephant in the car and she cleared her throat.

'It could be a really awks drive back if we don't clear the air.'

'"Awks"?' Pete smiled, tickled by an expression he'd never heard. Relieved that Charlie had brought it up.

'Look, we're good,' he said, more dismissively than he meant to.

'You seem angry with me.'

'I'm not angry! Not with you anyway.' He laughed. 'We're good.'

But it was clear they weren't, that there was a new distance between them, as Pete drummed his fingers on the steering wheel and peered through the windscreen.

'I'm sorry I led you on.' Charlie winced, the darkness giving her the confidence to push it, the way you could on a car journey when you were side by side without eye contact. 'I made a total dick of myself.'

'No! You didn't. Man, you don't have to worry about that even a smidgen. I mean, I kissed a girl and I liked it...'

Charlie smiled, relieved Pete was making a joke of it, further grateful of the dark as she thought about his juicy lips and the hardness in his trousers.

'But this...'

Under the streetlights of the busier road they were joining, she could see Pete's arm moving wildly as he pointed his finger between the two of them as if to say, *this isn't happening.* 'We're buddies. Mates. "Chums", as you say.'

'For the record, I *never* say chums.'

Pete was relieved to hear Charlie's humour again, he had missed it today, and he rubbed his palm over his forehead and up into his hair.

'I just didn't want you to think I was being opportunistic. Bringing you up to the woods to do that. I really wasn't.'

'I didn't think that!' Charlie was horrified he would think she would think that. 'I'm just so embarrassed what I did, then bringing the H word up.'

'First rule of being a Makris: always blame the ouzo. Ouzo and the heightened emotions, the mush among my parents. We've had some dramatic New Years. Really. We're cool,' Pete assured her.

'OK, good,' Charlie said, although still she felt that they were at an impasse.

* * *

Charlie looked out of the window and listened to the music, to try to focus on another woman's heartache, until the car's headlights startled a white-tailed deer with skittish eyes at the side of the road. She gasped, urging it not to leap.

'It's OK...' Pete said, to let her know he was aware of it. The deer didn't leap and Charlie exhaled a steady sigh of relief. Then took a deep breath.

'So why did your siblings close rank?'

'What's that?'

'Alexander was definitely colder today when I saw him. Irenie was whispering when I got back from my walk, she was pretty funny.' Charlie didn't say that she knew Pete and Agata were in there too, having some kind of emergency meeting.

'Irenie is always pretty funny.'

'Did they see us... you know...?' Charlie couldn't bring herself to say it.

Pete laughed.

'Oh, no! It wasn't anything to do with you!' he said, turning up the volume on 'Cry Baby'.

Charlie felt both relieved and insignificant as Pete let out a raspy wail to mirror Janis Joplin's, notably more relaxed than he was at the start of their journey.

'Now, this is a tune. But the original. Man, it's off the scale. Garnet Mimms, 1963.'

'I thought this *was* the original.'

'No!' Pete said in quiet outrage. 'Garnet Mimms and the Enchanters. One of the most criminally unappreciated soul singers ever from one of the most epic years in soul. What a song.'

They sat for a few seconds listening in exquisite awe as the song built to a crescendo before they both bellowed, 'Cry bay-beee!' in unison at the windscreen, smiles trying not to escape the corners of their mouths as they gave it their all. 'Cry cry bay-beee!' they yelled as the raw Gibson guitar echoed and the guttural voice of Janis Joplin, full of torment, pulled at their heartstrings.

'Janis did bring an edge to it that kicked ass,' Pete conceded. 'Maybe that's something only a woman has the power to do.'

Charlie looked at Pete driving in profile and felt the mood in the car lift, the way only singing could lift a car journey, because Pete's reassurances hadn't been enough. Something about him was holding back and Charlie knew it from her furtive glance. From the palpable relief he felt that they had moved on.

'It's one of my favourite records in my collection,' she said.

'You have a record player?' Pete said, giving her a suspicious sidelong look.

'A vintage Linn Sondek.'

'Nice! Why didn't you say?'

'Well, I'm no Mary. I like it though. Walnut finish. My cat likes to sleep on the turntable lid.'

'Sacrilegious!'

'I know, I don't even know why she does, it must be so cold and hard, the plastic.'

'She's guarding it. Mabel, guardian of the Linn Sondek.' Pete made her sound like a superhero and Charlie smiled. She missed Mabel and couldn't wait to see her beautiful regal face.

'I don't have even 10 per cent of the vinyl you do. Harry wasn't one for clutter—'

'Clutter?' Pete snapped.

'He preferred his music in digital format. And for there to be no visible sign of it.'

'Oh, man! But the warm analogue sound of a Linn Sondek...' Pete said dreamily.

'I only really own the albums I truly love. But *Pearl* is one of my most cherished.'

'It's a good one.'

'And *True Blue* by Madonna.'

Pete wasn't sure if Charlie was joking, but he loved the turn the journey had taken as the snow continued to fall.

'The amazing thing about these songs and this era – the thing I love most – is at first listen, they sound like love songs. You think they're going to be sweet and cute. But a few bars in and you realise they're just so... dark.'

Charlie looked at Pete in the shadows in puzzlement.

'How do you mean?' she asked.

'Baby Washington's song "I Can't Wait Until I See My Baby"... even though I've heard it a million times that first line still floors me.'

'Why?'

'Because you think it's a sugar and spice love song and this woman is just so happy to be reunited with the love of her fucking life... she can't wait to see him.'

'Right...'

'So she can look him in the eye when she dumps him. Like she wants to kill him! It's amazing.'

Charlie half smiled but didn't say anything. She knew the feeling. But Pete's passion for a musical era decades before he was born was a good tonic. She didn't want to keep mentioning Harry.

'That line catches me out even though I know it's coming.' Pete shrugged as they hit the Taconic State Parkway. 'Even Elvis. He released "(You're The) Devil In Disguise" in sixty-three, and that starts sweet.'

They listened to 'A Woman Left Lonely' followed by 'Half Moon' in silence as Charlie watched the moon draw them back to the city, a city she realised already felt like home since she had been away from it.

'So why *do* you like the dark songs best?' Charlie finally got the courage to ask Pete. If he was thirty-six and single with a penchant for heartbreak soul, he had obviously loved and lost. 'Or is this like your optimism for the geological end of the world? You thrive on darkness!'

'Hahaha, I don't know about that...' Pete said, and pondered for a minute, as if he was deciding whether to tell Charlie something.

Fuck it.

'Like my sisters.'

'What's that?'

Charlie didn't know why Pete was bringing his sisters into his music.

'They did sorta close rank earlier.'

I knew it!

'Alexander too.'

Charlie kept her mouth shut and urged Pete to say more, her

eyes wide and encouraging, although he couldn't see it as he drove in the dark. But he could feel it.

'They were just working on their strategy.'

'Their strategy? For me?'

Charlie was dreading what Pete was about to say. He had told them about their kiss, she knew it, and they hated her for sponging off the good nature of Pete and his family, then using him, reeling him in and pushing him away.

'For Martha.'

'Martha in the study?'

'Yeah...' Pete groaned.

Charlie tried not to think about her pert boobs and disingenuous smile. She hadn't liked Martha.

'Martha is... Martha was my fiancée.'

'Shit!'

Charlie liked her even less.

Pete rubbed his chin in the dark as the headlights of the cars passing in the opposite direction fluttered a zoetrope of sadness across his face.

'How long ago?'

'Almost two years. This spring, in fact. She left me at the altar.'

'She what?'

There really was no other way to tell people, so Pete did tend to keep it to a blunt and factual minimum. A need-to-know basis. He felt Charlie deserved to know, especially if she thought his family were being hostile towards her.

'You can't really get a bigger platform for all your anxiety nightmares to actually come true than at the altar of a Greek Orthodox Church wedding on the Upper East Side.'

Charlie felt sick. At Martha's smug, fake face; at how Pete had been nursing this, all while she was going on about Harry. At how sweetly his family had closed ranks to protect him. At how she might have hurt him too last night by making out that kissing him made her feel sick. Except he said himself he wasn't into her, it was the ouzo.

'How did she do it? *Why?*' Charlie couldn't imagine it. She had seen Pete in a tux and knew how dashing and lovely he was. How could anyone do that to his sweet face? Dammit, now she thought of it, Martha in her white dress facing him in the study, they looked as if it could have been their wedding, but for the tension.

Pete let out a big sigh as he leaned on the wheel, eyes tired after an emotionally draining day.

'I knew she was nervous, but I thought it was all the wedding build-up. The family craziness. All the pressure for everything to be just... so. She's a bit of a perfectionist.'

Charlie guessed as much from her contoured cheekbones and injected lips. Martha seemed to display a white privileged notion of perfection anyway.

'And she didn't tell you until the day? Didn't give you any clue?'

'Nope. She didn't.' Pete sighed. 'I rocked up at the Holy Trinity, nervous, excited, ready to declare to the world that this amazing woman was the woman I wanted to spend the rest of my life with. Have kids with. In front of family who had flown in from all over the fuckin' world... and she just didn't show.'

'I'm so fucking sorry, Pete.'

'Hey, don't be! It happened for a reason. "For the best", you could say. Tonnes of people said it to me at the time. "Better to know now than on your honeymoon!" they said, as if that made anything better.'

'How long were you left standing there?'

Charlie wanted to cry for him. For his sisters. For Soulla and Dimitri. For Alexander and Conor, no doubt planning their wedding in Big Sur at the time. No wonder they had scaled it down. She'd thought it was because Dimitri had been ill, but

Charlie remembered what Conor had said on their walk about the shit with Pete.

'Well, Martha was always gonna be late. Her timing was atrocious. Maybe that's why I'm so punctual, I dunno... So my groomsmen – Alexander, Mike, Isaac, a couple more buddies from college – we had a little laugh about it. Mike brought a hipflask of his nana's rum ready for the eventuality. Until we realised we might need a bigger flask.'

'Oh, Pete.'

'She liked everything to be perfect, so I imagined her getting her hair redone or having her dress retied or something. And then I started to worry something had happened on the way to the church, maybe an accident. People were getting really bored and tired and hungry. Man, you can't keep that many hungry Greek people waiting on a feast.'

Charlie's stomach churned and she realised she was hungry. She'd been so on edge she hadn't eaten enough of the canapés.

'And then, after one hour and forty-five excruciating minutes, her poor sister, Lydia, walked down the aisle on her own, her coat over her dress, so I knew something was wrong – I knew anyway – and she whispered to me that Martha wasn't coming.'

'Oh, Pete. How crushing. I'm so sorry.'

'Ah, it's OK.'

'No, it isn't!' Charlie sounded angrier than she should; more invested in his family than was perhaps healthy. She checked herself. 'Had you been together long? Not that it makes a difference... heartache is heartache.'

'Since our mid-twenties – but we'd known each other since forever, through our families upstate. I was doing my master's when we reconnected in Manhattan. She worked in corporate travel, so we had a fun ten years before I proposed. I thought we were ready.'

'Ten years!'

The lights of Manhattan glimmered ahead as silent tears fell down Charlie's cheeks. She felt so wretched for Pete. So guilty that she had been going on about bloody Harry not showing up, not knowing that it had happened to Pete in the worst way imaginable. She could barely speak.

'It was pretty fucking humiliating. I spent the next few days apologising to people who had put money and good faith into our wedding; leaving messages apologising to her; hoping to change her mind. Maybe I'd come on strong with the whole marriage thing and she wanted to keep travelling, but I genuinely felt she'd been as keen as I was. She'd talked about wanting kids and a family since, well since before I started talking about it. She'd say what cute kids we'd have and talk about little girl names.'

'Oh, man...' Charlie realised as she said it that she was using one of Pete's sayings. 'Did she not even tell you herself? Just a message via her sister?'

'She didn't answer my calls and shut off. Lydia said she needed space, she was conflicted.'

'How rotten.'

'Well, what I didn't realise was that she was getting space on our honeymoon. Holed up with some douchebag from work. In the hotels we were meant to be staying in. In Costa Rica.'

'What is wrong with people?' Charlie shouted, raising her hands to the roof of the car in desperation. Their accumulated anger almost making them laugh.

Pete raised his eyebrows and nodded slowly in agreement as he exited onto the NY-100 towards the city.

'How did you find *that* out?'

'Martha had booked the honeymoon through her work for the discounts, but I had booked us a bunch of fun stuff to do. White-water rafting. Zip-lining. That kinda thing.'

Charlie thought of Pete on a zip wire and her heart broke a little.

'I was trying to cancel some of the activities, so we didn't lose all our deposits. I only found out when I called a zip-wire operator we'd booked in Costa Rica, to cancel a cloud forest tour. The guy wouldn't let me – said we had already taken it because the weather forecast looked better. Told me we'd brought it forward a couple of days. I thought they were scamming me and said it was impossible, we hadn't gone to Costa Rica. He proudly said they'd taken the balance and the cost of the photo package off the credit card. Wouldn't give me a refund. I called bullshit on it and said I would take action.' Pete shook his head in the dark. 'They sent me the digital photo package to prove their services had been used. It was Martha all right. Harnessed up in a helmet next to some guy with a thumbs up and a cheesy grin. She didn't look very conflicted.'

'Jesus Christ, Pete, I'm livid for you.' Charlie shook her head. 'Who was the fucker? I'll kill him!'

Pete laughed at the defiance and slight twang of humour back in Charlie's outraged voice.

'A guy called Troy.'

'Urgh, Troy!' Charlie spat. 'He even sounds like a creep.'

'Right!' Pete said. 'They worked together. They had already been on lots of trips. She claims they only hooked up in the days after she jilted me, but I called 100 per cent bullshit on that.'

'Clearly.'

'They had a quiet wedding at City Hall six months later. She didn't come to our New Year's Day party last year. She wasn't welcome. I can't believe she came today really. It was the first time I've seen her since the night before our wedding.'

'Which is why your brother and sisters needed a strategy.'

Charlie felt embarrassed she'd thought it had anything to do with her.

'What did she say to you in the study?'

'She said she was sorry. She didn't mean to hurt me. She had fallen out of love with me and I had become more like a brother.'

'Ouch.'

'She finally admitted she'd fallen in love with Troy before we were meant to get married. Which I knew, of course. She suggested it made it easier for me, that they had ended up getting married.'

'What did you say?'

'It hadn't. I'll always carry the sadness and the humiliation I felt that day.'

'And, fucking hell, she was wearing a white dress today!'

'That's Martha for you.'

'Was Troy at the party?'

'God no. Martha's mom and dad were. But no, not Troy Boy. I imagine that was of his doing though. She has no shame.'

'That's what you meant – when you suggested on the way up here, it might be easier not to have to see Harry.'

'I guess. I'll never get satisfactory answers from Martha. You probably won't ever from Harry. Seeing her definitely didn't help today.'

Charlie thought about Harry. What she would give to see him, *still*.

'I'm so sorry, Pete.'

'Nah, that's OK. I'm just beat.'

Charlie was disappointed her time with Pete was coming to an end. She wanted to suggest they get dinner and carry on talking. Pete hadn't opened up about much to her until now and it felt warm and wonderful, despite the sad story.

'Do you still love her?'

Charlie shocked herself – up until an hour ago she hadn't even asked Pete if he had a girlfriend – but the dark of the car, the knowledge that their journey was about to end, gave her a freedom to be more candid.

'Nah. I loved the idea of her, the dream. What could have been. But she ruined that by ripping my heart out. So... going back to your earlier question – about the music?' He looked across at her as they slowed down in traffic. 'I did like this music before. The tragic, hateful stuff. I just *feel* it more now.'

Charlie took a deep breath. She felt it too.

They slowly drove through the Bronx, into Washington Heights and Harlem.

'You feel it on the streets here. All those artists I love, they're from here.' He hammered his finger on the dashboard behind the steering wheel. 'The Chiffons, The Exciters, The Ronettes... They came out of The Bronx, Queens, Spanish Harlem. How could I not love them?'

I love them now, Charlie thought.

They turned onto the Henry Hudson Parkway and down the west side of Manhattan. Charlie felt an urgency. After so long pining for her bed in the Jane Street Guest House, she suddenly didn't want to get there. She wanted to talk all night.

'How have you been, for the past two years?' she asked him.

Pete scratched his temple as if it would make the memory of Martha not turning up in church disappear along with her.

'I had to remember: it was my response that mattered.'

'Damn response. It's shit being an adult.'

'Even worse a heartbroken one. You can't eat, you can't sleep, you feel sick. I know how you feel about Harry, I really do.'

'I know.' Charlie smiled gratefully as they stopped at a traffic light. 'I bet you responded better too. All that crisis prep.'

Pete let out a casual laugh. 'Ahhhh, not nearly as fucking well as you're doing, I promise.'

'I don't believe it.' Charlie paused for a beat. 'What did you do?'

'I got really fucking angry.'

'Angry? You don't seem the type.'

'Well, she rocked my world and ripped it apart. Catastrophic. And then I forgot the whole *emotion* part of being pragmatic. I had the facts – Martha didn't want to marry me, she wanted to be with Troy – but I didn't factor in my emotional response. I could have been cooler.'

They sat at a light on 11th Avenue, waiting to turn onto W 24th Street as Pete reflected.

'Agata made me lots of stews. My mom kept bringing baklava. Mike and Erin, Mary... they were fucking awesome.'

'They clearly love you.'

Pete turned right onto the cobbles of Jane Street, all closed up for New Year's Night, and put the car into neutral.

'Here you go. New Year, New Us.' He kept the engine running to signal he wouldn't be coming in. 'The Transatlantic Jilted Hearts Club.'

Charlie laughed. Then stopped.

'Thank you,' she said. 'For everything. Look, I'm sorry about last night.'

'Forgotten it already!'

'I'm sorry about all week really. I made it all about me and I didn't even realise you were going through the mill too.'

'Hey, don't be sorry. I've had a great time with you. And I discovered the Chorley cake!'

'I'm really grateful, you know. You saved my New York experience. Saved New York and saved New Year.'

Charlie's emphatic hug took Pete by surprise. She sniffed in the scent of his loose white collar but pulled back so she didn't put make-up on it or confuse things again.

'Happy New Year, Petros Makris.'

'Happy New Year, Charlie... hang on, what's your name?'

'Brown. Charlie Brown.'

'Good grief!' Pete smiled, sorry he hadn't asked sooner, wondering why.

Charlie had heard it all before and gave a knowing smile.

'Thank you,' she said as she got out of the car.

* * *

It was only when Charlie had climbed the stairs and opened her door. Only when she had dumped her bag on the bed, kicked off her heels, peeled off her jumpsuit, and removed her strings of delicate gold necklaces. Only when she'd had a shower and washed off her make-up. Only when she lay on her bed in her Anthropologie PJs and texted her parents, then Saphie as they slept, to say she'd actually had the coolest New Year she'd had in a long time. Only when she got into bed and flicked on CNN that she realised she didn't have Pete's number. It was long since lost, on the cover of *People* magazine that she'd left on the train at Grand Central Terminal on Christmas Eve.

21

JANUARY

'Right, I have a weird proposition for you...'

Charlie was sitting in the window of a coffee shop she hadn't yet tried (and she'd thought she had tried them all) overlooking the Bleecker Street playpark, nursing a latte. She had been people-watching and daydreaming, trying to remember if she could find her way back to Pete's apartment, the frontage of which she had only seen in the small hours through hazy beer goggles, and which looked like so many buildings in so many of the streets she had paced in Greenwich Village, when 'Ruby' flashed up as her phone rang,

Charlie had already been to another coffee shop this morning, the one where she had bumped into Pete last Saturday, to pick up a mango, blueberry and granola yogurt pot. And to see if Pete happened to be there, which she knew was a long shot since he was going back to work today, wherever Columbia was. But she had decided to sit down in this one, with its vantage point and window to the neighbourhood.

Charlie's agent Ruby, with her clipped tones and confidence, had snapped Charlie out of her daydream when she called unexpectedly and excitedly from London, and Charlie sat up in her chair by the window. She had chosen this seat in case Erin or Mike were taking Téa to the park and she could get Pete's number from them. Which also felt like a long shot. And a little stalkerish. Outside, New York was going back to work and school. People were purposeful, people were on their phones. Kids had backpacks on. An off-duty theatre actor was taking her boy to school. A silver-haired man was clearing up the poo deposit of his bichon frise on the outer perimeter of the park.

'Are you sitting down?' Ruby asked.

'For once, I am!' Charlie laughed, although she felt a little nervous and thrown by Ruby's call and the excitement in her voice.

'OK, look, I know you're in New York having an amazing time and it's unlikely and all that, but production has been brought forward on a big new commercial show, and they've asked for you.'

Ruby was in her mid-twenties and her ridiculous confidence was matched by her ridiculous contacts book that was full to bursting and would get even fuller every time she drank at Mahiki, Bluebird or All Star Lanes. Ruby was the sort of agent who relished asking the questions most polite people didn't like to ask and managed to get away with it due to her charm. But Charlie admired her confidence. She wished she were so together in her twenties, or even now. It made her think of Jazz, who was only twenty-two. She missed Jazz. She'd had a text from her last night, chastising her for not updating her social media, and she hadn't been able to reply. Jazz was another person she hadn't wanted to let down.

Ruby had started at the talent agency doing work experience when she was sixteen, and last year, when Charlie's agent, Sue, retired, Ruby took over Sue's list of stylists, make-up artists, and nail technicians, most of whom were not surprised by Ruby's mete-oric rise either.

'This sounds ominous. "Weird" is ominous...'

'It's prime time, a new sort of talent show with a twist. Celeb judges do that "press the button" thing while other celebs appear on stage in disguise.'

'Oh, cool, like total transformations to anonymise them?'

Charlie liked big transformations.

'Exactly.'

'Prosthetics, wigs, paint?'

Hold your horses.

Charlie wondered why she was even asking questions as she pictured Peter Crouch in her make-up artist's chair, her trying to disguise him as a Smurf. She rubbed her tired eyes and looked out of the large window. A little boy in the playpark was wearing a Smurf backpack. That must be why she'd thought it.

'Erm... not quite,' said Ruby.

'What's the format?'

'It's pre-recorded, scheduled for spring, and yes, transformations. But they'll be wearing enormous costume heads.'

'What?' Charlie exhaled, shaking hers.

'Costume heads, made of papier-mâché or fibreglass or something. To conceal their true identity.'

'I'm not a model maker!' Charlie said, thinking this gig sounded better suited to her dad.

'No, you'd be doing the make-up for *under* the costumes.'

The boy with the Smurf backpack fell over and grazed his palm. His mother scooped him up and hurried him along.

'I'd be doing celebrity make-up – only for the celebrities to have their faces covered?' Charlie had never heard of such a concept. Weird was right.

Ruby spoke with a calming assurance.

'It's all about the reveal. Who's who. They come out, perform anonymously, and then the judges try to guess who they are.

Celebs don't want to take their mask off bare-faced. They still need to look TV Awesome underneath the head.'

'TV Awesome' was an expression Ruby often used. Charlie knew that TV Awesome was different from Red Carpet Awesome and High Fashion Awesome – which was different from Wedding Awesome, when Ruby occasionally booked Charlie to do a celebrity wedding.

'It sounds terrible. And I am in New York.'

'I know, but the money is *insane*. And they specifically asked for you based on your portfolio, so they're throwing money at you, and I think we could push for another couple of hundred on the day rate.'

Charlie went quiet as her eye followed a man in a baseball cap walking past with his head down, sheltering his handsome features from the cold. For a second she thought he was Mike.

'Why the hell haven't you posted any NY pics on Instagram, by the way? I mean, I know it's not about work, but it's great for your brand.'

Charlie groaned internally. First Jazz, now Ruby.

'Yeah, bit of a long story there...' Charlie said cryptically. 'Is Leyla doing wardrobe?'

If Leyla was doing wardrobe for this terrible-sounding show, it would make it more tempting.

'Bree Blackwood is wardrobe,' Ruby said flatly.

'Oh.'

Bree Blackwood was a celebrity stylist whose public #bekind postings and feminist manifesto didn't fit her most unsisterly of work ethics and she had trodden over and fallen out with every single woman she'd worked with. She was known in the industry as a one-series wonder because she was so unbearable no one rebooked her. During her one series on *Look Who's Dancing!* she repeatedly tried to sell Leyla, who she was assisting, down the river to take credit for her ideas that worked, and shit-stir about the ones that didn't. Bree also tried to stage an affair with a happily married contestant to get exposure: tipping the papers off that the male newsreader was sleeping with 'someone in Wardrobe'. She even ensured she was papped with the newsreader when she got a coffee with him during rehearsals and was over the moon when it made the *Daily Mirror*. Every time she reshared the story, she claimed to be a victim of the press while not shooting it down as a fake story she had planted.

'Anyone but Bree!'

'I know, I know, I told them you were in New York "working" anyway. And I am sorry to disturb. But I had to run it by you. It's double the *LWD* day rate. And that's before I negotiate.'

'What?'

'I do think we could get you more if I say you're in New York and super busy, but that you might consider coming back for it. If you *would* consider coming back for it, of course.'

'The money is crazy.'

'That's commercial television for you. Eight to ten week shoot. But... and there's a big but...'

'What?'

'It starts next week.'

'Next week?'

Then the penny dropped.

This was Charlie's out.

A job too tempting to turn down. She could go home with her head held high. Hug Mabel. Reclaim the flat and get rid of any trace of Harry from it. See her parents. Catch up with Jazz. Go straight back to work. Enjoy the distractions. Earn better money than she ever had. She could explain Harry away later. What was she doing in New York anyway, spying on kids in a playpark in order to get the phone number of the one friend she had in the city? And she didn't really know him.

'I'm in,' Charlie said.

'Amazing!' Ruby almost sang with glee. Even she was shocked by how convincing she'd been.

'Fuck it. Harry's dumped me, Ruby. I've cried more tears in the last ten days than I have in my entire life.' She thought back to being curled up on the bathroom floor. Perhaps that wasn't strictly true. 'Even Bree Blackwood can't bring me down.'

Charlie shuddered when she remembered Bree and her hypocrisy. Bree, an advocate for the love-yourself body-confidence cultural ideology on her social media channels, did one season presenting a style makeover show where women were torn apart for what they looked like and given a rating out of ten by strangers in the street. Usually contrived to be a low rating, which made for great TV when feelings were hurt, and made it easier for Bree to raise the bar when she gave the women a restyle. Charlie was glad she had turned that show down, and it was cancelled after one season, but she wasn't sure if she had the energy.

'Oh, my gosh, you poor thing,' Ruby tried. The sympathy and naivety in her voice couldn't quite outweigh the desire to get her 15 per cent. 'Are you OK?' she asked blithely.

'No, but I will be. I love this place. But not the way I feel right now. And I can't live in a bloody hotel for the next two and a half months out of stubbornness.'

'Wait, what? He broke up with you and made you move into a hotel?' Ruby's outrage sounded real.

'Something like that.'

'Urgh. I'm so sorry, Charlie.' She sounded almost compassionate. 'So is that a yes? If so I'll ping contracts and NDAs over to you in a flash.'

'It's a yes.'

* * *

Charlie hung up, shook her head and smiled. It was time to go home. Time to stop drinking coffee and mourning. Time to stop looking out of the window and plot and deliberate. Instead she looked at her phone and scoured flights, changing hers from late March to a flight leaving JFK tomorrow night. Then she wrapped herself up again, left the coffee shop, and walked the neighbourhood.

While she walked she called Saphie to tell her she had been offered a job and would be home on Saturday morning. Saphie was so pleased, not just because she was ready to move back in with Prash, but because she knew New York wasn't right for Charlie right now. She said she would come pick her up from Heathrow.

Then Charlie called her parents, who were also ecstatic – they were so desperate to give their daughter a hug.

'Oh, love!' her dad said. 'It'll be grand to see you.'

Then she sent Jazz a text, checking in to see how she was and to say New York had turned out badly, which was why she had neglected her social media, and she would be back in London sooner than planned.

Fancy a drag brunch when I'm back?

Harry still a cunt then?

Charlie was so shocked by Jazz's reply she almost laughed as she remembered Jazz the day she met her. Hostile, guard up, blunt. She tapped out a reply.

Seemingly so.

Charlie was so busy pacing the streets of Greenwich Village, thinking about her London life and how quickly she needed to turn around her packing – and how the hell she was going to find Pete and tell him – she didn't even recognise or notice his apartment building as she walked past it on Leroy Street.

22

Charlie looked up at the skyscraper in front of her and felt very small indeed. Small and dizzy and as if she were about to go into battle, as she looked up at the splice of sky she could see over Beaver Street, its clouds reflected in the building's façade. She stood on the pavement and dialled the switchboard that connected her to the receptionist on the thirty-third floor.

This was it. Closure. She had put on her make-up armour of a feline flick, dewy skin and peachy lips and was ready. Harry was back at his desk and this was her day of reckoning.

'Good afternoon, Goldcrest International, how may I help you?'

'Can you put me through to Isabelle Irving, please?'

'Who's speaking?'

'Tell her Harry Taylor's girlfriend is in the ground-floor lobby.'

* * *

Less than five minutes later the pinched blonde woman from Bedford Hills was coming down an escalator; stance awkward, arms hanging by her sides; twinset and pearls replaced by a navy blazer and cream silk shirt, matching navy skirt and a thick velvet Alice band. Somehow, Isabelle Irving knew that the woman in the lilac coat and red beret was the woman who had called her down, and she walked straight towards her.

'Hi there,' she said, manners perfect under a cold smile. 'Shall we grab a coffee?' Her bright eyes and thin lips scrutinised Charlie's determined expression.

'Sure.'

'There's a great little coffee shop over the road...' Isabelle said, chatty and businesslike as if it were she who had called the meeting. Isabelle led them out, coatless, hugging her ribs and clutching her phone in the icy wind that rolled through the Financial District, and they crossed over to a coffee shop.

'What would you like?' Isabelle asked politely, as if Charlie were an intern she was interviewing.

'Hot chocolate, please,' Charlie replied, irked by how the power had shifted; annoyed that she had chosen a jolly and childlike drink and not something that made her look more kickass like a double espresso.

Isabelle got the drinks while Charlie found a table by the window – she did always love a window seat – and took off her coat and beret.

She looked at her phone while she waited. Looking busy. Working out what to say. Determined to get this right. She felt sick.

Isabelle walked over clutching two paper cups and her phone. She still looked as if she was leading this meeting, *for fuck's sake.*

'So. You're the person who kept texting before Christmas. Harassing Harry at all hours.'

Charlie raised the cup as if to say thanks, although she wanted to tip it over Isabelle's head. Stain her awful velvet Alice band.

'Ahhh, he played the "crazy ex" card, did he? How utterly uninspired.'

An angry flash across Isabelle's benign mouth revealed a chink in her wall, a glimpse of self-doubt flickering across her prim lips.

Charlie slid her phone along the thin wooden rail table to Isabelle, open to her WhatsApp conversation with Harry. His face unmistakeable in a circle.

'OK, so I did go a bit batshit when he didn't show up to the airport like he said he would and left me stranded at JFK overnight. And I was rather miffed when I saw your cosy family Christmas scene up in Bedford Hills...'

Isabelle looked up from the phone and scowled.

'You followed us?'

Charlie nodded proudly. She was determined to stay proud.

'But scroll down. Go back a few days and weeks... read them all. Take your time. The *love you*s, the requests for magazines, Liberty ties and treats. Sending me selfies from his walks across the Brooklyn Bridge. Unmistakeably Harry Taylor.'

Isabelle's penetrating eyes scrutinised the screen; reading back the shopping requests, the question asking for a screenshot of his last P60. Messages saying:

Good luck with the show, love you.

And:

Give Mabel a goodnight kiss from me!

'Who's Mabel?' Isabelle asked with a furrowed brow.

'Our cat.'

My cat.

Isabelle soaked it all in. The diction and the date stamps. The tone and the normality of it all. She clocked the sweater and avia-tors he was wearing that sunny November day on the Brooklyn Bridge. And her face flushed red and dappled.

She gasped.

It was easier than Charlie had expected.

'Asshole, I was with him when he sent you that!'

Charlie shook her head gently.

'It was New York City Marathon day. We were cheering on my brother-in-law.'

Charlie wondered which pink-faced, potato-headed guy from the restaurant Isabelle meant, but it didn't matter. 'I *bought* him that sweater!'

'It's a nice colour on him. But he was sending me that in November, telling me and the cat that he loved us. In December he was giving me lists of things to bring out for Christmas. I had no reason to believe we weren't going to be together for my three-month stay here. I am not the crazy ex. Do not believe that narrative.'

Isabelle stared to the street outside, as if she was trying to find a strategy in that very efficient-looking head of hers.

'When *did* you break up?'

'We haven't broken up. Not that he's deigned to tell me anyway, but, you know, I got the message,' Charlie said, taking her phone back from where Isabelle had pushed it away. She had clearly seen enough.

'I feel sick.'

'I've felt pretty sick too.'

Isabelle looked to Charlie, almost in remorse, but she couldn't quite process it.

'I just... I just...'

'When did you and Harry get together?'

'Labor Day weekend, up in The Hamptons. I had a party...'

Isabelle threw a guilty look at Charlie. 'I had no idea. He said he had broken up with his ex by mutual agreement, before he had left London.'

Charlie shook her head.

'We were very much together. The plan was that I come out and join him.'

'Well, those relentless calls before Christmas...'

'When I was waiting for him at the airport...'

Isabelle put both elbows on the bar table and her head in her splayed palms, almost massaging her temples as she tried to make sense of it all.

'And did you go to London? With Harry? A friend spotted him on the Fulham Road late November.'

'Yes, we went to London. His mom was sick.'

'Clarissa?'

'She had a stroke, he was super worried, I wanted to be there for him and he said that would be nice.'

'Is she OK?'

Why would Harry tell Isabelle this, take her with him, and not me?

'She's improving.' Isabelle looked cautious, suddenly uncomfortable with being the guardian of such personal family information. Wondering who the hell Charlie was and what right did she have to know anyway.

She had every right, she realised, from the concern on her face. 'She was in hospital for a few days, she lost a lot of the usage of one side, her motor skills... but she's having physio and getting lots of help.'

'You went to Hawksworth? You met the family?'

'I mean, it wasn't the jolliest of occasions – but yeah, we checked in on his mom – she was still in hospital at the time. Stayed a couple nights at Hawksworth Hall. Then he showed me around London. Took me to The Ritz and a soccer game. I always wanted to go to The Ritz.'

'Jesus. What was he texting me, while you were in the UK?' Charlie pushed her phone back to Isabelle and she scrolled back to late November and the dates that corresponded with their trip.

'It was Thanksgiving...' she mumbled sheepishly as she found the right messages, and pushed the phone back to Charlie.

Good luck with the show tonight Babycakes. Wish I could get iPlayer here. Am walking the High Line. Can't wait to bring you here when you come. Love you Hx

Isabelle paused to work out what she and Harry had done that Saturday night.

'He took me to Le Gavroche,' she said under a crinkled brow. Her features almost childlike now.

'Well, you can have him,' Charlie assured her. 'I don't want him back and he clearly doesn't want me anyway. But can you pass on a message to him, given he's ghosted me?'

Isabelle's light blue eyes filled up as she listened intently.

'Can you let him know that you... that *he*... he broke my fucking heart. And that's not very nice.'

Charlie bit her lip to hold back her tears.

'I had no idea, I promise.' Isabelle's palms were shaking as she held them up. 'When you were sending those messages just before Christmas, making all those calls... I had no idea you were in New York. He told me you had heard about us and gone crazy. You wouldn't accept it. That you always drank too much at Christmas...'

'What?'

'I nearly answered a call myself and asked you to move on.' Isabelle looked terrible again. 'So... so he got a new phone.'

'Ah, the coward's way. That's Harry. Always saving face. Like not turning up at the airport rather than having to admit he's shagging you.'

Charlie thought about another time Harry fled rather than face a consequence.

Isabelle shook her head.

'He has form, you know,' Charlie spat. But none of this was Isabelle's fault, however annoying her prim and privileged face was.

'I'm so sorry. Do you have friends here?'

'I found my feet,' Charlie said proudly, and decided not to tell Isabelle that she was about to fly home; it would be nice to make Harry sweat for a bit. Think she was still hanging around.

'Do you want to...?' Isabelle nodded her head sharply and gestured up to the skyscraper opposite.

'No, I have to get going. I'll leave it with you, and however you want to deal with it. But good luck. I'm sorry I've caused you distress too.'

* * *

A rather large part of Charlie hoped Isabelle wouldn't forgive Harry. That he wouldn't live happily ever after with her and her billions while Charlie returned to London to start over, in the flat she had bought on her own the last time she and Harry had split up, doing make-up for celebrities who were going to then ruin it under a fibreglass head.

'I'm going to cut one of his fucking balls off,' Isabelle declared, with a dark venom that jarred with her face, as she grabbed her purse and phone and sloped off her stool.

Charlie nodded and watched Isabelle open the door.

She was doing that American thing of not saying goodbye, of

ending an encounter by leaving it hanging, which felt unsatisfactory to Charlie after all the hanging around she'd been doing.

'Wait!' she called.

Isabelle stopped in the doorway and turned around.

'Cut his other ball off for me,' Charlie said flatly, hoping that she would never see or hear of Isabelle Irving ever again. Isabelle gave a limp wave and hurried back to the Goldcrest building.

Charlie sighed and looked down at her phone. There was just one more goodbye to say.

23

Charlie emerged from the subway to see the afternoon light hitting beautiful red and white brick buildings with elegant arched windows that seemed to shimmer under the winter sunshine. The buildings dominated the entire block, and those either side of it, of the majestic avenue in front of her. Charlie couldn't believe this was Broadway, the same artery as all the razzamatazz of Times Square to the south. It looked so scholarly.

Charlie had jumped on the red line and travelled all the way up from Wall Street station to 116 Street/Columbia University, hoping that she could find Pete after her failed attempts in the Village. As she stepped off the train onto the white-tiled platform, she realised the rage in her palms that she felt when she boarded had dissipated with the rhythm and the hum, and she had a new-found sense of calm.

She looked at the grandeur of the building on the street in front of her and wanted to say, 'Wow,' to Pete next to her, to hit him on the arm, but she muttered it internally and crossed the street, vowing to find him.

She darted through a grand open gateway and weaved among

students, professors and alumni, pretending she wasn't an inter-loper. Most of the people she passed were wrapped in long coats and scarves for the bright and biting day. Scholars who looked as if they had come from all corners of the world, but that they all belonged. Charlie slunk a little into her scarf and stopped in front of a majestic bronze statue of Alma Mater, serene and learned, reclined with her arms open and a wreath crown on her head. The ten columns of the Low Library behind her strong shoulders framed her beautifully.

The campus was so grand, so huge, Charlie had no clue how to find one lovely heart in the heart of this institution, but she hoped to narrow it down with each question she asked.

A girl with a shiny black bob walked past in a black quilted coat.

'Oh, excuse me, please, can you point me in the direction of the Earth and Environmental Sciences faculty, please?' Charlie asked.

'Schermerhorn,' she replied.

'Erm, maybe?'

'That way!' The student smiled before carrying on in a hurry and Charlie followed her finger *that way*. The campus seemed enormous tucked away in this corner of Manhattan, but Charlie asked enough people until she was standing outside Schermer-horn Hall, which looked like a mansion, as did all the departments in this world-within-a-world.

'Excuse me, please,' she asked an older male student walking hurriedly along a corridor. 'Do you know where I can find Pete Makris?'

'Dr Makris?'

'Yes, Dr Makris, that's right.'

The man looked guilty.

'He's in II.I.B – I just left the lecture. I gotta get to my grandma's birthday.'

'I won't tell if you don't tell him I'm late!' Charlie winked, and the man laughed and hurried off down the corridor. After a few dead ends, Charlie managed to find theatre II.I.B where Dr Pete Makris was finishing a lecture on something called igneous processes, according to the large screen behind him. Pete looked deceptively small in the big hall as he stood at a wooden lectern with notes and a mug on it, in a chambray shirt and his beat-up burgundy tweed jacket. He wore thick black rectangular glasses that Charlie hadn't seen before, and they made his brown eyes look like the biggest part of him. Charlie slid in quietly and sat down at the back.

'Right, so, quick-fire round because you're all still suffering your New Year's hangovers and we gotta wake up and go home for dinner...'

There was a small murmur from the students.

'How much of Earth's crust is made up of igneous rock?'

Hands shot up and Pete pointed to a redhead in the front row.

'Yes!' he said.

'Ninety-five per cent,' she answered, coolly.

'Correct. What is the ocean floor made out of?'

A guy in a checked shirt with oily blond hair was chosen from the middle of the auditorium.

'Black basalt rock.'

'Which is...?' Pete enthused, back at the guy.

'*Extrusive* igneous rock.'

'Correct!' he called, looking as if he was running on empty himself. January 3rd must be a tough crowd but he was making them sit up and wake up.

'How big can a batholith be?'

Fewer hands went up.

'Take a guess...' he encouraged as a trickle of arms raised

unsurely. 'Erm, you!' he said, accepting an unsure hand on the left of the auditorium.

'Fifty kilometres across?' the student said in a mousy voice.

'Higher!' Pete shouted, and Charlie smiled. She thought Pete looked pretty sexy in his element, like a geology game-show host.

'Seventy-five?'

'Higher!' he shot back, looking around for another hand. 'You!' he said to the man sitting next to Charlie, and did a double take when he noticed her. He smiled. 'You!' he said again. Charlie smiled back.

'Actually, batholiths in the earth's crust can be up to 97 km across,' the student said knowingly. Charlie looked at the man next to her in astonishment.

'Bingo!'

Pete punched both his fists in the air.

'Final, easy-peasy one to send you on your way: what is the lightest igneous rock on this beautiful planet of ours?' He clasped his hands together.

'Pumice!' half the class almost groaned.

'Get outta here!' Pete joked as the students packed their laptops, phones and pens into their bags and sloped out, some tentatively going down the steps to talk to him. Pete engaged with his pupils and answered their questions, keeping half an eye on Charlie, anxious about keeping her waiting. She moved further down the auditorium, took a seat, and gave him a reassuring look to say *don't worry, take your time,* as if she didn't have a flight to catch.

From here he looked like a giant. Or his dad. Tall and commanding as he straightened his glasses frame and answered questions. Charlie liked watching Pete doing what he did well. She loved watching people deep in their passion. She thought it about Leyla when she was pondering her rails of clothes and costumes and putting something amazing together in her mind; she thought it about Saphie, sleeves rolled up sketching her next neon master-piece. She saw it in the pride with which Prash would stroke a piece of furniture he had made. Seeing people engrossed and excelling in their passions gave Charlie extra energy.

As she sat patiently, she marvelled at how strange it was that a city as fast-paced as New York had enabled her to slow down. Take stock. She was surprised to realise she felt so energised when she had been so drained.

'Bye, Dr Makris,' came a grateful voice, snapping Charlie out of her thoughts.

'I'm so sorry!' Pete said, rubbing his hands together.

'Not at all. That was cool. You made me wish *I* was studying basilisks!'

'Batholiths,' Pete corrected.

'Sorry, Harry Potter nerd,' Charlie apologised.

'Aren't we all?' Pete said kindly, before putting one hand in his pocket and raising the other to scratch his stubble. It made Charlie realise how clean-shaven he had been in his tux on New Year's Day. He was wearing the same shabby tweed jacket he'd been wearing in the Uber; which seemed more fitting now he was in his natural habitat.

'Erm, can I just confirm those are actual corduroy elbow patches on your jacket?' Charlie asked, stroking his arm in awe.

'Rumbled!' He laughed, and dropped his arm. 'You came for a tour?' he asked hopefully. He really did look sweet in his glasses.

'Actually, I came to say goodbye...'

Pete looked winded.

'Oh, now you got me saying wow...'

'I had a job offer come in yesterday.' Charlie suddenly felt nervous. 'Starting next week, so I've accepted it.'

'Cool, what is it?' Pete asked, taking off his glasses and looking at the lenses for smears, before tucking them in his inside jacket pocket.

'It's my ticket home,' Charlie answered cryptically. She didn't really want to have to explain celebs in papier-mâché heads.

'Do you have time for a coffee? You wouldn't believe it, but the canteen here even beats the coffee in the Village.'

Charlie looked at her watch.

'I'm afraid I don't. I came up here because I didn't have your number, and I wanted to see you before I went.'

'You didn't take it down?'

'I left Harry and Meghan on the train.'

'So you came all the way up here?'

Charlie looked around the empty lecture hall.

'Another cool place I would never have known about, were it not for you! This is just incredible...'

Pete looked proud, then his face dropped again.

'You have to go *now* now?'

Charlie nodded.

'My flight is at 10 p.m.'

'Well, at least let me walk you to the subway. I'd come back to the Village, take you to JFK, but I have a faculty meeting.'

'Don't even worry,' Charlie said, before saying a walk to the metro would be nice. Pete gathered his bag and picked up his empty coffee cup from the lectern. It had 'Geology rocks!' written in a comic sans font.

'Such a dork,' she said affectionately.

* * *

'At least take my number again,' Pete said as they stopped on Broadway, next to the green rails trimming the subway station entrance. The sun had set and cars were flying down towards

Manhattan's beating heart. Charlie's heart raced as she looked up at Pete in front of her. Suddenly lost for words. This abrupt ending to the most unexpected of weeks only just hit her. So she opened her phone and typed his name into a new contact before handing it over to him. "'Dr Petros Makris...'" He laughed to himself. 'Now you *are* taking the piss.' He typed in his digits and handed the phone back.

'I'll send you a text...' Charlie said briskly. She really did have to get going.

'You better had. We made a deal. I want my return tour of London.'

'Already working on it.'

They stood facing each other in a little huddle. Not sure of what to do next, except say goodbye.

'See you for Crustal Deformation?' Pete said hopefully.

'What?'

'My paper.'

'Ah, right. It sounds like some intense eye make-up remover.'

They laughed almost nervously as their smiles dropped and Charlie studied Pete's face. She really would have enjoyed their kiss on New Year's Eve were it not for the fact she'd wished he were Harry, which reminded her.

'Oh! I went to stick it to Harry.'

Pete's shoulders slumped a little.

'Oh, well done,' he said quietly. 'Did you kick him in the bollocks? Mike taught me what bollocks were...'

'Even better, I got his girlfriend to. I just couldn't cope with seeing him. I think you might be right about it being better not to.'

Charlie's eyes welled up as she glanced over at the headlights of the cars on Broadway and Pete wanted to put his hand out to her, but he kept them tucked under his jacket to keep warm. He really should have grabbed his winter coat hanging in his office, it was freezing.

'Ahhh, well done.'

'Thanks, Pete, you're a hero.'

He looked down at his battered brown shoes. 'Well, I think you're a hero.' He looked back up at her. Was that a blush Charlie spied, on the most easy-going face she had ever seen?

She raised on her tiptoes and planted a kiss, half on the corner of his mouth, half on his cheek.

'Thank you,' Charlie whispered.

'No, thank you,' he said, calmly now, pulling back a little. 'My family will never forget the New Year's when I brought a British girl home. My mother will forever ask Aunty Eleni if she has bumped into you yet...'

Pete pulled Charlie into his chest, warmed by the glow of her in his arms, and she slid her hands up his back and squeezed him tight.

'Text me!' he called cheerily as they released each other.

'Will do,' Charlie said as she flew down the stairs to the subway, feeling as if she might cry.

PART III

'So the reason I chose this outfit is because there's a real dichotomy...'

Bree Blackwood spruced her shaggy blonde seventies fringe performatively as she stood next to a mannequin. The mannequin was dressed in a costume prototype for one of the celebrities on *Triple-A Talent*, and Bree did some flouncy hand gestures in front of it as she spoke.

Here we go, Charlie thought. *Dichotomy*.

Bree used the word in every production meeting and most of her Instagram posts, never *quite* in the right context, but it impressed the juniors and the runners because, like Bree, they didn't realise either. When she said the word she elongated it, in her deep voice, as if that made her cleverer than the person she was talking to. *Die-cot-omeeee* always set the Bree Blackwood bull-shit alarm off in Charlie's head when she was bored in a meeting. She used gaslighting in the wrong context too, and had been known to gaslight her assistants.

'The *dichotomy* is that the folds of this piece look like labia, so the judges and the viewers are less likely to think a toxic male celebrity like John Tong will be inside...'

John Tong was a former tough-nut footballer turned Shakespearean actor, who probably wouldn't relish being labelled a toxic male when he had single-handedly raised his three daughters, although he probably wouldn't *love* being dressed as a vagina either.

Bree continued as she wafted bejewelled fingers in front of the costume. 'It throws the wolves off the scent, adds some intrigue and is a nice little "fuck-you" to the patriarchy.'

Is it though? Charlie thought. She wished Jazz were here. She knew how to say *fuck you* to the patriarchy without treading all over the sisterhood.

'Bree, can I just interrupt you?' Lauren, the executive producer, said. Lauren always asked permission to interrupt, even though she was going to do it anyway. You couldn't really argue with the boss.

'I don't get your point. Are you trying to make a statement or throw the judges off the scent?'

Bree scowled at Lauren and made a mental note to post an Instagram Story about women burning women in the workplace.

'Erm, well...'

'Don't get me wrong, I love the dress, I'm just wondering what the point is. You say it's a dichotomy but is that not a juxtaposition? Or a contradiction? Or even a red herring?' Lauren was also obviously irked by the dichotomy of Bree saying one thing when she meant another too.

'Can I just add...'? said Tabitha, a runner, gingerly raising her hand as if she were scared to speak.

'Yes, Tabs,' said Lauren.

Tabitha had a frizzy shock of red ringlets and freckles as if Orphan Annie had grown into a very tall, thin woman.

'I went to uni with John Tong's middle daughter, Maisie.' Tabitha looked around nervously. 'And he's totally not toxic. He's a really great guy.'

No one said anything and to compensate Charlie smiled encouragingly while Bree shot Tabitha a disappointed look.

'So what are we going to call him?' Lauren asked. 'John Tong is Sunflower on the production notes, right?' She looked to Dan, the series editor, who looked at his clipboard and nodded.

'Orchid,' Bree said in her deep and plummy voice.

'OK, fine,' Lauren said indifferently, 'but can we make sure it's not too labial? This is prime-time family entertainment, after all. Make it look a bit more orchidy up top.'

Bree scowled again, hurt under her shaggy fringe, as if her creativity was being curtailed even though the costume had been approved. Charlie wanted to point out that this was a joke costume used to conceal the appearance of a B-list celebrity, not the Met Gala, but she scribbled 'Text Jazz' on the page of her notebook and drew a cloud shape around the reminder. Today was her birthday.

'Charlie, talk to me,' Lauren said, and everyone turned to her.

'Yeah, so I'm going with classic traditional make-up really. Studio perfection for the male celebrities; cocktail-party glam for the women; whatever best suits their faces...'

What else the fuck can I do?

Charlie had only been working on *Triple-A Talent* for a few weeks but was already bored to tears planning 'TV Awesome' looks that didn't tap into anything she loved about doing make-up. Turning a mousy woman into Elphaba in *Wicked* had been exciting. Metamorphosising a middle-aged man into a zombie for TV was cool. Covering her own acne-ravaged teenage skin enough for her to feel able to step outside the cottage and go to school was empowering. Helping Jasmine learn to love her skin, and the hundreds of women she had helped get their confidence back after cancer, was rewarding. Nothing about this gig moved her. But she took a deep breath and put on her happy face.

'Great, any problems with schedule?'

'No, I have a team in place. The biggest issue will be retouching after the big reveal, so it's not too obvious we've done a refresh and so we don't kill the excitement in the studio.'

'Well, yes, we can't interrupt the reveal for hair and make-up,' Lauren confirmed.

'Of course.'

'But I'm sure we can cut, refresh, and make everything good before the reprise song.'

'Yes, my team will be super quick,' Charlie assured Lauren. 'I've got Eva Delgado and Phoebe Jones booked in.'

'Right, tech, talk to me. How's it going with the augmented reality...?'

Charlie looked at her phone, as everyone else seemingly did when it wasn't their turn to report in. She pulled it in close as she opened Instagram and looked at Pete's profile. The most recent picture was the same most recent picture from when she'd first found him online, when she was on the train out to JFK to get her flight home. Pete at Griffith Observatory, looking relaxed and happy at golden hour with the sprawl of LA behind him. It was posted in early September, she assumed when he was out in California for Alexander and Conor's wedding.

He clearly didn't post often. You couldn't scroll through his grid for days as you could with Charlie's, although she hadn't posted much of late, and most of her posts were about the work she had done. Make-up-artist shoots for partner brands; *Look Who's Dancing!* celebrity looks; prosthetics for a Marvel film she'd worked on at Shepperton.

Pete's grid told Charlie everything and nothing at the same time. He was well travelled but not showy: there were pictures of the Greek Islands, Paris, Toronto, Mexico, Bali and London. And there were hints of Martha in some of them. A swathe of long black hair just in shot on a pristine beach; the reflection of her at the top of the CN tower in Toronto. A small figure in a white puffa coat inside the Louvre. Pete had clearly deleted any photos where Martha was obviously *there*, or maybe he'd never posted them in the first place. From his Instagram grid you could tell Dr Pete Makris was a Columbia professor who wasn't vain, liked old soul record covers, food, travel and rocks. That was the measure she had got of him in New York. She looked up around her at mouths moving in slow motion with no sound, and was hit by how much more she wanted to know about Pete. How she hoped she would see him again in March. She stopped again at the Louvre picture and remembered Martha's face.

Charlie had pondered Pete's confession in the car, and felt terrible that he hadn't shared that with her for the week they were hanging out. In Charlie's outrage for him, she had even tried to look Martha up, but could only find something under Martha and Troy for a wedding-gift registry at Bergdorf Goodman that had since closed.

Charlie hadn't had much contact with Pete since she returned to London. She had sent him a WhatsApp picture of a vintage Jackie Shane album she had picked up on Berwick Street and Pete had replied:

Now you're talking!

She had sent a couple of emails to his Columbia address after she'd thanked him for taking her under his wing and he had said she was welcome. One was an article about a tourist who had died climbing Pacaya volcano in Guatemala and Pete had replied, assuring her that some volcanoes were safer than others. She'd sent another about a pregnant woman who ate pumice. He'd replied with a laughing emoji and signed that one off:

See you in March!

Charlie took that as Pete not being fussed about corresponding in the interim, so she'd decided to leave him alone.

Harry's social media was almost as disappointing, but for a different, crushing reason. Isabelle Irving hadn't chopped his balls off. Only last night they were at the opera seeing *Porgy and Bess*.

Arseholes.

Harry hated the theatre. He'd always declined to go with Charlie to see Jazz in an undergraduate play; if Charlie ever saw a West End show she'd go with Phil, Aidan or Saphie. Remembering this made her realise she didn't miss Harry as much as she thought she would. She was so busy yet so bored with *Triple-A Talent*, she hadn't had time to mourn him. Her flat felt sufficiently like her flat again. She and Mabel against the world since Saphie had moved back in with Prash and was spending more time on her upcoming exhibition. As Charlie had spent January and February nights in the flat with Mabel, she'd realised it had never felt like Harry's home anyway. That was why she hadn't got round to getting the last few traces of him out: a bag of clothes he hadn't taken to America, a few photos on the messy fridge, held together by magnets and stickers. She wondered if Harry would be thinking of her today. If he would remember.

* * *

'Right, so tomorrow we've got Flamingo, Jellyfish, Cactus, Hummingbird and Cheeseburger all good to go. Any issues?'

Lauren was wrapping up. Tomorrow they were going into the

studio to shoot the first ninety-minute episode – which would be broadcast late next month. Not John Tong's turn yet, but a selection of socialites, soap stars and washed-up pop stars, who surely had an unfair advantage when it came to a singing competition.

Charlie grabbed her smoothie and notebook and stood up.

Bree was pulling all her costumes into big blue Ikea bags as everyone filed out of the meeting room. Tabitha offered to help.

'I want a word with you...' Bree said, pointing at her.

Charlie looked up from her notebook to see Tabitha's nervous freckled face.

'Me?' Tabitha asked.

'Yes, you.'

Bree shot Tabitha a petulant frown from under her fringe.

'Why are you trying to undermine *me* in a team meeting?'

She gave a *don't you know who I am?* scowl and pouted.

'Oh, I didn't mean to...' Tabitha said, her earnest Orphan Annie face looking desperate and apologetic. 'It's just Maisie's dad... John... He's a really lovely guy. A really great dad.'

Bree looked as if to say 'And...?'

'He was lovely to me when I was transitioning at uni. I know for sure he's not a toxic male. He handled it much better than my own dad. I even stayed with them for a bit. He said I could stay as long as I liked.'

Tabitha had been Toby until partway through her first term at Manchester, and her new best friend Maisie Tong, Maisie's sisters and famous dad John had been understanding and embraced her when her own parents hadn't.

Bree scowled.

'OK, but women need to support women in the workplace, *Tabitha*...' Bree loaded her name with a sour unkindness so Tabitha's freckled face flushed a shade of aghast. Bree spoke as if she were giving a lesson in womanhood Tabitha didn't yet know, and so she had therefore failed.

Charlie choked on the last sip of smoothie – which was the best thing about this gig, the juice bar next door to the production studio and the lovely Portuguese couple who ran it.

'Sorry,' Charlie said, clearing her throat and almost laughing, except the look on Tabitha's stricken face wasn't funny. 'Did you really just say that?'

Bree glowered at Charlie but then saw it. That Charlie *knew* she had bullied women in the workplace, that Bree's pity posts might not wash with someone who had worked with her before. She backed down.

'I just think us women need to stick together,' Bree almost mumbled.

'Yes, we do,' Charlie concurred with a smile.

'Not make it about John Tong,' Bree added through gritted teeth.

'Well, he's the one on the show, and Tabitha was just saying he isn't toxic. Which is great, given we all have to work with him!' Charlie smiled and Bree gave her best effort to return it.

Dickhead, Charlie thought as she walked out of the meeting room and went back to her hot desk. *I hate this job.*

As Charlie gathered her coat and scarf she wondered what she would be doing tonight if she were in New York, not London. But first up, Charlie had a birthday to celebrate. Hers. Thirty-three and heartbroken was not a good place to be.

'Oh, God, it's awful! Awful, awful, I hate it!'

'Still bad?' Saphie groaned.

'What's up with it?' Aidan asked sweetly.

Charlie, Saphie and their friends Phil and Aidan were sitting around a circular wooden table admiring a plate of chutneys, black dahl, okra and roti, awaiting their main courses in an Indian restaurant tucked away behind Regent Street.

'The format is awful. I hate studio pre-records. And I suppose I've become so accustomed to live work with *LWD*, and other lovely projects, it's just a bit... soul-destroying.'

'But the money is great, no?' Everything always came down to money with Phil and there was little he wouldn't do for a good wedge.

'Tell them about the worst part...' Saphie nodded to Phil and Aidan.

'What?' Phil's eyes widened in juicy anticipation.

'Bree Blackwood,' Charlie said flatly.

'No!' the boys gasped in unison, followed by laughter.

'You know her, then?' Saphie asked. They were two cocktails in and already gossipy. Phil and Aidan had both come across Bree in their work. Aidan was the head of womenswear at Harrods, and Phil was the PR director for a chain of private members clubs Bree was always trying to blag free stays at – she even tried using the newsreader splash as currency, saying she had been dragged through the coals and needed to check out for a few days.

'She said she was in desperate need of a reset in the Cotswolds after all the media "hoo-ha" about her and the newsreader.'

'No one cared.' Aidan shrugged.

'She engineered the pictures!' Charlie said in outrage.

'So did you let her stay?' Saphie asked.

'I said we couldn't fit her in. She begged and said she'd Instagram the hell out of it but I told her: "Darling, the Obamas were here last week... we don't need your Stories..." She told me I'd made a big mistake.' Phil gave a bitchy chuckle.

'Well, you know what she did to lovely Leyla, right?' Saphie said.

Phil and Aidan nodded.

'She always starts fights or sells her colleagues down the river, then does a "poor-me" post on Instagram about how mean people are. The hypocrisy is insane,' said Charlie. 'I've seen it up close.'

'Tell them what she did when she finally got to stay,' Aidan prompted, elbowing Phil.

'Oh, yeah, so when she happened to be at the Manor a few months later, and legit staying for work, she took *all* her dry-cleaning from home: dresses, coats, cushion covers... even her living-room curtains. My press office got the bill from House-keeping for six thousand pounds.'

'Whoa!' Charlie said. She didn't know how she hadn't heard this story before.

Phil shook his head.

'Who paid it?' Charlie asked. 'Surely the people she was

shooting with should have covered it? Expenses would have been on them.'

'There were a lot of pissy emails back and forth but we had to write it off. At the time we wanted the production company to shoot with us again. But they won't book "Febreze" Blackwood again.'

'She's always trying to blag stuff from Harrods. She's like the Artful Dodger,' said Aidan, more quietly.

'I met her at an art launch once,' Saphie said, and grimaced, without bothering to elaborate that Bree had cornered her for forty-five minutes and ranted about her tricky relationship with her mother, making Saphie miss the chance to talk to an important dealer. Saphie was less bitchy than the others. 'She's quite draining.'

'Well, all that kindness bollocks doesn't wash with me,' Charlie said, remembering her takedowns of self-conscious women on her makeover show. 'She was admonishing a trans runner today; publicly telling her off for undermining her while also patronising her with a lesson in how to be a woman. It was awful.'

'Kill me now!' Phil spat.

'How long is the shoot?' Aidan asked.

'Only a few weeks left, it starts airing late March. I'll just have to grit my teeth and think of the money.'

'Well, cheers to that!' Phil said with a mischievous laugh.

'Anyway, happy birthday!' Saphie said, raising her glass.

'Cheers!' everyone chimed as they sipped beers and rose-and-cardamom bellinis to collective and mistimed cheers of 'Happy birthday!'

'Any word from the hot scientist?' Phil asked with a raised eyebrow.

Charlie looked flustered.

'Oh, please! He wasn't hot, he was... he was a teddy bear. And no, I haven't heard. Not really. I think he's still coming. I don't know.'

'He is hot,' Aidan said quietly.

'What?'

'I saw some TEDx talk he did about underground super volcanoes on YouTube.'

'You did?' Charlie looked at Saphie and did a double take.

'We all did,' Saphie confessed. 'Phil sent it around. He's sweet.'

'Phil!' She hit his arm.

'What? You told me his first name and his last name. I did what any good friend would do and googled him.'

'He's my friend!'

'Well, I want to meet your "friend" and I want him to bring a hot gay scientist out with him.'

Despite everyone assuming Phil and Aidan were a couple, they weren't. They were perennially single though, and Charlie and Saphie were always on the lookout for hot guys for them, but they were terribly fussy. Saphie had tried to fix Phil up with a beautiful mixed-media painter she shared a studio with in Bow, but Phil didn't like his teeth. Charlie had even tried to set Phil up with Blake Perry, but Phil said that, even though they looked the same age, Blake Perry was too old and he didn't want to be wiping his arse in ten years' time. Sometimes Charlie wondered if Phil was scared of commitment.

Through the window of the restaurant, someone caught Charlie's eye.

'Shit!' she said, almost choking on her cocktail. 'I just have to...' She was already up and out of her chair before she had time to explain.

* * *

Charlie followed a prim blonde woman into the Flickadelica store on the other side of Kingly Court and cleared her throat.

'Erm, Felicity?' she said, unsure of herself, even though it was clearly her.

Harry's sister Felicity Taylor-Miers owned the Flickadelica athleisure-wear brand and had eleven stores across London, this being the flagship. She had started the brand with the help of her husband, Timothy, and her oldest brother, Lawrence, who, like Harry, was a banker and had advised their banker friends to invest. Charlie hadn't seen Felicity since Harry's leaving party last summer, although she had wondered if she'd bump into her. Felicity and Timothy had three very pink and blond children, who reminded Charlie of sweets from the eighties in human form, and lived in St John's Wood. If she wasn't in her flagship store in Soho, she was often in the Waitrose on Finchley Road, and Charlie always looked out for her when she was buying emergency cat food and tins of gin and tonic.

'Felicity, hi!' Charlie said warmly as she followed her into the shop. Empowered by Bollybellinis. Bracing herself. Felicity was already behind the till, talking to the store manager. She looked up with a puzzled smile.

'Charlie? Fancy seeing you here!'

'I know, right?' Charlie laughed. 'When I should be in New York!'

Felicity looked confused, unsure of how to play it, but she tried to steer away from her usual Felicity Taylor-Miers lack of tact that was always getting her into trouble with Timothy's friends and the mums at school.

'How are you?' she asked, trying to knit her eyebrows into a sincere bow.

'Not great, but I was just wondering how your mum is. I heard she was poorly?'

Felicity relaxed a little – she had an uptight face despite her lack of filter.

'How sweet of you,' she said. 'She's doing better, thanks. Having speech and physio and her consultant believes she should be back to her tippity-top Mummy Taylor self soon.'

'Oh, that's great...' Charlie said, realising Felicity wasn't really going to bother with any other pleasantries or apologies on her brother's behalf.

'Charlie, this is my store manager, Bea, and my brand manager, Heidi!' she said as another familiar woman, this one with fishtail braids, walked down the stairs as electro beats pumped out of the shop's sound system. The women nodded warmly as Charlie looked around the shop.

'This is my brother's ex, Charlie, remember the make-up artist?' Charlie had done a few campaigns for the Flickadelica brand. Bea, the store manager, looked unmoved but Heidi remembered her from the shoot. Heidi had been one of the models.

'Oh, yeah, hi!' she said as she plonked the clothes on a table.

My brother's ex.

'Did you actually *go* to New York?' Felicity looked confused again.

'Yes, I bloody did. Why did no one stop me?' Charlie was feeling bold. Perhaps Felicity's bluntness was rubbing off on her. She used to love getting Charlie to do her make-up for events, parties, even her own wedding, but never held back in telling her if she didn't like Charlie's latest hair colour, or if a certain ensemble wasn't for her. Felicity only ever wore a white shirt tucked into prim navy jeans, so no one could ever say she was getting it wrong.

'We thought you knew.'

'About Isabelle? No! Why did no one tell me?'

'Well, I only met her when they were over visiting Mummy,

after she collapsed. She's very sweet. I'm sorry for your heartache, Charlie, but to be honest we had other stuff going on at the time.'

'Other stuff. Of course. It just would have been nice if someone had mentioned it. Especially if Harry had mentioned it, you know... before I boarded a plane. I went all the way out there for nothing.'

Bea and Heidi retreated a little and busied themselves with leggings and mannequins. Felicity tried to put her sympathetic face on.

'Don't be sad, Charlie, the Beans on Toast girlfriends are the backbone of this nation. Like the Land Girls. And they always triumph in the end.'

'The what...?'

'The Beans on Toast girlfriends.' Felicity said it as if it were perfectly normal. 'You stick with your man through the lean years, support them when they're studying and all you can afford for dinner is beans on toast. Then when they hit the big time and are dining at Le Bernardin or Per Se, bleurgh, you're cast aside!' Felicity said it as if it were something jolly.

'It happened to me before Timothy. You must have met Archie...?'

Charlie felt about one metre tall. She looked back at the restaurant across Kingly Court and couldn't wait to get back to her friends. Their warmth. Love. Compassion. Her birthday celebration.

'Don't worry, it all works out in the end!' Felicity sounded very upbeat about this, but then everything always worked out well for her. 'Have you seen our spring/summer range?' but her voice echoed into Charlie's past as she looked around the shop, almost feeling giddy, and walked out, back to her friends, who were definitely more like siblings to her than Harry's cold siblings were to him.

* * *

After the birthday curry, Charlie went back to her flat to prepare for an early start. A car was coming at 6 a.m. for the first day's shooting of *Triple-A Talent*, and this birthday was never going to be big anyway.

At the flat she put on *Any Other Way*, the Jackie Shane record she had picked up on Berwick Street and paid through the nose for because she was so pleased to find it and have a little bittersweet memory of New York. She sat back, listened to 'In My Tenement' and put her feet up on the pouffe. She looked at Mabel on the sofa next to her, looking back up with wide orange eyes. 'Happy birthday to me, missy,' Charlie said as she raised her glass of clementine gin and tonic as Mabel rolled onto her back, bent her paws and proffered her tummy for rubs. It was Mabel's way of saying, 'Happy birthday. I will deign to let you revere me and treat me like a princess,' and Charlie took a large slug of gin and duly obliged.

'Shall I call him?' she asked the cat.

Mabel purred and butted her with her wet black nose.

Charlie looked at her phone and hovered over the circle with Pete's face in it. It was his Columbia profile picture and in it he looked handsome, if a bit stiff, like Clark Kent in his black glasses, but clever and kind all the same.

'FaceTime?' she nervously asked Mabel. It was 11.50 p.m. in London, early evening in New York. She pictured Pete on the red line from 116th to 14th, reading a book, planning what to have for dinner. Pictured him at the little round dining table in his lovely apartment. She hankered to talk to him. His calm was what she needed while she was fretting about turning thirty-three with a broken heart.

'Nahhh,' she said, moving her thumb away. 'Early start.'

Plus she couldn't take the extra heartache if Pete didn't answer. Something innocuous like him being in a meeting or on the subway could feel like rejection, and she couldn't take a micro snub on top of the macro one from Harry.

Fucking Harry.

She looked at the picture on the sideboard of a bunch of friends. Her friends at Saphie's thirtieth birthday party. Saphie and Prash, Phil and Aidan, Harry and Charlie. Saphie had a festival-themed party in her parents' garden and it looked like a wedding, Charlie with a flower wreath on her head. Her nose pressed against Harry's neck.

Why haven't I got rid of it?

It was a truly happy time.

I don't want to get rid of it.

She gripped her phone, tempted to launch it at the photo as it enraged her. Mabel's purrs ramped up, she wriggled for another rub and Charlie looked down.

'I know Miss Mabel. Bedtime.'

FEBRUARY

Jazz Jenkins slid into the terrace looking like a queen behind her sunglasses; white blazer balanced on her shoulders like a cape. Lazy Oaf dungarees with smiley faces on. So much so that the drag artist, Coco de Mare, on the mic, even stopped her patter and followed Jazz's trail to the little table where Charlie was waiting. She looked so confident and composed, her white and brown patchwork face shimmering in the sunshine, it was hard to believe she was only twenty-three years old, and desperate to see her birthday twin.

'Charlie!' she said, almost as performatively as Coco followed her with a keen eye.

Charlie looked up and almost gasped. She'd been nervous to see Jazz. She hadn't seen her since she'd got her tickets for *LWD* one Saturday last November, and she felt guilty for having almost put her off.

'God, look at you!' Charlie said, standing up. Jazz didn't have a scrap of make-up on and she glowed.

They hugged tight.

'Happy birthday!' Jazz said.

'You too, my love.' Charlie squeezed. 'How was it?'

Charlie didn't meet Jazz through the visible differences charity she volunteered at, but Jasmine's mum, Monique, had found Charlie on Facebook and got in contact direct. She'd sent her a message and said that her once-confident-performer fourteen-year-old daughter was being teased about her vitiligo at school – and it was making her stop auditioning for plays. She had even dropped out of after-school drama club at an impressive stage school near their home.

'She used to want the best parts; she used to get the best parts!' Monique had lamented. 'Now she doesn't want to go out. She's started skipping school.'

Charlie had never been a performer, but she knew exactly how Jasmine felt so she'd called Monique.

'I'm sorry I messaged you, but I promised I wouldn't approach the charity,' Monique had said. 'She was angry when I mentioned it – she doesn't want to be a charity case. She's a bit of a firecracker...'

'I see...'

'So this is a sort of way around it,' Monique confessed. She was as shrewd as her daughter. 'She loves the theatre...'

'I love the theatre! I think I can help,' Charlie said.

Charlie spoke to a make-up-artist friend, Donna, who assured Charlie that she had all the kit and wisdom she needed to help a girl of colour with vitiligo, and Charlie took her skin-camouflage kit to meet the family at their house in Purley.

When they first met, Jasmine was like a sulky child. One part petulant and angry at her mum for arranging this behind her back, insistent she was fine and would get her shit together and go back to school; two parts desperate to know what Charlie had experienced in the theatre. Which shows she knew. Actors she had worked with.

Charlie won Jasmine around with behind-the-scenes chat as she showed her how to cover up her vitiligo, to even out her skin tone to make the patchy pink parts dark.

Jasmine cried when she first looked in the mirror and felt 'normal' for the first time since becoming self-aware. That she could blend into the background.

But something about it didn't sit well with Charlie. Jasmine was so brilliant, so beautiful, she wasn't a 'blending into the background' sort of young woman.

Charlie didn't think camouflage was the answer, but having it in her locker would be. During their chats about Harry Styles, Timothée Chalamet and the theatre they became unlikely friends, given Jasmine was born on Charlie's tenth birthday. But useful allies when it came to Jasmine helping Charlie stay cool enough and tech-savvy enough not to look like a dinosaur on social media, and Charlie being able to guide Jasmine through London life when she moved there to go to drama school.

Jasmine had since graduated from RADA, and was living her best life, sashaying through drag queens to meet Charlie for the belated birthday brunch they hadn't thought they would have this year.

She looked magnificent.

Charlie hugged Jasmine – who was now called Jazz since she went to drama school – and released her tall and willowy frame.

'Oh my God, you look incredible.'

'All thanks to you, Charlie Brown!'

'Well, *I* should have listened to *you*...' she said with a conciliatory wink.

They both sat down.

'I called it, Charlie, I said he was a prick.'

'You did. But then you say most people are pricks.'

'After what he did to you before... I would never have looked at the fucker.'

Jazz was only fourteen when Charlie hit rock bottom, and they had only recently met, so Charlie didn't tell her until she was twenty, when she was talking Jazz through all of her and Harry's breaks over the years. But still, it was enough for Jazz.

Jazz levelled Charlie with a look. It was surprising how scared she was of a kid.

'Anyway, enough about him. I promise I will listen to you in future on all matters to do with pricks, podcasts and when is the best time to post...'

'Yeah, what's with that, babe? You didn't post a single New York cliché. Who cares if you weren't living your best life? The whole point of socials is to make out that you are! The opportunities!'

Fleetingly, Charlie thought of another missed opportunity in New York.

'So tell me about this play...' Charlie said, after they both ordered poached eggs on toast.

'I've got a call-back next week, which is amazing. The lead in a Lorca play. Although I'm a bit worried.'

'Why?'

'She's a married woman wanting a child. It's going to be hard.'

'But is she young?'

'Yes.'

'Well, you're young – and you're full of empathy.' Charlie thought back to Jazz's reaction when she told her about the highs and lows with Harry. Jazz had been telling Charlie about her crush on Freddie, who had been her best friend since Welcome Week at RADA, and was worrying whether crossing a line might ruin their friendship. She had asked if Charlie and Harry started out at friends, and as Charlie went into detail and confided about their darkest of times, Jazz's eyes filled with compassion and a sort of sadness Charlie only just remembered. She never did ask Freddie out. 'You're so full of understanding. You can do it.'

'I don't know *love* though, do I? I've never been in love, and I don't know what it's like to want a child.'

'Yeah, but Chris Hemsworth isn't a Norse god, is he? You're actors. And you're an exceptional one. I'm sure you'll ace it.'

Jazz looked hesitant. Charlie wasn't used to seeing Jazz look hesitant, not for a long time.

'What about your mother? Think about the ferocity with which Monique loves you. How she would do anything for you.'

Jazz smiled.

'And think about how much you love Harry Styles. Channel that.'

'Fuck yeah,' Jazz said.

Charlie looked at her in awe. She knew that, call-back or not, Jazz was going to be a star.

'Anyway, what's with you? How are you getting on?'

Young and perceptive. Jazz could see right through her, that there was more to her than a post New York funk.

'Oh, it's weird. It's probably nothing.'

'What?'

'I'm just a bit all over the shop.'

'Well, I don't know much about relationships, but I know a funny face when I see one.'

27

FEBRUARY

Charlie stood in the make-up room – her office for the past few weeks – at her favourite chair, where she was applying foundation to the face of TV historian Leopold Leatherbarrow. Leopold was nervously wittering because he was terrified about singing 'You're History' by Shakespears Sister under a costume that made him look like a chess piece – a pawn.

Charlie's assistant Eva was working on the celebrity in the next chair and Phoebe was heading up the subgroup at the other end of the TV studio, the team who were doing the judges' make-up. Given they had to keep the contestants' identities secret from the judges, the producers split the studio into two camps so the two would never cross paths.

'I mean, Jesus Christ, why did I agree to do this?' Leopold was full of nervous energy and regret as Charlie dabbed foundation onto his domed head. She was going to need a lot of powder for this face. He was a sweater.

'Eva, can you pass me a couple of ice cubes, please?' Charlie asked, giving her a knowing look. Eva was working on Nancy Van

Cauter, the former Page 3 model in the next chair along, and she gave Charlie an obliging nod and walked out.

Leopold looked at Charlie in the mirror, pleading as if she were his executioner.

'My agent said it would give me wider appeal. "Bring history to a prime-time audience!" she said. Help my chances of an autobiography...'

'I'm sure you'll be wonderful, Leopold,' Charlie assured him. 'I heard you in rehearsals, you were great!'

'Really?' He flushed. 'Was I?'

He wasn't, but there was no turning back now, and there was something sad about seeing a man with four degrees who could enthuse anyone about the history of the House of Habsburg look so small and nervous.

'Yes,' Charlie said as she mixed concealer on the back of her hand and pressed it into the red nostrils of his drinker's nose. 'You're going to be fine!'

'Fine?' Leopold whimpered.

'You was great!' Nancy enthused from the chair next to him as she waved an arm and looked back at her reflection while she waited for Eva to come back. 'Way better than me anyway. I'm shitting meself!'

Nancy gave a laugh that belied her fear. She was dubbed a 'bubbly brunette' in her eighties heyday, and there was an enormous enduring effervescence in her laugh even faced with the most terrifying gig of her life. 'I'm not sleeping, I'm not eating, the song's going round in me bloody head. Darrell and the kids think I've gone doolally!'

Nancy Van Cauter was now head of a sex-toy empire and an investor in a Championship football team, and nothing about her was doolally, as much as people expected her to be. She was going to be fine, Charlie knew it. Better than Leopold Leatherbarrow anyway, and Charlie did feel terrible for him.

Eva came back in with a little bowl of ice cubes.

'Brilliant, thanks,' Charlie said, taking the bowl while Eva put her hands on Nancy's shoulders and looked at her face in the mirror. She was pretty much ready.

'What the devil are you going to do with those?' Leopold asked fearfully.

'Take one in each hand and hold it behind each ear for me, please, just while I finish your face.'

He narrowed his small blue eyes.

'They'll cool and calm you, I promise.'

Leopold obliged, taking a slippery ice cube in each shaky hand and placing them behind his ears. Anything to take the focus off his nerves. A man with a clipboard and earpiece poked his head around the door with a time warning.

'Ten minutes, Pawn and Poodle. Ten minutes to studio. Judges are in place.'

Panic ensued. Charlie kept her cool, calm demeanour while Bree walked in clutching a pair of boots.

'I mean, I can't remember what day it is!' Nancy said with a giggle as Eva applied one more lashing of waterproof mascara to her sparkly blue eyes.

'It's 28 February.' Leopold winced. 'I've had this day etched in my Filofax in *blood*,' he added dramatically.

'Wow, you still use a Filofax?' Charlie noted.

Eva gave Charlie a knowing look that made them both say *historians* without uttering a word.

'Urgh!' Bree scoffed, placing a pair of shiny black boots next to Pawn's chair. 'Leap year tomorrow. Now we have to hear the bull-shit about women proposing to men.'

She propped the boots so they were just in front of Leopold and looked at the clock above the mirror.

'Actually it's quite interesting...' Leopold countered, relieved for another distraction. 'The tradition is attributed to two women in history, not a male diktat: Brigid of Kildare, an Irish nun in the sixth century, and Queen Margaret of Scotland in 1288, according to which you believe.'

Bree looked blank. She didn't appreciate being mansplained to.

'Marriage is such a hetero-normative construct,' she replied flatly.

Leopold didn't catch the hostility in her voice. He looked at most things as if they were to be marvelled at. Apart from celebrity talent shows.

'I rather prefer the Queen Margaret theory,' he continued. 'Apparently she wanted it put into law that if a man refused a woman's proposal, he had to buy her a new gown.'

'Sounds good to me!' Charlie said jollily.

'I was proposed to by nine different men in my youth,' Nancy said proudly. 'Only said yes to my Darrell, of course. Best decision of my life – we've been married thirty years next June.'

Charlie and Eva smiled over Nancy's bouffant of dark, well-dyed waves, that were about to be flattened by a papier-mâché poodle head.

'Well, you're the exception,' Bree said, folding her arms and sucking on a lollipop as she looked at Nancy's reflection. 'Humans didn't used to live as long as we do now, we are not meant to be shackled to one person for so long. Marriages lasted in the old days because you were only married about twenty years before one of you died.'

Nancy looked a little crestfallen.

'And women weren't allowed to say if they weren't happy.'

'Oh, I am happy,' Nancy declared. 'We're planning a party!' She looked around contentedly but Bree didn't buy it.

'Name me one couple who lasted longer than thirty years pre-1900, because it just didn't happen.'

'Queen Victoria and Prince Albert?' Charlie suggested.

'Our dear Queen Victoria was heartbroken when Albert of Saxe-Coburg and Gotha passed away only twenty-one years into marriage...' Leopold offered apologetically.

'Oh, yes, I did make-up for a film about them,' Eva concurred.

'However, Lazarus and Mary Rowe of New Hampshire married in 1743 and were together for eighty-six years,' Leopold said helpfully.

'Yes, but how many of them were happy?' Bree argued.

Everyone looked around at each other, wondering what the dementor was going to say next. 'Well, the patriarchy has a lot to answer for,' Bree tutted. 'Making women who do buy into the construct feel they can only propose one day every four years.'

'I was going to propose to my boyfriend tomorrow,' Charlie blurted. The room went quiet. Nancy turned around intrigued. Eva's eyes filled with concern.

'Oh, really?' Bree said flatly, with a look that said *of course you would*.

Charlie stood a little taller in her shoes.

'Not because I didn't think I could propose to him on 1 May or 17 August, but because I felt ready for marriage and wanted to commit, to make the leap – so I thought it would be nice to say so; to ask him.'

Nancy clapped her hands together, thinking this story had a happy ending.

'Well, that didn't work out, did it?' Bree quipped.

Charlie's mouth hung open while Nancy gasped in dismay and Eva looked furious.

'Last call for Pawn and Poodle. Last call for Pawn and Poodle!'

Leopold went a shade of puce under his subtle 'TV Awesome'. Nancy lifted herself out of her chair, one eye still on Charlie, as Eva took her hand and Bree puffed the sleeves of her blue and white shoulders.

'Does that mean I'm going?' Leopold laughed but Charlie could see him shaking as he gingerly stood.

'Yes,' Charlie half apologised, face still flustered. 'You'll be OK.'

As she said it, she knew it was a lie. Leopold Leatherbarrow was about to be humiliated in front of a studio audience, only for him to be humiliated again in a couple of months' time when the episode was broadcast on TV. And Charlie wasn't OK either. All she wanted to do was get in a car and be as far away from poor Leopold, Bree, this show, and London, as possible.

'For fuck's sake, you forgot your boots!' Bree called.

28

MARCH

Charlie and Ruth Brown walked along the lush green edge of the bank of the Ribble river and stopped at the sight of a grand house sitting on the valley floor. The soothing, trickling sound of clear water, dotted with chub, barbel and trout, tempered their combined distaste as they stopped for breath and to take in the view. The house looked as tiny yet as grand as a hotel on a Monopoly board in the distance, only Hawksworth Hall was beige and grey and made of sandstone. The spring green of the valley floor surrounding it was so verdant it looked as if you could bounce or cartwheel there. Not that either Charlie or Ruth would want to. Instead, they soaked in the surrounding view of the wide valley with hills rising gently on each side, green fields made into a patchwork with darker green hedgerows and trees.

Ruth sighed and put her hand to her brow, resting her foot on the bottom step of a small stone bridge that crossed the river, and properly examined her daughter's face.

'How are you, love?' Ruth asked, candidly.

'Oh, you know. Knackered. We're filming the final this week and I cannot wait to get the hell out of there.'

'That's not what I meant.'

Ruth gave an ever so gentle flick of the head towards the Taylor estate, almost so the house and the people in it wouldn't know they were talking about them.

Charlie sighed and slumped down on the bottom step next to her mum's foot.

'I'm empty. Wiped out. Angry.'

Ruth had a soft and pretty face, her eyes were bluer and gentler than Charlie's but the love-heart frame of it was the same.

'I'm angry too,' Ruth said with a surprising darkness. 'I saw Clarissa Taylor in the butcher's a couple of weeks ago. I felt such rage I wanted to punch her in the face.' Ruth let out a small and surprising laugh. Charlie looked up in shock.

'Mum!' Charlie had never heard her mother utter a violent statement in her life.

'I know! I felt so bloody... furious. Then I remembered what the family have been going through. She didn't look well. And I felt... terrible!' She looked almost apologetic.

'Don't feel bad. But it's Harry you should be directing your anger towards. It's Harry you should punch. Not Clarissa.'

Ruth narrowed her eyes and comedically curled one hand into a fist and hit it against the flat of her other palm. It was so unconvincing they both giggled at how silly she must look. Then Ruth's face dropped and she took a deep breath.

'It's the most raw and powerful anger a person can feel... I think,' Ruth mused. 'I mean, Gordon Batley broke my heart before I met your dad...'

'Fuckin' Gordon Batley...' Charlie joked. Gordon Batley was a bit of a joke character in their house. He had both wronged Ruth Carnegie yet done the best thing in the world the night he dumped her at the Clitheroe disco, making way for Ray Brown to moonwalk into Ruth's life. Gordon Batley was almost revered now. Ruth ignored Charlie's joke, her face serious.

'But a wrongdoing against your child. When *their* heart is broken. You feel it ten times over because the person you love more than anything is hurt and there's nothing – *nothing* – you can do. Worse still when it's been caused by someone else's careless-ness. Carelessness with the thing you treasure the most.' Ruth's eyes welled up as she looked at the tabletop hill beyond the house in the valley. Charlie listened to the sounds of birdsong and river as she rested her elbows on her thighs and propped her head up in her hands, looking at Ruth and wondering what it would be like to be a mother. She said nothing. Her mum rarely spoke so candidly, she didn't want to interrupt her flow.

'Your dad lost a piece of himself, you know, that time...' She nodded angrily towards the house.

For a second Charlie didn't know what her mum was referring to, as if she had detached herself so much from it that she was a bystander looking down on the sliding timeline of her life.

'When he came to get you.'

Charlie hadn't forgotten. The pain of being bent double on the bathroom floor in a pool of her own blood. Mabel's large and alarmed eyes. Saphie coming in and making a phone call in panic; a call Charlie had begged her not to make, but she was too weak to fight it. She knew Saphie was just being a good friend. She remem-bered Ray's haggard face as he walked into the flat and saw his daughter, pale and listless. How he had made the back seat of his Skoda as comfortable as he could with a duvet and towels laid across it while he raced from London to Lancashire without saying a word, apart from to placate Charlie's moans as she curled into a ball drifting in and out of sleep. How he and Ruth had helped Charlie up the stairs and into the bed of her childhood home and called their family doctor to come and check her.

'He closed the front door on Dr Hammersley, put a fist to his mouth – it was an angry fist – and came into the kitchen sobbing.'

Charlie looked stunned. She had never seen her dad cry apart from the day he got the phone call to say his mother had died; she was shocked her mother was sharing this with her. Ruth liked to talk a lot, but she rarely talked about the nitty-gritty, she always wanted to keep things light, for everyone to be happy. 'He didn't want you to hear him cry. But when that kettle whistled, it all came flooding out.'

'Oh, Mum!' Charlie was about to hug her, half in apology and half to make her feel better, but an elderly couple came walking over the bridge from the other direction and interrupted them. The old couple nodded cheerily as Ruth stepped to one side and Charlie swung her legs out of the way to make room.

'Thank you,' said the woman.

'Morning!' The man nodded.

Charlie and her mum smiled, said good morning, and waited for them to pass along the riverbank from where they had walked.

'I'm sorry I put you through it.'

'Don't you be sorry, Charlotte,' Ruth almost scolded. 'Not for one second.'

Charlie was taken aback at the vehemence in her mother's voice.

'I'm not saying it to make you feel guilty. I'm just saying, you can imagine, the depths of your father's anger. How angry we both were with Harry.'

'He never really said.'

'Of course he didn't. We knew you might get back together.'

'We didn't really split up. Not properly.'

'Well, it wouldn't have helped telling you. Your father's aim in life is to make you happy. What's done was done and there was no point dwelling on it. We just had to get you better. To hope Harry would treat you better.'

Charlie half smiled.

'Is that why you weren't as upset for me as I thought you might be, about New York?'

Ruth looked across at Charlie as she leaned on her walking pole.

'We think you are stronger on your own, love. At least stronger without Harry. All your best decisions, about work and life... buying the flat, your cancer work. They came about when you were on your own.'

Charlie frowned as she looked at the Taylor house that she knew so well.

'I still want to punch that boy in the face or the goolies though,' Ruth said matter-of-factly.

'Mum!' Charlie laughed, while her mother gave the look of a guilty little girl and just for a second Charlie could picture her mother as a child. 'Goolies! Honestly. Join the queue...'

Ruth smiled, before they both spotted the blue flash of a king-fisher; pointing and whispering as they followed its trail around the curve of the river. They paused for a few minutes to be sure it wasn't coming back.

'Come on, Mum. We can throw rocks at their fancy stained-glass windows.'

They laughed conspiratorially and waited for a family with young children to pass so they could cross the stone footbridge and head home. Three generations. Grandparents, a couple of about forty, and three children, the youngest of which was trailing behind.

The adults nodded a grateful thanks to Ruth and Charlie as they walked past and crossed the bridge back towards the cottage Ruth had given birth in. The youngest child, dawdling in her own world, finally made it across the bridge and locked eyes with Charlie as she passed her.

The girl gave a serious frown, almost as if she were admonishing Charlie.

Charlie gasped, and slumped back down onto the stone step.

'What is it, love?' Ruth asked, puzzled by Charlie's sharp reaction as she straightened her walking socks. Charlie looked at the girl in red dungarees and a pink roll-neck top as she ran off with a scowl, and a chill ran down Charlie's spine.

'Mummy, wait!' the girl called out to her parents.

Deep breaths.

'Nothing,' Charlie said with a sigh as she stood up again. 'Just stood up too quickly. Let's get on.'

29

MARCH

Charlie wasn't planning on going to meet Pete when he landed at Heathrow airport. In an email exchange the week before, he'd told her his London trip was still on and the Earth Sciences department at UCL had arranged for a driver to meet his flight and take him to his hotel just off Tottenham Court Road. He said he would catch up with her before his 'drinks thing' in the evening.

But when Charlie woke on the morning Pete was landing, alert as a bird as the sun burst through the white slats of her shutters, she felt compelled to get up.

Even though it was different, crossing the Atlantic for a work trip, the memories of her arrival in New York and how alone she'd felt made her feel slightly nauseous and she couldn't get back to sleep. She knew what she had to do.

* * *

Finchley was quieter than she usually saw it, as she weaved among the early gym bunnies, bin collectors and office keen beans, who all seemed a bit miffed that the streets still weren't quiet enough, and hopped on the Jubilee Line.

After two Tubes, a Heathrow Express, and a good dent in her book, *The Goldfinch*, she got to the terminal to see on the board Pete's flight had landed only fifteen minutes late, five minutes ago.

'Perfect!' she said to herself as she went to a coffee shop and stood in line to get a...

Shit, what did he drink?

In the queue, a red heat crept up Charlie's neck as she panicked at not being able to remember something as simple as Pete's order. She knew it was ridiculous, she didn't even *have* to get him a coffee, he'd never know she even had time and it would probably go cold anyway. But her panic and the disproportionately sick feeling were making her face feel hot and her brow sweaty and she wondered how something so simple could make her spiral so suddenly.

I fucking hate airports.

Charlie and Pete had drunk so many coffees in the short space of time they were together in New York and she couldn't remember his simple order. He was a straight-up guy.

Was it a black Americano?

'Can I help you?' a pallid-looking man asked.

Maybe a flat white.

'What the fuck am I doing?' Charlie whispered, feeling a trickle down her spine. All her outdoor layers were adding to her fluster in the heat of the cavernous airport interior.

The young man looked confused.

'Erm, getting coffee...' he said flatly, waiting for Charlie to speak. She couldn't for a few seconds. 'The hot cross bun cappuccino isn't as bad as it looks in the picture,' he said, totally deadpan.

A small tornado spun in Charlie's head. And then she remembered.

It's how you react.

She inhaled intently.

'Two flat whites, please.'

I hardly remember him.

The underwhelmed barista took Charlie's payment, and while she waited for her drinks she pondered New Year's Eve and how she had pushed Pete away.

What am I doing?

She remembered how she had felt so close to him and such warmth in the cold of the garden as their hands gently touched. How the urgency to be with him was so immense, until a switch flicked and she suddenly felt entirely different. How it was Harry she wanted.

Maybe he doesn't want me to meet him.

Their exchanges in the interim had been brief and transactional, to the point Charlie wondered if Pete was just being polite about drinks this evening.

I might not want to see me if I were him either.

Charlie collected the coffees and took them to the metal barrier facing the Arrivals exit as she waited and watched the steady trickle of passengers coming through the doors. She imagined Harry and Isabelle walking through, hand in hand, excited by their first big trip together last November, keen to get to the family seat and see Clarissa.

It's how you react.

She thought for a second about whether Pete would look the same, or whether they would have anything to talk about. She looked along the line at other people waiting, wondering if Pete's driver were here – what if she'd missed him and he'd already gone?

It's how you react.

But there Pete was, walking through the doors. Tall, dark and doe-eyed in his weatherworn tweed jacket, a smarter coat thrown over his arm as he trailed a case on wheels behind him. Pete wasn't looking for Charlie, so he did a double take when he saw her waving, his eyes lighting up to see her, bright and breezy in the melee of suits and drivers and black coats on a spring morning at Heathrow.

It's how you react.

'Hey!' He beamed, pulling his case up to the barrier where Charlie opened her arms wide, like a scarecrow balancing hot coffee, and he carefully edged into her embrace and squeezed her shoulder blades.

'I wasn't expecting you!'

'I wasn't expecting me either! But I woke up early, and wanted to come.' They paused and appraised each other, unsure whether to kiss, slightly awkward for a second while they both reasoned the hug had covered it.

'Coffee?' she offered.

'My hero.' He smiled, taking the paper cup over the metal barrier. 'I did not get much sleep.'

'Here, let me get that,' Charlie said, taking Pete's coat.

'I'm meant to find my driver... unless you're...'

'Oh, no! I want a lift back to central London with you. I have a couple of meetings, near your hotel, if you're still staying around Bloomsbury way?'

They laughed and both smiled to themselves as Charlie down-played the enormity of her gesture.

* * *

In the car from Heathrow the driver listened to Heart FM while Charlie and Pete caught up in the back. Charlie was relieved their conversation wasn't awkward in the slightest. Pete was the relaxed and lovely man he was when they had first met, and he put her just as much at ease on her own turf as he had on his.

'So let me get this straight, you've been to London, right?'

'Right.' Pete nodded, his aeroplane bedhead bouncing a little across the seat from her.

'I need to know all the touristy things you've already done so I don't repeat them. Or if you do want to do them again, I need to do them better.'

'God, the pressure! I am feeling it for you.' Pete laughed.

'You set the bar high in New York!'

'OK, well, yeah. I've been to London a few times. As a kid en route to Greece. We stayed with family in Cockfosters one time, and Dulwich another, which I thought was called Dull-witch until my cousin, who I thought was hot, laughed at me so meanly I stopped thinking she was hot.'

'Well, that's for the best, I think. Anyway, Greenwich, Dulwich... same principle!'

'I lived in the Hudson Valley! I probably would have called Greenwich "Green-witch" then. We didn't go to the city that often.'

'OK, I'll let you off.'

'And then Irenie and I came Interrailing, in our twenties. Went to the Tower and Big Ben and all that jazz. Got ripped off for the worst burger we ever had somewhere near Piccadilly Circus.'

'You fools! None of that nonsense this trip. Was that the last time you were here?'

Pete looked out of the window, at the green banks of the M4, dotted with fledgling trees.

'No, I came a couple years ago, with Martha.'

'Oh.'

'We went to Buckingham Palace. Saw Diana's wedding dress at some other palace. Martha liked palaces and she liked wedding dresses.'

'Oh, cool. Your mum liked Diana's wedding dress too.'

'Who *didn't* like Diana's wedding dress?' Pete said sarcastically.

'I dunno.' Charlie shrugged casually. 'Before my time...' she said with a wink. Pete smiled but didn't take the bait. He was comfortable in his skin and with his age. Most of the time.

'Martha was a bit pissed I wasn't that excited. But I'm more into rocks than "frocks", as you say...'

Charlie smiled.

'But I did see a cool wildlife photography exhibition at your Natural History Museum.'

'Oh, yes, I've been to one of those, they do it every year.'

Pete rubbed his eyes, seemingly rubbing sleep and sadness out of the corners under his thick brown lashes.

'We...' He hesitated.

'Are you OK?' Charlie asked at the same time, putting a hand on his arm.

'Oh, sorry, you go...' they both said.

'No, you,' Charlie insisted.

'Oh, I was just gonna say, Martha and I... we did go on the London Eye. Actually, I hired a pod. I proposed up there.'

Charlie suddenly felt irked and she wasn't quite sure why but mainly that Pete had wasted his time and energy on that awful woman with the smug smile who had totally humiliated him and broken his heart.

'Ahhh, shit, I'm sorry.'

'Don't be. It was shitty weather. Foggy too. Then a bomb scare delayed us. And the champagne I ordered was warm. And the glasses were plastic.' He gave a wry smile. 'It was my fault for ignoring the omens.'

As the car weaved through west London, Charlie made a mental note: avoid the London Eye.

Pete put his dollars away and unzipped sterling from a travel pouch and tucked them into his leather wallet.

'But I really don't mind what we do. I don't have long, just hanging out would be great. I don't even *have* to do anything touristy, really.'

* * *

The car pulled up outside Pete's hotel, a beautiful 1930s neo-Georgian building on a Bloomsbury corner that looked so *London*, Charlie wished she had stopped to notice it before. The driver asked Pete to sign something, and Charlie watched him scrawl with his free hand; his forearm was tanned and brown. Something about the way Pete signed his name made her feel sorry for him. Sad for him and his heart.

'Thanks, mate,' the driver said, taking his clipboard before getting Pete's luggage out of the boot.

'Nice!' Charlie said, getting out of the car and looking up at the hotel, wishing the traffic hadn't been so easy. They'd hardly had a chance to catch up.

'You need dropping anywhere?' Pete asked, trying to hold onto the driver in case she did.

'Oh, no, I have a meeting, but it's around the corner,' Charlie said, nodding her thanks and waving him away, but the driver was already pulling off. They stood on the pavement, Pete clutching his suitcase. They held each other's gaze just fractionally long enough for Charlie to feel flustered again, so she checked the time on her phone.

'Ooh, good going! Not even eleven. For once I am not going to be late for a meeting with my agent.'

A doorman with a top hat craned his neck to see if Pete and Charlie were guests.

'Great job,' Pete said, rubbing the back of his head. He really wanted to go to bed.

'So what's your schedule, Dr Makris?'

Charlie knew Pete was in London until Sunday, but she didn't know any of the in between. 'Do you have time for a power nap?'

'Not really. First I'm going to take a shower, then I'm meeting the coordinating professor in the lobby and I presume for lunch, then drinks with some geologists later at Burlington House.'

'Fancy.'

'And then the conference tomorrow at UCL, which I'm told is near here.'

'It's just around the corner!' Charlie said chirpily, belying the slight disappointment she felt at Pete's lack of freedom compared with hers in New York. Blasted work. 'You sound busy, so just shout when you do have a window.'

'I'm sure I can duck out of the drinks later if you want to catch up? Get some dinner. They should be over early.' He sounded as if he wasn't sure whether to sound keen or not.

'Sounds great. I can meet you round Piccadilly way,' Charlie said vaguely. She didn't want to be a pain and get in the way of his work.

Pete felt a bit lost. He didn't want to invite her into a hotel he'd never been in, but this seemed all too brief a catch-up too. Maybe they could get some breakfast.

'What's your day looking like?'

'I have a meeting at half eleven. At my agent's office, on Dean Street, not far from here.' She pointed to Soho. 'Then I have to go to Selfridges about a job I'm doing there tomorrow with a big brand.'

'What's Selfridges?'

'It's a big department store, at the other end of Oxford Street.

It's our Bloomingdale's. I'm doing a tutorial in the window for Phlox.'

'Working in the window? That sounds fun.'

'It's stressful! I get a hot face.'

Charlie remembered how hot her face had got at the airport. How it had dissipated the minute Pete walked through Arrivals. Maybe it was just time to pack away her winter woollens. It was getting warmer and lighter. She could see blossom and magnolia blooming on the trees in the square behind them.

'I'm sure you'll be as cool as a cucumber,' Pete said with conviction.

'Thank you. Well, when the Phlox thing is over, I'm all yours.'

Charlie blushed as soon as she said it. Pete smiled wearily, and they both remembered the discomfort of New Year's Eve.

'So... I'll see you after my Geological Society thing, yeah?' Pete said. 'Burlington House?'

'Geology rocks!' Charlie said, hugging him briefly before putting two thumbs up as she walked away with a laugh.

30

'Right, sit down,' Ruby ordered, her panel of brown and gold hair swinging down her back. A big smile on her face.

Charlie loved Ruby's assuredness, her bossiness. She could never have dreamed of speaking to successful women the way Ruby did. She sank into the velveteen shell-shaped armchair in Ruby's office, where everything seemed to be blush pink and rose gold.

'So I have good news, I have great news and I have amazing news.'

'Wow!' Charlie said, almost choking on her water bottle. 'Today is a good day.' She thought of Pete around the corner, and wondered how he was settling in.

'OK, so *Triple-A Talent* launches Sunday and you've been invited to a watch party for the first show at the Charlotte Street Hotel.'

Charlie winced. That didn't fall into any of those good/great/amazing categories.

Pete would have flown to Italy by Sunday night – he had planned a geeky working holiday at the end of his trip to see some volcanoes before flying back to New York from Rome. Maybe she could go to the watch party on Sunday night. It would take her mind off however well or however badly the next few days were about to go.

'OK, RSVP yes, and I'll send Eva or Phoebe if I'm not feeling it. Was that the good, great or amazing part?'

'Oh, that was an aside. The good news is the Phlox tutorial has totally sold out and *maje* press are going: *Vogue* beauty; *Harper's*; *ELLE*, all the bloggers; BBC London. It's going to be big, so be prepared that you will be in the spotlight too.'

Gulp. What to wear?

'I mean, I'm going to try to get some book bods down there too, this is the sort of thing that could get you a beauty book, so I think it's really worth turning on the charm. I'll be there too.'

'Aces.' Charlie nodded gratefully.

'The great news is the new contract has arrived for *Look Who's Dancing!*. Usual time frame, they still want you as director of make-up.'

'Phew. Everything looking the same?'

'Yup – Leyla's in too, her agent told me.'

Even though it was now seven years in a row, there was always a slight panic around this time of year, when rumblings of pro dancers being dropped hit the press, in case their crew contracts weren't renewed. But knowing she was being invited back afforded Charlie the chance to relax a bit between now and June; to take the jobs she really wanted to do and not the soul-destroying ones, or anything with Bree Blackwood.

'And the amazing—' Ruby couldn't hold it in any longer, and jumped out of her chair squealing and clapping her palms together to the point Charlie could barely understand her.

'You got a BAFTA nom!'

'What?'

'You've been nominated! For a TV BAFTA! For *LWD*! I'm so proud of you!'

Charlie jumped up and down out of her chair, and Ruby's assistant, Jamie, and Sarra, the head of the agency, came in to share the news, since they had guessed that Ruby had just told her.

'Oh my God, this is *amazing*!' Charlie put her palms to her face in shock. 'I'm so fucking chuffed!'

'You should be! Long time coming!'

Charlie had always missed out on TV nominations to gritty dramas and period pieces.

'A BAFTA nomination!' She sighed to herself. 'That's mental!'

'Well done, darling,' Sarra said. 'We're very proud of you.'

Jamie revealed from behind his back a posy of roses he'd been sent to Jane Packer to buy and handed them to Charlie, who stood up and hugged everyone.

'Awwww, thanks!' she said.

She thought of Pete, knowing that he was probably in the shower by now, and felt an overwhelming desire to tell him.

'Noms are being announced at 6 p.m. but Sarra and I were emailed in advance. Can you believe it?' Ruby squealed, clapping her hands together again. 'Well, obviously I can because you're awesome, but *still*!'

Charlie blushed.

'This deserves champagne!' said Sarra, looking out for her assistant across the floor.

'I'll get glasses...' Jamie said helpfully.

'OK, steady, I've got to meet Selfridges at one...'

31

Despite rush hour squeezing Piccadilly with its footfall and fumes, the evening felt optimistic and light as Charlie wandered down Regent Street and turned right. After her meeting and impromptu champagne with Ruby, Sarra and Jamie, Charlie went to Oxford Street to meet Ariana, the PR for Phlox, plus Veronica, the events director at Selfridges, to run through the order for tomorrow. Model demos. Ticket-holder Q & A. Giving out the goody bags. All pretty straightforward, and Charlie's newly announced BAFTA nomination, which she was bursting to tell the Phlox and Selfridges teams about but couldn't, would only be a great talking point in the morning and help distract from her nerves. Despite loving what she did and knowing she was very good at it, Charlie still got ruffled in the spotlight.

Charlie hadn't called Pete to tell him – it seemed a bit needy, calling for praise or a pat on the head, and he would have been with his UCL professor friend by the time her thumb hovered over her phone, but she did call her parents, who were eating baked potatoes in the garden-centre cafe in Holden and were over the moon. She spent the afternoon with her laptop in a cafe in Mayfair working on invoices, researching runway looks from all the February fashion shows she had been too busy to take notice of while she was working on *Triple A-Talent*, and emailing the Look Good Feel Better coordinator to set up her next workshops at the Royal Marsden.

Now it was 5.30 p.m. and Charlie was walking along Piccadilly. Nervous and fizzing because there was suddenly something so exciting yet so reassuring about Pete being in town. Pete had made New York for her and she wanted to be a brilliant tour guide for him, even if he didn't have much time on his hands.

At Burlington House she had to look for the entrance to the Geological Society, discreet before the banners and brass of the Royal Academy in front, and followed signs for the Anglo-American Conference down grand corridors until she came to the room where the drinks soirée was being held.

Charlie felt a bit out of place in her bright red trousers and hot-pink jumper as she walked into a room with crimson walls and oppressive paintings of oppressive men standing about Making Decisions.

At least my legs blend in, she thought, laughing to herself as she imagined whether her bottom half might disappear if she stood against the wall. Her trousers were the exact same shade of red as the wallpaper under the dado rail. She sighed with a smile and looked around. People were standing in small groups clutching small wine glasses and talking rocks. It didn't feel very Pete, but he saw her before she saw him.

'Charlie Brown!' he called, from a corner. Charlie was about half the age of most of the men in there, and one of only three women, as she made her way across the room to join him. Pete looked relieved as he waved a palm in the air. She waved one back to let him know she was coming.

'Hey, you!' Charlie said as she approached his circle, trying not to laugh at the absurdity of her plus him in that room.

She stopped herself from kissing both his cheeks – geologists didn't look as if they kissed each other on the cheek – and gave him a hearty nod.

'Hey!' He beamed. 'This is my friend Charlie,' Pete said to two balding men, one tall, one stout, both with friendly faces and sprouts of white hair between their ears and their domed heads. One of the men had sprouts of white hair coming *from* his ears. They both looked a little enchanted to see a young, attractive woman in their space.

'Charlie, eh?' said one. 'Quite unusual for a girl.'

'Not really.' She smiled, quizzically. 'Charlotte?' she offered.

'Charlie is my tour guide in London,' Pete said. 'Charlie, these are GSL fellows Professor Openshire and Professor Karnak. It's down to these very kind gentlemen that I'm here in the first place.'

Wow, he does love fossils, Charlie thought.

'Pleased to meet you,' she said.

Pete looked around for a passing waiter with a tray of wine.

'What do you do, Charlie?' asked the taller, more kindly faced bald man while the one with the hairy ears took a clumsy sip from his glass.

'Oh, I work in minerals,' she said, with a wink of her shimmery grey eyelid.

Pete looked at Charlie in awe.

'Wonderful!' the professor said, with some confusion. 'In the energy sector? Mining?'

'No, I'm just kidding, I'm a make-up artist. I work in costume departments, that kind of thing.'

'Oh,' the professor said, looking delighted.

'So where are you taking the esteemed Dr Makris while he's here?' asked the shorter professor with the hairy earlobes.

Charlie suddenly wished she'd planned his visit better, but all the great things they had done in New York had happened organically, at a few hours' notice, so she hadn't put too much thought into it.

'Well, I can't give my secrets away yet,' she replied, trying not to wince.

'Wonderful!' said the tall professor again, Openshire or Karnak, Charlie hadn't caught which way around they were, but she liked that the tall one seemed to think everything was wonderful.

Pete managed to secure Charlie a glass of wine, and himself a second, and after an hour of people coming over, of a toilet break to check her phone, which was blowing up with the BAFTA nomination news, and messages from Phil and Saphie asking if Pete had arrived; after drinking her glass of wine, then another, too quickly and milling around the airless room, Charlie decided to call it a night, leave Pete to it and go back to Mabel. This really wasn't her scene.

'I'm going to get going,' she said quietly to Pete's shoulder, after she'd been to the loo and come back to a conversation about crustal deformation in the southern Andes with another two old men and a woman wearing a scarf with birds on it. 'You have a big day tomorrow; I have my tutorial.'

Pete gave Charlie a desperate look as if to say *please don't leave me*.

'Oh, OK, sure,' Pete said politely, while one of the men cleared his throat and started responding to the group about subducting Nazca plates.

'Take me with you,' Pete whispered into Charlie's ear. Pete's warm sweet breath and his gentle hand on Charlie's arm made her intake sharply, something between a laugh and a gasp, while she nodded reassuringly and they both pretended to listen to the man while Charlie hatched their escape plan.

'Uh!' Charlie gasped dramatically. 'Dr Makris! If we're to see out your second most important London engagement, I've realised, we need to go now...' Charlie said efficiently, as if she were his PA.

'What's that?' asked the woman with the bird scarf.

'Fortnum & Mason, before it shuts. Very important mission: Rose & Violet Creams for Pete's mother. He promised he would get them, and I said I would take him there myself.' She turned to Pete, like a forthright parent. 'This is your one chance. Plus you need your beauty sleep after that *hideous* flight.'

'Of course, dear chap!' said the man who had been talking, patting Pete on the back. 'You must be exhausted!'

Pete nodded, to back up Charlie more than anything. He was tired, but he would sleep it off on the plane home from Rome.

'We are all very much looking forward to tomorrow. Dr Sachse has been telling us what an orator you are.'

32

'Did you speak to my mom?' Pete asked as he and Charlie darted across Piccadilly to the beautiful department store on the other side. It wasn't quite Central Park, but it reminded her of one of her best days ever.

'No! It was all I could think of. Fortnum & Mason is over the road!'

'Well, you saved my bacon, thank you. I'm under strict instructions to get her and Agata some Rose & Violet Creams.'

'Oh, well, that's perfect!'

'Agata was so taken by them, she's been craving the flavours ever since. Said she even tried to eat a rose at the Botanical Gardens in the Bronx.'

'What? That's so funny!'

'Look what you made her do!'

'Well, we'll get her some too. How far gone is she now?' Charlie asked as they landed on the pavement opposite. A security guard was turning the lock on the door from the other side.

'Shit!'

'Oh, man!' They looked around. 'She's ready to pop any day!' Pete said with a smile.

'Oh, wow.'

They both peered through the door but the security guard shook his head.

'Damn, sorry,' Charlie said. But Pete didn't look too bothered.

'Hey, don't be, thanks for busting me outta there. The GSL fellows are lovely, but it's kinda stuffy.'

'I know, talk about fossils!' Charlie laughed. 'Is that who you were lunching with? The bald dudes. Long day!'

'No, lunch was with my buddy Dirk from UCL, he's a friend and the nicest guy in the world. He got me here; those guys in there paid for it. But even Dirk didn't fancy those drinks. Had a get-out, something about taking his kid to a Spurs game.'

'Ah, yes, Champions League,' Charlie said, looking at the ornate clock above the duck-egg-blue doors and wondering when they might make it back to Fortnum's in their short time frame. It was five past seven and the store was well and truly closed.

'Another time,' Pete said philosophically.

'Suppose we should get you back to the hotel before you turn into a pumpkin? You must be knackered.'

Pete rubbed his eyes, lit by the phone in Charlie's hand that kept illuminating and vibrating with missed calls and messages.

'Jeez, you're in demand!' Pete said.

'It's my friends...' she said, glancing down sheepishly at the notifications.

Heard the news!!!!

So proud of you!

Celebratory drinks!

We're in The Clachan.

There was one from Jazz.

Girl got a BAFTA nom! See you there one day!

And Phil kept asking:

Has the hot scientist arrived?

Charlie quickly slipped her phone away, hoping Pete hadn't seen that one, and urged them to walk down the road towards Piccadilly Circus.

'What's going on?' Pete smiled in anticipation.

'Oh...' Charlie's cheeks went pink in the dusk light. 'I've been nominated... for an award. My team has, anyway.'

'Hey, that's amazing, Charlie, for what?'

'A BAFTA, which is sort of our version of an—'

'An Oscar! I've heard of them!'

'Well, I was going to say it's our version of an Emmy, but, well, I haven't won. And I probably won't. It's taken me this long to be nominated. It's usually a period drama that gets it, but the nominations were announced at 6 p.m., so my phone was going a bit mad in there.' She nodded back to Burlington House. 'My agent told me this morning.'

'Hey, can you stop with the downplaying? You need to celebrate every triumph! It's a fucking BAFTA nomination! That's really cool.'

Charlie smiled.

'In fact, didn't I walk past their headquarters along...?' Pete stopped, put his thumb over his shoulder, looked around, and realised they were standing right outside BAFTA HQ next to Fortnum & Mason and both cracked up into laughter.

'No way!' she said.

'Too funny.' Pete smiled as he put his face to the window of the closed building and made a shield around his eyes so he could see in. In the lobby a large screen was showing lists of nominees with professional-looking portrait shots. Charlie's face eventually came up on a list of four people nominated for make-up and hair design. 'There you are!' he said, pointing. 'Charlie Brown! That's you! Not a team.'

'Well, Eva and Phoebe and me... my team make it all happen.'

'It's you!' He pointed, in awe.

This was perhaps the coolest thing that had ever happened to Charlie. The timing was impeccable.

'We gotta take a selfie in front of this! Get the screen in the background. We gotta celebrate!' Pete nudged the side of his body into the side of Charlie's with the fondness of a proud brother and took a picture. 'I'll message it to you...' he said.

'You, Dr Makris, "gotta" get some sleep!' Charlie chided. 'Although my mate Phil is already in the pub hassling me to join him.'

Charlie weighed up how dangerous it might be to introduce Pete to Phil. He would shit-stir massively, and she still felt like an idiot about New Year's Eve and how it had almost ruined everything.

'Let's go, then!' Pete grinned.

* * *

When word got out that Charlie was heading to The Clachan with the hot geologist, Aidan was there like a shot and even Saphie took a break from setting up her Covent Garden exhibition, which was opening in two days' time.

The four friends sat around the table, drinking, chatting, and trying not to make Pete feel as if he were being scrutinised, but Charlie's BAFTA nomination was a handy distraction tool and an excuse for a celebration on a school night. Pete sipped Camden Pale Ale and chatted amiably and *OK, just the one* soon turned into three vodka and tonics for Charlie before Saphie took a call from Prash saying she had to get back to Covent Garden to help him position her artwork.

'Have to love you and leave you, guys,' Saphie said, standing to put her khaki parka on.

Ten minutes later, Phil, Aidan, Charlie and Pete were standing on the pavement of Great Malborough Street saying their goodbyes.

'I fucking love him!' Phil mouthed to Charlie as he headed to Oxford Circus Tube, Aidan headed to Bond Street and Pete and Charlie jumped in an Uber to take them to Finchley, via Pete's hotel.

* * *

Back in the flat Charlie collapsed on the sofa and stroked Mabel's cheeks as she closed her eyes, smitten. Charlie was fairly tipsy and relieved the day had gone so well, surprised by how nervous she had been about Pete arriving, the responsibility of their pact. Relieved that he was every bit as lovely and easy-going as he had been in New York, that Morning After in Hudson aside. It hadn't ruined anything.

'I did it, Mabel! I finally fucking did it!' she said. Rapt that she could put BAFTA nominee on her portfolio. Mabel purred.

As Charlie kicked off her shoes and looked at her phone, she felt annoyed that, despite the sense of pride and contentment; despite the achievements after her toughest of months, despite this being one of the coolest days ever, part of her still wanted to tell Harry.

'You talk about patchwork make-up,' said a woman with tomato-orange lips, 'and I'm not sure what that means – I'm envisaging someone looking like a scarecrow!'

'Ooh, great point,' Charlie said as she sat on her stool next to Iris, her third and final model of the session. Iris sat with a hairband, half her face bare, half with make-up on, and both she and Charlie had their backs to the store window as the head of PR for Phlox, Ariana, stood with a mic managing questions from the audience.

The woman with the tomato lips was slightly distracted by a man on Oxford Street pressing his forehead and palm to the window, as lots of passers-by had, but it wasn't enough for Charlie to turn around and lose her train of thought. This woman was one of fifty beauty junkies who had bought tickets for the event with celebrity make-up artist Charlie Brown, either eager to be a make-up artist or keen for tips for themselves.

Charlie had been nervous when she woke up with a slightly foggy head – she was much better at helping other people shine in the spotlight than standing in it herself. But the BAFTA nomination had helped elevate her confidence – Pete was right, it was a triumph that should be celebrated – as had the buzz of Pete being in town.

Charlie looked at the woman who asked the question.

'Well, what I mean is, take Iris' face. If I'd put the same colour all over, she would have a mask-like look. We want to keep things natural, unless we're going *Ex Machina*... so I layer up using different colours and different amounts based on what the face needs. So here Iris needs very little. It's an approach I've used when people want to cover scars or strawberry marks.' She thought of Jazz and her bejewelled skin, how the natural patchwork of her beauty won out in the end. 'But sometimes, it's not necessary at all. We don't all want uniformity. I know I don't want to look like a Kardashian clone.' The audience laughed. 'Does that answer your question?'

The woman nodded.

'Can I ask you one?'

The woman nodded again but knew what was coming.

'Morange. MAC.'

'I thought so,' Charlie said. 'It's a hard colour to wear but you wear it beautifully.'

The woman nodded gratefully.

'Any other questions?' Ariana asked into the microphone.

A man asked what the best way to get a Cleopatra eyeline was, and Charlie duly demonstrated on Iris, before Ruby made a gesture to Ariana that it was time to wrap it up. Ruby had the satisfied look on her face of someone whose artist had done well and provided lots of lovely content for the agency Instagram, and Charlie had the satisfying epiphany of an idea for what to do with Pete later.

* * *

At 6 p.m. Pete was already waiting for Charlie in the opulent orange and gold bar of The Bloomsbury Hotel, sitting in a curved armchair under a palm plant.

'Hey!' she said, looking around in appreciation. It was a nice bar. Pete looked comfortable there, reading *The Times* with his glasses on, which reminded her of him at work in the lecture hall at Columbia. The glasses suited him.

'Hey!' he said, startled, as he stood eagerly, knocking his head on a palm frond that sent his glasses askew, reminding him to take them off, which he did and tucked them into his pocket. 'Just catching up on your news! Westminster seems even crazier than the Senate.' He ruffled his hair while Charlie smoothed hers.

After lunch with Ariana, Veronica and Ruby in the Selfridges cafe, Charlie had stayed on and spent a productive afternoon at her laptop updating her website and posting about the Phlox beauty event on Instagram, which had got lots of lovely traction, as had a repost about her BAFTA nomination.

'How did it go?' they both asked keenly, as they embraced each other with a kiss on each cheek – it really did feel the most comfortable greeting to Charlie, their lips a safe distance apart – before they each slunk into a blue velour armchair side by side.

'You first,' he said.

Charlie sighed.

'Really well, thanks. Good turnout; lovely people. The beauty industry really is a collaborative and friendly one, despite what people might think.'

Pete nodded as if he already knew it would have been a triumph.

'What might people think?'

'That it's shallow. Skin deep.'

Pete shook his head.

'From what you said about what you do, it changes lives.'

'It does.'

'Well, I have no doubt you were brilliant.' Pete smiled and paused. 'Plus you're glowing from your success,' he said in mock adoration.

'No, that is Charlotte Tilbury Wonderglow – and I haven't won the award yet – but thank you. How was your paper?'

A waiter brought over two blood-orange drinks in low tumblers.

'Thanks, Luis,' Pete said. 'I ordered you a Sazerac.'

'A what?'

'Luis' recommendation.'

The waiter placed the drinks on the table in front of them.

'Cognac, absinthe, Peychaud's bitters...' the waiter said proudly. 'With a Coral Room twist...'

'What's that?' Charlie asked, looking up at Luis' handsome, bearded face.

'If I tell you I have to kill you...' he said in a thick Spanish accent.

Pete laughed.

'They're good. I had one last night before bed.'

'Did you, now?' Charlie said, picturing Pete, sexy and brooding at the bar. A warmth ran down her body with the liquid gold.

'So how was your paper?'

'Yeah, it went well, thanks. Got some great feedback. Dirk and I work really well together; he's not like the dinosaurs you met last night.'

'They were friendly dinosaurs...'

'He's invited me back already.'

'Oh, that's great!'

'Although not before he comes to Columbia.'

'Oh.'

'Cool, huh?'

'Cool! And crustal deformations in the Andes aren't putting us in imminent danger?'

'Possibly. My paper was about crustal deformations in great California earthquake cycles. Elastic lithospheric plates and the San Andreas fault.'

'Damn elastic lithospheric plates...' Charlie joked.

'Dirk knows more about the Andes, and he seemed pretty chirpy, so I think we live to see another day.'

'Well, I'm glad.'

'It was at the British Museum, just along the road too. Not a lecture hall at UCL, so it was even better than I could have imagined.'

'Oh, crap.'

'What?'

'I was going to take you to the British Museum. See the Egyptian rooms. The Rosetta Stone. Grayson Perry's Tomb of the Unknown Craftsman...'

'Really?' Pete smiled, half in awe, half in apology that he'd already been.

'Oh, no! You saw them all?'

'Maybe not all those things. It was pretty cool. I got to see the Parthenon sculptures you pilfered from the Greeks over lunch.'

'Like Americans never pillaged art...' Charlie laughed, giving Pete a playful nudge.

'True.'

The sunny day had given way to a grey evening, where a dark and dirty mist had lowered on the street outside.

'I did see the Grayson Perry. I love him. And the Ramses statue and the mummies were beautiful.'

Charlie gave Pete an unsure glance.

'Beautiful? How can someone so chill be so macabre? About natural disasters and dead bodies anyway.'

Pete laughed as he swirled the ice cubes in his glass. There was a sense of relief about him, to have got the work out of the way. He might look relaxed but he took his work very seriously.

'So what's the plan? Want to get another drink?' Pete gestured to the bar but Charlie had just had another, better idea.

34

'Welcome to London's most haunted Underground station!' said a man dressed as a Victorian undertaker, with what appeared to be a dead fox slung around his neck. His get-up looked bizarre and somewhat stuffy for a muggy, drizzly March night, and Charlie and Pete looked at each other and tried not to laugh. The man surveyed his crowd and Charlie followed his eye to see the usual mix, she imagined, of European families, Asian couples, young lovers and old eccentrics, all looking to see London under a different lens. Charlie briefly wondered how she and Pete fitted in; how people might perceive them. Tourists? A couple?

Jazz had been on a spooky walking tour with some college friends last Halloween because an actor friend of theirs played a ghost halfway through it. She said that, despite *knowing* actors were drafted in, it was so good that 'No fucking way am I ever using Bank station ever again' – which Charlie didn't think was a good thing as it sounded inconvenient, but it was helpful when she was trying to come up with something different to do with Pete.

They were gathered outside Bank, where the walking ghost

tour was set to depart at 7 p.m. sharp, and Edward, the man with the fox slung around his neck, was good to go.

He told the story of the Black Nun, a nineteenth-century woman who roamed the station groaning and wailing as she looked for her brother, hanged for forgery at the Bank of England, where she'd turned up every day since, in her lifetime and beyond it.

'Do you wonder why Bank is the deepest Underground station in Central London?' Edward asked as he waved a theatrical hand over his audience. Pete looked at Charlie in anticipation. 'The next station on the line – Liverpool Street, to those of you not from around here – was built on top of one of London's biggest bubonic plague pits!'

Pete raised a quizzical eyebrow that made Charlie laugh.

'OK, so maybe this is not an *exact* science...' she whispered.

'And let's not forget that the ticket hall in Bank was built on a church crypt...' Edward almost oohed at himself as he said it. 'The station was bombed in the Blitz in 1941 and fifty people died. Ladies and gentlemen, you are standing on the site of London's most haunted station! Late-night commuters, hedonists and libertines might think the woman in black roaming the tunnels and the ticket halls is a figment of their addled imaginations, but the ghost of Sarah Whitehead is very much real...'

He widened his eyes.

'Now, if I may, we are going to walk up this way, to London's most haunted pub!' He gave a 'follow me' signal but then paused for effect, turned, tossed his fur and widened his eyes. 'Wonder what that putrid smell is?'

Those who understood stopped to inhale.

'It's no coincidence Bank is built on an ancient burial ground. People going about their business, going to work with a pit of dread in their stomach, aren't just worried about the day ahead –

the sense of foreboding, the accompanying stench, might just come from walking on an open to-o-o-o-omb...'

At that point a bin truck went past and Pete playfully nudged Charlie in the ribs.

'More likely that!' He laughed.

As they walked along Poultry, past the banks, businesses and closing shops, Pete leaned into Charlie.

'You OK?' he asked. 'Not spooked?'

'Hahaha, yeah, I'm OK. Are *you*?' she asked unsurely.

'Yes! Look! There's St Paul's!' He gazed up in wonder.

'Did you go there before? Maybe we should go there now if you'd rather?'

'No, this is hilarious!'

They stopped outside a pub on a dark corner of Newgate Street opposite the Old Bailey. Its exterior was deep mahogany; Charlie could see ceiling roses and large etched mirrors in the interior as they walked past and shuffled into a quieter side street.

'There is nothing like a cold pint with a cold shiver running down your spine as your body is flooded with the demons and debauchery of a Victorian gin palace...' Edward said, hand creeping over his small crowd as he shepherded the group into a specific nook.

'Rumour has it, the Butcher of Bank, who worked in Newgate Prison over the road, would come here after a shift and confess his sins to Molly Smith, a woman of the night who worked behind the bar, but one night she went mysteriously missing...'

Suddenly, a figure came out of the shadows, a woman dressed in a dirty corset and grey frilled skirts, with blackened teeth, wild hair and what appeared to be an axe wedged in the back of her head. Charlie wondered if this actor was a friend of Jazz too.

The group gasped in amused and fearful shock as the woman weaved through them, demented eyes and speaking in a cockney accent, making little sense, laughing maniacally between cries. Edward looked pleased with himself. The older man in a couple of steampunk eccentrics looked at the ghost with admiration. A pair of Italian teens derided each other for having screamed when the woman first jumped out.

Then another figure came out of a stairwell. A man in stripy bloodstained clothes, a meat cleaver in hand. Charlie wasn't expecting this one, and screamed with the surprise, burying her face into the arm of Pete's coat, seeking solace in the smell of his clothes; embarrassed by how ridiculous it was. She knew they used actors on these tours, and it was as much cabaret as it was horror.

Pete, who was a mixture of shaking with laughter and feeling bad for Charlie at quite how much the man had made her jump, leaned over and whispered in her ear.

'Are you OK? They're heading away now...'

Charlie nodded as she weaved her arm around his, his hand still in his pocket, her body curved into his side, her face now at the back of his bicep as she looked away behind the group and listened to the ghoulish actors, their voices getting quieter as they retreated off down the road.

Charlie kept her gaze behind Pete's arm, into the stairwell the actors probably came from. And then she saw her. It was the little girl she had seen twice in New York and three times now in her dreams. The little girl she thought she had seen on a walk with her family in the Ribble Valley. The little girl was crying under the stairs, just as she was at JFK. Red dungarees and pink roll-neck, as if they were clothes from Charlie's own childhood. Only today the girl was covered in blood; her eyes rolled, her mouth open, petrified in death.

Suddenly Charlie felt a wrenching punch in the gut that made her gasp again and her rooted legs tremble.

'It's OK, they've gone,' Pete said calmly into Charlie's ear. 'Just actors...'

Charlie couldn't speak and her teeth started to chatter.

Edward laughed at how great he was and pondered what he might have for dinner tonight, before suggesting the walking tour continued.

'If you will, my ghost hunters, let's turn this corner and head to the hospital of St Bart's, where the coffin lift will unsettle the nerves even of the calmest of surgeons...'

Pete could feel Charlie's legs shaking where her body was leaning into his, as if she were trembling with cold. She buried her face back in his arm.

'Hey, what's up?' he asked carefully.

'Can you see her?'

Pete looked over his shoulder to where Charlie was hysterically jabbing her head, sobbing into his arm.

He couldn't see anything, but he knew he needed to get Charlie the hell away from here.

'What is it? A ghost?'

'Everything all right?' asked a bemused Edward as he read-justed his top hat, really pleased with himself at how convincing tonight's walk was turning out to be from the look of the woman crying into her boyfriend's arm.

'We'll catch you up!' Pete said, shooing them on with one arm while keeping a protective curtain around Charlie with his other.

A few of the group gave Charlie a confused look as they ambled away. That chick really was hypersensitive.

'Heyyyyy,' Pete said, lifting Charlie's crying face from his arm with two careful palms.

'You wanna sit down somewhere? Find a bench?'

It was misty and eerie and the day had turned cold, and,

Charlie realised as she fell into Pete's hug, she just wanted to be in his arms, in the warm, in a pub.

She couldn't really articulate any of that through her sobs.

'Shall we get a drink?' Pete suggested. Charlie nodded, the colour still completely drained from her face. 'Not here… let's head to St Paul's way.'

Pete put his arm around Charlie and crossed them over the road to the lure of St Paul's graceful dome. 'Dude was creepy anyway!' He laughed, trying to make light of it all; completely baffled as to what had just happened.

Charlie tried to laugh but it got lost among another sob.

They stopped at the steps of St Paul's Cathedral, lit beautifully in the night.

'I'm so sorry…' Charlie eventually said.

'Don't be!' Pete said, whipping a pack of tissues out from his pocket and handing her one.

'It's all been in my head, Pete,' Charlie said as she dabbed the tissue under each eye and fanned her face. She was one part embarrassed but two parts unable to stop herself crying. All her anger and rage and shame about the past few months – the past few years – was tumbling out, and all thanks to a crap tour guide.

'Come on, let's get outta here…' he said, wrapping his arm around her again as he nodded to a tiny pub that jutted out of a corner opposite St Paul's as if someone had bent space and time and shrunk the Flatiron Building to make a drinking den for Shakespeare.

* * *

Pete found a quiet table and sat Charlie in a seat at a frosted glass window as he went to the bar to get two gin and tonics. When he returned she was wiping the black smudges from underneath her eyes with her forefingers and trying to work out how to explain it all to Pete without him running a mile.

'All that talk of Victorian gin palaces made me think... when in Rome,' Pete said as he placed the glasses on the bar mats on the little table.

'Thank you,' Charlie said, trying not to glug it as if it were water in a desert. Pete slipped off his coat, settled into the cosy round table in the window and waited for Charlie to offer up. If she even wanted to. He didn't really think she had seen a ghost, but he didn't want to pry either.

'Who wears a fox around their neck?' Pete laughed, trying to shift the focus. 'I know he's playing a role but...' He shook his head. 'I bet he's a data-entry nerd by day or works in a comic-book shop.'

Charlie's crying lines faded out as the laughter lines creased in. *That's better.*

'I guess you have to be weird to do that job, huh?' Pete suggested. 'Us, on the other hand...' He gave a self-deprecating shrug before sipping his drink and putting it down. 'Perfectly normal!'

Charlie gave a half-hearted smile, before taking a deep breath. Pete deserved an explanation for her meltdown out of nowhere.

I can do this.

'I know this is going to sound mad...'

'We've just paid a guy wearing a dead fox and feathers in his top hat twenty bucks to show us some questionable hauntings. Try me.'

She smiled gratefully, then took another deep breath.

'I think I've been having some questionable hauntings myself.'

Pete put his glass on its mat, twisted it around, and listened.

'When I was at JFK waiting for Harry, I saw a little girl. Or at least I could have *sworn* I saw a little girl. She was there. She looked like she was lost, crying under the stairs, and I asked her if she was OK then went to look for a parent because she looked scared and alone. And I didn't want to freak her out by going too close.'

'Right.'

'Then, quick as a flash, she was gone.'

'OK.'

'Her disappearance was so sudden, I didn't think she was real. She couldn't have gone anywhere that quickly, so I put it down to my tired and stressed brain. My timings were all out and I was sleep-starved.'

'Sounds reasonable. Although New Yorkers do move fast.'

'And when we were in the tornado room at the museum, all those kids – I thought I saw her there, happy and carefree.'

'When I was there?' Pete thought out loud, realising of course it was when he was there, as that was the only time Charlie had been to the American Museum of Natural History. Charlie nodded and continued.

'So I was relieved for a second, thinking she must have found her mum at the airport. Or her mum had found her. I didn't even say it because it was probably a coincidence, or she just *looked* like the girl from the airport. It wasn't worth mentioning.'

'Right...'

'But then she looked at me, through the tornado machine. Her face turned to alarm, her eyes were wide, and she was mouthing, *Help me!* at me, looking almost furious.'

'Why didn't you tell me?'

'Because I felt sick, and it was so noisy, and before I knew it she was gone again. You would have thought I was mad.'

Pete shook his head to assure her he wouldn't.

'And when the lights went up and I knew there wasn't anyone who needed helping, all the kids must have happily filed out, I thought I was going crazy. Had I imagined it?'

'Maybe it was the same girl from the airport on a field trip. Stranger things can happen. I bumped into you twice in New York, didn't I?'

Charlie didn't tell Pete about her nightmare. The dreams she had been having since.

'Then I saw her up in Lancashire.'

'What?'

'A few weeks ago, I went home. My mum and I went for a walk in the countryside, and she was bloody well there, in the middle of nowhere. The same girl, I swear. And I thought I was going mad so I couldn't bring myself to tell my mum.'

Pete played with his drink on its mat, his brow furrowed. He was a man of science and explanation – he could cope with any disaster, as long as there was a reasoning for it. But there was none for this, other than perhaps Charlie wasn't well.

'You think she was an apparition?'

'I saw her back there, in that stairwell by the pub. I saw her, Pete.'

Charlie's khaki eyes filled with fear and water again. 'Same girl. Same clothes. But she looked ghostly and dead.'

Pete was silent for a minute and Charlie felt ridiculous.

'OK, well, if it wasn't Fox Guy messing with your head, perhaps it's someone you keep seeing. Like an imaginary friend or a little totem... when the stakes are high or you're feeling stressed. Even if you don't know you're feeling stressed. You've been through a period of incredible upheaval.'

'You believe me?'

'I believe in your responses.'

Charlie studied Pete's thoughtful and gentle face, unsure whether to tell him. Nervous about how he would react.

'I think I know who she is.'

Charlie finished her G & T and put her hand on the base of the stem.

Pete waited.

'When I was twenty-four, I had an abortion.'

Charlie's face flushed as she spoke. She had only ever said those words twice out loud. Once to Jazz a couple of years ago. And now to Pete. And she had no clue what Pete, a family guy from a very different place, with very different values, who had been set to get married at a big Greek Orthodox church, was going to think of her. His face was still, his eyes wide.

'Harry had finished his masters at LSE, he was doing an internship at Deutsche Bank. He was winning at life.'

'And what about you?'

Charlie took a deep breath and locked eyes with Pete. Pete had a pathos about him that always made her feel as if he was feeling things with her.

A slurring city boy knocked into their table, spilling a little of his pint onto its curved corner, snapping Charlie out of her warmth for Pete with a flimsy apology they both nodded away.

Charlie continued to talk about Harry. Always Harry.

'He was renting a flat in Barnes, but I was doing OK freelancing. I had bought my flat the year before... when we were on a break,' she added sheepishly. 'Saphie rented out the spare room so I could cover a mortgage.'

'You and Harry didn't live together?'

'Not then. He'd always wanted to rent with his friends and said he didn't want to commit to buying yet. I wanted to buy before I was priced out of London. Our timing never aligned. So it didn't seem like we were in a place to have kids. We weren't ready for kids. I was starting to get some really good TV work. He was applying for Goldcrest.'

Pete put his hands up.

'Hey, you don't have to justify anything to me. I am not one of *those* Americans. If it's not right, it's not right. Your body, your choice.'

Relief fluttered at the corners of Charlie's mouth.

'I know – it's not even so much that. But, well, as you say, it's how you react.'

'How *did* you react?'

'Harry made it clear he did *not* want a baby, and he totally freaked out when I said I needed a few days to consider it. I'd always seen motherhood in my future – what if that was my one shot? I had to think about it.'

'Of course.'

'So I thought about it. I went to Marie Stopes, I had a consultation and was offered counselling...'

Charlie didn't feel the need to tell Pete about the STI testing and the dating scan. She didn't tell him about the sadness of taking the first pill on her own at the clinic; the agony of lying on the bathroom floor after taking the second tablet and Saphie calling her parents in panic. The vomit, the diarrhoea and the blood. The feeling that her insides were being ripped out of her with perhaps her one chance of having a baby all over the bathroom floor. And she didn't tell him the worst part: Harry, knowing that she had taken both tablets and that her body was expelling their baby, went on a jolly with the Deutsche boys to Val d'Isère and turned his phone off.

'I was looked after,' Charlie said as she thought about the kindly women who had treated her, given her time and space to talk and think, and told her how she could safely end the pregnancy. She thought about Ray driving her back to Lancashire and lifting her into the house, her limp arm around her dad's neck, blood running down her legs. How she didn't realise it at the time, but her parents lost something too that day.

'But I had terrible nightmares afterwards. I'd dream about being pregnant, or giving birth to a Haribo-like baby. Or having had the baby but being careless with it – like I'd left her in a plastic tub in the boot of a car while I went shopping. And I came back to find her dead.'

'You knew the baby was a girl?'

'No, it was too early – I was nine weeks – but whenever I dreamed about the baby she was a daughter. And I was unfit to care for her.'

They sat in silence for a second, Pete not quite able to join the dots.

'I think the girl I've been seeing – or imagining – I think she's my daughter.'

Pete looked concerned.

'I know it sounds crazy. But, well, ever since Harry, and that chapter ended, maybe I subconsciously thought of her. Conjured her. I started seeing her the night Harry didn't turn up. She would have recently turned eight. The girl in the dungarees, she looks about eight. She looks like me as a child.'

Charlie looked at Pete, expecting him to get up and walk out, she sounded so crazy. Who actually saw ghosts on a ghost walk?

Pete was still there.

'You've got a lot to process,' he said measuredly. 'Maybe if you do see her again, you can reach out to her. Take some comfort from her.'

'But sometimes, she frightens me.'

'Did you take the counselling they offered you?'

'I had a couple of sessions before the abortion.' Charlie looked around at the pub. The jovial faces. 'But none since.'

'Well, all my siblings and I have therapy. I can recommend it.'

'You're American. Brits are stoic. All that "keep calm and carry on" bullshit. Lancashire lasses even more so.'

'I hate "keep calm and carry on".' Pete waved his hand dismissively. 'What about "wake the fuck up and act now"? There is no shame in getting help.' Pete was surprised by how impassioned he sounded and tried to shrug it off. 'Well, it helped me through a ton of shit anyways. But I am like the Michelle Obama of my family in terms of being calm and composed,' he said with a playful smile.

'I don't doubt that.'

'I still see a shrink...'

'Oh,' Charlie said sadly. 'Are you not in a better place?'

'I'm in a brilliant place right now,' he said, meeting Charlie's eyes with his, and there it was again. Confusion. Before his features fell a little.

'Martha and Troy... they're expecting.'

'Fucking hell. I'm sorry.'

'Hey, it's OK. Well, it's shitty. She messaged me to tell me last month. Two years ago I imagined being a dad by now. And although I woke the fuck up and got help, it sometimes gets me down. In those dark corners of the night.'

'I hate those corners.'

They held each other's gaze again.

'But you, man...' Pete said, trying to batten down those bubbling feelings. 'You're so cool and competent! You've been through the mill, no wonder you're starting to see things.'

Pete finished his gin and tonic and looked as if he had something else he wanted to tell Charlie. 'Want another?' he said, already getting up.

'Just a small one...' Charlie smiled.

* * *

Charlie watched Pete at the bar, relieved he hadn't run away at her disclosure of ghosts and demons. At the revelation of the thing she felt most terrible and conflicted about in her lifetime. She watched him wait patiently, bank card in hand. His face keenly observing the unfamiliar around him. Serene and self-possessed as the barmaid served someone else. And Charlie knew at that moment that Pete wouldn't have left her curled up on the bathroom floor.

He came back and placed two more balloon glasses on little mats.

'I went orange and rosemary this time.'

'Nice. Thank you.'

Pete sat down, rubbed his hands on his navy chinos, and cleared his throat.

'You know, I saw you. At work.'

Even though Pete always sounded relaxed, he sounded as if he was *trying* to sound relaxed now.

'Huh?'

'At Selfridges.'

'Oh, wow!'

'I had breakfast with Dirk and we set everything up at the Great Court in the museum. But I wanted to catch your thing and, er, my app said it was an easy walk from A to B. Just down Oxford Street. So I popped out for some air. To see you.'

'Oh no! I didn't see you!' Charlie's thick brows knitted in a bow.

'Just as well, it was a disaster!'

'How come?'

Charlie looked confused.

'I didn't realise how *long* Oxford Street was, so I had to break into a run. Then I realised I didn't have time to come in and say hi or ask a question – and you were already doing your thing...'

Pete didn't say how he had longingly put his palm against the window as he pressed his forehead to the glass. 'So I had to turn around and find a cab to take me straight back. And my cab got stuck in traffic.'

'Standard. Oh, God, I'm so sorry!'

'Don't be, it was my mess-up. I made it back to the museum just in time for my paper. Dirk looked a bit flustered though...'

'Ha!' Charlie mock winced.

'But I knew, even from seeing the back of you at work...'

Charlie blushed to think of her arse spilling over the stool while she was sitting next to a model whose legs were bent in three. 'I knew that you were cool and competent and brilliant at what you do. Without Harry. Just you. Even if you don't win the award. You're already the winner, Charlie Brown.'

Charlie blushed and looked up at Pete. He was probably the kindest and sweetest friend she had ever made.

'Ahhh, mate, that's really lovely,' she said, opening her arms out and wrapping them around Pete's neck for a hearty hug. 'Thank you!'

He sat looking a little befuddled.

'Well, I mean it,' he said, patting her purposefully on the back.

'What question would you have asked?' she said with a raised eyebrow.

'Huh?'

'In the beauty tutorial. What on earth would you have asked?'

And this time Pete blushed. Not knowing how to react.

35

MARCH

'Good morning!' Charlie called as Pete walked towards her, waiting under Marble Arch.

'That's better!' he said, laughter lines cutting into the olive skin at the corners of his eyes. 'I prefer this street when I'm not running down it in a shirt, tie and glasses!'

Pete was wearing black jeans and a cream shirt – he'd even ditched his tweed jacket today – and was clutching two cups from Joe & The Juice.

'Oh, totally,' Charlie joked, because she never ran anywhere. Exercise had always evaded her, despite Harry's attempts to get her to go to the gym.

Pete offered her a cup but saw Charlie already had two of her own.

'We are going to be wired!' Charlie said as they laughed.

'How did you sleep?' Pete asked, worried that the little girl might have haunted Charlie's dreams.

'You know what,' Charlie said, as if it had only just occurred to her, 'I slept well last night for the first time in months!'

'Nothing like a ghost walk to exorcise the demons. I'm going to see if they do them in New York.'

'Hahaha, imagine! The ghosts of John Lennon, Heath Ledger and Malcolm X. Very cool.'

As they weaved past Speakers' Corner Charlie explained that it was… just a corner, where people sometimes spoke, and felt a bit bad that there wasn't a glitzy podium or anything, until she remembered Strawberry Fields.

'OK.' Pete nodded. 'So what are we doing today?'

'Well, given that you have rather selfishly done *all* of the big-ticket London tourist items on any tour guide's list—'

'And managed to ruin most of them…' Pete held a coffee cup up in the air, as if to accept the blame.

'*And* managed to ruin them, I'm taking you somewhere different.'

'Intriguing.'

'Well, you took me to learn about tectonic plates and rocks and stuff, so I'm sort of fusing our passions…'

'Ooh, sounds great!' Pete enthused.

Charlie gave a hopeful wince.

'But first, we walk!'

* * *

As Charlie and Pete strolled through Hyde Park, along the edge of the Serpentine, past runners, under blooming trees and across the bridge over the lake, the sweet smells of orange blossom and hawthorn bushes reminded Charlie of her childhood and filled her with a sense of calm. As they sipped their double coffees and talked, Charlie internally thanked Mother Nature for providing the perfect London weather day. Sunny with a few wisps of cloud; warmer than it had been in months yet not too warm to stroll. One of those spring days where optimism beamed through the cherry blossom and the tinkles of the ice-cream man felt uplifting, even at 11 a.m.

As they approached the Albert Memorial in Kensington Gardens it glimmered gold and Pete gasped, taken with something beyond it.

'Shit!' he said, his mouth hanging open.

'Oh, yeah! There's the Royal Albert Hall.'

'You pointed out Speakers' Corner but we were going to walk past this? I gotta get a photo!'

Pete looked like one of the kids being drawn towards the off-key tune of the ice-cream van back by the lake, his smile and his stride getting more urgent with every step.

He put their stacked empty cups in the recycling bin, stopped on the south edge of Hyde Park, opened his arms out in rejoice and looked up.

'Diana Ross 1973.'

'Huh?'

'I watched that concert over and over with my family when we were kids. We had a VHS of it.'

'Cute.'

'Irenie and I would duet to "Ain't No Mountain High Enough".'

'Can you sing?'

'Fuck no.'

Charlie was pleased there was one London landmark Pete hadn't already been to as they crossed the road, and she made him stand outside it so she could take a photo. She took a few and checked them over – in every one of them Pete looked sweet and earnest, and his eyes were open, so that was good. But something happened to her heart as she looked from the photo up to Pete. It swelled as she saw him as a child, boyish features making a guest appearance in his adult face. The sweetness and the enthusiasm of a little boy who pretended to be Marvin Gaye to his sister's Diana Ross, and sang his heart out even though he couldn't.

'Perfect!' she said, as she dropped the pictures to him.

'Can we?' he said, suggesting they walk around the building.

'We can try...'

They got most of the way around, then continued down Kensington Gore, to High Street Kensington, past bistros, cafes, high-street shops and little mews terraces shooting off it, past a beautiful church, until Charlie crossed them over and they stopped outside a brutalist 1960s block, with a window-walled gallery and a stretched canopy roof.

'The Design Museum?' Pete read with interest.

'We're marrying my love of beauty and your love of rocks. Well, of sorts...' Charlie laughed, pointing to a poster that read 'Make-up in Rock: from Baby Love to Bowie; Gaga to Gen Z' across a poster of stars in iconic looks spanning decades.

'Looks great,' Pete said. 'Let's do it!'

* * *

Inside, Charlie and Pete wandered the permanent Design Museum exhibition of trinkets, typewriters, logos and gadgets, marvelling at the evolution of the everyday. Items that seemed like relics from their childhood that had shaped their lives. The Fisher-Price toy telephone. The Game Boy. An iMac mouse.

In the Make-up in Rock hall they saw beauty and music merge through the ages. From The Supremes' heavily winged frosty eyes and pearlescent lips of the 1960s to Madonna, Bowie, The Cure and KISS in between.

'Ahh, here you go!' Pete said, stopping at a wall all about Rick Baker's special effects for Michael Jackson's 'Thriller' video in the eighties. 'Your inspiration?'

'He was!' Charlie said as she looked at the exhibit in awe. 'Although I should confess, my inspiration was born of necessity. Which is less cool.'

Pete looked at Charlie in profile.

'Necessity? Not your love of transformation?'

'A *need* for transformation. What I didn't say is *my* skin was so cripplingly awful...'

'Really?' Pete couldn't imagine it.

Charlie nodded.

'I feel shit about it now, given it was teen acne, and not something permanent like scarring, vitiligo, or the side effect of some terrible disease...'

'Well, you live with what you live with.'

'But yeah. I could barely live with it. I would skip school when I had particularly bad outbreaks.' Charlie didn't want Pete to think of her looking like that. 'It would hurt even to open my mouth wide enough to eat an apple. And it looked vile.'

Pete couldn't believe it. To him Charlie's skin was flawless and he wanted to reach out and smooth his thumb over her cheek.

'Make-up was my mask. My lifesaver. I actually got anxiety about it. Was scared to leave the house.'

Pete looked on in awe but was disconcertingly quiet.

'I never would have got my GCSEs if it hadn't been sorted.'

'How did you sort it?'

'I tried everything: Chinese herbs, toothpaste on my spots. I went dairy-free, I used salicylic acid and rolled ice cubes I'd frozen with green tea in them over my skin – everything!'

'So what did work?'

'Drugs, I'm afraid. Industrial ones. My parents were worried about side effects: depression, fertility...' She tailed off. 'But I was getting pretty depressed as I was, so I gave it a shot.'

'Wow, and it worked obviously.'

'Yeah, for some it doesn't. And it's not permanent. I'm lucky. My mental health improved massively, I could live a normal life. I mean, I never would have even had the nerve to look at Harry if I hadn't got my skin sorted. Luckily he started at my school soon after it cleared up.'

Pete felt a flicker of irritation.

'Trust me, Harry was the lucky one.'

They weaved their way around the exhibition, much smaller than the geology rooms at the American Museum of Natural History, but glittering all the same.

As a baby of the eighties Charlie didn't actually remember Annie Lennox made up to look masculine, Nick Rhodes in lip gloss, or Robert Palmer's 'Addicted to Love' video, but she had seen them replayed on MTV, studied them assiduously and emulated those looks on shoots, such was the timelessness of their beauty.

As they stepped out into the daylight of the gift shop, Pete thanked Charlie for the insight into her world and what inspired her.

'I don't think it's a shallow industry, you know,' he said.

Charlie looked at him quizzically.

'Sometimes you almost apologise for what you do, but you're changing lives, Charlie, starting with yours.'

Charlie thought of Jazz. She wasn't the first teen girl she had helped coax out of her shell, but she was the one who reminded her of herself. Of the woman she wished she were because Jazz had had the balls to do something Charlie hadn't. To wear her 'flaws'. 'Look at how many women and men you touch. I think that's pretty awesome.'

Charlie's cheeks really did flush now.

They wandered past a wall of postcards into the furniture area of the gift shop, filled with chairs, lampshades and plates that looked too good to hang on the wall, let alone eat off.

'I need to get some new bits for the flat,' she said, surveying the shop floor. 'Reclaim it. Not that Harry was ever really there...'

Pete followed Charlie around, his hands in his pockets.

'Oh. Wow!' Charlie said, stopping at a long lounging chair in brown, white and black cow hide.

'The Cassina LC4 chaise longue,' Pete said coolly.

'You have one?' Charlie gasped, not remembering seeing it in his apartment.

'I wish. Alexander does out West. It's more of a California recliner, with the views he and Conor have, than a tiny New York apartment thing. Most comfy chair in the world, try it!'

Charlie looked around for a shop assistant, to see if it was allowed, but Pete egged her on.

'Designed in Paris in the twenties, made to put the person it was designed for at the centre of it. The perfect marriage of ergonomics and geometry. Tilts almost upright and goes almost fully reclined.'

Charlie edged on, dropped her bag to the floor next to her and lay back. She closed her eyes. Pete looked at her face in relaxed state. Much better than the distress he had seen last night. She looked luminescent.

'It's a hug in a chair!' Charlie concluded.

'Isn't it?'

'Your brother is a lucky bastard.'

Pete nodded.

Charlie sat up and looked at the price tag.

'I think I'd better get a postcard of it...'

* * *

After the exhibition, Charlie and Pete walked back towards the West End, via Harrods on Knightsbridge to see if Aidan was free for lunch, but he'd already eaten by the time they managed to locate him in the womenswear department. Aidan attempted to chastise Charlie for doing her Phlox event at a rival store when his beauty department had been trying to secure it for months, but he loved Charlie too much to really give her grief.

'Are you going to Saph's private view tonight?' Aidan asked, leaning over a rail of Paige jeans.

Charlie looked at Pete first to check he was keen, although she wasn't going to miss it for the world. It was Saphie's first stand-alone exhibition, in the market of Covent Garden. Surely that would tick off another great tourist sight for Pete.

'Of course!' Charlie said.

'Yeah, count me in,' Pete added. He wasn't leaving until Sunday morning, and until then he was happy to be in Charlie's hands.

'I'll see you there, then,' Aidan said, looking at his watch. 'I have to dash – autumn/winter merch meeting. Typical. Warmest day of the year so far and I'm in a cupboard looking at knitwear.'

'You wouldn't have it any other way!' Charlie said with a wink as Aidan kissed her twice, kissed Pete twice, and peeled off with a wave. Charlie looked around the floor.

'Do you want to do some shopping while we're here?' she asked. 'I mean, your mum might like something from Harrods. Princess Diana was a big fan...'

'No, man, I gotta eat, I'm starving.'

'Wait a minute, you took Pete for fish and chips in *Soho* and not to the seaside?' scoffed Phil. Phil was from Scarborough, which he claimed had the best chippie in the world. He claimed Yorkshire had the best *everything* in the world: beaches, cricket, curries, fish and chips. Not that Phil ate much deep-fried food, he was too vain to. 'You could at least have taken him back up north – fish and chips in the dunes at Bolton-le-Sands. Even if it is on the wrong side of the country...' He gave Charlie a wink.

'I wish!' Charlie mused. 'But we are sort of time limited.' She gestured to the neon art lighting up the walls and railings of the Covent Garden market all around them.

For lack of a teleporter, Charlie had gone with her best option, an artfully no-frills fish and chip shop on Old Compton Street that was just the right level of downbeat to look authentic but the chequerboard floor and jukebox gave it an edge, even if it was a contrived one.

'They were good fish and chips,' Pete mumbled.

'I'm so happy this is finally happening!' Charlie said, looking around her in amazement.

Pete walked away a little, towards a neon bird. Most of Saphie's art was animal or tropical, based on time she had spent in India with Prash and his family, or on trips to South America: Indian pittas in yellow, green and turquoise; a Malabar hornbill; a hyacinth macaw in static flight halfway up a wall – that was Charlie's favourite piece, although she felt bad for Prash that it was inspired by the trip to Iguazu where Saphie had rejected his proposal.

Prash joined them with a glass of juice and shook Pete's hand.

'Lovely to meet you!' he said sincerely. 'We've heard a lot about you.'

'Thank you, great to be here!' Pete replied, bottle of beer in one hand, his other hand in his pocket as he studied the wall. 'She's so talented!'

Prash nodded proudly.

Phil turned and mouthed to Charlie.

'I. Fucking. Love. Him.'

'Who?' Charlie mouthed, although she knew who he meant.

'Both of them! But particularly yours...' he said in a stage whisper.

'Oh, stop it!'

As they watched Pete and Prash deep in conversation, Charlie noted the gentle nods of the backs of their heads, and felt so relieved that all the stars aligned. Pete was here. They had had a good day. He was soaking in her best friend's work and going to efforts to talk to her friends about it. She couldn't remember a time Harry ever supported anything Saphie did. She couldn't remember a time Harry supported much of what she did either.

Saphie's curator, Kit, chinked a fork on a glass, and Saphie reluctantly stood next to him so he could make a speech.

'Welcome, friends! Welcome, Saphie Simpson fans.'

Charlie felt Pete return to her side as they both listened, and everything felt wonderful and everything felt right.

* * *

'Let's get an Uber...' Pete said as he, Charlie, Phil and Aidan stood on the pavement outside Covent Garden Tube station.

'You guys and Uber, you're so sweet...' Phil said pointedly as he nodded to the station and said he was going that way. Aidan hugged Charlie then Pete, and said he would get the Tube too, which left Charlie standing on the pavement looking at Pete as if to say *are you sure?*

'It's easy for me to get the Tube too...' she said.

'It's fine, I'll drop you at your place and go back to my hotel. It's not a problem. Expenses and all that...'

The problem was, Charlie didn't want Pete to go back to his hotel.

* * *

It was the little touches that made her feel as if she was on the edge of something giddy. The way Pete put his hand on her back as she unlocked the downstairs door. The way their hands brushed as they walked up the stairs to her flat. The way Mabel came tiptoeing to the door to greet them and gave Pete a little mew.

All of these things conspired to give Charlie a charge she hadn't felt since she'd put her foot onto the stone step of the Makris house at midnight on New Year's Eve. A cautious voice in her head reminded her how that ended.

'Awww, Mabel, I've heard so much about you!' Pete gushed as she slumped onto her side at his feet and rolled onto her back like a diva. 'What a beauty!' he said, crouching on his haunches and rubbing her tummy at her effusive invitation.

'Wow, she likes you,' Charlie noted. 'You're allowed in, if you can get past her.' Charlie turned on lamps and went to the kitchen and the fridge. She didn't want another drink, but she offered Pete one.

'Just some water, thanks. You are gorgeous! Softest thing ever. Can I take you home with me? Can I?'

Charlie listened to Pete from the kitchen and smiled.

'How old is she?'

'She's nine now. A grande dame.'

'She's beautiful! Look at those eyes!'

'They were blue when she came to me. Blue eyes and blue-grey fur, but they changed orange in the first year.'

'They're stunning.'

'Have you ever had a cat?' Charlie called from the kitchen.

'We grew up with cats. Had three up at the house in Hudson. Zack, then Ziggy, then Smoky... But Mom and Dad never got another after Smoky died. Not sure why. And I wanted to get one when Martha and I got a place, but she's allergic.'

Charlie busied herself getting the best glasses and adding ice cubes and mint as if she always did that; straightening things and putting on the nice lights that showed her flat off best. She dragged her less flattering underwear that was drying on the clothes horse into the spare room with all her flight cases full of make-up and boxes of wigs and brushes.

Pete finally stopped stroking Mabel so he could actually walk in and take his shoes off. He looked around as Charlie handed him a glass of water.

'Thanks. May I?' He gestured to the doors of the deco balcony.

'Sure!'

She opened it for him as they carried their glasses out onto the narrow tiled balcony, and leaned over its ledge, side by side.

'Shame about the air pollution, but this is London.'

'Hey, I live on Manhattan, I'm used to it.'

'If you had longer I'd take you up to Lancashire.'

She thought about how much she would love to take him home; show him her village and the Brown cottage. Take him on the Tolkien or Sculpture Trail. Walk up Pendle Hill and kiss him at the top.

They leaned in towards each other, their foreheads drawn like the gravitational pull of a very slow magnet. Charlie looked at Pete's full lips.

'This is a really cool apartment!' he said, pulling back. Charlie felt flummoxed.

'Erm, yeah, I was lucky to buy when I did. And I could only do it on the proviso I rented out the second room, or I never would have been able to afford the mortgage.'

'Was that Saphie?'

'Yeah, the first time, before we met Prash at a retreat.'

'You're a yogi?'

'Am I fuck!' Charlie laughed as they walked back in. 'I was only in it for the dahl.'

Pete walked back inside and looked around the room admiringly. He wanted to ask if Harry had ever lived there, but he could see a photo of who he assumed was Harry with Charlie and a group of friends on the sideboard by the TV and he didn't want to bring Harry up now.

'Good job you have this place. A sanctuary.'

'That's exactly what it feels like,' Charlie said, locking the balcony doors again. 'Me and Mabel against the world!'

'I'm glad Martha and I never lived in my apartment together. We rented somewhere else before. Midtown.'

'You want to put some music on?' Charlie said, gesturing to the record player. She wanted to talk about Martha about as much as Pete wanted to talk about Harry. 'I'll get some nibbles...'

'Ahh, the Linn Sondek. Why, thank you!' he said, eyeing it appreciatively.

Pete looked through Charlie's modest vinyl collection and saw she was definitely more of an indie girl than old-school soul. Editors. Interpol. Bjork and Beck.

He ran his finger along the line, stopped at *Pearl* by Janis Joplin and remembered the car journey from Hudson back to New York.

Mabel jumped up on the sofa next to the record player as Pete took the record out of its sleeve.

'You wanna listen too?' he said, stroking the soft grey hair between her ears. Mabel let out a plaintiff mew. She didn't like it when the record player was in use. It meant she couldn't sleep on its see-through plastic lid, but Pete's soft touches made Mabel wrap her tail around herself like a ribbon and close her eyes in contented bliss on the arm of the sofa.

Charlie came out from the kitchen with a bowl of olives and another of crisps and looked at Pete stroking Mabel. He couldn't hear her there as the music had started to crackle. 'Cry Baby' began to play. It was sexy and rhythmic and it stopped Charlie in her tracks, overcome by that overwhelming urge to touch Pete again. To run her fingers up his back.

'Here you go,' she said, trying to break her febrile feelings. She put the bowls on the table. 'Snacks!'

Pete turned around. He and Charlie locked eyes again, standing frozen but for the beat of the music drawing them together, their gazes unflinching. This time their heads came together gently. Their lips met with caution, nervous not to hurt each other again, and Charlie put her hand to Pete's chest as they started to sway together. With each button she carefully unfastened, the sureness in her green eyes grew, her determination ever more resolute. When they both reached the point of certainty they nodded, and the passion and longing unleashed.

On the arm of the sofa, Mabel had fallen asleep.

37

MARCH

At 4 a.m. Pete woke up in disbelief, but felt reassured by Charlie's naked body pressing into him from behind, her hand on his thigh.

He rolled over hazily.

'You OK?' he whispered.

'Very. You?'

'Undeniably.'

They gave each other dreamy smiles and drifted back to sleep.

At 6.30 a.m. Charlie woke to Pete marvelling at her beauty, and without saying a word they had sex again until she came under the weight of his body pressed against her, and fell back asleep.

At 9 a.m. Charlie woke Pete with a question.

'Why didn't you tell me?' she asked softly.

'Why didn't I tell you what?'

'Why didn't you tell me that you'd come to see me at work? At Selfridges. Until we were back in the pub?'

'Isn't it obvious now?'

Charlie looked puzzled.

'I'd been flown over by a colleague at UCL, paid for by the Geological Society of London, to deliver a paper to a load of well-respected peers, only for me to almost blow it by running out to watch you at work for two minutes. It was quite a desperate move.'

'I wish I'd seen you.'

'It made it pretty obvious I had fallen for you. Even I realised it then.'

Charlie looked pleased with herself.

'I didn't want to freak you out again, after what happened at my parents' house...'

'Look, *I* freaked me out in Hudson. It was such a gorgeous evening. I wanted to kiss you and hold you. So much! But I didn't believe it could be possible, or healthy, given what I was going through.'

'It wasn't.'

Pete didn't say he wasn't sure if it was healthy now. He had seen traces of Harry all over the flat. He knew how long it had taken for him to get over Martha. Charlie was the first woman he'd slept with since.

'I mean, down-on-their-luck women I know don't meet gorgeous men in the back of an Uber the day they're totally broken-hearted, do they? Life isn't as seamless as that.'

'It isn't.' Pete kissed her nose. 'But looking at it from my perspective, down-on-their-luck men don't meet gorgeous, funny, talented, lovely women less than two years after they're totally humiliated and ditched at the altar, do they?'

Charlie smiled.

'Everything looks so much better now,' she declared, looking up at him looking at her, his head propped on his hand. She kissed him on the lips.

'What do you want to do today? Last day in London!' She tried not to let out a groan.

'You got blueberries?'

'Probably.'

'Then I wanna make you some pancakes, then I want to make you come again, and then I gotta get a few things from the shops.'

'Fortnum & Mason! We have to get your mum and Agata their Rose & Violet Creams, and some Chorley cakes.'

'Confession: my mom didn't really like the Chorley cakes. She was being polite.'

Charlie laughed.

'That's OK, I don't really like Chorley cakes either.'

* * *

As Pete poured batter into the frying pan he ignored the photos of Harry looking down on him from the kitchen pinboard as he dotted blueberries into each sizzling silicone circle. As he drizzled the pancakes in honey he noticed the pair of Glastonbury tickets stuck to the fridge by a magnet, making him imagine Harry and Charlie in straw trilbies. As they sat on the kitchen stools and ate their breakfast gazing into each other's eyes, Pete tried to shut out the photo-booth-style picture of Harry and Charlie next to the council tax bill over Charlie's shoulder, Harry in blue Kanye-style shutter shades and Charlie in a red wig.

And when he carried her, bare legs wrapped around him, into the living room and onto the dining-room table, then the sofa, he tried to ignore the group photo by the TV, with Harry's arm slung around Charlie's neck.

'Best. Breakfast. Ever,' she said afterwards, looking intently into his eyes.

'Best tour guide ever.' He laughed. 'You have definitely taken me places I've never been.'

They kissed again and laughed.

'Although I think next stop needs to be the shower,' Pete said, lightly turning towards his armpit. 'Yeah, I definitely need to shower...'

Their tired limbs resisted sex again in the shower but they did wash each other, Charlie examining every mole on Pete's shoulders. Pete loving how Charlie's wet lashes made her eyes glisten. He remembered the sun bursting through the large windows of the museum at Ellis Island, highlighting them and making his heart stop.

Charlie got out of the shower so she could get ahead with her hair and make-up, while Pete stayed in a bit longer to let it all sink in.

'I need to go back to my hotel, get some clean clothes,' Pete said as he rubbed his hair with one towel while another was tied at his waist. Charlie looked at him from the reflection in the make-up mirror of the spare room. He was definitely buffer than she ever would have imagined under all those New York layers. His soft demeanour belied him.

She felt a pang of sadness that they had less than twenty-four hours together, and she didn't want to spend a single one of those hours apart.

'There are some spare clean ones in there...' She pointed to the long thin Ikea wardrobe on her left. 'Middle drawer down.'

'Really?' Pete grimaced. 'Harry's, right?'

Charlie was surprised by the look on his face.

'Oh, yeah, bad idea. It's just he didn't take everything to New York...' she said sheepishly.

'I don't want to wear your ex-boyfriend's ex-smalls, if that's OK.'

'Oh, some of them are new!' Charlie said helpfully. 'Still in their packet. He just never...'

Pete didn't ask why Charlie still had some of Harry's underwear, old or new, but gently shook his head.

'Too weird.'

'Can you go commando? Get some in Primark or M&S when we're out?'

'OK.' Pete shrugged, considering his options. He was acutely aware of the ticking clock too. He had to be at London Luton airport, wherever the hell that was, for a flight to Catania at the godawful time of 6.05 a.m. tomorrow. And although Dirk had kindly booked him a car for 4 a.m., and he could sleep on the plane, he also knew that every second was precious.

38

Charlie and Pete looked like any other happy couple out shopping on a Saturday afternoon, fingers interlaced as they walked down Regent Street, stopping at Penhaligon's, the Apple store and Hamleys, to get gifts for sisters, nephews and Agata's baby, who was now a week overdue. Nestling into each other, giving each other little kisses while they waited in queues to pay. It was a strange and heady mix. Both felt the most blissful concoction of excitement and newness they had in their lifetime; both had a pit of dread in their stomach that they were on borrowed time.

They happily ate sandwiches on the go, and kissed again when they remembered all that they had learnt about each other in the past twenty-four hours. If it was weird it didn't feel it, until a flash of a moment in the queue in Fortnum & Mason, when Pete gave Charlie his credit card and he ducked out to make a phone call.

'I'll meet you outside,' he said as he looked at his watch.

Charlie waited, tapped his card and paid for his souvenirs, a slight sick feeling lingering beneath the joy.

'Everything OK?' she asked five minutes later as she joined him on the pavement outside. They were facing Burlington House and the Royal Academy in the sunshine. The view from the other side of the street. Three nights ago seemed like a very long time ago.

'Yeah, great,' Pete said. 'I just gotta do a couple of things.'

'Can I do them with you?'

'No,' he said cryptically.

'Oh.'

'I gotta go pack my stuff up,' he said. 'It's such an early start tomorrow.'

Charlie couldn't hide the disappointment in her face.

'It's OK,' Pete said, leaning to kiss her lips again, but Charlie didn't respond. 'You go home, and I'll pick you up, at seven? Take you for dinner somewhere, I'll sort it. We can come back to my hotel. If you want to.'

That was what Charlie was hoping. If Pete was leaving at 4 a.m., she wanted maximum time with him. There would be time to lie in his hotel bed and cry after he'd gone, but she didn't want an enforced two-hour break from him now, on what might be their last day together.

Maybe he needed some space. She didn't want to freak him out. It had all happened so quickly.

'OK.' She nodded, forcing a cheery smile. 'I'll go and make myself look Dinner Date Awesome.'

'You already do.'

They kissed under the blue and gold clock, and this time Charlie's lips met his again as two figurines dressed in red frock coats and green breeches exited the machinery above them, as if they were blessing this exciting new union with a salute. Charlie and Pete looked up and laughed.

'It's five. I'd better go,' Pete said, with slight fluster. 'What do you fancy eating? I saw a nice couple of places on Charlotte Street I can check out.'

'I don't care,' Charlie said. 'I would happily just eat in your hotel room.'

'I'll fix something and come pick you up.'

He looked at his watch. 'I gotta go. See you at seven!'

Charlie watched Pete disappear into the crowd of Saturday evening shoppers on Piccadilly. She had two hours to go and make herself look her Most Fucking Awesome because she did not want this to be her last night on earth with Dr Pete Makris.

39

Charlie put an Arcade Fire record on, ran a bath and luxuriated in it, easing her limbs and shaving her legs in disbelief. She hadn't had sex in over six months – *no, nine!* – she thought as she soaked her tired body. She certainly hadn't expected to have so much passionate, tender sex in one night (and morning), with a man she didn't know until Christmas Eve. Until Harry stood her up. *Fucking Harry.*

How dare he infiltrate her headspace now? She tried to push the thought of him out of her mind as she lathered up and glided the razor up her calf. She wanted tonight to be wonderful. She pondered her look. Khaki jumpsuit slathered in delicate gold chains; smoky eyes. A pop of colour with some acid violet heels. 'Sprawl II (Mountains Beyond Mountains)' came on and lifted Charlie like a call to arms. This was definitely music she could get ready to, which was rudely interrupted by a rapping on her flat door.

Shit, she thought, trying to ignore it, except whoever was at the door would know she was in because of the music. Perhaps it was her neighbour knocking to complain. The knuckles rapped again.

'For fuck's sake!' Charlie said, getting out of the bath with suds stuck to her calves. She pulled her Liberty print dressing gown off the back of the bathroom door, wrapped a towel around her hair, and padded out to answer the front door. She hoped it was her female neighbour rather than an Amazon delivery guy who had got through the front entrance, although they never bothered to come up three flights of stairs.

'I'm coming!' Charlie hollered as impatiently as the person at the door, as she took the chain off and opened it with a gasp. The record ended, the needle crackled in its repetitive groove, and suddenly everything stopped.

40

'Harry?' The force of the blow Charlie felt to her stomach almost made her fall back, but she secured her dressing gown as tightly as she could and gripped the door handle for support. 'What are you doing here?'

Harry stood looking shattered and sheepish. The collar on his black knee-length coat turned up as if to point to his ruddy cheeks.

'Hello,' he said quietly.

'What the he—?'

Charlie wanted to extend her arms out and rage at him like a windmill, but Harry already looked broken.

'My mum died.'

'What?' Charlie said breathlessly, her hands now to her mouth. She stepped back to let Harry in but Harry almost fell onto her, so she extended her arms and took him in them. Over his shoulder stood a lonely, neat wheelie case with its handle upwards on the landing.

Charlie inhaled the familiar scent of Hugo Boss and hair pomade and tried to gently release Harry but he sobbed into her collarbone, gasping for breath like a lost child who had just been found. Charlie kept her arms around him, the familiarity of the shape of him filling her with comfort and confusion.

'I'm so sorry,' she kept repeating, stroking her hand up and down his back as he cried.

After a few minutes Harry came up from their clinch and Charlie pressed her palms to his cheeks, so torn between wanting to prop him up and wanting to punch him. All she could think was to be practical.

'Sit down, bring your case in, I'll get you a tea.'

'Mabel!' Harry said as he saw her curled up on the sofa. He wheeled his case in, propped it by the TV and slumped down next to the cat, who got straight up and padded into the kitchen to see what Charlie was doing.

'Good girl,' Charlie whispered, kneeling and stroking Mabel's cheek, glad the sisterhood was still strong in her sphere.

While Charlie made the tea and the record continued to crackle with every revolution, Harry sat back on the sofa and clicked the TV on with the remote. Joyful Saturday night telly that had no time for death, duplicity or desertion. Charlie looked at the kitchen clock and put some cat biscuits out for Mabel while the tea brewed and pulled herself together. She rewrapped and tightened the belt of her dressing gown, conscious of her nakedness underneath.

'I made you a green tea,' she said as she walked back into the living room clutching two mugs, wondering what Harry thought of the flat as he looked around the room. Not much had changed to look at. Saphie's neon macaws still hung above the TV. Mabel still clearly didn't use the bed Charlie had bought for her almost a decade ago. A clothes horse hung in the spare room. Harry wouldn't know that Charlie's life had changed enormously in the past twenty-four hours from his view from the spot on the sofa.

For half a second, Charlie felt a pang of guilt, but it soon evaporated as she placed his green tea onto the arm of the sofa, and took her mug of milky builder's tea to the table. She pulled out a chair, sat down, and primly crossed her legs.

'How did it happen?' she asked, hugging her mug. 'Was it to do with the stroke?'

A fleeting flash whisked across Harry's face, not knowing how Charlie knew about the stroke, but he was too consumed to go into that right now, and talked openly.

'They think so. It was a heart attack, but apparently Mum was at higher risk of having one after the stroke, and she'd had a few little mini strokes that were never picked up.'

He sat forward and leaned his elbows on his knees as he soothed his face with his hands. Harry, who had always had a young face, suddenly looked older, in the realisation that life wasn't always going to be kind to him.

'When did it happen?'

'Thursday night here. Thursday lunchtime. I got a call from Lawrence at my desk to tell me.'

'Shit.'

'I've come straight from Heathrow, been flying what feels like all day. I'm going up to Lancaster tonight. My train leaves Euston in a couple of hours, but I had to see you first.'

'What time is it?' Charlie panicked, craning her head to look at the clock on the wall.

'Shit.'

Six-twenty. Dinner Date Awesome was fast going down the pan.

'Look, I'm really sorry, but I have plans to go out – so I have to dry my hair and get changed, you can't really wait here…'

Now wasn't the time for retribution. Harry's mum had just died and the clock was ticking on her time with Pete. She just wanted to get ready. Like most arrogant cheating boys, Harry was going to get away with it.

'I want you back,' he said, looking rigid and flushed on the sofa.

Charlie stopped towel-drying her hair.

'What about Isabelle?'

Harry's face went terribly pink.

'We broke up.'

Charlie sighed. She was too broken herself for this. Her first instinct was to wonder where she had left her phone – probably steaming by the bath – so she could have a quick look at the Instagram accounts she had become so familiar with, to see whether he was lying again. Although she realised he never had actually lied to her.

Harry was always so terrified of being seen as the bad guy, of people hating him, that he wouldn't lie when he was hurting someone, he would just go underground. At uni when he first cheated on her, she didn't hear from him for a fortnight when they used to talk most nights; when she had the abortion and he went skiing with work and switched his phone off as she lay on the bathroom floor. When she arrived in New York. Harry was so frightened of confrontation, of being a disappointment, he would just go off grid. How he had lied to Isabelle about not being with Charlie was a mystery, but perhaps she was so neatly tucked away in London, and so busy with her work, that she was easy to compartmentalise in his head. He just didn't have the courtesy to let Charlie know.

His declaration now, however, must have been terribly uncomfortable for him and untrue to type. He was going to have to confront his nefarious nature and lies. But then grief had a funny way of turning behaviours on their head. Charlie almost felt sorry for him.

'Oh,' was all she had the energy to say. 'Look, I *have* to get ready—'

Harry stood grandly, like Westlife getting up for the big key change.

'I'm so fucking sorry, Babycakes. I freaked out.' He looked pleadingly at her while Ant and Dec chirruped. 'I've done a lot of soul searching.'

The volume of the TV, the abrupt end to her bath and her music, the shock of seeing Harry's face were all starting to irritate Charlie beyond measure but she had to park it. And she had to get ready.

'You've changed?' she said flatly.

'I've changed. I've had an epiphany.'

'Really? Because that was a shitty thing to do. I have never been treated so badly, by anyone, ever. And I would never treat anyone like you did me. You were meant to have my back.'

'I know!' he begged.

She felt hot and angry as she remembered their baby on the bathroom floor.

'Wasn't the first time either, was it?'

'I'm so sorry, Charlie. Losing Mum has made me realise...'

'You only lost her two days ago, Harry.' The barb in Charlie's voice sent a shock to his heart and raised another pang of guilt in Charlie.

'And all I've thought about in the past two days is you. How great we were together, how you were my right arm.' Mabel walked past and looked at Harry with disdain.

Charlie looked at Harry with a sigh and realised she didn't want to cut his balls off any more, she just wanted to get dressed, to dry her hair, and to put on her make-up. Her armour. She felt so vulnerable and exposed right now, but knew she had to cut through his bullshit and get where she needed to be.

'Look, I must get ready,' she said as patiently as she could. It was 6.30 p.m. She didn't want to have this conversation now and she definitely didn't want to have it mostly naked. 'Just give me a minute.'

'Anything,' Harry said as he slumped back down, throwing his coat on the arm of the sofa and loosening his shirt.

Mabel followed Charlie into the bedroom through the open crack in the door and Harry kicked his shoes off, turned the TV up even more while he tried to pop his aeroplane ears, and decided to grab a beer. He needed a beer.

In the kitchen Harry rummaged in the once-familiar fridge, took out a bottle and gave a cursory glance through the slightly open door at Charlie in her underwear as he walked back.

A studio audience howling with laughter almost drowned out the sound of a gentle knock on the flat door.

Harry padded across the living room to open it, beer in hand, to a flustered man, with dark eyes and a trickle of sweat running down one temple.

'Oh, hey...' said the man, out of puff. 'Is Charlie there?'

Harry flushed again, slightly thrown by a man with a New York accent when he'd just got back to Finchley.

Pete recognised Harry from the photos on the pinboard, the fridge, the sideboard. Photos he thought it was weird Charlie hadn't taken down. He had removed every trace of Martha's face from his life.

Harry gave his most bashful public schoolboy look and ruffled the top of his hair.

'Erm, she's a bit indisposed at the moment...' he said, looking pleased with himself. 'In the bedroom... getting dressed,' he added with a wink.

Oh, Harry could lie. He was very good at it, it turned out.

'Harry!' Charlie bellowed from the bedroom. 'Can you play

with Mabel? She's clawing at my dressing gown! I have to get my clothes on. Fast!'

Pete's olive features turned to ash as he peered over the shoulder of the man who clearly wasn't going to let him in. Behind him he saw the dining table and beyond that, through a chink in the bedroom door with a coat slung over it, the bare knees and ankles of Charlie rushing about.

'I don't want to get caught...' she added.

'Shall I relay a message?' Harry asked quietly and helpfully. 'Are you a delivery driver?'

Pete looked at his feet. He felt a familiar feeling of humiliation and heartbreak careering through his body from his little toe up to his throat until he thought he might be sick.

'OK, I'll just, erm... Tell Charlie I called. I was obviously early.'

'And your name?'

'She knows it.'

Pete turned and hurried down the stairs, two at a time, before slinking out onto the road and walking as fast as he could to the Tube.

Harry quietly closed the door and took a swig from his bottle.

'Harry!' Charlie called. 'Shake a toy for Mabel, will you? I don't want to get caught on her claws!'

Harry looked around the flat for a toy.

'My jumpsuit is silk and she's wanting to play!'

'Sure thing. Mabel!' he shouted, in an old-familiar call, as he waved a feathered stick with a bell on the end. Mabel came padding out of the gap in the bedroom door and chased the stick, which Harry twirled absent-mindedly as he slumped back down and watched the TV. 'Good girl.'

'And can you turn that down? It's so friggin' loud! Or turn the record over, will you?'

Harry had never dared touch the record player while he lived there, so he wasn't going to now. He turned Ant and Dec down and thought about the man at the door. Thought about the outrage that simmered inside him, that he had to keep in check.

'Look, Harry...' Charlie said, coming out of the bedroom in a khaki silk jumpsuit, threading thin gold loops through her ears. 'We need to talk, but now isn't the time. You're in shock, I'm in shock. And there is so much to unpick. And... and I'm on my way out.' She walked across the living room to Saphie's old room, now her make-up and wardrobe, to get the almost-neon lilac heels out of their box.

'Where are you off to?' Harry asked nervously as she whisked past. 'You look beautiful.'

Charlie came out of the spare room, clutching the heels, and put them on the floor next to the chair, where she looked into a portable mirrored light so she could do her make-up. She'd have to forgo the nails, she was running out of time.

'On a date, actually.'

'Oh. Well, I hope it doesn't change any considerations you might have about me. About us. About giving us another go. There are certainly no hard feelings from me...'

No hard feelings?

'Harry, I just can't process any of this at the moment.' She looked in the mirror on the table and hurriedly lined her eyes with a smoky grey smudge. Behind the mirror she could see the blurred naked bodies of her and Pete entwined in the shower. She remembered how beautifully the day had started.

Deep breath.

Charlie paused, her eyeshadow brush balanced between her thumb and forefinger, and turned around.

'I'm really – really – sorry about Clarissa. I can't imagine what you're going through.'

Harry looked down at his socks. 'But you fucking broke me, Harry,' Charlie said, as kindly as she could.

Harry quietly took another sip of beer.

'I've tried to move on.'

Harry sighed.

'I get it. You have every right to be angry.'

'Damn fucking right I do!' Charlie spat, shocked by the venom she felt, how bitter she sounded. She didn't want any of that right now.

'Well, can I just hang here while you wait for him?'

'Er...' Charlie didn't want Pete and Harry to meet. If Harry instilled the same feelings in Pete that Martha had in her – before Charlie even knew what she had done – it wouldn't be great.

'Finish my beer... have a snuggle with Mabel? My train isn't until nine, so I thought I'd kick about here before I head to Euston.'

Charlie reluctantly conceded, thinking she had five minutes to come up with a plan.

'How's your dad doing?'

'Not great. You know he doesn't talk about his feelings at the best of times.'

Henry Taylor was anal. Worried about appearances. Always kept a stiff upper lip and put on a brave face.

The apple doesn't fall far from the tree.

Except none of Harry's faces looked brave. Harry Taylor was more about saving face.

Charlie finished with a hurried plump of peachy pink lips and went to find her phone in the bathroom. She begrudgingly let the curtailed bath water out before returning to the table, where she continued to check her make-up was *just so*. Harry had made her rush it.

She fired off a message.

Text me when you're downstairs, I'll come down x

Two blue ticks and no answer.

The comfort with which Harry sat there drinking Charlie's beer and watching her TV irked her.

His mum's just died.

She focused on her corner lashes, slathering them with her favourite mascara.

Go easy on him.

As 7 p.m. came and went, Charlie kept anxiously glancing at her phone. In the few times they had rendezvoused, Pete had never kept her waiting. He was never late.

Charlie hovered over her phone to see if he was typing. Harry kept his eyes firmly on the TV.

In the ad break, a trailer for *Triple-A Talent* came on – loud and shouty and adding to the noise in her head, even though she was grateful for the distraction. From Harry's loss and declaration, from the feeling of dread in the pit of her stomach that Pete was going to Not Turn Up the way Harry had Not Turned Up.

'That's what I've been working on, the past couple of months,' Charlie said, nodding towards the screen, although she didn't think Harry should be privy to all she had been up to.

'Oh, right,' he said, mind elsewhere.

Charlie told Harry that it was awful. That Bree Blackwood had even got a job on it. That she was meant to be going to the watch party for the launch show at the Charlotte Street Hotel tomorrow but couldn't bear to. She wondered why she was wittering at him and telling him, sharing parts of her life when he hadn't her, but she figured it was easier than the other elephants in the room.

'Cool,' he repeated, unconvincingly.

'Well, it wasn't really, but it was an outlet, a distraction.'

Harry looked boyishly sheepish, as if he were charming, and changed the channel, as if he'd never gone to New York. As if the past nine months hadn't happened.

Charlie looked at her phone: 7.15 p.m. She texted Pete again, to check he wasn't waiting downstairs.

I mean, I'm sort of glad you're late because I needed to get my face on, but this is most unusual Dr Makris...

One tick. Two ticks. Both blue. No answer.

Charlie felt a discomfort in the depths of her stomach. The clock was ticking, but with it lurked the familiar bleakness of being dumped. Harry was cutting into precious minutes of a night she could feel slipping away from her.

She looked at her watch again. Seven thirty. Her hair looked amazing. Her make-up was perfect.

'Mind if I grab another beer?' Harry asked, halfway to the kitchen. 'Do you want one?'

Charlie shook her head and stood up, pacing up and down between her bedroom and the balcony like a panther, waiting for Harry to leave the kitchen before going in and getting herself a tin of Pimm's from the fridge to steady her nerves. The cold bubbles fizzed in her mouth.

'Why?' she finally snapped.

'Well, I-I-I,' he bumbled, 'I sort of need a drink after the flight, before I see my family...'

'*Why?*' she snapped louder. 'Why didn't you have the courtesy to tell me you had hooked up with a billionaire's daughter?

Why didn't you tell me you'd brought Isabelle to the UK? Why did you sneak around London? *Why the fuck* did you let me get on a plane to New York and put me through that utter humiliation?'

Harry slumped back into 'his' side of the sofa with a look of horror and pain, but such was Charlie's agitation, she didn't actually care that Clarissa had just died. He'd treated her appallingly before his mother had died.

'Babyc—'

'Don't call me that disgusting name!'

Harry looked stunned.

'You made a total idiot of me! You actually put me in a dangerous situation. I was alone, all night, in New York! Wandering around the airport in distress. In a place I didn't have any friends or family. Why? Why would you do any one of those things to me, let alone all of them? Just because you couldn't tell me the truth. Are you that much of a coward?'

Harry held his bottle between his knees and put his hands to his face, groaning again.

'I just don't know. The thought of hurting you made me feel sick. I just couldn't bring myself to tell you.'

Charlie was furious.

'So you'd rather I felt the pain of *not* knowing. The worry I was going through about whether *you* were OK? The pain of walking around New York in the days after, on my own?'

She thought of Pete again.

Where the fuck is he?

She didn't even care if Pete walked into the flat right now. He would be by her side, as he had been in New York. He might even do her a favour and throw Harry out.

She looked at her phone again, which she clutched like a grenade, desperately hoping Pete hadn't done to her what Harry had. He'd seemed shifty and desperate to get away from her outside Fortnum & Mason. After his mystery phone call.

She looked at her phone again. He'd read her messages and not replied.

Sometimes, I'm even a little early.

Then it hit her.

No hard feelings.

How the fuck dare he? Grief or not.

Can I just hang here while you wait for him?

A tingling in her fingers and the condensation on the can made Charlie drop her Pimm's.

'How did you know Pete was coming to the flat?'

Harry ruffled his hair.

'Beg your pardon?'

'How did you know I was waiting for him here? Or indeed that it was a guy. I just said I was going on a date.'

Harry's ruddy cheeks flushed red and he pushed his hair upwards as he spread back on the sofa, doing that 'bashful schoolboy' look Charlie had fancied when he was a schoolboy. Now it had all the hauntings of an arrogant, dangerous man.

'Umm...'

There he went. Incapable of admitting his failings.

Charlie opened the flat door and ran down the stairs in her bare feet. The road beyond the mansion's door was busy with Saturday night life. People going about their business. Plans and bustle and excitement. A huge box lay next to the communal door with a bow on it and a Sharpie scrawl she recognised from the magazine cover in the Uber in New York. Harry and Meghan's foreheads. This time it said:

To Charlie, Love Pete x

'What the hell?'

Charlie ran back up the three flights of stairs to her flat.

'Was he here?' She scrunched up her face and pointed her finger at Harry, who stood up. 'An American man? Did he knock?'

Harry pushed the collar of his rugby shirt up.

'Calm down, Charlie, you're getting hysterical.'

'Was he here?'

Charlie stared at Harry's face, floundering for something to say, weak when faced with confrontation. And then she realised why Harry always went to ground. He couldn't lie to her. She knew him too well. He was too terrified of not being adored; of the reality of the crushing disappointment he was to people. It was written all over his face.

She took a deep breath, wheeled his case to the stairs, pushed it down the first flight, and lowered her voice.

'You absolute piece of shit, Harry. Get out. Now.'

* * *

Charlie grabbed her blazer and left the neon heels by the chair in favour of her Vejas so she could run to the Tube, where she sat, eyes prickling as she looked at the photos on her camera roll. The ones she had put a love-heart tag on without realising why. Pete outside the Royal Albert Hall with his hands in his pockets. Pete and Prash chatting at Saphie's launch. Pete from the side on their ghost walk, raising one eyebrow at the tour guide's questionable spiel. Him leaning thoughtfully over the Staten Island ferry. Then she saw the only photo she had of them together was from the boat on New York harbour. The golden hour lighting their smiles; Manhattan glittering behind them.

Fucking Harry, she cursed. Harry had led her to Pete, and now had possibly pushed him away, although she knew she could explain it all if she could just look him in the eye. She thought about the selfie of them on his phone outside BAFTA that he never got round to sending her.

She looked at her last two texts to Pete: they made her sound so complicit, she groaned.

Jesus.

At Bond Street Charlie got off, and rather than run up and down escalators from the Jubilee to the Central Line, she went to street level and darted between the last of the shoppers; past Oxford Street Tube station; past the shops closing up after a busy day. Charlie's feet fell clumsily, her breath weary. Her heart raced as the skyscraper of Centre Point at one end of Oxford Street pulled her in, and she turned left up Tottenham Court Road and darted onto Great Russell Street to Pete's hotel, where she had to put her palms on the wall outside to catch her breath.

'Dr Pete Makris,' she said to the receptionist between puffs. 'Can you put a call in to his room, please?'

'Just one second,' said an efficient-looking woman with a French accent and a shiny ponytail.

She typed into a system, looked at the screen, then nudged the man next to her and pointed to something.

'Is that correct?' she said under her breath.

The man turned his back on Charlie as if he were a judge conspiring with the local parish councillors to choose the winning pumpkin at a village fete.

'Very good.' The woman nodded.

She looked back at the screen and then to Charlie after measuring her face.

'I'm so sorry, Dr Makris checked out this afternoon.'

'No, he didn't!' Charlie scowled. 'Come on!'

'Yes, I'm afraid he did,' the woman said in a neat voice.

'Please, can you tell him Charlie is in Reception. And it's not what he thinks.'

The woman paused as if she were considering it.

'I would, because I am a fan of *le romcom*, but he isn't here I'm afraid. He check out.' Her male colleague walked away, busying himself and avoiding eye contact.

Charlie frowned at the woman and held her gaze for a second.

'For fuck's sake!' she shouted up to the ceiling, before looking around the lobby and wondering what his room number was, if he were still there, but the woman was clearly not going to tell her.

'Is there anything else I can help you with?'

'No.'

Charlie went to the bar area and called Pete's mobile, but he didn't pick up, so she sent another message.

That was Harry. And I don't know what he said, but don't believe it. He's a liar and a shit and I am so, so sad. Please let me see you. I have to see you. I'm in your hotel bar Cx

The ticks didn't turn from grey to blue this time, however much she willed them to.

'*Fuck!*' she yelled, causing the few people in the bar to look round at her in alarm as she walked out.

* * *

Charlie decided to walk up and down Charlotte Street, whose restaurants were buzzing with couples, families and groups of friends, on tables spilling out onto the pavements, high on London life in spring. Pete still needed to eat, surely? She traipsed up and down in her silk jumpsuit, hair askew as she peered in the windows to see if a beautiful lone figure was hunched over a book, eating alone at the table he had booked for two. Once she'd been up one side and down the other she did it again, this time going into every single restaurant and eatery, saying, 'I'm just checking to see if my friend has arrived...' to get past the waiter or the concierge. He wasn't anywhere.

Dejected and devastated, Charlie returned to her flat.

'Shit!' she whispered, on seeing the huge box left at an angle in the doorway. She was lucky no one had nicked it, given the downstairs door was often open. She knew she had to drag it upstairs to get it out of the way, to not piss off her neighbours, and secretly hoped one of them would hear her heaving and help. But her neighbours had better things to do on a Saturday night.

By the time Charlie had slid and heaved the box up three flights, around three corners and into her apartment, she could feel an antagonising trickle of sweat running down her spine, being soaked up by the silk of her beautiful, wasted jumpsuit. She collapsed on the sofa, kicked Harry's empty beer bottle off the table, apologised to Mabel for making her flinch, and put a record on. Janis was left out from last night. She knew putting on 'Cry Baby' would make her cry, but she had to let it out.

As she sat contemplating the box, Mabel jumped on it.

'Is that where Pete went? To get this?' she asked the cat.

Charlie had thought he was freaking out, that he needed space. But he had run off to source whatever was in the box.

Cautiously she got up, ripped one end open to have a look in, and her heart hit the floor when she saw the LC4 Cassina chair, tag still on it from the Design Museum shop.

Charlie took her make-up off, curled up on her bed, and cried harder than she had ever cried for Harry, before falling into a deep, unsatisfactory sleep.

41

MARCH

'He's gone, Jazz. I blew it.'

'Gone? Who?'

'Gone. Left London. Left the country. Italy maybe. Maybe home. He won't answer my calls or emails. I'm screwed.'

'Who's gone?'

'Pete. A man I met in New York. Who I thought I couldn't possibly fall for but I have.'

'I knew something was weird with you!' Jazz said, defiantly.

'It's all mad, but he came over to London, and we got together on Friday night, but Harry rocked up and—'

'Wait, what? You hooked up with another guy?' Jazz sounded delighted.

Charlie was walking towards Charlotte Street as she spoke to Jazz on her phone, still hyper vigilant and looking left and right, *just in case.*

She explained what had happened, about her pact with a stranger from New York, who she had fallen for, in as succinct a way as possible.

'Oh, mate!' Jazz said.

Jazz did get the lead in the Lorca play, and for the past month had been holed up in rehearsals ready for the big opening in the summer.

'What do I do?'

'You're asking me what to do?' Jazz almost choked. 'You're the person I want to be when I grow up!' Jazz declared.

'Me?' Charlie stopped in her tracks and pulled into the doorway of a Turkish restaurant. 'But you have more self-respect in your little finger than most people my age – of any age – I know.'

'Me? Fuckin' hell, Charlie.'

'Yeah, you. I often think: *what would Jazz do?* It's sort of why I didn't tell you what was going on. You would have made me face the bleeding obvious with Harry.'

'Wow.' Jazz went quiet, and Charlie thought she could hear groans in the background.

'Oh, hang on,' Charlie said. 'Is this a bad time?'

'I'm just rehearsing.'

'On a Sunday night?'

'Yeah, sort of off-script... Turns out my oppressive husband in the play – Jack IRL – is quite wonderful off stage.'

'Oh God, I'm so sorry!' Charlie said, half laughing and half blushing as she pictured Jazz being taken from behind by an Andalucian farmer. 'I'll leave you to it. I'm so sorry!'

'Hey, don't sweat. But you know what? Sounds like crossed wires more than anything. We all retreat when we're hurting, eh? I've not been in love but that much I know. Hang in there. He'll be in touch. Or go back to New York and find him! What's an ocean?'

Charlie wasn't sure if she could put herself through that again.

'Look, do you want me to get rid of Jack? I can come meet you?'

'Oh, thank you – you're the best, but I've got to go into a screening anyway.'

'What is it?'

'Oh, that shitshow I worked on. It's on air at 6 p.m. Don't worry. You work on your chemistry anyway with – what's his name? Jack?'

'Yeah, it's going to be something else. We'll watch your show in bed.'

'Don't, it'll be a buzzkill.'

'Love you.'

'Love you more. Sorry to disturb.'

And with that, Charlie didn't say goodbye as she hung up and walked under the sage-green candy-stripe awning, through the glass doors of the hotel.

* * *

'Right, so, guys, I want to start a feminist debate about OnlyFans. I'm thinking of going on it.'

Here we go.

Even before Charlie walked into the private screening room in the basement of the Charlotte Street Hotel, she could hear Bree's low and privileged voice dominating the room.

Urgh.

She was not in the mood for Bree.

Charlie waved hi to her colleagues and Eva came over and gave her a hug and a pornstar martini while Bree continued her monologue about why she thought people should be paying for her content.

Charlie pondered Bree's content. Last week she had posted about the untimely death of a popstar and how #tragic it was. Charlie remembered Bree hating the popstar when she was a contestant on *Look Who's Dancing!*, the series Bree worked on it, and it reminded Charlie how Bree had done this before. When a celebrity died too young, of cancer, suicide or some other tragedy, Bree would clearly go through her camera roll or search on Getty

Images, scrabbling to find a photo of them together asap. So she could post as quickly as she could and claim they were great friends, even if they weren't. It made the story about her again, claiming ownership of someone who had died tragically – she revelled in it *more* if they died tragically. It got her traction.

'I'm really interested in this,' Tabitha said. 'My friend does foot fetishes on OnlyFans, makes a killing.'

Lauren, the executive producer, was milling around like the host, making sure Charlie and anyone else who came in after her – the judges, videographers, floor manager and gaffer – had a welcome cocktail in hand. She had two kids back at home she would rather be watching *Triple-A Talent* with, but had to show willing for the launch.

'But what about the patriarchy taking twenty per cent?' Lauren asked.

'What's OnlyFans?' asked Patrick, a sound engineer.

'Porn and fetishes by subscription,' Tabitha helpfully explained, and Patrick started to sweat. 'You film and own your content and upload it, then people subscribe and engage. Some sex workers find it really empowering... but it can be a dark place,' she added nervously.

'And the patriarchy takes twenty per cent,' Lauren restated.

'No one would want to see my feet,' Charlie mused. She thought of her abandoned pedicure last night. How she just wanted to see Pete.

'The dichotomy is, I'm massively underpaid in this industry,' Bree bemoaned.

Where's the dichotomy? Charlie thought.

Lauren shot Bree a look. She had employed her for *Triple-A Talent*, and it wasn't prudent to bite the hand that fed you, but Bree hadn't noticed and continued to hold court, talking about herself *all the fucking time.* 'I mean, there's a bit of a dichotomy there, isn't there?'

Charlie looked over at Lauren.

'I post loads of sexy pictures to my Insta, I'm comfortable with my body, why not monetise it, even if I am willing to let The Man take twenty per cent?'

No one cared, except for Tabitha, who didn't think Bree understood what happened on OnlyFans. Most of her friends on it – foot fetishists aside – were filming themselves having sex: with their partners, strangers, or 'content creators' they had met through OnlyFans. One straight friend joked that he was 'gay for pay', but Tabitha had seen the sadness behind his glint when the laughter stopped. They seemed more miserable than empowered.

'What's that about sexy pictures?' asked Ryan, the *Triple-A Talent* host, as he walked in and air-kissed Lauren. 'Not guilty!' he said with a wry chuckle. Bree shot him a look.

'Great! Do it!' Charlie said, knowing Bree didn't really want a feminist debate, she only wanted to hear what she wanted to hear.

Bree looked a little confused, and fiddled with the heel of one stiletto while she leaned on the arm of a cinema seat.

'Bree wants to join OnlyFans, for a side hustle,' Lauren said. Ryan widened his eyes.

'Yah, I'm just fed up of the endemic abuse of women, of men making money from women. Of treating women in the workplace like shit.'

'But the patriarchy take twenty per cent...' Lauren said again, flatly.

Bree's very chic, very high stiletto was starting to smart her heel.

'Tabs, be a poppet, will you, and nip to Boots on TCR? I need some plasters.'

Tabitha wondered if Bree would have spoken to her like that if she still identified as Toby, and, crestfallen, went to get her bag.

'Sure thing, which sort?'

Ryan and Lauren exchanged a look. More people entered: a sound engineer, production coordinator and key grip.

'Not Minions or branded ones – unless they're D&G...' Bree chortled.

As Tabitha headed out of the door, Charlie gave her a smile.

'I'm not sure Boots is still open, Tabs,' she said. Tabitha shook her head in defeat and conceded to missing her first ever launch show. She had to try, even if it meant traipsing to find a chemist open on a Sunday evening.

'I just see it as a fuck-you to the patriarchy, making filthy men pay me to get off on my content.'

'While also lining their pockets.'

'Girl gotta have a side hustle when she's not paid as much as the man, hasn't she?' Bree glowered at Lauren pointedly under her thick blonde fringe.

'Bree, you keep mentioning pay. Do you feel you were under-paid on this show?'

'Well, I bet I wasn't paid as much as Ryan,' she shot back.

Ryan put his hands up as if to say, *What did I do?*

'Nope, you weren't. He works across three prime-time shows for the channel, so that's unlikely. But he's not paid as much as me... because I exec-produce four.' Lauren smiled smugly. 'And none of us earn as much as the judges, because they get a shitload from all their voiceovers and advertising.'

'Hey, I lost a little bit of my soul when I did that haemorrhoid cream shoot!' said Andie, the funniest of the three judges.

'It's five to!' someone shouted. 'Turn the volume up!'

Bree realised she had lost the room, so she slunk around to

near where Charlie was sitting, and perched against the wall next to her.

'You know, I think I'm done with all this shit. Am thinking of going to the States. You went, didn't you?'

'Well, I went to New York.'

'Yuh, I'm thinking LA.'

'Of course.'

'How hard was it to get a visa?'

'Oh, I didn't go for work, I went out there to—'

'Oh, shit, yeah! You went out there and got dumped.'

'What?'

Charlie picked up her bag and gave Lauren a friendly nod as if to say she couldn't stay a second longer. She gestured to Eva chatting to Ryan across the room that she'd text her. She had to get out of there. She paused before she walked out and turned around.

'You know what, Bree...'

'What?'

'Here's a dichotomy for you: asking for a feminist debate and then shooting down any woman whose opinion doesn't fit your narrative or doesn't kiss your arse. Or making up stories, tipping off the press and then claiming you're a victim of the media. Or posting about "being kind" when you're really not very nice to people.'

'You what?' Bree looked flabbergasted.

'So what I'll say is this: if you can be anything... just *don't* be a dick.'

Charlie slung her bag over her shoulder and walked out of the stifling underground cinema room, out of the hotel and back down the street she had scoured last night without so much as a backward glance.

Charlie knew what she had to do.

42

MARCH

Under a wooden structure wrapped in grapevines, Charlie soaked up the spring sunshine through the dappled shade of the green frilled leaves. She closed her eyes, leaned back on her chair and basked. She hadn't felt such pure warmth in months, and it felt restorative after the exhaustion of her journey. Refuelling with a beer and some olives made the whole mission seem almost worth it.

I'm not there yet.

She opened her eyes and immediately narrowed them. She literally had a mountain to climb, and she stared at its smoky peak. Willing herself to be up there.

I can do this, she thought, a little bead of sweat fizzing above her top lip. She wiped it and stood up, smiled to the waiter to signal she wanted to pay, and walked over the terrace to the water's edge. Down below the Tyrrhenian Sea was gently lapping the black gravel sand.

The waiter nodded.

'*Prego.*'

Charlie rested her arms on the weather-worn woodwork of the

balcony. She felt slightly light-headed, and didn't know if it was from the latent seasickness, the mid-afternoon beer, fatigue or all of it.

Charlie had woken at 4 a.m. when her phone alarm startled her, left a shitload of food out for Mabel, and got an Uber to Luton Airport, where she looked out of the car window the entire time and wondered how Pete had seen the world twenty-four hours before.

She was so tired, she was asleep by take-off, and the soporific hum of the engine kept her under for the entire flight to Catania, which was convenient as she had to preserve her energy. After asking lots of men milling around at the airport how to get to Stromboli, she made her way to the coach bay marked Messina and onto what felt like an out-of-service fun bus from the past, eighties upholstery and all. On the road past Taormina she realised she'd heard of the place before. Ruth and Ray had been there on holiday while Charlie was at university, and she still had a postcard they'd sent in a keepsake box. The memory of the card brought comfort, even though she hadn't looked at it in years.

At the busy port town of Messina, Charlie took a hydrofoil to Lipari, where she puked most of the way from the bouncing sea as the sun glimmered on the breaking water.

Thank God I didn't do this in New York, she thought as she stood as close as she could to the front of the boat staring at the horizon, the wind giving her a medicinal reminder to take deep breaths.

'*Un'ora!*' the man at the hydrofoil stop said for the boat to Stromboli, but it was lunchtime and, now she was no longer seasick, Charlie stopped in a cafe for a *piadina* to replenish her.

As she watched scooters circle a fountain, she considered her mission: to get to Stromboli with enough time to climb the volcano and hit sunset. And hope that Pete hadn't already been and gone. Perhaps he was already on his way back; she couldn't remember when he was going to Rome, which day he was flying back to New York. All she knew was that she didn't have long.

As the passengers got off the inbound hydrofoil from Stromboli, Charlie looked at every face. Like a flickbook of people whizzing through in fluttery stop motion. Charlie's eyes darting as she checked every face that passed her as she waited in line. Pete definitely hadn't got off the hydrofoil. He wasn't there, but the sight of a few green-faced children with claggy bits of vomit in the corners of their mouths made Charlie groan again.

An hour later, the Stromboli hydrofoil approached a small island with black beaches, green olive groves, and a craggy peak, smoking gently. If she looked closely, the volcano's contours looked as if they might move, like the prehistoric muscles of a sleeping dragon, inhaling and exhaling peacefully.

Or perhaps it was the seasickness messing with her head.

'Wow!' she said, wishing she were saying it to Pete, before groaning internally, *get me off this boat.*

An old man with a scooter offered to drive Charlie to the cafe at the base of the volcano for ten euros and she took it. It was the most enjoyable leg of her interminable journey, imagining she were in a Federico Fellini or Roberto Rossellini film.

She'd settled down at the terrace bar for a quick loo stop and drink before the climb ahead, resting her weary head and tired stomach muscles.

Uber. Plane. Coach. Ferry. Hydrofoil. Scooter. Never before had Charlie taken so many modes of transport in one day. Now all she needed were her feet. Charlie knew she wasn't the strongest of athletes, but her feet hadn't let her down in New York and they wouldn't now.

'*Prego,*' a waiter with jet-black hair and bright blue eyes said as he handed Charlie her bill on a tiny silver platter. She turned around from the balcony. The smell of salt water and lemons reinvigorated her, as had the beer, she realised as she put down a ten-euro note – everything seemed to cost ten euros – slung her slim backpack on her shoulders, and set off.

* * *

The sun was lowering but Charlie started to work up a heat in a pair of apple-green capri pants she had dug out and worn with gold trainers and – foolishly – a white broderie top. As she walked through the shrubs of the lower mountain slopes, cicadas started to chirrup, a sweet alluring soundtrack to walk to. With every step Charlie took, Pete was with her. The hope of seeing him; the memory of their first encounter when she slumped into the Uber-Pool on 8th Avenue and into his world. Thoughts and memories darted in non-linear directions. How she wanted to stroke the back of his neck as they looked at a wall of photos in Ellis Island, not realising then the depth of her feelings. The power of him inside her on the dining table on Saturday morning. The look of him, flustered and flummoxed in his tux on New Year's Day.

I have to see him.

Then the anxiety hit her. A sense of desperation. Pete still hadn't read her messages. What if he had changed his plans? What if he went straight to Rome? What if he climbed Stromboli yesterday – after all, she was managing to do the hike on the day she'd travelled, on the same flight out of Luton. What if he had been and gone? What if he were planning to do it tomorrow?

Oh, God, I can't do this again tomorrow.

What if he were already halfway back to New York?

Charlie stopped and turned around, to get out of her head full of catastrophic thoughts and take in the view of the blood-orange sun dipping towards the sea. The six other Aeolian Islands dotted neatly before her like stones she had skimmed that hadn't sunk.

As she paused, halfway up, hands on her hips, to take in a slug of water, she felt her first volcanic rumbles underfoot and gasped out loud. A harbinger of something that felt like doom but she hoped beyond hope would be something wonderful.

'Cool, huh!' said a German-sounding man as he almost ran past her, overtaking her uphill like a mountain goat. He didn't wait for Charlie's reply, he too was desperate to get to the summit, and a little more physically able.

Is this even safe?

Once the sun dipped the light changed instantaneously, as if a veil had been gently laid over Charlie's sphere like a shawl dimming a light. Everything felt a little eerier.

A couple of handsome, bearded men came down the slopes, speaking Italian, supporting an older man, who was limping, an armpit over each of their shoulders. Charlie moved to the side of the dry brush path.

'Are you OK?' She thrust her phone out. 'Do you need help?'

The men each waved a hand and muttered something back in Italian as they hastened back to the village at the base. Something serious must have happened to make them abort the hike before sunset.

Charlie clutched her phone and realised she didn't have much power left on it – she hadn't charged it since 4 a.m. and had used it to navigate her way there. She would be lucky if the torch was working for the way down. She rubbed a dusty palm on her white top and realised she was most unprepared.

Half an hour later, a couple not much older than Charlie's parents headed down the mountainside, carefully sidestepping in dusty walking boots and crampons to ease their shaky knees. It gave Charlie an opportunity to pause for breath again, to step aside.

'Evening,' she said, jovially. 'Everything OK?'

The couple had tanned faces and white hair, they looked Scandinavian and wholesome, with affable smiles and silver blue eyes.

'Hallo!' the man said, watching his footing.

'Everything OK up there?' Charlie asked nervously.

'Our guide couldn't make it today and we don't feel confident to come down in the dark on our own,' the man said.

'Oh, is it dangerous?'

'It's an active volcano!' The kindly woman laughed.

'We think it might be wise to watch the eruptions from ground zero,' the man said. 'Come back with our guide tomorrow.'

Ground zero? This was starting to feel like a really bad idea.

Charlie watched them pass and knew this was probably a crossroads moment. If she went down with them she would have safety in numbers. If she carried on alone, she might be walking to disaster. This couple looked healthier, more sensible, and better equipped than Charlie. What hope did she have if they were turning around?

Her paralysis to call out to them was buoyed by her drive to get to Pete.

The Scandinavian couple continued down, and she watched them go, the rumbling ramping up underfoot. The soles of Charlie's trainers felt as if they might start to melt. Perhaps they had already – dusk was giving way and it was harder to see in the dark. She looked at her phone again: the battery was on 13 per cent. The torch would kill it on the way down, if it hadn't died already.

When the first flares burst from the crater into the sky Charlie let out a yelp. It looked like the most magical fireworks display she had ever seen, except they weren't the fireworks in the garden of the Makris family home in the Hudson Valley. This was a live volcano and Charlie was on her own.

Fuck!

Charlie almost whimpered. She had been walking for two and

a half hours, her thighs ached with fatigue and her mouth felt parched, but the summit was in sight, it was do or die now. The air got thicker, hotter and more sulphurous as Charlie's brow began to sweat. She wished she'd brought another bottle of water; that she hadn't had that beer.

As the trail curved around another corner and the rumbling and heat intensified, Charlie felt immense relief to see small blurs – people – at the top, on a ledge where tourists and their guides seemed to have gathered. She could hear voices oohing and ahhing, much like at the fireworks on New Year's Eve, which made her feel so relieved, she wanted to cry. She would get down OK. She was always OK. Her feet were reliable and strong. Whatever happened, she knew she would be OK.

* * *

Then she saw him. In the light of the lava that obscured the moon. Wearing an olive-green T-shirt that was dusty and damp in lines on his shoulder blades, where a backpack had hugged him. Set apart on his own. Head tilted up, sideways facing the crater. Mouth open in fascination.

'Pete!' Charlie called, but the rumble, the crack, and the astonished cheers drowned her out. 'Pete!' she said, louder this time.

Pete didn't hear her, but he turned around with a half-smile, as if he *knew* someone had come for him.

'Charlie?'

Pete forgot about his confusion and his hurt. He momentarily forgot the betrayal. He was so taken aback and so happy to see her, he asked the obvious question with a befuddled laugh.

'What are you doing here?'

And then he remembered and his shoulders dropped in defeat. 'It wasn't what you thought!'

'You... you *hiked* up here? On your own?'

'Well, how did you get here?' Charlie lifted her head and met his eye almost with a challenge. 'And why the hell didn't you answer my messages and let me explain?'

She saw the sad look in his forlorn eyes and realised exactly why.

Martha.

She walked towards him and set her backpack down at her feet. Another shot of sparks erupting into the air startled them and bought her some time to think of the words she'd been trying to come up with all day.

'Remember in New York, you told me—'

'What? What did I tell you?' Pete looked defeated. As if he'd been hanging on for her for ever.

'Science helps us assess the likelihood, but you and only you can act based on what you know *and* how you feel.'

The lava roared as another explosion of orange and red sparks burst into the sky, raging in their hot faces. 'You looked at a situation and you weighed it all up. But you got it wrong, Pete! You went with your emotions before getting the facts. You responded and ran.'

Pete looked almost proud of her.

'You said Harry's name in your sleep,' Pete said sadly.

Charlie scrunched up her face.

'Did I?'

Pete nodded.

'You've still got his photos all over the place...'

'I dream about Keir fucking Starmer!' she shouted, red faced. 'That doesn't mean I'm in love with the guy!'

'You were naked with him...'

Pete knew how petty he sounded now. That he should have trusted her.

'I was getting changed! I wanted to look my most awesome for *you*. He turned up out of the blue and told me his mum had died. I had to let him in. Still, all I could think about was you, and getting to you.'

Pete winced.

'The pictures, come on...' he pleaded, trying to get her to admit she was still in love with Harry. He would understand if she was. But Pete could see his argument weakening.

'That's just inertia. And because I like some of the pictures.'

'I just thought...'

'Look, I know what you thought and I realise now why you might have been so quick to think the worst. But... Mr Disaster Reaction. You got it wrong this time and I'm devastated.'

Pete looked embarrassed.

'You put the hypothesis to me!' Charlie was shouting now, against the wind and the boom, lava lighting up her eyes. '"Our response to what happens to us is more important than that which we cannot control".'

A bittersweet smile flashed across Pete's features and he hung his head, looking at his dusty boots before looking up.

'I went with what I felt and not the facts.'

'And you're the scientist!'

'I know,' he said mournfully. 'So why are you here? Taking this risk? To tell me I'm a shit scientist?'

Charlie paused.

'I'm here to thank you for the chair.'

'Oh.'

'It's beautiful, and you're too kind and too generous, and I love it.'

'Well, you're welcome.'

'And I think I love you.'

Another incandescent arc shot from the rumbling earth and lit

Charlie's face as she kept her gaze firmly fixed on Pete. She didn't know how he was going to respond. But a fact was a fact.

Pete let out a laugh that was overshadowed by a blast of sparks. This one felt dangerously close, so he crouched for cover quickly, pulling Charlie down to her haunches under his arm.

'What?' he whispered, suddenly nose to nose.

'I love you!' Charlie said, almost astonishing herself. 'Which I know is crazy.'

'Based on what you know or how you feel?'

'Both.'

The rumble subsided and they stood up slowly together, clutching each other's forearms for balance as they rose.

'I felt it in your parents' garden on New Year's Eve,' Charlie confessed. 'I felt it dancing with you on Alphabet. I even felt it in the bloody tornado simulator at the museum!'

'That *was* cool...'

'But I didn't *know* it until about 7 p.m. on Saturday. When you didn't show up.'

Pete looked at Charlie's tired and dirty face and crumpled.

'I'm so sorry, Charlie, all the shit from Martha came back and I—'

'Shhh.' She put her hand over his mouth and removed it, then slipped her arms around his waist. 'They're all ghosts, Pete: Martha, Harry, the child I will never know. And they're gone now.'

Pete nodded, and pressed his dusty forehead to hers.

'So how do we react to this?' Pete asked.

'Well, I wanted to see you and I wanted to see this. And I'm not walking down from this volcano without you.'

Pete looked at Charlie's face in as much awe as he had that moment she lowered her head and hesitated before getting into the Uber on 8th Avenue.

'Nor am I,' Pete said, and their lips met.

'At least not without a head torch anyway. Please tell me you have a spare.'

* * *

As they walked down the volcano, under the comfort of a star-spattered sky, Pete and Charlie held hands and talked. Charlie told Pete she had done something empowering in her work and walked out on a job she would never accept again. They compared journeys from London to Stromboli. Pete told Charlie that Agata had given birth this morning, to a healthy daughter named Rose Violet Brooksbank. Their sandy, dusty, shrub-strewn path was lit by the moon and Pete's head torch. And as they held hands and negotiated the path together, a small girl in red dungarees peeled away, off the volcano's edge, and slid contentedly into the sea.

EPILOGUE
DECEMBER

As Charlie Brown waited in the queue, clutching her passport, she looked among the rows of border control cops, wondering if the man who *wasn't* called Benjamin Steakhouse still worked there. And if he did, whether he might be working today. He had been one of the unexpected faces of kindness Charlie had come across in New York during that traumatic trip one year ago.

Deep breath. Trust in the universe. Trust in Pete.

Charlie looked down at her immigration form. Pete lived at 23 Leroy Street, Greenwich Village, New York, New York 10014, and his address was firmly on it. Since their kiss on the top of Stromboli they had seen each other three times: Pete came back to Europe and met Charlie for a holiday in the Greek Islands in May; Charlie went to California, where Pete was delivering a paper in San Diego, and they stayed with Alexander and Conor for 4 July (the four of them also belatedly celebrated Charlie's BAFTA win); and Pete came to London, and briefly Lancashire, which he loved, in October. He was even a guest in the *Look Who's Dancing!* studio audience for the Halloween special, and was cooed over by cast and crew alike. Leyla seemed to go very giddy in his company and could barely get her words out.

The rest of their relationship had to be conducted on phones and laptops, through WhatsApp and FaceTime, with the odd protest grumble from Mabel when she would deliberately sit across the laptop keyboard and plonk herself in front of the camera. Charlie wasn't sure if it was because Mabel was being possessive of her, or whether she wanted Pete to come back too.

And here Charlie was again. Another season of *Look Who's Dancing!* wrapped, Mabel now shipped off to Saphie and Prash's, and her flat rented out on Airbnb. Three months with no work on the horizon. Pete assured Charlie there *was* a TV industry in New York and that with her credentials she could get work easily, but there was the small recurring issue of a work visa, and, for now, she wanted Christmas with Pete. Friendmas with Mike, Erin, Téa and baby Maynard. New Year with the Makris family up at Hudson. She wanted to just be. But there was the small matter of Pete turning up first.

'What's the purpose of your visit to the United States, ma'am?' asked a woman with a stern face. Benjamin Steakhouse was nowhere to be seen.

'To see my boyfriend. Vacation.'

'Where will you be staying?'

'With him, on Leroy Street, West Village.'

'How long will you be staying?' the woman asked.

'Ninety days, if you'll have me!' Charlie joked.

The woman gave nothing back.

'Do you have the financial means to support your trip, ma'am?'

'Yes, I do,' Charlie said proudly.

The woman stamped Charlie's passport and nodded her in.

* * *

Charlie's orange suitcase took what felt like forever to appear on the carousel in the baggage reclaim hall and she exhaled another sigh of relief when it did. Flight. Immigration. Case. She was jumping all the hurdles. She just had to jump the big one.

Have you landed love ? c

I mean x .

A text from her mum. Charlie's hands were too shaky to answer, so she put her phone away for now and focused on getting through.

She propped her heavy case upright and wheeled it beside her, desperately hoping that Pete would be there; knowing that she would be OK if he wasn't.

The doors were automatic now, they'd been upgraded since her last visit, and they glided seamlessly open as she walked through. She saw the barrier. The Travelex currency booth. The Metro News. The Dunkin' Donuts. All signposts to her heartache of one year ago. As she looked at the familiar logos, and the blurred unfamiliar faces in front of them, she gripped the handle of her case and willed herself not to travel back in time as she thought that her legs might not go on.

Her eyes darted left and right, which made her miss the man standing right in front of her. In his shabby tweed jacket, holding a huge bunch of deep orange, fuchsia and red roses; ranunculi and snapdragons in the most dramatic of carnival bouquets it almost obscured his face.

'There she is!' Pete said, and, on cue, three women and one man stepped out from the crowd behind him, playing trumpet, saxophone, tuba and French horn. It took a second for Charlie to

recognise the song – 'Reach Out (I'll Be There)' by the Four Tops –
as she fell into Pete's arms, found his face among the enormous
stems and blooms, and kissed him.

Tired travellers and expectant families, friends and drivers all
stopped to take it in, in their slightly bemused, still hurried, New
York way. And while all around them the airport buzzed, Pete and
Charlie stood, the centre of their own tornado.

'Too much?' Pete asked quietly as he pulled back and looked at
Charlie's heart-shaped face.

'Never.'

'Welcome home, my love,' Pete said with a smile. Charlie took
the bouquet, Pete took her case, and the brass band followed them
out to their future.

ACKNOWLEDGMENTS

Firstly, thank you to my readers for making it this far on the journey with me, from the commuter town of *The Note* to the far corners of upstate New York in this book – my sixth! I love going on this roller coaster with you and am grateful for each and every book bought, downloaded or borrowed from the library, and all the messages you send me to talk about them.

I'd like to say a special thanks to John Hodson, who messaged me in 2020, aged eighty, with terminal cancer to say he loved my books; how they had helped him escape the drudgery of cancer, chemo and isolation, and how excited he was to be approaching his sixtieth wedding anniversary with his beloved wife Jean. He was determined to get there, and they celebrated their diamond anniversary in September 2022. Thank you for the inspiration, John, I often write with you in mind, and wish you and Jean more happy days together.

Thank you so much to my editor Sarah Ritherdon for her vision, faith, and sending me the email of my life on 6 October 2022 saying quite how much she loved this book. (A lot.) Authors are mostly solitary, self-doubting creatures, but that email gave me a boost just when I most needed it. It's pinned to the board in front of me.

Thanks also to Rebecca Ritchie, my amazing agent, who is off growing the army of little boys the three of us now have – future lunches will just be all boy talk, right? Thanks to Florence Rees for stepping in and holding my hand, Team AM Heath is a wonderful one to be on.

Thank you to the Boldwood badasses, Nia Beynon, Claire Fenby, Jenna Houston, Marcela Torres, Isabelle Flynn, Emily Ruston, Tara Loder, Caroline Ridding, Emily Yau, Ben Wilson, Leila Mauger and the visionary Amanda Ridout – you all make it a very exciting time to be a Boldwood author.

Thank you Alice Moore for the ever-so-pretty Central Park cover and to Sue Smith, Sandra Ferguson and Sue Lamprell for moving the copy, proof and production process along like a dream.

In researching this book I'd like to thank Irenie Ekkeshis Wilson for confirming just how lovely big Greek families can be, and for checking that I didn't get my *melomakarona* and my moussaka in a twist. Thank you to the women who shared their abortion stories with me; to the Look Good Feel Better charity for helping me understand how they help people face cancer with confidence; and to the Changing Faces charity, who helped me learn what life with a visible difference might be like.

Thanks to my author friends who remind me just how fun this hustle can be: Kathleen Whyman, Paige Toon, Jo Carnegie, Lorraine Brown, Caroline Khoury, Samantha Tonge, Jackie Middleton, are all women I have sought advice from and enjoyed dinners, laughs, hot chocolates and voice notes with. The sisterhood is strong in this industry. Ian Critchley brings the football exasperation (his Watford, my Spurs), laughter and outrage. Thank you, Ian.

I'd like to thank my friends and family for being the best support network a midult woman could wish for. Especially one going through grief. I lost my dad just after I submitted the first draft of my last book *The Three Loves Of Sebastian Cooper*; I lost my mum after I submitted the first draft of *Fairy Tale Of New York*. I have been enveloped inside the walls of grief and sadness I couldn't have broken through had it not been for my friends, my family – especially my brilliant sister Clare and my amazing stepmum Gerlinde, two inspirational women – and the privilege of escaping to another world through my stories.

Last and definitely not least, thanks to my pillars: my husband Mark – loveliest man ever – and our beautiful boys Felix and Max. What an honour to wake up with you every day, I love you more than you can possibly know (although I do harp on about it because you're all total babes) xxxx

You can message me on Instagram or Twitter @zoefolbigg

ABOUT THE AUTHOR

Zoë Folbigg is the bestselling author of many novels including *The Note*. She had a broad career in journalism writing for magazines and newspapers from Cosmopolitan to The Guardian. She married Train Man (star of *The Note*) and lives with him and their children in Hertfordshire.

Sign up to Zoë Folbigg's mailing list for news, competitions and updates on future books.

Visit Zoë Folbigg's website: https://www.zoefolbigg.com/

Follow Zoë on social media:

ALSO BY ZOË FOLBIGG

The Three Loves of Sebastian Cooper

Fairytale of New York

Boldwood

Boldwood Books is an award-winning fiction publishing company seeking out the best stories from around the world.

Find out more at
www.boldwoodbooks.com

Join our reader community for brilliant books, competitions and offers!

Follow us
#BoldBookClub

Sign up to our weekly deals newsletter

https://bit.ly/BoldwoodBNewsletter

Made in United States
Orlando, FL
06 November 2023

38639800R00222